Considering what had happened that day, this shouldn't have surprised Ryan, but still…

As Ryan entered the station's lobby, Firenzo flagged him down from the reception desk. "Hey, Doherty! Your brother's here to see you." The sergeant nodded toward the waiting area chairs lined up against the front wall.

"I don't have a—" Ryan turned to see the strange task force agent who had been staring at him in the meeting. "*You.*"

The man stood up slowly to greet him. He held out palm and said, "Agent Doherty."

"Detective," Ryan corrected him. "I'm *Detective* Doherty."

"Yes, I know. *I'm* Agent Doherty. Devin Doherty. Pleased to meet you." He shook with an unexpected vice grip, one that could've rivaled Ryan's own. "I tried to catch you at the other police station, but you and your partner left so quickly." He paused for a response, but Ryan gave none. "I'm sorry, I didn't mean for you to find out this way. It's just that the desk sergeant asked for my identification, and, well, when he saw my name, I had to explain. Is there someplace we can talk? In private?"

"You didn't mean for me to find out *what* this way?" Ryan asked.

"That you had a brother."

Someone has been picking off the women of Chicago's most notorious mob families. Detective Ryan Doherty is on the case with his partner, Matt Di Santo, walking a tight line between the Chicago PD, the feds, and the Outfit. From the Windy City to Sin City, Ryan and Di Santo travel to Vegas to chase down the assassin brave enough to take on the mob—and face shocking secrets of their own pasts.

KUDOS for *Friend of the Family*

In *Friend of the Family* by Jennifer Moss, we are once again reunited with Ryan Doherty and Catharine Lulling from Moss's *Ryan Doherty Mystery* series. Ryan, who is a Chicago homicide detective, is called upon to investigate the murders of the wife and a girlfriend of two of the organized crime leaders in Chicago. No sooner does he start investigating these two murders when another mob leader's sister is killed. Then the investigation gets even more screwed up when a federal agent, claiming to be Ryan's brother, shows up with other federal agents who want jurisdiction of the case under the RICO act. But Ryan really takes offense when the feds start trying to use his partner's distant family connections to the mob to make Di Santo an "inside man." Like the three books in the series before it, this one is well written, has a complicated plot with plenty of twists and turns, and will keep you turning page from beginning to end. ~ *Taylor Jones, Reviewer*

I love a series, especially one where the author gives us realistic characters who become like old friends. Take Jennifer Moss's *Ryan Doherty Mystery Series*. Her latest addition to the series, book number four, is *Friend of the Family*, apparently a mob term meaning guys on the outside who aren't "made" men or mob members, but who are friendly or sympathetic to the mob—or, in Detective Matt Di Santo's case, very distant cousins. Our main hero, Matt's partner in the Chicago PD Homicide Department, Ryan Doherty, is called to the scene of a murder on his day off and told his partner is already there. When Ryan shows up at the crime scene, he discovers that the victim is the wife of the local mob boss (godfather), and the reason Matt was there before anyone else is that the mob boss called him instead of 911, as Matt is the mob boss's distant cousin. When the feds show up, naturally Matt is the prime suspect and they take him in for questioning. Ryan rushes off to save his partner, reluctantly agreeing to cooperate with the federal task force working to take down organized crime in Chicago, in exchange for them getting off his partner's back, thus unleashing a chain of events none of them foresee—and that change Ryan and Matt's lives forever. Moss has created a cast of realistic and likeable characters and put them into situations that make them grow and change over the course of the books. In Ryan Doherty she has given us a strong, driven, unpredictable cop with plenty of human foibles, and you can't wait to see how he screws up next. She always leaves you wanting more and waiting hungrily for the next book. ~ *Regan Murphy, Reviewer*

Author's Note:

Friend of the Family is the fourth book in the *Ryan Doherty Mystery* series. Although the books don't have to be read in order, I recommend it for story continuity and maximum entertainment value.

RYAN DOHERTY MYSTERY SERIES:
(in order)

Town Red
Present Tense (a Kindle short story)
Way to Go
Taking the Rap
Friend of the Family

Other books by Jennifer Moss:
The One-in-a-Million Baby Name Book

FRIEND
OF THE
FAMILY

JENNIFER MOSS

A Black Opal Books Publication

Dedicated to my amazing daughter, Miranda,
whose love and strength saved me from drowning
in the sea of loss these past two years.

"There are three sides to every story.
Mine, yours, and the truth."
~ *Joey Massino*

PROLOGUE

Two Years, Eleven Months, Twenty-One Days Ago:

The first week after his partner's death had been a blur of people—people in his apartment, people at the funeral, people in the squad room. People gushing condolences and reiterating their disbelief that Detective Jonathan Lange had died so young. Especially since he didn't buy it on the job, but in a freak highway accident. It was the same week that Kelly had left him—during all of the chaos, when Ryan couldn't even stop for one minute and discuss it with her. Then again, he wasn't sure if there was anything left to discuss.

So he'd let her go.

The second week he holed up in his apartment. Didn't answer any calls, texts, or emails. The sarge told him to take at least three weeks off before returning to work, as he'd had six saved up in unused vacation time.

The third week he showered. Shaved. Even ventured to the corner store to replenish his groceries—and the liquor cabinet. He had consumed everything possible in his apartment down to the last two-year-old package of ramen. Now he'd become antsy and wanted to get back to work.

Ryan Doherty loved serving as a Chicago cop and had been promoted to detective four years earlier. Before that, he had been on patrol for almost ten. He and Jon had asked to be partnered when they both passed the detective's exam within weeks of each other. Working together made them better friends, and being friends made them better cops.

Ryan stood outside the blond oak door in the beige hallway of a nondescript medical plaza. His knuckles hovered just under the nameplate, prepared to knock.

James Sullivan, PsyD.

Ryan had never been to a shrink before. Sergeant Besko reminded him it was a prerequisite to returning to the job. Even though Jon hadn't been killed in the line of duty, it was standard operating procedure in the death of a partner. At least three sessions, Besko told him. Ryan was banking that he could get all three done this week and be back to work by Monday.

He knocked.

After getting no response, he turned the handle and entered a small waiting room, clearly designed to be tranquil. Low lighting cast a glow on several bamboo plants while a tabletop water fountain trickled in the corner. He had his choice of four blue overly-cushioned chairs, took one and checked the time on his phone: 1:25 p.m. He flipped through several tattered magazines, giving up on *Glamour*, as he had no interest in how to apply the perfect blush.

At exactly 1:30 sharp, an inner door opened and a man appeared. He was in his early thirties—thirty-two at the most—dressed conservatively in black slacks and a beige button-down.

Ryan stood up as the man held out a hand and addressed him with a wide smile. "Detective Doherty?"

"Call me Ryan," he said, completing the handshake.

"I'm Jamie Sullivan, nice to meet you. Come on in." He held the door open, letting Ryan into the inner sanctum. With similar décor as the waiting room, the walls were an earthy green offset by a warm red and yellow braided rug on a bamboo floor. A large mahogany desk stood along the far wall, while a more casual seating area took up the left.

"Take a seat anywhere you like," Sullivan said.

Ryan smirked, spotting the proverbial psych sofa. "Should I lie down?"

"Only if you want to. But most of my clients just sit," Jamie Sullivan quipped. The man was confident and amiable. From his mannerisms, vocal inflection, and the rainbow Pride sticker on the window Ryan concluded the doc was gay, which surprisingly made him more comfortable.

When meeting a straight guy for the first time there was always an air of competition, especially when the dude found out Ryan was a cop.

But with gay guys, all he had to worry about was being hit on, and there was little chance of that happening in a therapeutic environment.

He took a seat on the sofa and scanned the room. Several framed university degrees hung on the wall, along with Dr. Sullivan's Chicago P.D. certification. The bookshelves contained true crime books, psychology texts, knick-knacks and several framed photos. He recognized a man in one of them.

"Hey, that's Sully…*Captain* James Sullivan. I never got the connection. I assume you two are related?"

"He's my father. Do you do know him?"

"Definitely. Sully was my FTO back when I was a rookie in the Sixteenth. Great guy."

Sullivan sat down in a wingback chair facing him. "He is a great guy. And a great training officer, I've heard. But mostly from him," he said with a warm smile.

"A cop's son ends up being a cop shrink. What would Freud say about that?"

Jamie laughed as he opened the folder. *Ryan's* folder. "I'm not sure. That I want to fully understand my father? It's pretty transparent, isn't it?" He handed Ryan a form. "This is our privacy statement, I'd like you to sign it. I want you to know that everything you say in here is completely confidential. No matter who my father is, nothing goes outside of these walls. I do have to report back to your supervisor whether you are ready to go back to work or not. If not, then I would have to share a diagnosis. Like PTSD, for example."

Ryan nodded. "I understand." He reviewed the language, signed the form and handed it back. "So, how long have you been with the Department?"

"Three years. Before that I did clinical work."

Ryan nodded and crossed one ankle over his knee. "You like it? Working with cops?"

"I love it. It's fantastic that the C.P.D. takes the mental and emotional health of its officers seriously. It's so important for you to do your job. Do you like your work, Detective?"

"Oh, we're starting now?" Ryan sat up a little straighter and cleared his throat.

"Have you ever been in therapy before, Ryan?"

"No."

"It's not scary by any means. It's just a conversation."

"That's exactly what we say in an interrogation so the suspect doesn't get upset."

"Do you feel like you're being interrogated?"

Ryan scratched an imaginary itch just above his ear. "I just want to say I wouldn't be here if it weren't ordered by the Department. My sarge says if I do three of these sessions I can get back on the job."

"The *minimum* requirement is three sessions, Detective, but it's my decision when you return to work."

Ryan frowned. "What are you saying? That it could be longer?"

"I should say that it most probably *will* be longer," he said, reviewing the one piece of paper in the file. "Judging from your closeness to the victim. And some other circumstances."

"What other circumstances?" He scrubbed a hand over his face. "Shit. I was hoping to go back Monday."

"Let's not concentrate on when you're going back to work. Let's just get through this first hour and see how it goes."

Ryan stared at the floor and started to flex his right hand, getting increasingly pissed at the situation. Wondering if he had to talk about his fucked-up feelings.

"Ryan? Are you okay?"

He stretched his neck both ways until he heard it crack. "Yeah, I'm okay. Go ahead and ask away."

"It's not a race. Why don't you tell me about…Jonathan."

Jon's full, formal name sounded strange. Jon never used it, himself. Formal names were meant for births, weddings and funerals, and it was repeated too many times at his funeral: *We're here to honor the life of Jonathan Lange…*

"What about him?" Ryan finally answered.

"Where did you two meet—at the Eighteenth District?"

"Jon and I met at the Academy. First and second in our class. I was first."

Sullivan scribbled that in his notebook. "And you stayed friends since?"

"On and off. After the training period, we were assigned different districts, and took different paths. He went from patrol to tac team to Homicide. I went from patrol to Robbery Division, and then asked to be reassigned when an opening came up in the Eighteenth. We asked to be partnered and we worked well…" His throat constricted to the point he couldn't finish.

Jamie shifted in his chair. "Do you like working Homicide?"

"Yeah, I do. Helping the families. Solving the puzzle." The doc scribbled some notes, and after a few moments glanced back at him without speaking. "What?"

"Sounds like the standard answer you give everyone who asks that question." Ryan shrugged. It was. "It must be very emotionally taxing work," the doc prompted.

"Yeah, well, in Homicide we deal with the worst of the worst that humanity can produce. But you just have to balance it."

"And how do you balance it?"

"With my friends and my…" he trailed off.

"What were you going to say, Ryan?"

"I was going to say 'my friends and my girl.' Both gone."

The doc scribbled in his file. "And so what will you use now?"

"Whisky and gin." Sullivan frowned. "C'mon, I'm kidding!"

"Are you?" He poised his pen.

"Don't write that down," Ryan said pointing to the file. "It's a joke. That's how we cope. Murder cops. We have to joke about this shit or we won't get through it."

Sullivan nodded, turned a page in the notebook, and then took a deep breath. Ryan recognized the doc's expression from the multitude of interrogations he'd conducted. The man was about to take a different tack.

"Tell me what you've been doing since Jonathan's funeral."

"Jon. He went by Jon." Jamie nodded, still awaiting his answer. "Eating. Sleeping."

"That's it?"

"Drinking." Jamie lifted his gaze in inquisition. "Hey, you're Irish, right? Sullivan? You understand." Ryan tried flashing his killer grin. The doc didn't return it.

"How much drinking?" Jamie asked.

"Oh, now don't go there. I was in mourning and you're judging my alcohol consumption? Shit." He squirmed in his seat.

"I hope I didn't come across judgmental, that's not my job. I just asked how much…on average. One beer? A couple of shots? Or did you go through a bottle a day?"

"Depends on the day. Some are worse than others." And of course, he had to write that in the fucking notebook. "Look, this isn't going to affect me going back—"

Jamie held up his hand. "We're not going to talk about that, remember? And I don't want you to tell me what I want to hear just so you can get back to work."

'*Busted.*' Jon's voice rang out. Ever since that night—the night he was killed—his partner's voice would sporadically chime in from nowhere. Ryan chalked it up to grief, convincing himself it was all in his head. Probably all in his head. But there were times he talked back and they had lengthy conversations, as if Jon were still around. Or on the other side of the phone. But that was one thing he wasn't about to reveal to Dr. Jamie Sullivan—hearing voices would definitely go in the mental file.

"Tell me about this girl you lost," Jamie said.

"No."

Dr. Sullivan gazed up at him from under his brows.

"I'd prefer not to talk about her."

Sullivan sat back in his chair and punctuated his exasperation with a sigh. Ryan knew that trick: the longer the silence, the more uncomfortable the other person became. So uncomfortable that they'll try to fill the quiet by gabbing. This doc was good. He decided to stare straight back until Jamie lost the game by blinking and went back to the file.

"Your sergeant. He said he was a friend of your family's?"

"I've known the sarge for a long time. He actually worked it so I could serve under him. When my dad died, he was a sort of a mentor to me."

"Is that why you wanted to become a cop? Because of Sergeant Besko?"

He shrugged. "That and other things."

"What other things?" Ryan checked his watch to see how much time he had left. In turn, Jamie glanced at the wall clock. "Thirty-three minutes to go," he said with a smirk. "What other things made you want to become a cop?"

"I wanted to save the world and all that," he threw out.

The doc blew out a breath, snapped the folder shut and stood up. "You know what, Detective? I think we're done for today."

"What? You just said we had thirty-three minutes to go!"

"It feels to me that you're not taking this seriously, Ryan. Come back when you're really ready to talk. Until then, go buy a bottle. I'm sure that will be very productive." The doctor got up from his chair and started to cross the room.

"Wait. Jamie. Dr. Sullivan. I'm sorry."

"Please exit through the left door. That will take you straight back to the hallway."

Ryan followed the doc to his desk. "You don't understand. I *have* to do this. I have to stay."

"So you can get back to work, right." The doctor took a seat at his desk, turned on his computer screen and ignored him until Ryan slammed a fist on his desk.

"*No!*"

That got the doctor's attention.

"No," Ryan rasped. "I mean, yes, I have to go back to work. Because my head is a mess and work is the only thing that can clear it. I can't stay at home one more day or I'll—"

Eat my gun, he almost said.

Dr. Sullivan cocked his head. "You'll *what*, Detective?"

"I'll go crazy. And isn't that what you're here for? To help me stay sane? I want...your *help*. Please. Give me my thirty-three minutes."

The doctor dropped his gaze to Ryan's file, with an expression of both anger and pity.

He made a bold decision to give the doc what he wanted.

"My sister was raped." Sullivan lifted his head. "I was at U of I and Erin was in high school," Ryan continued. "Her prom date didn't understand the word 'No' and, well—anyway, Besko was the investigating officer. We'd just lost our dad a couple of months earlier. My mom and my sisters lived alone in the house. Besko and his wife—they sort of adopted our family. Took us under their wing. That's how I met him and that's what solidified my decision to become a cop. My sister was raped."

Jamie got up from his desk, picked up the file and his notebook and returned to the other side of the room. Ryan followed. The doc gestured for him to sit back down, and they both took their previous seats.

"You said you were in college at the time?"

"Yes, University of Illinois in Champaign."

"And?"

"And I felt guilty that I had left them alone, without a man in the house. I should have been there."

"It wasn't your fault, you know."

"You can forget the platitudes, I've heard it all before. That's what we tell all the families of victims."

The doctor let it hang for a beat. "How's your sister now?"

"Erin? She's fine. She's divorced now. Lives in Phoenix with her kids and my mom. It was a long time ago."

"What about your other sisters?"

"Finn's in L.A. She's a reporter for the *L.A. Times*. My sister, Siobhan, lives in Ireland. She's a Bohemian sort of person, a singer. She's actually pretty popular there. Released three albums. We hardly ever see her."

"So you have no family left here in Chicago?"

"Extended family. Aunts, uncles. None that I see regularly."

"When was the last time you saw your mom and sisters?"

"Mom, Finn, and Erin came back three weeks ago, for Jon's services. Siobhan sent me a video of her singing a song she'd written about loss. It was really nice, actually. Made me realize how much I missed her."

Jamie nodded, appearing pleased that he was opening up. "Are you close with them?"

"Yes, our family is very close. But all the Doherty women together in one room are...how should I put it? Overwhelming. Especially during all that was going on. And then the whole thing with Kelly—" *Shit.* He didn't want to go there.

"Kelly left you," Jamie said quietly.

After a pause, Ryan asked, "Are you married?"

"Engaged," Jamie replied, holding up his ring finger. A thick silver band encircled it, with three embedded diamonds.

"Congratulations."

"Thanks. How long had you and Kelly been dating?"

He almost checked his watch but decided against it. "Fourteen, fifteen years, on and off."

"Fifteen years! Wow. That's a long time. And you weren't engaged?"

He rolled his eyes. "No."

"Why'd she leave?"

He shut down again. Sniffed. Scratched his ankle. Checked the clock on the wall. Seventeen minutes to go. "How long have you been with…your fiancé?"

Jamie narrowed his eyes, recognizing the deflection. "Three years. And I thought that was a long time."

Good try, but that wasn't going to work on him. He'd been honing his own interrogation techniques for a good four years now. "He a cop?"

"No-o-o, Tim works for the city. Film Board. He's a liaison between the City of Chicago and the entertainment industry."

"That's cool. Get to meet a lot of movie stars?"

"Occasionally. So then I presume we're done talking about Kelly?"

"For now."

"Okay, I won't push it." They sat in silence for a couple of minutes. "Tell me," the doc finally said. "How do you envision it when you go back to work?"

"How do I envision it? What do you mean?"

"Walk me through it. The day you go back to your squad in the Eighteenth. What's it going to be like? What are you going to do?"

"I'll walk in the door, Sarge will hand me a case and I'll work it. I don't get what you're going for—"

"Alone? You won't be reassigned a partner?"

Shit, he hadn't thought about that.

"Yeah, Sarge will let me work alone. I've worked alone before."

"And how will the other detectives treat you?"

"The Department's lost guys before. We pat each other on the back and move on. Keep pursuing the bad guys."

"So that's it? Business as usual?"

"God, I hope so." Sullivan nodded and unconsciously began tapping his pen on the file. "Why? Do you know something I don't?"

"No, no. I just want you to run through it in your head. Sometimes it's extremely traumatic for a PO to go back to the station after his partner is gone. It's where they worked together. You'll see his desk. His coffee cup. Any of his items left behind."

"His family went by last week to get his stuff," Ryan said, picturing Jon's desk across from his. He couldn't imagine it empty. Without Jon. Without the gleaming white smile greeting the week. Without the morning handclasp as they each recounted their weekend exploits.

"What are you thinking about?" Jamie said, breaking through his vision. Ryan glanced at the clock, and so did the doc. "That's my last question, Ryan. And I'd like you to answer it honestly. Verbalize your thoughts. Then we'll be done for today. What are you thinking about?"

His eyes stung with tears as the scenario sunk in.

"That he won't be there."

CHAPTER 1

Current Day:

Ryan fumbled with his keys in the hallway while Catharine stood waiting behind him. He didn't know why he was so nervous. In the past sixteen years since he'd rented the Rogers Park apartment, he'd brought a litany of women back to his place. But Cat was different. He cared about her opinion, and worried about her state of mind.

"You okay?" he asked, as he found the correct key. He inserted it into the lock and then glanced back at her for the answer.

She graced him with her gentle smile. "I'm fine. I haven't really had a bad outing since that day at the Rose Garden, but since we went back a couple weeks ago, I've done very well!" Cat squeezed his arm in anticipation of entering, and he took her positive energy as an answer more than her words. He'd become adept at sensing when Catharine was about to go into agoraphobic shock. It began with the trembling. Then she'd drop eye contact and start repeating words. Her fear of stepping outside her home was the main reason why—after nine months of dating—she had never seen his place.

Ryan took her into his arms, kissed her forehead, and

then opened the door to his apartment as if it were the Promised Land. But first, he stepped in to do a quick scan and made sure everything was in place. "Okay, this is it." He pulled her inside and shut the door behind them. Catharine took it all in with wide eyes. "So this is the kitchen," he said, beginning the tour. "It's kind of small." He gestured to the galley-like space. The white tiles on the floor and Formica on the breakfast bar dated back to the last time the landlord had updated the place, around the mid-nineties.

Catharine entered the kitchenette and executed an effortless pirouette. "It's good!" she announced. "Functional. What are you making me for breakfast?"

"Well…um…I can make omelets. That's about the extent of my cooking skills. That and macaroni and cheese, but that would be a weird breakfast."

She laughed and then stepped past him into the living room. Her gaze wandered around the room and she pointed to the two books she had lent him, displayed prominently on the coffee table. He'd read them eventually. She acknowledged them with a nod and then made her way to the entertainment center on the far wall.

"A turntable! I'm impressed. And look at all your records!" He watched her as she crouched down and flipped through the twelve-inch albums ranging from Louis Armstrong to classic rock.

She turned back to him with a smirk. "Aerosmith?"

"Yeah, well." He scratched an ear.

"I like them too," she said, replacing the album. Somehow, he imaged that Catharine Lulling only listened to classical music, since she was trained in ballet and he'd only ever heard piano concertos and string quartets and such playing in her estate.

"I like it, Ryan," she said, taking another look around his living room. "I like your apartment. It's very you. Ryan's lair!"

He beamed at the compliment and watched as her attention turned to the view outside his bay window. It wasn't much, but he liked being able to see the collage of trees, fire escapes, rooftops and the el tracks, situated a half a block east.

The morning sun created a halo around Cat's long, brown curls. Her blue eyes sparkled as she glanced back at him. "Nice view! Very urban."

He pointed east. "If you look through those buildings, you can see the lake," he said.

She stood on her tiptoes, a move he found to be completely adorable.

"I can! I can see the lake."

"Are you—oh, sorry. Not asking." He put his hand on her back, rubbed it a bit, and pulled her close.

"Yes," she replied, as if surprised at her own comfort level. "I'm good. I like being here." She toured slowly through the living room, making her way to the hall.

Halfway down, she pointed to a door. "What's this?"

"Bathroom."

She peeked into the small space. He had cleaned off all his shaving stuff from the sink and stuffed it away in the medicine cabinet. It hadn't been this clean since his mother had come to visit last year. Catharine stepped in and pointed to the ocean-themed wallpaper. "Sea horses?" she said, teasing him with a snicker.

"Yeah, well, it came with the place."

It did. He'd never even thought of redecorating, not even after sixteen years. It was a rental, after all. He figured he'd get into all the DIY stuff once he bought a house.

Catharine bypassed him back into the long hallway. He followed, flipping on the hall light. "What's this?" she said, opening the door on the left to the hall closet. "Oh my god, *Ryan!*"

"What?" He rushed up to her, concerned that she was having an episode.

"It's your *uniform!*" She swung out the hanger that held his full Chicago blues and ran her fingers over the epaulets on the shoulder.

"Yeah, we have to keep them for official ceremonies and stuff."

She took the matching navy blue hat from the top shelf and placed it on his head.

"That's *so* hot!" She stepped in and kissed him, deeply.

"Mmm. What is it with women and the uniform?"

"I don't know, it must be an evolutionary thing," she said. "You know, we're attracted to the ones who can protect us, and the uniform is a symbol of protection. And power."

"You're hot when you talk evolution," He put his hat back on the shelf and pinned her against the wall.

"That's funny, coming from a Catholic." She squirmed out from under him to investigate farther down the hall. She got to the door at the end. "What's in here?"

"My bedroom."

She glanced back at him with a wicked grin, opened the door and peeked in. He followed and peered into his room after her—hoping it presented well, trying to see it from her perspective. He made sure he'd made his bed before he went to pick her up and hoped she hadn't noticed the remnants of his "stuff" sticking out from underneath it. To the right of his bed sat a modest dresser with some dollars and change, a couple of receipts and a stick of deodorant on top of it. He should've put all that in the drawers. She moved around his room and pretended to inspect it, running her fingers along the top of the bedside table.

"I like how you look in here—in my place," he said, stepping into the room behind her. "Like a normal woman."

She turned around to face him and feigned offense. "As opposed to what?"

"As opposed to a queen in her castle."

Catharine ignored the comment and sat down on the edge of the bed. She bounced a couple times and then lay back, burying her face in the pillows.

"Mmmmm, it smells like you," she purred.

He crawled onto the bed until he was hovering over her,

supporting himself on his elbows. His bangs fell down onto her forehead.

"You know what else smells like me?"

"What?"

"Me."

He took a moment to gaze into her deep blue eyes and then lowered his body onto hers. He was just about to kiss her when she made that little humming sound that he loved.

"That's it, right there," he said, and continued his seduction. In his bed. In his place. He felt like a Roman conqueror as Catharine allowed him to be dominant in the lovemaking they shared for the next thirty-eight minutes.

"It's so dark in here," Catharine observed after they had rested for a while in each other's arms.

"I know, it's the charcoal gray walls. I never did repaint. That first morning I woke up in your bed, it was so bright I thought I was going blind. And then I got distracted by the woman beside me..." He pulled her close, kissed her, and peeled away the sheet that was covering her half of the bed. He loved to study her full, unclothed body.

"When is this breakfast that was promised to me? It's..." Catharine turned to look at the digital clock on his side table. "It's after eleven!"

"I'm making it, don't worry. I want to just look at you. Here. In *my* bed." She softened and snuggled in closer to him. "I love you," he whispered. He brushed away some of the wisps of hair that had fallen onto her face and gazed into her eyes.

"Is that a statement or a question?" she asked.

She was way too smart. "Both."

"Then I love you, too," she whispered.

"I've been thinking..." He had to just let it out. "Another

reason I wanted you to see the apartment sooner rather than later is because…well…maybe it's time I did move into the grand Lulling Estate. I mean, I'm there all the time anyway, and so's half my wardrobe." Cat's eyes widened. "Is—is that okay? I mean, does your offer still stand?"

Cat wrapped her arms around his neck. "Of course! Oh, Ryan, I'm so happy." He pulled back to make sure she was really okay with it, but she seemed truly delighted at the prospect. "But what about the Department? Doesn't every-one who works for the city have to live in the city? I don't want it to come in the way of your job."

"Sarge told me as long as I kept this place and picked up my mail, this could still be my official address. Our paychecks are auto-deposited, so that's not a big deal."

They were interrupted by the buzz of Ryan's cell, vibrat-ing on the nightstand. He leaned over to check the caller ID. "Here's the Sarge now." He answered with his usual greet-ing, "Doherty."

"Yah, D. We caught a big one this morning." Sergeant Bob Besko's voice blared from the phone. "I'm gonna need you to come out to River Forest."

Ryan mouthed *"Damn it!"* then went back to the conver-sation. "River Forest? But that's not our jurisdiction. What's up?"

"We've been asked to assist on a homicide over here. Actually *you've* been asked to assist. They're asking for you by name, D. Probably because you're one of the best detec-tives we've got, you know." The transparent compliment couldn't dull the sting of giving up his day off.

"I'm kind of in the middle of time with my woman, Sarge," he said running a palm over Catharine's bare shoul-der. He was hoping to get at least one more round in before the omelets. He kissed that same shoulder, waiting on Bes-ko's response.

"Well, if someone had whacked your woman, wouldn't you want the best detective on the case?" Besko's said, his voice escalating. "We may have a serial here, D. Women.

Wives. Daughters. Sisters. *Women!* How soon can you get here?"

Shit. Sarge knew that personalizing the victim would appeal to Ryan's sense of duty. It worked every time. He sighed in submission and looked to Catharine for an answer. By the frown on Cat's face, she had heard Besko's proclamation.

She mouthed "Go," and started to gather up her clothes. She wasn't angry—she understood the requirements of the job—but he could feel the disappointment hanging in the air, on both their parts.

"Leaving now, Sarge. Text me the address." He disconnected the call and apologized to Cat. "You're welcome to stay, if you'd like. But I don't know how long this will take. I'll drop you off on the way."

"Don't worry, I'll call one of the boys." Catharine grabbed her delicate sky-blue blouse from the floor beside the bed. "The killings will continue," she said cryptically, "if you and Matt don't stop it." She had stopped dressing and was staring out of the bedroom window.

"Matt's on vacation," he answered. "Week one of two."

The Department had implemented a new policy for every cop who'd accrued over six weeks—they had to start taking it.

"No," Catharine responded, shaking her head. "Matt's going to work this with you. In fact, he's already involved."

Ryan knew from experience that Catharine's intuition shouldn't be ignored. He'd first met her on the Town Red case and had no idea what to expect when he'd read the file on the elusive woman who had thirty million dollars in the bank and claimed to possess special metaphysical powers. He certainly didn't expect the intelligent, well-spoken woman that he'd met in that strange house of her own design. And he hadn't expected to fall so hard for her.

Since then, Catharine's "abilities" had helped the Department close more than one case. Besko had been so impressed that he put her on the official consultant's list for the

18th District, Chicago PD, although never once uttering the word "psychic." But Cat's intuition went beyond psychic—she could also find things. Lost items, people, suspects, and even bodies, if necessary. Ryan couldn't explain it in full, and neither could Catharine. She was certainly a unique individual, and from that first day he'd met her, he'd had his own vision that this unusual woman would change his life.

And she had.

CHAPTER 2

The last time Ryan had seen so many officers at a homicide was when rapper Terrico James had been found crucified on stage. The entire residential block was cordoned off and bookended by black and white patrol cars from the local River Forest Police Department. Ryan flashed his badge through the windshield, and one of the officers pulled aside a wooden blockade. Coasting at ten miles per hour, Ryan noted five additional Chicago P.D. patrols and several unmarked black sedans peppered throughout the block. He passed the driveway cordoned off with yellow tape and parked two houses down wondering how the hell he fit into all of this.

The door on his vintage '66 Mustang tended to stick, so he inadvertently announced his arrival with the slam of its door.

"D! Good, you're here," Besko shouted. His sergeant weaved his way through the crowd of uniforms and suits and slapped Ryan on the back in greeting. The sarge was in his early fifties, with a full head of white hair and the stout, muscular body of a former wrestler. He was old-school, blue-collar Chicago, born and raised in the heart of the city with the iconic Dese-Dose accent to prove it.

He pointed to a late-model fire-engine-red Cadillac CTS sedan, parked in a wide driveway of a large property, surrounded by a brick wall. The driveway's automatic iron gate stood open, inert, almost pointing to the Caddy. In back of the car, a children's tricycle lay toppled on its side.

"Victim is forty-four-year-old Robin Ricci," Besko said. He paused for Ryan to recognize the name. Ryan shook his head. "Mrs. *Ricardo* Ricci…or 'Richie Rich,' as they call him in the Outfit." Sarge whispered the last word, a term used exclusively for the Chicago-based mob.

Ryan acknowledged the implications with a nod as he made his way over to the victim in the vehicle. He wasn't too up to speed on the organized crime families in Chicago, but there were certain names every cop knew, and Richie Rich was one of them.

"Where is Mr. Ricci now?" Ryan asked, pulling out the next textbook question.

"Where do you think? At River Forest PD giving his statement."

"So, they think he's good for this?"

"Well, that's the thing," Besko said, scratching his mop of white, wiry hair. "That's why you're here. They're thinking this may be part of a bigger thing. A serial."

Ryan took in a deep breath as he peered into the driver's side window. The wife, a pretty Caucasian brunette, lay motionless, slumped to the right side of the steering wheel. A bullet hole the size of a dime was ground zero for the trail of dried blood down her left cheek.

The shot had definitely come through the driver's side window with significant force, yet the body had been held in place by the seatbelt.

Peering through the car and out the passenger side window, Ryan could see several uniformed officers rifling through the contents of a large black handbag and handing items off one by one to a man in a suit.

"Did she hit a child?" Ryan asked, nodding to the tricycle behind the left wheel.

"No, thank God," Besko answered. "We believe the trike was put there so Robin Ricci would intentionally hit it and brake at the prime location for the hit. When she put the car into park, *KA-POW!* Bullet through the head."

"I assume they're going to print the tricycle, then," Ryan said, just thinking aloud. Sarge nodded. "So how do they think this is part of something bigger? Do they think it's an Outfit thing? A rift between families?"

"We're not sure, D. The feds have tied this to another homicide. Another woman."

"Yeah, you said something like that on the phone," Ryan responded. "So who was the other victim?"

"Miss Sandy Orlando. She died ten days ago. Vehicular accident on the Dan Ryan. That particular incident was not investigated as a homicide, as she had a cocktail of prescription drugs in her system. They put it down as an overdose. Thing is, though, Ms. Orlando was a longtime companion of another one of the crime bosses, Victor Basso."

Ryan glanced back at the body. "And you don't think it's a coincidence? These two women in two weeks?"

One of the suits approached and inserted himself into the conversation. "We can't take that chance, Detective. I'm Agent Jensen, Federal OC Task Force."

Ryan put out his hand and the man mashed it, as if arm wrestling in a bar. "Ryan Doherty, 18th District Chicago PD"

"I know who you are, I was the one who requested you."

"Well, thanks for fucking up my day off," Ryan said with a tight grin. It was meant as a joke. And not.

Jensen chuckled in camaraderie, nonetheless. He was about Ryan's height, with sandy blond hair, slightly graying at the temples, with the kind of Nordic coloring where even his eyebrows and eyelashes were blond, and a hint of childhood freckles. Ryan put his age at forty-five, forty-eight at the most.

"Feel free to take your time at the crime scene," Jensen said. The way he gave permission sent a clear message establishing himself as Ryan's superior in this whole mess. "When you're done, meet us back at RFPD headquarters and we'll do some brain share before we decide on an investigation strategy."

Ryan raised his eyebrows at Besko.

"Yeah, they trump us, D. So you'll have to report to both of us."

Ryan accepted his boss's answer. For now. He hated taking orders from anyone who hadn't yet earned his respect.

Ryan took in the surrounding area, concluding that the neighborhood was fairly quiet with the exception of police radios creating occasional snippets of conversation. No looky-loos, no traffic, no neighbors peeking through curtains. The intersection of Oak Park and River Forest was not the usual placid Chicago suburb where PTA meetings and neighborhood house walks were the main events. This particular community was infamous for housing the Outfit's elite, all the way back to the 1950s. Ryan suspected that the neighbors had a habit of minding their own business.

It appeared as if the local officers were well in control of the scene, even convincing a news crew or two to turn around and drive away. Besko interrupted his thoughts with a poke in the shoulder.

"Looks like some kind of sniper rifle," he said. "Military grade. Angle suggests the perp was up there in that tree." He pointed to a mature oak, two properties down from the Riccis' driveway. The tree stood about one foot from the curb, with a delta of branches that sat fairly low, enabling the murderer to climb it and await his prey.

"But it was clear daylight," Ryan said. "How did he perch up there without being seen?"

The sarge shrugged and scratched his head again, looking up at the tall oak. "It may not be that they didn't see it, D. These neighbors know who lives here, and nobody's talking. Catch my drift? We have several uniforms doing a canvass but the residents either don't answer or don't know nothin'. Almost as bad as the projects."

Several evidence techs were crouched at the base of the tree, taking samples of the dirt while stopping occasionally to study the bark at eye level. Ryan stayed a safe distance, knowing he should let the techs do their job without contaminating the area. "You calling Matt back in on this?" he asked, remembering Catharine's vision. "He may have some insight on it , with his family—"

"*Shhhh!*" Besko said, two inches from his face, and pulled Ryan aside by the crook of his arm to an uninhabited corner of the Riccis' front lawn. "Apparently your partner was already at the scene when the locals arrived."

"*What?* Di Santo was here?"

"Yeah, Richie called Di Santo instead of 911. As a 'friend of the family,' is how he put it." The sarge punctuated the phrase with air quotes. "That's what the Outfit calls the guys on the outside—not made men, but sympathetic to their activities. Well, as you can imagine, that didn't sit well with the feds, so the other D's back at the River Forest station giving his statement."

Ryan cleared his throat, trying to erase the thought. He didn't like his partner being identified with organized crime. "I don't get it. He came to a crime scene before calling it in? Why didn't he call me? Di Santo's my partner, he should've called me."

"This isn't about you, D. There's something bigger going on here."

Now Ryan was torn between wanting to scrutinize the crime scene and saving his partner from the feds. Di Santo was barely three years out of his blues, and was sometimes a bit naïve when it came to agency jurisdiction and the chain of command.

"The evidence team seems to have it covered here, so I'm going in," he announced.

"Okay, D. I'm heading back to the station. Let me know if you need anything, but as of now, you're both on loan. Be nice to your new boss and don't pull any shit."

Ryan chuffed before heading back to his Mustang. He asked for the address of the River Forest station from a uniform and punched it in on his phone.

He always compared other station houses to his home at the 18th District. Like a couple of months ago when they went to Atlanta—that headquarters had been a massive, modern building constructed of glass and steel, a stark contrast to their district's late 1960s cinderblock design. Here in River Forest, the station was somewhere in the middle of the spectrum between Atlanta and the 18th: a red brick building with newer, double-paned windows.

Before exiting his Mustang, he tried texting Jane Steffen. As an assistant state's attorney, maybe she would know why the feds were in town and could fill him in on their investigation. After a minute and seventeen seconds with no response, he decided to call her later. He had to get inside and see what was happening to his partner.

Ryan entered the River Forest station and checked in with the desk sergeant, handing over his shield. While signing the visitor log, his partner's signature popped out at him a couple lines up on the sheet. He needed to find Di Santo before the task force did a number on him. The sergeant handed him back his credentials and gave him directions to the Robbery/Homicide Unit.

The squad was fronted with double doors, exactly like theirs, yet only the right one gave way when he pushed on it.

"Doherty! You're here!" Jensen shouted from across the room.

Shit, the fed had beaten him. "Where's Di Santo?"

"Interview Room Three," the agent responded, nodding to a video screen.

The screen showed his partner at an interrogation table from the perspective of the top corner of the room. "What the fuck? Get him out of there, now!" Ryan knew all the tricks of the interview from the buddy-buddy system to "do yourself a favor," but Di Santo was a greener cop and there was a possibility that he could slip up.

"Hey, hey," Jensen said, trying to deter him. "It's just a conversation."

Which meant that they were interrogating his partner. "I need to talk to him. *Now.*" Without waiting, he took the initiative and burst into the interview room. "Hey," he nodded to Di Santo. "Can I talk to you for a minute?"

Di Santo glanced at the other guy as if asking permission to leave the room.

Ryan addressed the agent. "I'm going to speak to my partner, Detective Di Santo, before this thing blows up any bigger than it has to. I've just been assigned lead of this case. So, whoever you are, you're relieved of this conversation."

Jensen came in behind him and addressed his man. "That's okay, Powell, you can release him," and then turned to Ryan. "You can have ten minutes, Detectives, and then we'll all convene in the conference room."

Ryan already regretted his decision to come in on this case, and he might have refused if it weren't for his partner's involvement. "We're not talking in here," he said, beckoning his partner with a wave.

Di Santo rose from the plastic chair and dusted off his suit jacket. How he went from being on vacation to donning a full double-breasted number was anybody's guess, but that was Di Santo. Always dressed for the occasion.

"Glad you're here," Di Santo stage-whispered as Ryan led him out of the room by his elbow.

Ryan glanced around for somewhere private to talk, and tried one of the closed doors. Supply closet. "In here," he whispered back.

"Geez, it's dark!" squawked Di Santo. "You can't at least find a light switch? You better buy me dinner afterward!"

Ryan found the switch and flipped it. A pair of fluorescent bulbs sputtered and hummed to life above them. The detectives were sandwiched between two utility shelves bearing various office supplies, intermixed with white document boxes.

"Did they Mirandize you?" Ryan asked, glancing around for security cams. There were none.

"No, D, they said I'm in the clear, for now. But they *are* holding it over my head. Like why I was called before the locals. And you know what? I was the one who fuckin' convinced Richie to call 911. I was the one who said to do this by the book. Now I've got this organized crime task force all up in my grill."

"Wait, wait. Start from the beginning," Ryan said, checking his watch. "We've got eight minutes and twelve seconds."

Di Santo puffed out his chest. "Fuck their ten minutes! We'll get there when we get there!" There he was: the Di Santo Ryan respected. "Okay, so I get a call from my cousin—third cousin, mind you—Carlo. He says I gotta get over to the Riccis' house. Said something really bad went down there. I go, 'Why me?' and he goes, ''Cause they need your expertise.' Apparently Ricci asked for me by name."

"That's not good."

"That's not anything. That's normal in our culture. You know someone who knows someone who can help, so you help. What I was worried about was that they wanted a cover up or something. And then when I see his wife's body, I just about blew a gasket. I go, 'Oh, hell no, I'm not covering this, you need to call the cops.' But then I see Richie is bawling. Distraught. Inconsolable, even. Sitting on the front steps of his house howling his wife's name. So I go up to him, and he tells me he found her like that. Half outta the driveway and slumped over dead."

"Yeah, I saw her. She had a bullet in the skull—they say it looks like a sniper rifle. So what did Ricci say? Why did he call you in first?"

"He knows I'm a murder cop. He wants me to find the person who did it."

Ryan absorbed that for a moment. "And then tell him first?"

"You got it! So then the feds show up with this guy Jensen and he starts salivating at the thought of me being a cop and also a friend of the family—which you know I'm *not*, I barely know any of them. But Jensen gets it in his head that I could be an asset. He says to let Richie think I'm gonna be working for him, so I can get in with the family and feed the task force incriminating information. Apparently, they've been working on the Chicago mob since it reared its ugly head again after Family Secrets."

Operation Family Secrets was the infamous takedown of fourteen of the major players in the Chicago Outfit, where its own members broke their code of silence and sang like canaries.

Ryan shook his head at the thought of his partner being a federal asset. It was way too dangerous. "That's fucked up, D."

"I know! I know it's fucked up! But now I'm between this task force and the head of a crime family. Neither choice is good for my health, know what I'm saying?" Di Santo said, pulling at his necktie as if trying to escape a noose.

Ryan rubbed the stubble on his face as he thought about the situation. He hadn't even had time to shave before reporting to the crime scene. He'd been too wrapped up in Catharine…literally.

Di Santo continued, "So I told Agent Jensen out there that the only way I'd work this double-spy fiasco is if you'd work the actual case with me. Enter the great Detective Doherty." He put a hand on Ryan's shoulder.

"Gee, thanks."

"You gotta keep the feds at an arms' length for me, or else Ricci will smell it. I'm telling you, these wise guys are not idiots."

"But Ricci knows you're a cop. Does he know you're not dirty?"

"I made that extremely clear when I was convincing him to call in the homicide, believe-you-me. I'm worried that if he thinks I'm going along with this, he's going to pull me in for other bad shit. And you know what they say: once you're in—"

"Yeah, yeah. I've seen *The Godfather*."

There was a knock on the door, causing both of them to flinch.

"What?" Ryan answered.

The voice on the other side of the door did not belong to Agent Jensen. "Yo, I was looking for Di Santo and they said he was in this closet."

Di Santo shook his thumb at the door and mouthed *Richie Rich*.

CHAPTER 3

Ryan nodded toward the door and Di Santo opened it. In walked Ricardo Ricci, the godfather of the contemporary Chicago syndicate. Ricci was in his late forties and stood about an inch taller than Di Santo, with a barrel chest that made him look twice as wide. He had thinning brown hair, slicked back on a round pate, and wore his button-down shirt unbuttoned just enough to expose a thick tuft of Italian chest hair.

"Nice digs they give ya here," Ricci jibed, with no smile to accompany it. He threw a nod to Ryan as he moved between him and his partner. "So's I heard they're trying to recruit you for the task force," he said directly into Di Santo's face.

Ryan squeezed his eyes shut and mumbled, "What a *clusterfuck*. Already."

"No!" Di Santo said, almost simultaneously. "No. I'm not working for them."

"So you're working for me then, right?"

"No, Richie. I'm not working for you either. I work for the city. My boss is Sergeant Bob Besko with the Chicago PD Eighteenth District. I and my partner here—" He gestured to Ryan. "—have agreed to work your wife's case. I'm not getting in the middle of any RICO situations. We're here to find Robin's killer."

And with that the man crumbled. His shoulders shook as he covered his face with his hands. Ryan and Di Santo swapped a glance while Ricci pulled a white cotton hand-kerchief out of his pants pocket and blew his nose with a honk.

"That woman. She was the love of my life. I—I—*Madòn*, she's the mother of my children, God bless her soul, now what am I going to do? She was the love of my life, Di Santo. Love of my life. We met back when I was running for Charlie Bobs."

Di Santo patted the crime boss on his shoulder in an awkward move. "We'll find the guy, Rich," he said, in a tone quieter than Ryan had ever heard from his partner. "I promise you, we'll find him."

Ricci blew his nose again. "And then tell me first, right? Because we gotta do what we gotta do."

Di Santo threw a look to Ryan and Ryan shook his head, almost imperceptibly.

"I'm a cop, Richie. I can't condone anything you 'gotta do.' But we'll keep you posted every step of the way. In honor of you being family of the victim."

The man clenched his jaw as if chewing a horse. He pointed at the detectives with a chubby hand while grabbing the door handle with the other. "You will tell me. Because if it weren't for the families, Di Santo, you wouldn't be where you are in the Department. You'd still be a beat cop wag-ging your stick and arresting taggers. You'll tell me." He then pointed at Ryan. "And you, whoever-you-are-Mick, you will *not* get in our way."

Ricci opened and shut the door behind him just as Ryan was about to pounce. "Did he just call me a *Mick?*" he asked, turning back Di Santo. "Really?"

"They're throwbacks. To them, it's still 1945 and the city is divided in two: the Italians versus the Irish. It's not per-sonal."

"What did he mean about you getting where you are in the Department?"

"I have no fucking clue," Di Santo answered. Ryan narrowed his eyes while staring his partner down. "I swear to Mother Mary, ask Besko. Anyway, they don't have that kinda pull in the Department." Ryan remained silent. "*Really?* Really you gonna do me like that after almost three years of being together? Richie probably just threw that out to pit us against each other. They're not dumb, you know. It's all street smarts. Now let's get back out there before they think we're going at it in here. Shit."

Ryan accepted that answer. For now. But he'd put it on his mental shelf until he could ask Besko about it later. Not that he didn't trust Di Santo. He'd never doubted that his partner was completely clean. Di Santo had admitted his distant ties to the Chicago Outfit early on in their partnership. It was never a secret. He had described his connection as extremely peripheral—cousins, in-laws of cousins. As far as Di Santo was concerned, he was never personally involved in any mob activity and neither was his immediate family.

But they had a murder case on their hands, and now that he had gotten his partner out of the clutches of the feds, Ryan surprised himself at how eager he was to start working the case. Robin Ricci was a mother, a daughter, a wife, and there were people suffering that loss. A loss that he knew very well.

"Hey, look at the guys from the Eighteenth!" a River Forest cop announced as they re-entered the squad room. "They're comin' out of the closet! Together!"

The room broke out in applause. The detectives acknowledged the ribbing with smirks and accompanying waves.

Jensen beckoned them over to a conference room on the far side of the squad, hidden behind vertical blinds. Ryan took in the room as he entered: brown file folders and some loose papers divided into several piles on the conference table, along with yellow legal pads and half-empty coffee cups saving seats for members of the task force who were filing in again. On the far wall hung a white board with a massive org chart labeled *Chicago Outfit*.

"Take a seat, gentlemen," Jensen instructed. "Ricci just left. We'll try to give you a general overview on the organized crime families of Chicago, as they exist today, to help with your investigation. This has to be a co-agency initiative."

Ryan and Di Santo took two seats near the head of the table that didn't have obvious occupants. Ryan scanned the task force agents at the table. Aside from Jensen, there were six male agents in matching suits, one female.

"We've got four families, dividing up Chicago by territory," Jensen began his lecture. "They split up the city according to a pact created in the mid-nineties called 'The Four Corners.' Basically north, south, east, and west. Our friend Ricardo Ricci—or Richie Rich to his friends—has the sweetest territory: the Loop and the East Side, along the lake. Victor Basso, also known as 'The Big Fish,' covers the South Side and Chinatown." Jensen pointed a laser to the org chart. "Joseph Giordano, aka 'Joey Bones,' has the West Side, and the Leone twins cover the north, from Lincoln Park up to Howard Street."

Ryan leaned toward Di Santo. "How come we've never heard of the Leone twins if they're operating in our district?"

"The Leones have been pretty quiet the past couple of years," Jensen answered, as if Ryan had thrown the question to the room. "Danny and Desirée Leone are only twenty-three years old, with barely a high school degree between them. The two started apprenticing with their father instead of going to college. They took over the rackets of the North Side after Paul Leone died, about a year ago. But the kids are more about spending the money than making it, and they really don't know what the hell they're doing. Because of this, the rackets activity on your North Side has slowed and their business has too. Bad for them, but good for us, as we don't have to keep watch over them too closely."

Ryan nodded. One of the agents on the far side of the table caught his eye, as he'd noticed the guy staring at him for the last couple of minutes. When he decided to make direct eye contact, the bespectacled agent flashed a grin, lasting no more than 0.8 seconds, then dropped his gaze to his notebook and continued to scribble. Ryan had come across some strange characters in dealing with the feds in the past, but this guy was an oddity. Solid, broad-shouldered, but sat with his shoulders hunched, as if he wanted to fade into the background. There was something about him that Ryan couldn't quite grasp. Despite the nerd factor, the agent looked vaguely familiar. Maybe they'd met on a previous case.

Ryan dropped his scrutiny of the man when Jensen continued. "The families are into three rackets and you can remember them using the acronym PUB: Protection, Unions, Bookmaking. Most of their income comes from the bookmaking. Big connections with Vegas. However, nowadays the Outfit covers its tracks. They pay their taxes, thanks to Uncle Al, and they can launder money like champions. Their newest venture is The Chicago, a hotel, casino and resort in Las Vegas. All four families went in with a developer and have different ownership percentages in the resort. Our task force is currently working with the Las Vegas PD to figure out how they're getting the money there and washed."

Jensen paused and cast a gaze straight at Di Santo, as if he was going to respond with the answer. But the silence created awkward shifting from several of the task force members.

Ryan spoke up. "Well, this is all very informative, but we're here to investigate the Ricci homicide and see if it's connected to the death of Sandy Orlando. Can you explain the connection between the two vics?"

"Absolutely. Victim number one, Sandy Orlando, was a longtime companion of Victor Basso—he's our South Side guy. The two were apparently together while his wife was alive and when she died (of ovarian cancer) they continued the relationship, making it public. Well, *more* public. These guys, they're not ashamed of their *'gomattas.'* In fact almost every one of them has something on the side, with the exception of Ricci. He seemed pretty devoted to his wife. Anyway, Ms. Orlando was killed when she hit the divider rail on the Dan Ryan, spun out, and hit a semi which couldn't stop in time."

Ryan flashed on Jon's death. Something he hadn't witnessed, although the scene had repeated hundreds of times in his head like a bad newsreel. On his way home from their monthly poker game, Jon had stopped to help a driver change a tire on the shoulder of the highway—even off duty, Jon was first and foremost a public servant. A truck driver had sideswiped the wreck, instantly killing Jon and the man he had stopped to help.

Out of the corner of his eye, Ryan saw that the strange agent at the end of the table had taken up staring again. He decided to ignore it, hoping the guy would lose interest, and turned his attention back to the agent in charge.

"The Medical Examiner ran tests and found that Ms. Orlando had a lethal dose of prescription drugs in her system," Jensen continued, "and it was put down as a straight OD/DUI. No one else was injured in the accident. The day of the incident, we interviewed Basso and associates and there was no motive whatsoever for him to have offed the woman. For one, it's extremely rare that the mob takes out hits on women. We know from our research that wives and girlfriends are all usually off limits. Number two, from all accounts, Basso and Orlando had a good relationship. And three, she had no money of her own. So there was just no motive for Basso to have offed her. He did say she'd been on several legit prescriptions, so we chalked it up to an overdose."

"Until Robin Ricci," Di Santo concluded.

Jensen pointed at him. "Yes. Until Mrs. Ricci. We actually came forward to the RFPD as soon as we heard about

Mrs. Ricci this morning, informing them there may be a connection. Two women, companions to the major family heads, dead within two weeks. Just doesn't sound kosher to us. Especially since Ricci's death is an obvious homicide by firearm. Now, according to our official definition, this isn't a serial murder unless there are three proven victims. So even if these two cases are related, we can't classify it as such until there's a third."

Silence hung in the room while they all considered the connection. Ryan turned to his partner. "What do you think? Gut instinct?"

Di Santo studied the org chart before answering. "So who's next?" he answered—both to Ryan and to the room.

Jensen frowned. "Who's…"

"Next," Di Santo repeated. "If we assume this is on its way to being a serial, who would be next? I'm seeing that we've got two scenarios: either one family is targeting the other three, in which case you still have one more victim to go, or we have someone outside of the families targeting all four, in which case there are two more potential victims. I'd start there."

"Interesting," Jensen replied. Apparently, their super task force brains hadn't gotten that far. "So, we use the remaining families as bait—"

"Not *bait*, asshole! We *protect* them!" Di Santo responded, flying out of his seat. "These aren't animals, these are people—*loved ones*—we're talking about."

Ryan placed a hand on Di Santo's arm, and stood up next to him. "We'll get the case files from the sergeant on duty," he said, attempting to dissipate the tension. "Agent Jensen, if you could get us a list of family members for the remaining families, the Leones and Giordanos, we'll interview them and organize a plan of protection. I think that's all we need from you at the moment." He pulled several business cards from his wallet and splayed them on the table. "My cell and email are on there. We'll be in touch."

Di Santo took the cue, tearing off the notes he'd taken on

the yellow pad and folding them into equal quadrants.

"But what about what we need from you?" Jensen protested. "It's a huge advantage to us that we've got a guy on the inside."

Before Di Santo could scream bloody murder, Ryan responded with authority, "Let me make this clear to all of you. You *don't* have a guy on the inside. Detective Di Santo has no involvement with the families whatsoever. He's no more on the inside than you or me. In addition, he's not *your* guy. Out of respect for another law enforcement agency, we'll keep you informed of our investigation. But no fucking way will we *inform on* them. That's not our job." And with a final "Good Day," Ryan practically pulled Di Santo out of the conference room and out of the building.

CHAPTER 4

Two years, Ten months, Twenty-two Days Ago:

D r. Sullivan had finally sent the form to Besko with the approval for Ryan to return to the job. He had been out on leave for over a month and had badgered the doc at the end of each session to set a return date. The last session of last week they had finally agreed that it was time.

A couple of uniformed officers waved at Ryan as he pulled his easily recognizable '66 Mustang into the cops' lot at the 18th District house. He paused for a moment to look at the station. Not that he expected anything to be different, it was just that life had changed so drastically that it was jarring that it all looked the same. As if nothing had happened. As if they weren't a man down.

"Hey, look who's here!" the desk sergeant shouted as he opened the glass door.

Ryan greeted the man with a firm handclasp. "How's it going, Firenzo?"

"Great, D." The desk sarge ruffled Ryan's hair over the desk. "Great to see you back. We missed you. You look good! A little thinner, but good." Ryan took the compliment and combed his bangs back with one hand. "Besko was on cloud nine, getting everything ready for you."

"Getting everything ready? There better not be balloons or anything."

"Nah, nah. Nuttin' like that," Firenzo responded. "But I think some guys from the squad are planning to take you to lunch. That's it. No surprises."

Good. He hated surprises. He ended the conversation with a wave and took the main stairs to the second floor. About a foot from the double doors of the detective squad room, Ryan stopped. The hallway was lined with headshots of officers who had died. At the end of the line hung a new photograph of his partner, Jon Lange, smiling back at him like he was going to live until a ripe old age. Like he was looking forward to finding a wife, having kids, and eventually rocking his grandchildren on the porch.

"You couldn't have just let me walk in there without stepping right out in front of me, could you?" Ryan said to the photo.

'*I want you to go in there and kick ass,*' Jon replied.

"But you're not going to be in there."

'*Oh yes, I will, my man. I'll always be there.*'

Ryan took a deep breath, slapped on a smile to match Jon's and strutted into the squad room. As expected, everyone rose to greet him en masse. He slapped hands, assuring his colleagues that things were good, he was good, and he was ready to get back on the job. And then something caught his eye: an unidentified male individual occupied the desk across from his. Jon's desk. A little guy in a dark suit, watching the crowd of detectives with a smile, tapping a pencil on the desk as if he was waiting his turn.

Ryan thought the guy might just have been lost or visiting, until he saw the nameplate: *Det. Matthew X. Di Santo.* A slap on the back interrupted Ryan's confusion, and he turned to see his sarge, Robert Besko, in all his glory.

"Glad to have you back, D!" Besko announced, accustomed to projecting his voice above the din of cops. "Have we got a caseload for you! C'mon, let's talk in my office."

"Yes. Let's talk," Ryan said through his teeth. He nodded

to the "Catch you laters" and "Really good to see yous" as the other cops dispersed back to their desk pods and cubicles. On his way to Besko's office, he laser-eyed the guy at Jon's desk, who turned away and began typing on his laptop.

As soon as Besko shut the door behind him, Ryan started in. "Who the fuck is that kid? You reassign Jon's desk the minute he's gone? How can you—"

"D, if you shut the hell up, I can explain the situation to you. Now sit down."

Ryan shut his mouth and pulled out a guest chair in front of the desk. Besko's office was tight and cramped, with a desk that was a little too big for the 150 square feet that the sarge was allotted. Two file cabinets testified that Besko was not ready to go paperless, despite the twenty-two-inch computer screen sitting behind him.

"To answer your first question, Detective Di Santo is the newest member of our team," the sarge said, easing himself into his executive chair.

"How old is that guy?" Ryan responded. "He looks like he just started shaving."

"Older than you think, but one of the youngest to make detective in quite a while. Really smart fellow, and we're lucky to have him." Ryan let out a *humph* of disbelief and crossed his arms in denial. "And to answer your second question, Jon's been gone over a month. You haven't been here, but the squad has been mourning just as much as you have."

"Not possible."

"Okay, maybe not. But don't think you've cornered the market on grief. We all felt it. We all loved him. And now it's time to get back to work. That doesn't mean we've forgotten him. That means we're gonna honor Detective Lange by doing what we do best: catching the bad guys."

It was evident that Besko had prepared this speech specifically for his homecoming. Ryan sighed and scrubbed the bottom half of his face with his hand. It was the first time in weeks that he had shaved and he wasn't quite used to the smooth skin. "So you said you've got a lot of cases going? Who's that Demento guy paired up with? Terry?"

Besko dropped his chin and grimaced at Ryan, as if saying he was an idiot.

"No," Ryan balked at the unspoken response. "No, no, no. No way."

"Nobody works alone, D. Everyone gets a partner. Including you."

"Anyone but *that* guy. C'mon, Sarge. It's my first day back and you spring this on me? Let me at least have someone who's gone through puberty. How about Mitchell? Isn't his partner on paternity leave? And when Corrigan gets back, he can take Demento—"

"Di Santo."

"He's a new father. Corrigan will be used to infants."

Besko couldn't help but guffaw at that one. His bouncing belly brought a smile to Ryan's face, too. He missed this, the cop banter. It was the only thing that kept them all sane. "Aw, D. I wish I could. But something else happened while you were gone. The Department is implementing a new program called POMP. Police Officer's Mentorship Program. We have to match one senior detective with a junior detective, and I thought this would be the perfect opportunity for you to get to know the new guy. After all, you're one of the best cops we've got."

Ryan narrowed his eyes. "You trying to flatter me into this?"

"I don't have to flatter you into this. I'm your fucking boss. What I say goes. And this goes. You and *Di Santo* are officially participants in the program as of today." The sarge slapped a green form on the desk in front of him. "You will evaluate the guy after six months, one year, and two years."

"*Two years?* I have to be with that little shit for two years?"

"And he will evaluate you too, as a mentor. Now it's about time you two meet, officially."

Ryan rubbed his eyes, trying to erase this whole scene. "Is there anything I can do to get out of this?"

"Well, I could give you another month off to think about it," Besko said, his index finger hovering over the speakerphone button. After a long sigh, Ryan shook his head and gave in, pouting nonetheless. Besko pressed the button. "Detective Di Santo to my office!" he shouted into the phone. The echo rang out on the other side of the sarge's door.

In under five seconds, the door opened and the guy in the suit entered with a notebook in one hand and pen in the other. He hooked the pen into the spiral and held out his hand to Ryan.

"Hi, Detective Doherty, I'm Matt Di Santo," he gushed. "It's such an honor to finally meet you. I've been reading up on all your cases. Do you know what's funny? The guys in the squad, they started calling me D, too. They've been calling me 'the other D,' so isn't that perfect? We're both D! You're D, and I'm Other D, like we were meant to work together. I've been really looking forward to today."

Ryan blinked at the verbal barrage. "*Sarge?*" he whined.

"Shake his fucking hand, Doherty. D, meet D. Now we've got the Double-D. Hey! The Double-D. I just made a joke."

Ryan ignored Besko's attempt at humor and stood up, intentionally using his six-foot frame to intimidate the new squad member while he shook his small, sweaty palm.

"I'm so sorry for your loss, too, Detective," Di Santo said with a somber frown. "Such a tragedy."

Ryan remained silent.

"Doherty, take the form," Besko barked. "Di Santo, bring him up to date on the latest cases, and let's all make nice. Now get out of my office. Welcome back, Doherty."

Ryan left Besko's office without a second glance at Di Santo. *Double-D*, his ass. He was the only D on the squad. There was no other D. Especially this little...Chihuahua-like creature in a suit. Ryan and Di Santo were nothing alike, nor was he going to put any time into mentoring the little shit. He could learn how to police like they all did, from the experience. Street-educated.

Ryan crumpled up the form and tossed it into his top desk drawer before dropping down into his chair. He took his laptop out of its carrying case, powered it up and proceeded to check his email. He could feel Di Santo's stare as he went about his morning business.

"So when do you wanna go over these cases?" the guy said, tapping that pencil again.

Ryan let his email download while he pushed out his chair and headed to the break room. He heard patter behind him like a baby duckling following his mother.

As he poured himself a mug of coffee, Di Santo caught up. "Ya know, I was expecting there to be a little adjustment period, but you don't have to be a dick about it. I mean, seriously. I'm not the new kid in school. We're all adults, here. This job is my life, and if you don't think I'm going to give it my all, well then you don't know me. I can be every bit as good a partner as Detective Lange—"

Ryan dropped the coffee mug and pinned Di Santo against the wall, with his arm across the throat. "Don't you ever—*ever*—mention Jon's name to me. And if you compare yourself to him again, I will kill you. Outright. And there won't have to be a fucking investigation because I'll leave my DNA all over your fucking body. Do you understand me?"

Di Santo attempted to choke out several syllables, failing at each one.

"*Do you understand me?*" Ryan shouted. The little guy's eyes bulged and his face started to turn blue when Ryan realized what he was doing and released him. Di Santo fell to the floor, inhaling with a gulp and a wheeze. "And what the fuck are you wearing? This isn't a used car lot. We don't wear suits here."

Ryan left the new guy on the floor of the break room and went back to his desk. Back to his email. After four minutes and thirty-three seconds, Di Santo emerged from the break room and returned to Jon's desk. Fuck the nameplate, it would always be Jon's desk. The squad remained abnormally silent, while no words whatsoever passed between Ryan and the man across the desk pod. At 11:57, Di Santo got up, brushed off his suit, and announced he was meeting a friend for lunch and left.

"He's only twenty-six, you know," Ostroski said to Ryan's back. "He definitely talks too much, but the kid's on the ball. Got one of the top scores on the detective's exam. It was big news around here."

Ryan took in Ostroski's words without turning around.

Detective Pike added, "We already gave him a pretty hard time when he got here a coupla weeks ago. He's been through the hazing, D, so you could cut him a break."

Ryan jiggled his leg as he absorbed what the guys were trying to say. He wasn't pissed at Di Santo. Not really. He was pissed at the sarge for assigning him a new partner. For the idiotic POMP program. And for springing everything on him the day he got back. Even an email would have softened the blow.

"C'mon, Doherty, talk to us," Terry Cornell called out. Ryan rotated his chair to face them. "We're really glad you're back. In fact, we wanted to give you this." Cornell walked over and handed him a small rectangle gift-wrapped in blue tissue paper. Ryan tore it open, his anger diminishing. When the tissue paper had drifted to the floor, he was looking at a framed photo of him and Jon, both beaming at the camera, their arms around each other's shoulders.

"Remember that day, D? The Memorial Day game when we beat the CFD six to zero?"

Ryan couldn't help but crack a smile at the photo and the memory of how the Chicago PD had shut down the Fire Department in the annual exhibition ballgame at Wrigley. It was a good day.

"Yeah. Thanks, guys, this is great. I'm going to keep it right here."

He swiveled back to face his desk and placed the photo right next to his computer.

He then took the framed photo of Kelly and tossed it into the garbage.

CHAPTER 5

Current Day:

After they left the River Forest police headquarters, Ryan drove Di Santo back to the crime scene where he'd left his car. The red Caddy holding Robin Ricci's body had been removed from the driveway along with the tricycle. Evidence techs had come and gone, leaving streamers of broken caution tape waving in the warm September breeze.

"Hey, thanks for standing up for me back there with the feds," Di Santo said, as they pulled up beside his car.

Ryan nodded. "We have to be really careful with this one, D. We're walking a thin line. If Ricci gets to the perp before we do, there's a chance you could be indicted as an accessory."

"I know, I know. Like I said, I have no intention of letting him take care of business. This is our case and we're gonna get the perp behind bars. What Richie does with him then is not our call. I'm not even sure how far his reach extends."

Ryan slapped his partner on the back. "Exactly. See you back at the—"

A knock on the window startled both of the detectives. Di Santo rolled down the passenger window of the vintage

Mustang by its manual crank. "Tootie, what are you doing here?"

The man could have been a gorilla in a designer suit, half busting out of the seams. His greased hair had comb tracks in it from front to back. "Hey, Matt. I'm here because I work for Mr. Ricci. He wants to talk to you. Both of yous."

"Fuck, really? My sister never—" Di Santo stopped when Ryan interrupted by clearing his throat. "D, this is Tootie—well, *Tony,* actually. I told you about him, he's my sister Gina's boyfriend."

Ryan ruminated on that new tidbit, which didn't bode well for his partner. "Look, we really need to get back to the station house and start the investigation," he replied, hoping Di Santo would interpret it as a command.

"I think you really want to talk to Mr. Ricci," Tootie said. "He wants to tell you guys that he thinks he knows who killed his wife."

Ryan and Di Santo exchanged a look, and Di Santo sent him an unspoken plea. He wasn't sure if it meant *please let's hear him out*, or *please let's get the hell out of here*. Ryan made an executive decision and pulled the car into a spot just ahead of Di Santo's white Fiat, out of earshot from The Hulk.

"You think Ricci's messing with us?" Ryan asked his partner, shutting off the engine.

"We gotta hear what he has to say," Di Santo responded. "And I swear to God, I'm going to give my sister hell about this guy. What was she thinking?"

"You didn't know Tony was connected? For real?"

"No, he said he worked construction. Although, come to think of it, he was always dressed a little too nice for a construction worker. *Fuck!* My ma is going to have a fit. She's really sensitive about our cousins being tied to the Outfit and raised us to stay far, far away from the business."

They got out of the Mustang and entered the estate through a pedestrian entry gate that Tootie held open with one of his thick arms.

On the front steps, he insisted on taking their cell phones and then patted both detectives down.

"You asked *us* to come in here, how could we be wearing a wire?" Ryan asked him.

Tootie ignored the question and led them into the house, where they were greeted by Ricci, amped up on something much stronger than caffeine. He was almost frenetic as he herded them into the living area, a room lush with ornate white and gold furniture. Not Ryan's taste by any stretch of the imagination. He'd seen this style of décor in other homes of working-class hoods who'd made it rich—high-end drug dealers, pimps. Those who mistakenly thought gaudy and flashy was how you showed off your wealth. In their circles, it probably was.

"Sit down, sit down, *sedetevi*," Ricci instructed. "Can I get you anything? A drink? Bourbon?"

"No, we're good," Di Santo said. "So, Tootie said that you might have a lead for us?"

"Yes! Yes! Shit, let me pour one for me."

Ryan almost reminded the man that it was not yet noon, but considering the day he'd had, maybe he needed it. And anyway, Ryan was the last person who could preach prohibition to someone in mourning.

Ricci came back with a tumbler of brown liquid and sat down opposite the detectives. "My children, bless their hearts, are with my sister. I just couldn't take their faces. *Madón.*" He threw back a healthy portion of the bourbon, while Ryan and Di Santo remained silent. They were trained to let the family member of a victim speak freely, without interruption, as there were really no words of consolation that could help them in their time of grief. "Anyway, I was thinkin' about the details of the hit. They told me at the station that it was a sniper attack. That the guy was up in a tree. A fucking tree!" He stretched his neck to the side, then leaned forward in his chair. "Well, I started to think on the drive back—who the hell could sit up in a tree in broad daylight—with a fucking sniper rifle, no less—and lay in wait for my beautiful wife to exit our house, without anyone seeing him? And then it hit me! *The Ghost!*"

"A…ghost?" Ryan was worried the man had just lost his mind in grief.

Di Santo scrunched his face in confusion. "Richie, you think a *ghost* did it?"

"Yes. And no. And yes." Ricci scratched between his legs and then took another drink. "So this is all off the record, right?"

Ryan was getting tired of the games. "We're not journalists, Ricci. And we're not your lawyer. We're cops. So if you're about to confess something—"

Di Santo held an arm out in front of Ryan. "Yeah, yeah, Rich. If you've got evidence that someone did something and it's related your wife's homicide, nothing else matters right now. Unless you were an accomplice."

Ricci's eyes bounced around the room, as if he was trying to plan an escape route. He twisted his head again from side to side before continuing his story. "Okay, so there's this independent contractor that works for the families. He has always stayed really incognito. But he's the best at what he does, know what I'm saying?"

Ryan took a breath. "You mean he was a hit—"

"Yeah, yeah, we know what you're saying," Di Santo interrupted. "Tell us more about this guy."

"Well, he's the best because nobody knows what he looks like. He never met any of us—his clients—in person. And when he does a job, he gets in and out of the situation without nobody noticing. A true master of his craft, he leaves no trace. So you know, internally within the organization, we started calling him *The Ghost*."

"Sounds like he's benefitting from the relationship, though," Ryan said, without exactly acknowledging the reality of said relationship. "So why would he suddenly turn on you and come after your loved ones?"

Ricci shifted on the sofa and cracked his neck, in what was becoming a nervous tick. "This Ghost guy, obviously he was an associate of ours, but then he started getting greedy. Sent us messages about maybe taking his own territory. This guy's a hired hand, not even vouched for by nobody. What was he thinking? I told him 'No go,' and don't ever ask for anything like that ever. But then he writes back, mentioning that he had a lotta incriminating information, and we wouldn't want it to get out to that fucking task force."

Ryan pulled out a small spiral notebook from his back pocket and started taking notes. "So he was blackmailing you? You said he wrote you. How did you guys communicate?"

"Through secret websites. I didn't do it. The young guy, Leone, is real good with computers. He would communicate with him. What's that?" Ricci said, suddenly noticing Ryan's notebook. "You're not writing this down, are you?"

"I have to write it down in order to remember it," Ryan responded. "You want us to help you or not?" Ricci seemed to accept that, so Ryan continued with the interrogation. "So you think this Ghost guy is targeting your families because he's pissed about the rejection?"

Ricci threw back the rest of the bourbon, emptying the glass. "If he is, he's in big trouble. I don't know, guys. Maybe it's him, maybe it isn't. I can't think straight. But all's I know is this shit ain't right. And it has his MO all over it. *The Ghost.*" He slammed down the tumbler, punctuating his theory.

"Do you have a real name for this guy, Rich?" Di Santo asked.

"No, no information whatsoever on who he is or where he came from."

"A picture? A description?"

Ricci shook his head and Ryan re-read his notes. "So if you needed this Ghost's services, you said that Danny Leone would contact him through a secret website?"

"If—theoretically—people would need his services, they would—theoretically—place an ad online on a certain underground website with certain wording and all that. But listen, guys, no one, and I mean *no one* goes after wives and kids. That breaks our code. They're off limits. That's why none of this makes any sense." Ricci fell into a slump, tears rolling down his face again.

"I'm so sorry," Ryan said, changing back to a sympathy tack.

Ricci pulled the cloth handkerchief out of his pants pocket again, blew his nose for an inordinate amount of time, and dabbed his eyes with the same rag.

"That's a lot of good information to start the investigation, Mr. Ricci, and we thank you for it. We'll do our best to close this as soon as possible. This has been a tough day for you, and now we'll let you be with your family." Ryan nodded a *let's go* to his partner and they left Ricci's house, with Tootie following close behind.

When they were back out in the drive, the man returned their cell phones and Di Santo stuck a finger in his chest. "You bring my sister into this bullshit, Toots?"

"Man, she has no knowledge of nothing," the guy said. He twisted the handle on the front gate and held it open for them.

"We're not done with this conversation," Di Santo warned. Ryan stood beside his partner in solidarity until Tootie waved the threat away with a laugh and retreated back to the house. "What am I going to do now?" Di Santo complained to Ryan, while unlocking his Fiat with a chirp. "I'm going to have to tell her to drop the guy. No-good piece of filth."

Ryan scoffed. "I dunno, D, I've got three sisters and I don't believe any of them would let me give them dating advice. The more you protest, the more she'll want to be with him—Romeo and Juliet syndrome, and all that. I say let it alone and she'll figure it out." He checked his phone to see if Jane had texted him back. She hadn't.

"Can I at least tell her who the thug works for?" Di Santo said, breaking into his concern.

"Yeah, I think that could come up in conversation: 'You'll never guess who I ran into at the home of one of the top Chicago crime bosses. Your *boyfriend!*'"

"That's exactly what I'm gonna say. Thanks."

Ryan rolled his eyes. "Well, good luck with that." Before Di Santo could get into his car, Ryan added, "But I'd do it sooner rather than later. On top of everything else, this Tootie connection is not going to make life easier for you."

"I know, I know. You don't think I know that? That big thug makes me two degrees from Richie Rich. That's too fucking close."

"Too fucking close."

CHAPTER 6

Ryan pulled into the 18th District lot and parked next to Di Santo's Fiat. The guy was so proud of his heritage that even his car was Italian, and he yapped incessantly to anyone who would listen that it stood for Fabbrica Italiana Automobili Torino. Ryan would've barely fit in the car, but it was perfect for Other D…until he made enough to get a Ferrari or Lamborghini.

As Ryan entered the station's lobby, Firenzo flagged him down from the reception desk. "Hey, Doherty! Your brother's here to see you." The sergeant nodded toward the waiting area chairs lined up against the front wall.

"I don't have a—" Ryan turned to see the strange task force agent who had been staring at him in the meeting. "*You.*"

The man stood up slowly to greet him. He held out palm and said, "Agent Doherty."

"Detective," Ryan corrected him. "I'm *Detective* Doherty."

"Yes, I know. *I'm* Agent Doherty. Devin Doherty. Pleased to meet you." He shook with an unexpected vice grip, one that could've rivaled Ryan's own. "I tried to catch you at the other police station, but you and your partner left so quickly." He paused for a response, but Ryan gave none. "I'm sorry, I didn't mean for you to find out this way. It's just that the desk sergeant asked for my identification, and…well, when he saw my name, I had to explain. Is there someplace we can talk? In private?"

"You didn't mean for me to find out *what* this way?" Ryan asked.

"That you had a brother."

Ryan let out a nervous laugh. "Yeah, sorry, pal. I don't have a brother. Three sisters, that's all. And that's enough. You must have the wrong guy." He turned to dismiss the agent.

"I'm pretty sure I have the right guy. I figured our paths would cross one day, since we're both in law enforcement. And when I was assigned to the Organized Crime Task Force here in Chicago, I was hoping to meet you."

Ryan took a longer look at the man. He couldn't deny that there was a resemblance. The agent was the same height and build as Ryan, with the similar Black Irish coloring: milk chocolate hair and dark chocolate eyes, as his mom would say. The agent's hair was styled in military fashion, buzzed on the sides, and his face was longer. Almost as if Ryan was staring into one of those distorted fun house mirrors.

"Can I see that ID that you showed to the desk sergeant?" Ryan asked.

"Oh, yes, of course." The agent patted all of his pants pockets as if he'd forgotten where he'd put his wallet, and eventually pulled a billfold out of his jacket and handed it over with his driver's license.

"Maryland?" Ryan asked, raising an eyebrow.

"I normally work out of the Pentagon."

The date of birth was April 30th, same year as Ryan's. Two months, one day older. The name on the license read *Devin Joseph Doherty,* causing Ryan's stomach to sting with recognition. Ryan's father had been one of six sons, so there was a sea of Dohertys out there in Chicagoland, and across the entire country. This guy could very well be a cousin.

"Impossible. I don't have a brother," he said, handing back the man's identification. Sergeant Vic Firenzo cleared his throat, reminding them they weren't alone in the lobby.

"I realize this is an extraordinary situation," Agent Doherty said in a slightly stilted tone. "Like I asked previously, is there somewhere private we can talk? I can tell you the whole story."

Ryan opened a mental investigation: Agent Doherty's posture was similar to his father's, who had been a solid six-foot and stocky but never quite owned up to his height, often hunching his shoulders like someone twice his age. And then there was the name. Through the years his mom had relayed the story about the Doherty children's naming pattern that she and Dad had agreed on: they had to be Irish, and they had to end in the letter N to honor Dad's mother, Eireen. Hence the children were named Ryan, Siobhan, Erin, and Finn, in order. Devin not only fit the naming pattern, but he also bore Ryan's own father's name as his middle name: Joseph.

It was enough to earn him a conversation.

Ryan gestured for the agent to follow him.

As they made their way upstairs, the agent tried to make small talk. "So, do the police officers call this the 'oh-one-eight'?"

"No, because this isn't *Dragnet*," Ryan replied. "We call it the Eighteenth."

When they entered the squad room, most of the cubicles stood empty with the exception of two detectives who'd pulled the Sunday shift. And Di Santo. Besko's office was dark, indicating that he'd taken off after his appearance at the crime scene.

Di Santo glanced up from his desk, and when he saw Ryan had a guest, he stood up and buttoned his jacket, expecting an introduction.

Ryan stopped to oblige. "This is my partner, Matt Di Santo. You saw him at the meeting, earlier. D, this is Agent Devin…Doherty."

"*Doherty?* Seriously? What're the odds? Are you two related? Ya gotta be related. Now that I see you standing side by side, you kind of look like brothers!"

Ryan sidestepped the accusation. "Um, Agent Doherty needs to speak to me in private. We'll be in Room One."

Di Santo nodded, acknowledging the coded message. Anytime they mentioned a specific interrogation room it was a signal for the other to either observe or record. Or both.

Ryan led the agent to the interview rooms in back and into IR1, closing the door behind him. "Have a seat."

Agent Doherty glanced around the cinderblock-lined room, wiped his palms on his pants, and did as instructed. His eyes went everywhere but on the man opposite him, as if he knew that he was about to be interrogated like every criminal who sat in this room before him. That gave Ryan a bit of comfort. This was his territory and he wanted to be alpha in this conversation.

He waited for the suspect to speak first. Nobody likes a quiet room.

"I know this must be really strange for you…" Devin began, fidgeting to get comfortable. His knees kept hitting the underside of the metal table. "Like I said, when I found out we'd be working together, I figured this would be a great opportunity to connect. I don't expect you to take my word for it, so I brought evidence. I have my birth certificate, but I wish to explain it to you, first." The man spoke in an almost robotic manner. Ryan gestured for him to continue.

"Okay. So I was born and raised in Milwaukee. My mother was never married. She had always been vague when it came to my biological father, but had told me some things about him. About how I looked like him, about how she and my dad were never married, and how they separated before I was born. That was all I knew, until I was an adult. When she was diagnosed with leukemia and knew she was dying, she told me the rest of the story."

Ryan thought about the history of the situation, imagining this man coming into the world at the time when his mother was seven months pregnant with him. "So, what you're trying to tell me is that my dad was a cheating scumbag. Sorry, Agent What-ever-your-name-is. I don't buy that. My parents had a great marriage. They loved each other very much and, furthermore, my mother would never have put up with that."

"Joseph Andrew Doherty. He died nineteen years ago, correct? I remember the day well. I was at the University of Wisconsin in Madison. My mother called me and left a message that my dad had died. It was ironic, since I had been planning on visiting Chicago that summer…I don't know…perhaps to meet him. Perhaps to say something, introduce myself, get to know him. I don't know what I was going to say. But then when she told me he had died, my dream of meeting my father died along with him."

Ryan recalled the day his father died. Upon returning to his apartment from Econ class, he found his roommate pacing back and forth.

"Oh, Dude, I'm so sorry," Chuck had greeted him. "You really need to call your mom. Your dad just had a heart attack." By the time Ryan had returned his mother's call, his father was already gone. DOA at Rush Medical Center.

Ryan studied the man who shared a resemblance, the man who'd refused to make steady eye contact since he'd sat down in the interview room. Occasionally, he'd look in Ryan's direction but then would scratch behind his ear or check his phone. Historically, a lack of eye contact meant the suspect was lying.

"Sorry, man, I call bullshit. How did your mom know that my dad had died if they weren't in touch?"

"Fair question, fair question."

Ryan clenched his teeth at the compliment.

"She saw his obituary online. She still read the *Chicago Tribune* religiously and kept up with her sports teams. She was a Chicagoan at heart."

Ryan frowned, not quite wanting to accept this new reality. This new brother.

Devin pulled out a sheet of paper, and proceeded to unfold it. He placed it face up on the table in front of Ryan. "Here, this is a copy of my birth certificate. You can keep it."

Ryan scrutinized the certificate. *Devin Joseph Doherty* was born in the city of Chicago, county of Cook. Not the same hospital as Ryan, but one close to their old neighborhood. Father: *Joseph Andrew Doherty*. Mother: *Mary Elizabeth Rafferty*.

"How do I know you didn't just Photoshop this crap?"

"You are a police officer and therefore have the ability to pull public records. So why would I even attempt to make it up?"

He had a point, but Ryan didn't like the guy's arrogance. "Who was Mary Rafferty and how did she know my father?"

"My mom's family lived next door to yours. She was young and still living with her parents at the time of their…affair."

"*How* young?"

Devin Doherty took a deep breath and cleared his throat before responding. "Eighteen."

The number hit Ryan like a wrecking ball in the chest. "Okay, let me get this straight: you want me to believe that *one*, my father had an affair while practically a newlywed, and *two*, that he was such a piece of shit that he slept with the teenager next door? No. That wasn't my dad. What the hell do you want?"

"I didn't come here to ask for anything."

"Of course, you want something. Is it money? If it's money, you're out of luck, because my dad only had a couple thousand left after all the bills were paid. And that's long gone." Ryan was shouting before even realizing he had raised his voice.

"I said, I don't want anything!" Devin raised his voice in

turn. He then took a breath, visibly calming himself down. "Look, I only want to connect with my family. My mom died last month. She was only fifty-eight. And now I have no one. I'm—I'm just searching for my family. That's it. I was an only child of a mother who was estranged from her family because they were so ashamed. I was the 'Big Mistake,' a reminder of one tragic error in judgment. My mom made me promise not to contact anyone on Dad's side until after she was gone. She didn't want to start trouble. That's why she moved away from Chicago to Wisconsin—she went to live with her aunt. But now I feel like I have no one, nothing. Well, I have a good career. I love my job." He pushed his glasses up the bridge of his nose. "But I want a family."

Ryan got up from the table and began to pace the room. None of this made sense. In response, Devin got up from his chair, shuffled his feet and waited for a response.

When Ryan could gather his thoughts he got up into Devin's face. "Does my mom know about you?"

"Not that I'm aware. My mother said Shirley knew about the affair, but she didn't know about the baby—about me. But I've done my research on your mother, too. She lives in Phoenix, right? With your sister Erin—"

Before he could finish his sentence, Ryan leaned back and swung a fist at his so-called brother, connecting with his nose.

"*Ow! Why did you do that?*" the man cried through his hands. Ryan grabbed Devin's collar and pinned him against the wall, looking up into his bleeding nostrils.

"I'm telling you now: leave my mother alone. And my sisters, for that matter. It's up to me to tell them. *If* I tell them. *You understand?*"

"Yes, yes, of course. You are the first person I've even told. I swear. I figured you being a police officer—"

Ryan held a finger in front of the agent's face. "Me being a police officer, I *will* investigate this, until I know the truth. But stay away from my family."

A knock sounded, the door handle turned, and Di Santo stuck his head in. Ryan released Agent Doherty from the wall.

"Sorry to interrupt, D, but we need to get going," Di Santo said, ignoring Devin's distress. "We should get to the Giordano and Leone families ASAP before the news spreads and there's a real mafia war."

It was an obvious ploy. His partner had been watching through the observation glass and interrupted to ensure Ryan didn't slaughter the agent right there in the district house. Di Santo also offered up a box of tissues, from which Devin pulled three sheets and pressed them under his nose.

"We're almost finished here," Ryan responded. Satisfied that all was good, Di Santo nodded and closed the door quietly. Ryan turned back to Devin. "You—I just can't deal with you right now. We've got to get going on this case."

"If we could just have more time...to talk?" Devin pleaded.

Ryan studied the man for at least a full sixty seconds, deciding how to handle him. He hadn't exhibited any obvious signs of deception, other than the lack of eye contact. And then there was the birth certificate. And the name. Ryan calmed, deciding to give the agent a break.

"I'll tell you what. My girlfriend, Catharine, is having Sunday dinner tonight. It's always open to guests, so you're going to be there. That way we can have more time and talk about this whole...mess." He gestured to the birth certificate. "I'd also like her input."

"I heard that she consults with the Department. What, exactly, does she do?"

Ryan snickered at the question that didn't have a simple answer. "You can ask her, tonight. She'd be happy to explain." They exchanged cell numbers and Ryan texted him Cat's name and address. "Dinner's at six-thirty. I'll see you there."

"I appreciate it, Ryan, and I look forward to having dinner with you and your girlfriend. I know this must be quite disturbing to you, and honestly, you handled it better than I'd imagined."

"You expected worse than a punch in the face?"

The agent shrugged and conducted a fingertip check of his nasal cartilage. "It doesn't seem broken."

"I'm sorry. I overreacted."

"No harm, it appears to have already stopped bleeding," the agent said. "Look, I'd like this to be a great beginning for both of us. I mean, yesterday neither of us had a brother and today we do."

"Yeah, right. I have a brother and now my whole entire childhood was a lie and my dad's an asshole. Thanks." Without further conversation, he walked the agent back through the squad. Devin tossed the tissues into one of the wastebaskets before he exited out through the double doors. Ryan waited until he saw Devin Doherty disappear down the main stairs before turning back to see Di Santo already retrieving the bloodied tissues with the eraser end of a pencil.

"You could've just asked for a cheek swab," his partner said, dropping them into a DNA envelope. "I'm sure he would've complied."

"Yeah, but this way was a lot more satisfying."

Di Santo handed him the DNA envelope along with a brown case file marked *RICCI, ROBIN*. Attached to the file was a yellow sticky note with the address of Desirée Leone. Ryan filed it in his case beside the DNA envelope and followed his partner out of the squad room.

"So what do you think about that agent guy?" he asked Di Santo as they exited the building. "I couldn't tell whether he was telling the truth or not. He seemed nervous, wouldn't look me straight in the eye during the whole interrogation. But his birth certificate looks legit."

"The guy is a little strange—the way he talks—all formal and shit. But he is a fed, after all. I think they're required to take Stick-Up-Your-Ass Class at Quantico."

They chuckled together as they left their personal cars in

the lot and found the unmarked brown Impala sedan assigned to them from the Paleozoic period.

Di Santo patted Ryan on the back. "I say just see what the test concludes. You can't refute the DNA, my friend. It's like ten billion to one. I'll tell you one thing, though."

"What's that?"

"It's not fair there are two of you in this world with that handsome mug. Just not fair to guys like me."

CHAPTER 7

Ryan swung by the lab to drop off the DNA kit along with a sample of his own blood that he'd smeared on an evidence card before driving over. He gave the Ricci case number in order to expedite the process, knowing that the lab would give priority to a federal case. If the task force wanted favors from them, this would be a quid pro quo.

From the lab it took only seven minutes and change to get to 159 East Walton Place, a Chicago landmark originally known as the Playboy Building but now called The Palmolive. It was a prime example of Chicago's Gold Coast, an art deco structure, now devoid of the giant iconic PLAYBOY letters that had topped the building during Hugh Hefner's reign.

Di Santo parked the Impala in the building's turnaround and the detectives checked in with a uniformed doorman who boasted he had every resident's cell number on speed dial. As the man waited for the line to pick up, he took a handkerchief to his hairline and patted a trail of perspiration.

Ryan sympathized with having to wear a full uniform in the heat and humidity as summer had lingered into fall. He recollected the misery from his patrol days.

"Yes, Miss Desirée, I have a couple of police officers

here to see you." Pause. "No, no warrant." Pause. Then to Ryan, "She's asking what this is in regards to."

"Her own safety. We believe there may be a threat—" Desirée Leone must have heard him because the security guard nodded and opened the door.

"Unit 10-C," he instructed, and then tipped his hat to them in a charming, twentieth-century sort of way. Ryan had never been inside the building and was half-hoping he'd run into its most illustrious resident, Vince Vaughn, who had purchased a penthouse consisting of the entire thirty-sixth and thirty-seventh floors. The elevator arrived, and to Ryan's disappointment, the car was empty.

The tenth floor hallway was cream-colored chic with elegant light fixtures and dark wood-stained doors, located far enough apart so that you knew the condos behind them were huge. Ryan took the lead and knocked on 10-C.

"Who is it?" a man's voice responded behind the door.

"Detectives Doherty and Di Santo, Chicago Police." They held up their shields by rote to the peephole. Several lock clicks and a chain later, the door opened a couple of inches and a man peered through.

"Yeah? How can I help you guys," he said, without the upturn of a question.

"We'd like to talk to Ms. Desirée Leone." Pretending to be check a text in his phone, Ryan started the voice recorder on his cell.

The man opened the door for the detectives to enter, stepping aside. "She's in the bedroom. Putting away her new shoes," he said, rolling his eyes. He gestured to two large shopping bags bearing the logos of Prada and Jimmy Choo.

"And you are…"

"I'm Danny, her brother," he said, holding out a hand. Both detectives took turns shaking while they stepped into the opulent vestibule. Two black suitcases stood behind Danny, with the initials DSM engraved into the leather handles.

"Those yours?" Ryan said gesturing to the luggage.

Danny Leone pulled them aside. "Yeah, sorry, come on in."

"You going on a trip?" Di Santo asked.

"Vegas. Trying to get Dez to come with. Things are getting a little stressful around here. We need a…vacation."

"A vacation, right." Ryan nodded, taking in the place, which appeared upscale metropolitan and most definitely designed. Not one of the occasional chairs appeared to have ever been used, not even occasionally. As far as he could see, a crystal chandelier graced the ceiling of every room. A very large dog crate took up a far corner of the room, even larger than the one Catharine had for both of her dogs. On instinct, Ryan checked his weapon.

"*Dez!*" the brother called out. "The cops are here."

Expecting the woman to appear, Ryan flinched when he saw a fully-grown male lion round the corner instead. Di Santo squealed and jumped back.

"What the—" Ryan reached for his gun and the lion stopped at his sudden move. The animal turned his attention, then his trajectory, straight toward him.

Ryan froze.

"*Bae!*" a high-pitched female voice commanded.

Ryan had been so focused on the beast that he hadn't seen the woman enter the room behind it. The lion turned, accepted a pat on the mane from her, and then leapt onto the couch.

"Sorry, that's our bodyguard," she said with a wide smile. "Hello, I'm Desirée Leone, by the way. You can call me Desi." She swept her long dark hair from her face and pulled it over her shoulder in a flirtatious move.

Ryan knew that his rugged good looks had an effect on women and it came in handy during interrogations. A couple more years, though, and he'd have to rely on his shrewd wit. He nodded a cursory greeting to Desirée, keeping a hand on his Glock and an eye on the feline. The lion had curled up into a ball on the sofa. A very large butterscotch fur ball.

"He's just a kitten, really." Desirée pulled up her skirt to show off the tattoo on her left thigh: an almost photo-realistic image of the animal with the letters B-A-E arched at the top of its mane. "He's my baby. That's why his name is Bae. But if someone tries to harm me or Danny, that's it. Bae is not shy. He will go on the attack. We've trained him that way."

"Attack?" Di Santo's voice cracked like a pre-pubescent boy.

Ryan shook his head in disbelief. "And the condo board, they approve of this?"

What he really wanted to do was arrest the twins on the spot. He was pretty sure exotic animals were illegal in the State of Illinois, but since he wasn't up on the legalities of wild animal possession, he'd call it in later.

"The homeowners' association? Hell, they let me do whatever the fuck I want," she answered, waving a long red fingernail in the air. "We're Leones. You see, that means lion, and that's what's on our family crest: a lion. Just like Bae!"

Danny stepped a little closer to Ryan, as protective of his sister as the beast beside him. "Now, why are you here, Officers?"

"*Detectives*, actually," Ryan corrected, flashing on earlier when he had corrected Agent Doherty. He had to get that whole situation out of his head. "Ms. Leone, we have reason to believe that you might be a target for a contract killer. I'm not sure you're aware, but Robin Ricci was killed this morning."

"I'm aware, but I don't know how that has anything to do with me." She punctuated the sentence by shoving a stick of Juicy Fruit in her mouth.

"I told you, Dez!" her brother said in a stage whisper, as if Ryan and Di Santo couldn't hear him. "This doesn't feel right to me. I think we need to get to Vegas, like Richie told us to."

"I thought that was a vacation," Di Santo countered.

"Did Ricci tell you to go to Vegas?" Danny hesitated to respond. "Look, Dan. We just left Richie's place and he told us all about *The Ghost*, so you can let us in on this. We just need to know where you and Desirée are going to be located, so we can arrange protection."

Danny seemed to ponder this for a moment, then nodded. "He wants us to meet up in Vegas at our resort. We're having a Commission meeting about the hits. He says it's to put together a plan."

Ryan tried to follow his narrative while keeping an eye on the dozing lion. The classic song ran through his head: *In the jungle, the mighty jungle, a lion sleeps to-night.*

"A plan for what?" he asked Danny.

"To find this motherfucking son-of-a-bitch," Desirée answered in a sudden rage as she made a Z in the air with those fingernails. "If someone thinks he can pick off our family members, we'll string him up so fast—"

"Dez," her brother warned. The lion leapt off of the sofa, probably sensing his master's discomfort, and stood in front of Desirée, emitting a low-decibel growl.

"Good, Bae," she responded, and allowed the animal to take a long sniff of Ryan's jean cuffs. After he was satisfied with the scent, the lion turned his face up and made direct eye contact, panting, showing off the size of his incisors. Droplets of lion saliva landed on Ryan's shoes. *A-wimoweh, a-wimoweh.*

"Can you please…call him off?" Ryan said, unlatching his holster. "I really don't want to put a bullet through this guy's head."

"Good luck with that. He'd snap your neck before you took aim." Desirée took a hold of the lion's gem-studded collar and pulled the animal back behind her.

Ryan composed himself, took a breath, and continued the conversation. "It's not going to look good, everyone fleeing, leaving town," he said to both of them. "And why on earth would you all go to the same place? Aren't you just making it easier on him? On the killer?"

"That's what I said!" Desirée turned to her brother to make a point.

"It's our own resort," Danny answered. "The Chicago Hotel and Casino. You don't have to worry about us. The Chicago was specifically constructed to be a safety bunker for the families. There's no way anyone is going to do anything there. It's got five times the video and security than the other casinos, and the best response team on the floor. No one will be able to get through, and if they do, they're dead. Dez, are you sure you won't come with me today? I don't want to leave you alone here."

Ryan was glad he had thought to start the recorder on his phone before he knocked.

Desirée smacked her gum. "Stop overreacting. No one is going to get to me with Bae in the house. Anyway, I have a date tonight that I'm *not* going to miss. I'll fly out tomorrow. Just send the jet back when you get there."

"I got a commercial flight out. I'll leave the Cessna for you."

"What-evah!" Desirée said with a wave of the fingers. She turned back to the detectives. "And good luck to you two trying to find that Ghost. Why do you think he's called the Ghost in the first place? Because he gets in and out without anyone knowing who the hell he is. Nobody ever sees him. Nobody has even seen or talked to this guy, so if you think you're going to catch him now, you are delusional. You need to just let the families handle it." The lion roared behind her. "Bae agrees with me!"

Ryan tried to ignore the animal, but the gooseflesh on his arms betrayed him. "Well, I'm sorry, but we can't let you handle it. The police have to handle it. What do you know about this Ghost guy? So you are positive you've never met him?"

"Naw," responded Desirée. "We've never needed his services. He mainly worked for Richie and Joey. Sometimes Vic, I think."

"Dez. Shut up," her brother warned.

Desirée threw him a look that indicated that she really had no clue that she had just informed on the other three families. No wonder these two couldn't run the North Side.

Danny pulled out his billfold and started to count out hundreds. "Let's be friends, guys. Here, you look hungry. Have dinner on the Leone family."

"Aw geez, put that away," Di Santo said, shaking his head. "We're not looking for a payout here. We're trying to help you out before one of you becomes the next target. You say you had no interaction with The Ghost, but Ricci said you were the one who contacted him on some kind of message boards."

"I have no idea what he meant. And I'm done speaking to you without an attorney."

Ryan sighed. "Look, we're just trying to help you. We have two females dead in two weeks, both related to the families. You may be next, Ms. Leone."

"He better not get near me!" Desirée screeched, her arms waving wildly while Bae started to pace back and forth behind her, chuffing every couple of seconds. "I haven't done anything to that guy and I've never met him in my life. If he's got a beef with Vic and Richie, that has nothing to do with us."

"Please calm down, or secure your—bodyguard—before we continue," Ryan ordered. Desirée grabbed the lion's collar and led him into the crate, incarcerating the feline as he roared his discontent.

Ryan's true agenda in this interview was to try to determine if the Leones were behind the first two hits. To see if they had hired The Ghost to go after the other families. But the twins appeared agitated enough that he believed them, and they honestly didn't have the brains between them to pull off such a big move. "What about the Giordano family?" he asked them. "They haven't been hit yet. Is it possible they had something to do with this? Maybe they got tired of the Four Corners arrangement."

"The Four Corners," Danny chuckled. "That's what

those two-bit feds named it. They try to come up with that shit for the media. Like I said, Richie called and told us all to get to Vegas. Why would he put us in danger?" Danny paused. From his expression, Ryan's theory was sinking in. "Nah, this isn't a family war, man. No way." He thought again. "I mean, it goes totally against everything my dad agreed to with the other families. We've all been respecting each other for over a decade. Why would they change now?"

"And if they did want more of the business, we'd just meet about it," Desirée chimed in. "That's it. We're like a company. I mean we *are* a company. We're legit!"

Ryan hadn't questioned their legitimacy. These two weren't criminal masterminds. They were privileged, simple-minded adult children in expensive shoes.

"Well, okay then, I guess Bae has you covered," he said, acquiescing to the siblings. "We just wanted to check in and see if you needed any protection. Here's my card, just in case you need anything. Keep us posted on the meeting and anything you find out."

"Yeah sure," Danny said with another irritating chuckle. "Thanks, Detective, but I think we'll be fine."

Ryan wanted to believe the boy. But as the door closed, his last image of the Leone twins was Desirée almost cowering behind her twin, chewing the paint off of a thumbnail.

Ryan called animal control on the elevator ride down. Since Bae was such a large animal, they said they'd have to coordinate with one of the zoos, but they promised to send someone to check on the situation in the morning. When he hung up, he saw a text had come in from Agent Jensen. He read it aloud to Di Santo:

– *Giordano family off to Vegas. Let's regroup at 18th in the AM. We'll discuss how to proceed.*

The detectives drove back to the 18th, abandoned the Impala for their own cars, and called it a day. Before pulling out, Ryan checked check the messages on his phone again. Jane still hadn't texted him back. She *always* texted him back. They were buds. He and Jane Steffen had met in court a couple of years ago, but they hadn't really been friends until the Town Red case. She was an amazing prosecutor and proved handy to have on his side. Ryan knew Jane had a thing for him, but when he made it clear he was with Cat, that seemed to subside, and they settled into a comfortable platonic friendship. He decided to call, just to make sure she was okay.

"Hey, this is Jane. Leave a message if you want. If this is urgent, call the SA's office at…" He cleared his throat while waiting for the beep.

"Hey, Jane. It's Ryan. You'll never guess what I just encountered in an interview at the Palmolive. I'll give you a hint: *Hakuna Matata!* So anyway, call me. I'm on a big case and I need your input. Hope all is well. Okay, bye."

He ended the call, put Baby Blue into gear, and resumed the drive to Catharine's for Sunday night dinner.

CHAPTER 8

The sun still shone brightly at 6:42 in the evening, casting orange-golden rays onto the grand Lulling estate. Ryan punched his code into the security box and the black iron gate opened to reveal one of the most unique homes in Evanston. Designed by Catharine, the estate mirrored her elusive personality: gleaming white columns fronted by marble steps leading to a grand, pristine entrance. Ryan followed the circular drive and stopped directly in front of the steps. Her sons' twin SUVs were parked side by side, along with a black Chrysler 300. A fed car.

"Shit, Devin!" Ryan shouted to no one, as he took the steps two at a time. He made it to the front door of the mansion just as it opened and Catharine appeared. She greeted him, as always, with an all-encompassing hug. He kissed the top of her head, relishing the sweet floral scent of her hair.

Cat pulled back slightly and tipped her head up to speak to him. "I was just about to text you. Apparently your *brother* is here for dinner—"

"I'm *so sorry*, I forgot to tell you he was coming."

"You also forgot to tell me that you had a brother," she said, closing the door behind him.

"Yeah, well, the jury's still out on that one. I can explain if you ply with me with alcohol." He put his arm around her waist as Catharine's two dogs ran up to greet him, circling around their legs. Bully was a huge Rottweiler, adopted for protection along with his goofy sidekick of a Shih Tzu, Buddy, whose tongue hung out of his mouth as he panted hello. Ryan leaned over and gave both a little love before they made their way down the two steps and onto the path that led to her fantastical, whimsical indoor garden. The atrium was surrounded by a square of rooms in four wings. Rooms that seemed only to exist because of necessity. If Cat could, she'd live and play solely within her gardens, like a fairy.

The air remained humid inside, a mix of the moisture off of the lake and the indoor greenhouse effect from the lush plants, flowers, and trees that constituted the atrium garden.

"Devin just got here, actually," Catharine said as they took the short walk to the center. There the new guest stood, gazing up to the massive skylight that illuminated the two-story oak trees.

"This is…incredible," the agent said. "I have never seen anything like it. Not in a residence, anyway. Can you identify all the species of flora in your garden?"

"I could, but it would take a while," Catharine said, accepting the compliment. She gestured to the Gothic table in the center of the atrium's courtyard. "Please, sit, Devin, and help yourself to some iced tea. The boys can give you a full tour of the house and back gardens after dinner."

Ryan threw a wave to the agent, who nodded back and took a seat at the table. An awkward silence befell the group, with the exception of Ryan tap-tap-tapping the table with his cell phone. Bully rested his head on Devin's knee, which appeared to make the man more uncomfortable. Catharine pulled both of the inquisitive canines away from him and led them out the back doors.

"Are the boys here?" Ryan asked. He'd hoped there would be more than just the three of them at the dinner table to diffuse the tension.

"Yes," Cat responded. "They're grilling the steaks, out back. I need to go bring in the rest of the food, I'll be right back."

Ryan jumped up. "I'll help!" He followed her along a path to the far side of the house, where they pushed through the swinging door to the gourmet kitchen. Catharine was an amazing cook and enjoyed having at it when her personal assistant, Sara, was off duty.

As soon as they were in the kitchen, Cat turned to him. "So? Who is this man?"

"He's a federal agent, assigned to the Ricci case with us. We met him in River Forest, but then he followed me back to the Eighteenth to unload the story on me. He claims to be an illegitimate son of my father. Can you believe it? He turns up just like that, tells me my father cheated on my mom and he's my older brother."

Catharine's eyes widened. "My gosh, Ryan! Do you believe him?"

Before answering, he made his way to Cat's fridge and pulled out cold bottle of Goose Island Beer, his favorite. "Shit, I don't know. The evidence seems to support it. He showed me a birth certificate. The guy is two months older than I am. *Two months!*" He held up two fingers to emphasize before popping the cap on the bottle. "So that would mean my parents were newly married when my dad goes and gets the teenager next door pregnant, and then eight weeks later gets my mom pregnant too? I just can't wrap my head around that scenario."

"*Teenager?*" Catharine's hand went to her gaping mouth.

"Yeah, he claims that his mom was eighteen at the time, lived next door to my family with her parents. When she got pregnant, they sent her away to Wisconsin to live with her aunt. That's where he grew up."

"I can't believe that! How scandalous. I'm so sorry. Have you talked to your mother about this yet?"

"No, I haven't had a chance." He started to pace the length of the kitchen. "This guy just sprang it on me this afternoon. Then we had to go do an interview, and then I came here. And plus: what do I say? 'Hey, Mom! Remember that teenager who used to live next door to you? Well, guess what? I have a brother!'" He let out a breath and perched on one of the kitchen bar stools.

Catharine came up to him, brushed aside his bangs, and kissed his forehead. "You'll figure it out. Think on it for a bit before you call Shirley. I suspect that she knows about the affair, at the very least. Women always know."

"Not all women are like you, Cat. They're not all in-tune with the universe."

She laughed. "When it comes to our men, we are. You don't need any special abilities to know if your partner is getting a little something on the side. Believe me, women always know."

"Is that a warning?" he said, pulling her petite frame in between his legs.

She took the opportunity to plant a kiss on his neck. "Never. I trust you." The oven buzzed and she broke free from his embrace to pull on two oven mitts. "Now help me serve dinner and we'll discuss this over the meal."

"But wait a second—" He stopped her with the platter of steamed vegetables in her mitts. "Do you have any feeling…you know, your thing…I mean, I'm getting our DNA run…"

Cat gazed over his shoulder for what seemed like hours but was really closer to seven seconds. She shook her head slightly. "I believe Devin's intentions are good. I'm not getting any bad vibes from him."

"That's not what I'm asking, you know that."

"You mean *is* he who he says he is?"

"Yes."

"I think…that you already know the answer to that question. I mean, you can't deny the resemblance. I almost kissed him at the door! Grab the pasta salad, please." Catharine turned and exited back into the atrium, and Ryan followed, salad in hand.

He placed the bowl on the table, a little disturbed at her declaration.

Catharine's nineteen year old twins had joined Devin at the table along with two platters of New York strip steaks. Hank and Duke Lulling were fraternal twins and aside from their linebacker builds, had their own distinct appearance. Hank was paler with sandy blond hair and brown eyes, while Duke had a darker complexion and brown hair, but had inherited Catharine's ice blue eyes. As far as personalities, Hank was definitely the alpha and Duke more introspect. But this evening, Duke started the conversation while Hank hung back, silent.

"Devin was telling us about his job with the NSA, it's really fascinating," Duke said, as they sat down at the table. "I'd like to do something like that."

Ryan narrowed his eyes as he took a seat next to Catharine. "NSA? I thought you were FBI. You're with the task force." He forked a steak onto his plate and passed the platter on.

"The Organized Crime Task Force is comprised of members of several agencies, actually. FBI, NSA, and Homeland," Devin answered.

"He's a data profiler," Duke added. "He catches perps through their data footprint, he says."

Devin's geeky vibe suddenly made sense. He wasn't a street investigator, he worked with computers all day. "I've read about that," Ryan said. "You use things like purchasing patterns, online footprints, and GPS to narrow down the identity of a criminal?"

Devin nodded. "Yes, absolutely." He paused for a moment, taking in the people at the table, the flowers, the trees. "I must commend you, again, on the design of this house. I never would have thought an indoor garden to be practical, but it is quite lovely and a serene place to take a meal." Catharine and the twins smiled, always proud of the grand Lulling Estate. "Did you have it built after you came into the money from Town Red stock? I'd read that you had accumulated a significant level of wealth from that—"

"You researched Catharine?" Ryan asked, putting down his fork. "Wait, did you *profile* us?"

"No, Ryan, I didn't profile you. Not extensively. I just wanted some insight into my family. See who you were. But I'd never invade your privacy."

Ryan scoffed. "Yeah, that's funny, coming from the NSA."

"I know, I know, the public perception is we spy on every US citizen. That's just not the case. In fact, that would be logistically impossible." He mused at his own statement and shoved a forkful of meat into his mouth.

"Just us," Ryan said under his breath.

"Honey," Cat said, softly placing a palm on his forearm. "Please. Let's have a pleasant dinner, and get to know each other."

He didn't like this new alleged brother. He didn't like the fact that Devin worked an agency that had jurisdiction over his, had access to private information, and had just used it. He felt invaded in all aspects of his life, and he certainly didn't like Cat sitting there defending the man. A man she'd "almost kissed." He sliced his steak as he eagle-eyed the agent.

"To answer your question," Cat continued, mitigating the tension, "yes, I used a portion of the money I earned from the stock sale to build this estate. My grandparents owned the land originally, but their house was in disrepair. I wanted to build my dream house, so I did."

"Do you work?"

"What, you didn't get as far as her website?" Ryan said. "I have a hard time believing that."

"I admit, I did look at it," Devin answered. "But I don't quite understand what you do."

"Mom's a psychic," Hank stated outright, his first words at the dinner table. Between the two boys, Hank had more of a problem with Ryan than Duke. He was fiercely protective of his mother and had resisted their relationship from the start, always taking the opportunity to initiate conflict.

"Well that's oversimplifying it," Catharine responded. "And not entirely accurate—Hank, you *know* that. I'm an empath. I can get information from people by feeling what they feel. Almost similar to what you do, Devin. You get data about people and interpret it. I do the same, only the data that I receive…just comes to me."

"She can also find things," Duke said. "She's found everything from missing keys and dogs to missing kids. That's why she consults with the Chicago Police Department."

Ryan scrutinized Devin, gauging whether he would judge or mock Catharine for her abilities. If he even so much as smirked, Ryan would kick his ass out.

But the agent remained somber and respectful, waiting to speak until he had wiped his mouth with his napkin. "That fascinates me. Although I can't say I totally understand it, I do believe there is so much out there that we have not quantified yet. As a scientist, I believe that one can interpret another's thoughts and intentions through microexpression, body language, and voice. Law enforcement officers like Ryan and myself are taught that extensively for interrogation, and perhaps, Catharine, you are subconsciously interpreting those data factors when you meet someone. It's possible that you are innately talented at interpreting a person's data, so much so that you can create a distinct and accurate profile on them."

Cat pressed her lips together, plainly put out by having her abilities grounded in practical logic, no microexpressions needed. "I've never heard it phrased that way, but I'm not closed to that interpretation," she responded, before she took a small bite of broccoli.

"That could explain the empathy," Duke said, in defense of his mother's metaphysical identity. "But how can that explain her finding things?"

"The brain is an amazing computer, Duke. I'm not saying your mom's not intelligent, by any means. I'm saying that maybe we need to redefine what psychic means. It is, in fact, an over-simplified word, as Catharine said. Our brains are taking in millions of data points a day—even an hour—data that your brain stores in all cortices, from each of your experiences, whether it be personal or perceived from another, like television, the Internet, the news. So when you hear that a child is missing, for example, and are given the baseline data like where the child was last seen, what he was wearing, relationships with the family, and community dynamics, your brain sieves through that data. Information that's been stored from all of the input during your entire life to give you a best-case scenario on where to look for that missing dog or child. Someone who has a high accuracy rate, like your mother, could be just a masterful data analyst of her own stored data. That's how I see it."

Ryan and the boys looked to Catharine simultaneously for her reaction to Devin's hypothesis.

She responded with a smile. "I don't mind being labeled a master data analyst, if that's how you define it. It's as good an explanation as any."

Ryan wanted to list every detail of every case Catharine helped with and why the data analyst explanation was bunk, but he, too, was an officer of the law who depended on evidence and facts. Maybe his love for Cat had clouded his rational judgment when it came to interpreting her abilities. He'd just accepted them as part of the amazing woman who had agreed to become his mate. And because of that, he'd never questioned it.

"So, long-lost brothers, eh? How did *that* happen?" Hank said leaning back in his chair.

Devin threw a glance to Ryan for permission to discuss the issue. Ryan nodded. He might as well get used to the humiliation. But when Devin proceeded to explain the situation to the table, the boys listened intently, sans humor. No one even spoke until Catharine took the initiative.

"Well, if it turns out to be true, I think you should embrace the positivity of the situation," she said as she folded a napkin into her lap. "See it as a blessing. You will both now have an extra loved one, an additional family member. I'm an only child, and I used to dream about finding a long-lost sister."

But Ryan couldn't quite embrace the concept at this point. He was perfectly content being the oldest sibling and the only male. He didn't know how this extra brother would fit into their family dynamic, and he wasn't sure he wanted to know. He was protective of his mother just as Hank and Duke were of theirs.

"I met a lion today," he said, changing the subject. Even the boys were riveted at the story of Desirée and Bae, how the large feline acted like a pet, and his recounting of the animal that drooled on his shoes. And how Di Santo screamed. Everyone at the table laughed and the family scandal faded, at least for the rest of the meal.

When the forks and knives had long rested on their empty plates, Hank and Duke got up to help their mother clear the table while the two Dohertys were left to converse.

"I would like to strategize about the case, if you have a moment," Devin said. "Give you some tips on how to identify the perpetrator."

"Sure. We can talk in the library." With almost seven years' experience as a detective, Ryan was a little annoyed that this man thought he needed *tips*, but he forced himself to keep an open mind. After all, that's what he'd just asked of Devin when it came to Cat's abilities.

He texted Catharine to inform her of their whereabouts and led the way through the atrium to the eastern corridor of the estate. The library was one wall of windows, two walls of floor-to-ceiling bookshelves and a grand fireplace to the south of the door. A wide desk ran the length of the windows, and there was a cozy seating area in front of the fireplace. Devin took a seat in one of the side chairs, while Ryan splayed down on the sofa, running his hands over his full belly.

"Catharine and her sons are very pleasant people," Devin said. "How did you two meet?"

"On a case, actually. Cat was initially a suspect in a double murder." He chuckled at the phrase, never having said it aloud. "Long story short: she obviously didn't do it. So what did you want to talk about?"

"We need to start putting together some data on the suspect. Although most of the time I prefer to work alone, I've been told that it helps to do this with another person. Since you've conducted some interviews today, I thought maybe I could show you how I set up my algorithm for profiling a perpetrator and you could add some valuable data points."

Both of Catharine's cats jumped up onto Devin's chair. Pyxis, the one with the suede-gray coat, started to knead his thigh, while Perseus the black cat leapt onto the back of the chair and circled behind his head.

In an unexpected move, Devin reached up and petted Perseus with one hand while he scratched Pyxis behind the ears with the other. "Now *cats* I like," he explained.

Ryan smiled, even though the man had just insulted their dogs. "Tell me, how exactly do you catch perps with an algorithm? Can you really do that with just math?"

The agent sat up straighter, visibly pleased that Ryan was interested in his work. "Yes! With math, data, and databases. My work has brought in five unknown perpetrators for the FBI in the past two years. It's very simple, actually." He pulled a spiral notebook from his briefcase and tore out a blank page. He folded the page vertically as a guide for drawing a straight line down the middle. He then labeled the two sides: *HARD DATA* and *SOFT DATA*.

"Hard data are pieces of information that are absolutes," he explained. "They're proven. For example, we know the perpetrator's exact location between eight a.m. and nine a.m. this morning: on the nine hundred block of Franklin Avenue, River Forest. That's a hard datum." He wrote *LO-CATION: 900 Block River Forest, 8–9 a.m.* and the date on the left side of the paper. "Soft data are pieces of information that are probable or possible. Not yet proven. For example, the perpetrator is *probably* military trained because of the weapon he used. A sniper rifle takes expert training. But we don't know that for sure, so we put it in the right column." And he did.

"Once we've gotten ten to twenty hard facts on the left side, I can start cross-referencing them through the NSA databases."

"Those databases that supposedly don't exist, like GPS, cell phone conversations, and text messages?"

"I am not at liberty to discuss the details of our databases."

Ryan smirked. "Yeah, got it. And this can narrow everything down to one person?"

"The more data the better," Devin explained. "Every single datum narrows the pool down to only certain people that could fit the profile. It's like a fingerprint. Or the DNA sample you're running on our blood."

"How did you—"

"Data points. One, you are law enforcement, so one, you will want concrete evidence; two, you have access to a DNA lab; and three, you drew my blood. Not difficult to conclude your intentions. I left you the bloodied tissue on purpose because I know it will validate our familial relationship."

Ryan was impressed. "Okay, so you're not so bad at this."

"I'm actually very good at this. I'm more accurate at analysis than most investigators because I'm on the spectrum."

"You're *autistic*?"

"Asperger's Syndrome. A highly-functioning form of autism, yes."

"But you don't—"

"*Look* autistic? *Act* autistic?" Devin said, completing his thoughts. Ryan shrugged, nodding his head. "That's why they call it a 'spectrum,' Ryan. There's a wide variety of traits associated with what we call autism. Those who are neuro-*atypical*, like me, don't have trouble conversing, per se, but we do have trouble identifying social cues. But by the time we hit adulthood, we've pretty much learned to compensate and mimic what is socially acceptable in terms of conversation and body language. Asperger's individuals are also known to have the ability to intensely concentrate and excel at complex tasks, like computational theory."

The door opened and Catharine entered the library with a tray of iced tea and her famous cinnamon cookies. "Would you gentlemen like dessert?" she said, with a soft smile.

Ryan was grateful for the interruption, as he didn't know quite how to respond to Devin's personal confession.

"Cat, I'd like you to stay and join us, if that's okay with Devin." Then to the agent, "Like we said at dinner, she's an approved consultant with the Department, so she's covered under our confidentiality agreement."

"That's fine," Devin responded, taking a cookie. "The more brains the better when it comes to analyzing data, and Catharine seems to be good at it. Like me."

She took a seat next to Ryan and he showed her the chart Devin had constructed in the notebook, relaying the difference between hard and soft data. She understood it immediately. She was smart that way.

Ryan grew excited about Devin's new process. "I have some more information about the perp, from the interviews we conducted today," he said, eager to test the algorithm. "They believe this is the work of a guy nicknamed 'The Ghost.' He is a contract hit man for the four families, although none of them have met him. He is not a member of the Outfit, he's considered a Friend of the Family. That's someone who is peripheral to the mob, maybe does work for them, but not a 'made man,' so to speak."

Devin picked up the pen and notebook, filling in the chart as Ryan spoke.

"When his services are needed, they put an ad online."

"The dark web," Devin responded.

"What's that?"

"Those are websites not discoverable by the general public because they're not indexed in search engines. What *you* think of the web is only the surface of what's out there, Believe it or not, what shows up in search results is only about point-zero-three percent of the total web pages that actually exist. Criminals operate on what we call the dark web—it's a network of websites specifically hidden from search engines for criminal activity. Child porn, drug sales, and even murder for hire. We've got many agents seeded on these websites. I'll put someone on checking the message boards for this guy's MO."

"So you'll be able to track him by his computer address?"

"No, probably not. Most of the Internet's criminals use a special web browser to connect to the dark web. It allows them to access sites without leaving any trace about their identification or location, as they connect through a string of servers all over the world."

Ryan took notes. He'd had no reason to investigate the dark web before, but he had heard of it. He'd research it later. "So Matt and I think there's one of two possibilities: the Ghost is acting alone, as he'd asked for a territory and they declined him. Or someone hired him to do the hits."

"Possibilities, all speculative. So they go on in the SOFT DATA column."

"Okay. So what else can we put in the hard data column?" Ryan asked.

"Bullets."

"Bullets?"

"Yes, criminals will often obfuscate the purchase of a firearm. Either they purchase it illegally, steal it, or borrow from another criminal. They know that weapons, especially high-caliber or military-grade, are easily traceable. But they forget about the bullets. It's easier to track someone down on the purchase of bullets. So in this case it would be the purchase of the cartridges for the M24 sniper rifle. Goes in the hard data column."

"Fascinating," Catharine responded. She took a breath

and then added, "How about this: he must reside—or at least stay—in the Chicago area, since he's basically on call to the families?"

Devin pointed to her with an affirmative nod. "Yes! That would go in hard data." He wrote it on the left side. Cat smiled, visibly pleased to have contributed.

Ryan thought about the money trail. "If this guy's an independent contractor, he has to run the income through some kind of business, for tax purposes. He also has a flexible schedule. Can we say he is most likely self-employed?" asked Ryan. "I guess that would go on soft data, since it's speculation."

"You're getting this!" Devin beamed. "I'm a good teacher."

The three of them chuckled.

Recalling the Ricci crime scene, Ryan leaned forward and studied the chart. "He's intelligent. And likely fit—to be able to go up in that tree and balance in it."

"Hard data," Devin said, writing the facts on the page.

"And he must have gone to the Riccis' neighborhood prior to this morning. He must have cased it to find the best perch. The best place from which to shoot at her," Ryan added. Devin noted that as well. Catharine flinched a bit. "What?" Ryan said, turning toward her.

Cat was staring into the empty hearth, her eyes blinking every few seconds. "The Ghost has two more targets," she stated softly. "Two more families. He's sending a message…" She paused for a bit, cocking her head to the side. "Women. He's going for the women."

"Yes, well, the perpetrator has killed two women so far," Devin said. "But we don't yet know if they're related. And I can't use any of that because you're basically just making it up."

"I am not making it up!" Catharine said, her back stiffening.

"Look, Devin, I know you don't quite believe in Cat's abilities, but—like you—she has a great close rate."

"I can't use any of that premonition stuff. It has no place in my calculations," he reiterated.

Catharine and Ryan locked eyes. "Devin," she said softly. "May I do something with you? Show you what I do? Maybe that will help you understand."

The man appeared a little annoyed that she had interrupted his case work, but was curious enough to agree with a nod.

Catharine switched seats with Ryan and held out her palms to Devin.

"What are you doing?" he asked.

"Give me your hands. I need a physical connection."

He complied by holding out his hands, although his skeptical frown spoke volumes. She closed her eyes and instructed him to do the same. They sat in silence for about twenty seconds and then Cat took a deep breath. "You're suffering from the loss of your mother. Very deeply. However, you are using your work to compensate. To get through the pain."

"Well, I had told Ryan my mother had died a month ago and the rest is good guessing. That data analysis in your brain is quite powerful."

Ryan bristled. "Will you just listen to her and stop being defensive?"

"Fine."

Catharine's breathing settled into a slow and steady rhythm. "You and Ryan are very much alike in both personality and basic morality." Devin scoffed, then straightened up, an obvious attempt to humor them. "You—you have heard—" Catharine paused, and then dropped her head. "No, no, I'm not getting anything further." She released Devin's hands and smoothed her skirt.

"What?" Ryan asked. "You always get something." He wish he could wipe the told-you-so smirk off of Devin's face. "Of course you got something."

"No, I'm sorry. Sometimes it's just not the right time. Or vibes or something."

"Can we get back to reality now?" Devin asked, specifically to Ryan.

It didn't make sense. He'd never seen Catharine fail at a reading. She was specifically hiding something. He gave in, and they listed a couple more data items on either side of the chart.

"Given the data, I believe that he is not done," Devin concluded. "He will strike again. There is either one more victim to go—on the theory that he's been hired by one of the families against the other three—or two more victims if he's working for himself or hired by an outside source."

"But how do we know for sure it's The Ghost? That was only Ricci's guess."

"The data supports it: this is an accomplished professional killer, familiar with the Outfit's organization and structure, able to kill two individuals without being witnessed. And well—Occam's Razor: usually the simplest answer is the correct one."

Ryan nodded. "I use that a lot too. And that does makes sense. The Ghost is the best lead we've got, so we have to pursue it. Cat, you said you feel like he's acting alone, right?" He glanced at her to find she was once again in a semi-trance state. "*Cat?*"

She doubled forward and put a hand to her mouth. "Excuse me!" she said, muffled through her hand. She jumped up off of the sofa and ran out of the room. By the time Ryan caught up with her, she had slammed the door to the powder room down the hall.

"Cat, are you all right?" He heard the sounds of purging, and tried the door handle to the bathroom. It opened. Catharine was kneeling in front of the toilet, heaving her dinner. Ryan crouched behind her, gathered her long hair and pulled it back, out of the way. "What happened?"

"I saw something terrible, Ryan," she rasped and then heaved one more time, but nothing was left. She flushed the toilet and wiped her mouth with a tissue. "It was a—a— crime scene. A body. Not good." Catharine stood up, turned on the faucet, dampened a washcloth, and held it to her face.

Ryan came up to the side of the sink and addressed her image in the mirror. "Any other clues? Did you see who the victim was?"

"Unidentifiable. Woman, I think. I saw a nightgown."

"It was that bad?"

Catharine turned to him, completely ashen. "That bad."

After she cleaned up, they returned to the library only to find it devoid of Devin. They headed back out to the atrium, which was now illuminated by soft footlights along the path, as the sun had since set and was no longer coming in through the skylight. Ryan called Devin's name several times, thinking he might be lost in the mansion. Only the dogs barked in response until Duke came out of his bedroom upstairs and called over the railing, "He left."

"*He left?* As in, left the house?" Ryan asked. Duke nodded. "Well, that's rude. He didn't even say goodbye."

"I dunno. He said goodbye to us," Duke said, his voice echoing through the atrium.

Ryan turned to Cat. "He's a strange dude, I tell you."

"It's the Asperger's," she responded, clearing some residual glasses from the table. "The afflicted tend to not follow social convention if they don't have to."

"Wait, how did you know he had Asperger's? You weren't in the library when he told me."

"Oh, he told you? I was just speculating. *Right column*," she quipped. "I've known several autistic savants in my healing work, and he just seemed to fit the profile."

"Well, it's left column, because he told me he's definitely been diagnosed." Ryan helped her carry the glasses to the kitchen, where she placed them in the sink and ran water over them.

"I'll have Sara finish up tomorrow," she said, visibly drained.

"Cat, what did you really get when you were doing your reading on Devin? Is he a fraud or something? Is he lying to us?"

She shook her head and dropped her gaze to the floor. "No, it's nothing like that. I just saw in my mind…" Catharine took a deep breath, like she didn't know how to formulate the words.

Ryan lifted her chin with a finger until she met his gaze. "What? I'm dying here."

"I think Devin has heard Jon Lange speak to him, too."

"It's better to live one day as a lion
than a hundred years as a lamb."
~ *John Gotti*

CHAPTER 9

The next morning, the Organized Crime Task Force set up in the 18th District detective squad. They gathered in the middle of the room, with eight suited federal agents surrounding Ryan and Di Santo's desk pod. Since their meeting in Catharine's library, Devin had converted his data chart into digital format where it was being projected onto a screen for all to see. He didn't have to explain the chart to his colleagues who were already familiar with his process, but he did review it for the benefit of Di Santo, Sergeant Besko, and the several detectives in the squad who were noticeably eavesdropping.

The main Homicide phone line lit up and Di Santo took the call. He hunched over his desk and plugged an ear to drown out Devin's lecture. "Mm-hmm, Mm-hmm" he said, prompting the caller, and then leaped out of seat with the receiver still held to his ear. "Shit! No way! The Palmolive? We'll be right there." He slammed down the receiver and locked eyes with Ryan, shaking his head. Ryan knew immediately what had happened and dropped his head in grief. "It's Desirée Leone," Di Santo announced to the group. "She's dead."

The meeting broke up so Ryan and Di Santo could rush to the scene. They jumped into their assigned Impala, which took a couple of grinds to start. They were due for a vehicle from the new fleet, although they had been waiting months for one. As ugly as it was, the sedan was designed to be responsive with decent pickup speed. Ryan activated the built-in light bar, placed just above the visors, which got them to the building in only six minutes and forty-two seconds.

One blue and white Chicago PD patrol car had already parked in the turnaround, along with an animal control van and a truck emblazoned with a photograph of an elephant, with the Lincoln Park Zoo logo on the door.

"How the *fuck* did the perp get around the lion?" Di Santo said. "I nearly wet my pants when that thing appeared in the condo. Less than a foot from our shins! Nothing between him and us."

They flipped open their credentials to the same doorman who had let them in just yesterday, and he waved them in with a solemn expression. Ryan saw a woman in a Medical Examiner's jacket at the elevators. She stood pushing the up button with one hand while balancing a cardboard box in the other.

"Dr. Bhandari?" Ryan said, approaching her. "Here, let me help you." He took the box and greeted her simultaneously.

"Detective Doherty, Di Santo. Nice to see you again," she greeted them, a slight East Indian accent still coming through. They had worked with Nina Bhandari on several other cases, although Zachary Sloane was their usual ME since he was specifically assigned to the North Side.

"Where's Zach?"

"Back in the lab," she responded. "He's working on Mrs. Ricci, so I got this one. I heard there was a lion up there at the crime scene?"

"Yeah, we met him yesterday. He's a pretty hefty cat," Ryan responded as the elevator car arrived. "I called animal control yesterday to report it. Do you have any idea what happened up there? Did they say anything about COD?"

"No, but they said it's pretty messy and to come prepared. I brought full forensic suits—I have extras for you."

She nodded to the box in Ryan's arms. "Animal control is already up there. I hope they didn't contaminate the scene."

The elevator door opened and they made their way down the hallway to apartment 10-C. Officer Ann Waleski and her partner Jordan Weiss flanked the doorway, reminding him of the lion statues on either side of the Art Institute's steps. Or maybe he just had lions on the brain. Waleski was old-school blue-collar patrol, towering above most of the men in the 18th at six feet and one-half inch. Her white-blonde hair encouraged some of the guys to call her Brienne of Tarth after the *Game of Thrones* character. But she didn't take offense. Waleski was proud to be associated with such a strong woman and considered herself a Knight of the Chicago 18th.

"Heya, Doherty, Di Santo, Doc," Waleski said, nodding her respect. "This ain't a clean scene in there, people. Be prepared."

"Where's Animal Control?"

"Who's all in there?"

"Where's the lion?" Ryan, Di Santo and Bhandari asked simultaneously.

"Whoa, whoa, whoa. Three zoo people are inside with two animal control officers. They've got the big guy sedated, and are discussing where to take him. The body's in the bedroom. I told all of those yo's not to go near the DB or touch anything in sight or they'd feel my wrath!"

Ryan put down the box of Mylar suits and pulled out three—for him, Di Santo, and Bhandari. Each sky-blue bodysuit included a pair of gloves that snapped onto the sleeve, which they helped each other to fasten.

Ryan took the lead in entering Desirée Leone's apartment. The first thing he spotted was Bae's massive mane splayed on the carpet. The lion's eyes were shut and his tongue lolled from his open mouth. That fucking massive tongue. Ryan's breath hitched when he saw the brown-crimson bloodstain encircling Bae's mouth. "What happened here?" he asked the group behind the beast.

One of the uniformed animal control officers stepped over Bae's leg and introduced herself, her partner, and the two zoo employees—a large animal handler, and the director of the large cat sanctuary.

"We were waiting for you until we moved him," she said.

"Did he—"

"It appears as if the lion attacked the owner and then…consumed part of her."

"I'm going to need this animal in my lab, then," Dr. Bhandari interjected. "I have to take evidence from his fur, remove the stomach contents…"

"I'm sorry, but our first priority is to put him down. After that, you may have access to the body, but I assume that Lincoln Park Zoo is better equipped to deal with the size of his body than the human morgue. We'll meet you there."

Bhandari accepted that answer with a nod and handed each of the animal handlers her card.

"What time did you arrive and discover the scene?" Ryan asked.

"We got here just before nine-thirty. We knocked, but there wasn't an answer. When we heard the lion roar—several times—we called a patrol to help us break in. The zoo technicians were able to corral him in the corner and sedate him within about five minutes. It was a long five minutes, believe me! I've never seen anything like this."

"Did any of you enter the bedroom?" he asked. "We have to know for forensic purposes."

"No. Not at all. John, here, followed the blood to the bedroom. None of us had any desire to see the scene that he described in there."

"Okay, thank you. You have my permission to remove the—animal—from the scene. Dr. Bhandari will be in touch to examine it."

As they prepared to remove Bae, Ryan gestured toward the bedroom with a nod. He led Di Santo and Bhandari down the hall, setting the pace, deliberately sidestepping the trail of blood that increased in saturation as they neared the crime scene.

The view was shocking, even to a seasoned homicide cop like Ryan. The walls were like Pollock paintings, spattered crimson. Pools of blood and entrails marked Bae's kill. What was left of Desirée Leone lay supine on the bed—a female form, with most of the flesh ripped from her upper body. No face. But fairly intact from the waist down. The torso was splayed open and entrails spilled out onto the tousled sheets. Strips of blue patterned cotton intermixed with the body parts, most probably the remnants of a nightgown. And there on a remaining thigh was the tattooed likeness of Desirée's murderer, Bae. The three of them stood just inside the doorway, taking in the scene in silence. Ryan couldn't help but reenact the homicide in his head, while he flashed back twenty-four hours to when the creature had stood just inches from him.

Dr. Bhandari made her way slowly to the other side of the bed, keeping her sight on the victim. Ryan forced himself to study the remains with her, attempting to interpret what he was seeing.

"Can you identify all the biologicals?" he asked the ME.

Di Santo circled the perimeter of the room, studying the blood patterns on the walls.

"Shoulders and arms—well the bones, really—are on this side of the bed, discarded." Ryan took her word for it. Dr. Bhandari leaned over the bed, taking inventory the rest of the organs. "Most of the upper body flesh and muscles are missing. But I don't quite know what this is—" She pointed to a line of brown masses, which Ryan had already assumed was biological. "It's not what you think."

Di Santo came up to the bed to check out the mystery meat while Dr. Bhandari ducked her head to smell it.

"Beef. It's cooked beef," she concluded.

"Was she…eating in bed and maybe that set off the lion?" Ryan asked.

"Not sure, Detective. It's possible. All I know is that it

appears that the lion feasted on his owner. People are crazy keeping exotic animals as pets. There are laws against it for this very reason. They're wild. *Wild!* They might appear cute and cuddly when they're fuzzy little cubs, but these things grow up. They can't help their instincts. They're on top of the food chain." She shook her head while she extracted some tools from her kit.

"This can't be a coincidence," Di Santo said in that high-pitched adrenaline-fueled squeal of his. "This is the third murder! The third family! The third *female* of the third Outfit family! This is not a fluke accident from a rogue wild animal. There's something—or someone—behind it."

Ryan agreed, and yet struggled to visualize the process of this particular homicide. He took in every piece of detail from the room. The body, the sheets, the blood spatter. The brand new shoes sat in their boxes to the right of her dresser, not even worn yet. "I just don't understand how The Ghost could have orchestrated this whole scene."

"I don't know, but this is not natural. We have to find evidence that says he was here. Somehow."

"At least her stomach is intact. That's it right there," Dr. Bhandari said, pointing to a pouch of flesh, ombred pink to gray. "That will tell us whether she was eating the beef and if she had any pharmaceuticals in her system."

"Can you get any inkling on time of death?" Ryan asked the doc.

The doctor rolled the torso forty-five degrees to check lividity, replaced it back to its resting position, then felt a knee joint for rigor. "Body temperature's not going to help in this case, since it's been…aerated. Also, the air conditioning unit is still on. Unfortunately, we can't gauge rigor in the facial muscles, since the flesh is most likely in the lion's stomach. From the organs and legs, though, I would venture to guess about ten to twelve hours."

Ryan glanced at his watch. "It's 11:13 a.m. now, which would mean the attack took place last night between eleven and one a.m." He scanned the bedroom windows, which were latched shut. No sign of entry, forced or otherwise. He and Di Santo conducted a tour of the rest of the apartment, which showed the same. Windows and door latches intact, no forced entry.

"She said she had a date, remember?" Di Santo said.

Ryan glanced back at the entry, where he noticed one of the dining room chairs near the front door. He glanced back at Bae's crate, which stood wide open.

"The perpetrator may have been the date," Ryan said. "He could have rendered Desirée unconscious, covered her with the beef—whatever—and then let Bae out of his cage. He could have backed out of the apartment, protecting himself with a chair like a lion tamer. Then left through the front door."

Di Santo agreed with the theory with a nod just as Sam Matello entered with his evidence tech team.

"Doherty! Di Santo! You caught this, too? I hear we got a fun scene to process here."

They greeted the head of the tech team without shaking, as they were already suited up. "Yeah, really fun. On prelim, this is a lion mauling," Ryan explained. "We've got buckets of blood all over the bedroom and a very full feline over there." The tech team strained to look behind the detectives and reacted to the unconscious lion. "Since there were no signs of forced entry, the perp most likely was let into the apartment by the victim. So print everything and look for hair and fibers. Dr. Bhandari will process the lion's body over at the zoo, after they put him down."

Several members of the evidence team let out an "Awwww."

Matello saluted Ryan without emotion, then led his team into the apartment. Within seconds they heard Matello's signature expletives from down the hall.

Before leaving, Ryan took one last look at the sedated Bae, being hauled out in his crate. "Be careful of the door jamb," he told the zoo people. "There may be prints there."

They folded the two sides of a stretcher so as not to

scrape against the doorway and successfully removed the animal from the condo. Ryan actually felt sorry for the big baby. He didn't ask to be imprisoned in a condominium ten stories above Lake Shore Drive. Dr. Bhandari was right: exotic animals were not pets.

A-wimoweh, a-wimoweh…

Ryan sent Bae a mental "Good night" before leaving the condo.

CHAPTER 10

Ryan and Di Santo took the elevator back down to the lobby, shedding their blue Mylar suits on the way down. In the front of the building they met up with Agent Jensen, who was huddled with Devin and the rest of the task force agents, awaiting their report of the crime scene.

"At this point, the preliminary cause of death is attack by lion," Ryan explained to the group. "The animal was kept by Desirée Leone as a pet—and for protection. They did mention to us yesterday that he'd attack anyone who threatened her or her brother. We'll have to speak with Danny Leone about the animal's volatility and if he had a history of violence. Has anyone notified him yet?"

Agent Jensen spoke up. "I just got off the line with him. He's already in Vegas and refuses to come back to Chicago. I'm sure he's still in shock. I think the next step is for all of us to get on a plane and go there. The Giordano family is the last potential target, and Joey flew his family to Vegas last night. Obviously the wife of Joey Bones is now in critical danger, from either The Ghost and/or the other three families who will suspect he ordered the hits unless and until something happens to her. They and their five-year-old daughter, Angelina, have already checked into their suite at The Chicago."

"So all four family heads are in Vegas now? Giordano, Danny Leone, Richie Rich and Victor Basso?" Ryan asked.

"Yes. Are you in?"

"Vegas is out of our jurisdiction," Di Santo responded. "I'm not sure the Department's gonna let us go."

"We'll talk to your sergeant. I'm sure we can get him to approve the travel. I'll explain to him that it's technically your investigation so it should be your collar. We'll continue to work on bringing down the Outfit, and you guys solve the murders. We'll give you all the resources you need." For a fed, Jensen was pretty solid. He seemed to truly want to cooperate and wasn't playing the territorial game. "You can fly on the agency jet with us. We'll leave at fifteen hundred hours. Meet us at Midway thirty minutes prior. That will give you two time to pack, and will give me time to brief Sergeant Besko." Jensen and the task force team took turns signing out of the crime scene. "See you at Midway, gentlemen."

Ryan's phone buzzed and he pulled it from his pocket. A text from Zach Sloane:

– Double-D: stop by the morgue ASAP. Found something on Victim Ricci.

He showed it to Di Santo and they made plans to head over there before packing. *The more data the better*, as Devin would say. Shit, Ryan was even starting to think like the guy. But maybe that wasn't altogether a bad thing.

The Cook County Medical Examiner's office was five miles from the Palmolive, to the west of the Loop. Ryan decided to take side streets. Chicago Avenue to Ogden would get them there faster than trying to jump on the Eisenhower, even for just a couple of miles.

The sweat on his brow nearly froze when they entered

the morgue itself, as the temp was at least twenty-five degrees cooler than the heat wave outside.

"Double-D!" Zach shouted, greeting the detectives as a unit. "Interesting stuff here, interesting stuff." He opened a drawer from the wall of metal compartments and rolled out Robin Ricci's corpse. This was the one part of the job that disturbed Ryan the most: seeing the bodies stuffed into the wall like Thanksgiving turkeys and then rolled out into the lab with a V of stitches emblazoned on the torso. It turned a human into a specimen. Just a body without the human component, without a life story. But an autopsy was an important part of the investigative process, and he was thankful they had doctors on staff who were sensitive to the fact that these people had lived human lives.

Zach pulled Robin Ricci's hand out from under the thin blue cloth that discreetly covered her midsection. "Turn off the lights for a sec?" Di Santo obliged by finding the bank of switches and throwing them. As soon as the room went dark, the purple glow of a black light appeared. "Check this out, on her hand." Zach waved the black light over Robin Ricci's body, a forensic procedure that often revealed biologicals or other material that glowed under ultra-violet light, like bleach. Evidence that was not apparent to the naked eye.

As the black light hovered over Robin Ricci's hand, the word "BOO" lit up in sketchy block letters. The doc flipped the lights back on, fascinated with his own discovery. "It's special invisible ink that only shows up under UV light. They use it at night clubs, frat parties, stuff like that."

"You think Robin Ricci had attended a night club or a frat party?" Di Santo asked. "She's, like, forty-something and a mother of three!"

Ryan shook his head. "No, but it could be the killer's calling card. Remember, Ricci's hit man is nicknamed *The Ghost*."

"*Boo!*" Di Santo cried, getting the connection. "So you think this guy is for real?"

"There's only one way to find out. We're going to have to exhume Sandy Orlando's body and see if she's got a matching stamp. If that is the killer's calling card, it's the only way to find out for sure if these two homicides are connected." He turned to the ME. "Zach, can you get the paperwork started on that? If you need help with the judge, call Jane Steffen, one of the assistant state's attorneys. She owes me a favor...or five. Di Santo and I are flying out to Vegas in a couple of hours."

"Vegas?" Zach replied. "You're taking a vacation in the middle of all this?"

"No vacation. The feds asked us to go. If this is a serial murder, the next victim—and possibly the killer—are both headed there."

Zach pulled out a form to get the two licenses necessary for exhumation. Ryan signed the bottom and thanked him for the additional "data."

He had a feeling Sandy Orlando's hand was going to light up in black light. As he turned to head out, he stopped, realizing that they had a third body currently on its way to the morgue.

"Do me a favor?" he called out to the ME. "Call Nina Bhandari and ask her to scan the Leone scene with a black light, and what's left of Desirée body. The evidence techs will have one. Text me immediately if anything shows up."

After they left the Cook County Morgue, Ryan dropped Di Santo back at his car in the 18th lot and drove back to his apartment.

He pulled his battered old black suitcase from the closet, placed it on the bed, and called Cat while he started to pack.

"Hey, you," she answered in that sing-song lilt of hers. Even remotely, he could envision the stunning smile that accompanied her greeting. "When are you coming home? See? I'm already saying 'home.' How does that sound to you?"

"Sounds great, but I'm not coming home. Matt and I are off to Vegas this afternoon for this mob case."

He pulled several dresser drawers open, wondering what the dress protocol would be.

"Las Vegas? Today? Why?"

"We think this Ghost guy will be pursuing another victim. And all the families have gone to a hotel they own there, on the Strip. I really wish we knew what he looked like, but no one has ever laid eyes on him. He worked strictly through the Internet. Maybe you can do your thing and try to get some kind of identifying characteristics? That would really help, Cat, whether Devin believes you or not."

"I have an idea. Let me come with you!" Catharine gushed. "I can get a feeling for him if I'm there. If I'm close to him. I'm almost certain I could pinpoint the man if I could feel his presence."

Ryan burst out in laughter and sat down on his bed. "Cat, of all the places you should *not* go, Vegas is at the top of the list. The crowds, the energy, your head would explode in three minutes."

"But I've been so successful, lately, in my excursions—"

"I know you have, and I'm so proud of you. But an outing to my apartment is one thing when we were alone, and you felt safe. But Vegas is a zoo. You going to Vegas is like teaching a baby to swim and then dropping her in the middle of the ocean. Trust me, it's not a good idea." He could almost hear her disappointment on the other side of the line. "I know you want to help, and I'll let you. From there. I'll call you with the information when we have it and you can work the case with us. I promise."

"All right. I just really feel I can assist with this Ghost guy. I've already received visions, you know."

"Yes, and I meant to tell you that the horrible scene you saw last night? It happened today. We had another victim, and she was mauled by a lion, apparently. Unrecognizable, just like you said."

"Oh, that's horrible, Ryan."

"It was. It really was."

Catharine paused for a beat. "Did she…have a…tattoo? Of that lion? I see it as a tattoo."

"Yes. We haven't released that information yet. But it helped us identify her. It was one of the messiest scenes I've ever had to witness."

"I'm sorry, honey. I wish I could hug you. How long will you be in Las Vegas?"

"I don't know. Hopefully not long." Ryan hated the thought of just taking off without seeing Cat in person. "We have two missions: to protect that last family and to catch this Ghost. Any impressions or visions you get, let me know. I trust your talents, and I don't necessarily have to share all this with the feds."

She sighed. "I know you do. Is Devin going to Las Vegas also?"

"Yes. I'm kind of looking forward to the time with him—see what he's like—determine if he's on the up and up."

"Communication is always good," Catharine said, in her New Agey philosophical way.

"Hey, that reminds me. Speaking of communication, I've had a hard time getting a hold of Jane. I've tried texting and calling her, but she's not responding and it's seriously getting me a little worried. I have a mission for you, if you choose to accept it: I was wondering if you could try stopping in on her? Maybe the two of you could have lunch or something. Just find out if she's okay. I'll text you her number and addresses."

"Sure, I can do that." She was silent for a couple of seconds, and he knew what that meant.

"Cat? Are you trying to clue into her? Is she okay?"

"I believe she's doing well and is still here in the city," Catharine responded. "Don't worry, she seems to be fine. But I'll find her, just to verify. Have a great trip."

"Thanks, babe. I love you. Stay safe."

They said their goodbyes and Ryan finished packing by stuffing in his black shaving bag and zipping up the suitcase. He hesitated for a moment, his hand hovering over his Glock, until he remembered they were traveling in a private, government jet. Firearms allowed. He dropped the gun into its holster and clipped it to his belt before he left, pulling his suitcase and laptop behind him.

CHAPTER 11

Two Years, Nine Months, Four Days Ago:

The light snowfall didn't deter Ryan from his plans for the evening of December first. He'd been back on the job for six weeks now. Six weeks of hell. He'd been so eager to return to work he had begged the shrink to sign the form, just to get out of his damned apartment. There was no way he could spend one more day watching mind-numbing daytime TV or trying to remember chords on his old guitar. He hadn't even considered how painful the alternative would be: policing without his partner.

He pulled up and double-parked outside R&R's Liquor on Clark and placed a tattered CPD vehicle card in the windshield. He pulled his wool coat snug to his body as he made his way across the walk and into the store. The proprietor greeted him with a nod from behind the counter and Ryan flashed his badge in return. He had no idea what possessed him to flash his credentials, as he'd been off duty for all of seventeen minutes. Maybe he just didn't want to spook the guy, rushing in here.

"What can I do you for you, Officer?"

"What's your best single malt scotch? But in my price range," Ryan joked.

The man had both hands on the counter, a gesture to

convey he wasn't going to go for the shotgun which Ryan sensed was within his reach. The proprietor thought for a minute, then slapped the counter top. "Glenfiddich!" he proclaimed, pointing directly at Ryan. "Won't break the bank, but it goes down smooth. You celebratin' somethin'?" He turned to the shelves to retrieve the Scotch whiskey.

"Birthday. It's my best friend's birthday," he answered. Jon would have been thirty-five.

The shield had proved useful, since it got Ryan a 20% city worker's discount on the Scotch. He thanked the man and jogged back to his car with the brown paper bag tucked under his arm. Inside, he placed it on the passenger's seat next to the two shot glasses he had brought along from home this morning. Baby Blue started up on the second try and he headed for the Kennedy Expressway.

Jon's parents were originally from the South Side and had moved to the Ashburn area after he was born, a neighborhood on the southwestern edge of the city that had been known to attract more middle-class blacks. Ryan had been completely unaware of these stats—or the area—until Jon brought him to dinner at his parents' house for the first time. It was funny how insular the ethnic pockets of Chicago remained and how there were folks who were born, grew up and died staying within their ten-block radius of a universe.

Although Evergreen Cemetery would have been closer to their home, Jon's family decided to inter him at Cedar Park, way down on the far South Side of the city, near Riverdale. Cedar Park was better maintained, they said, and nearer to the forest preserves where Jon had enjoyed visiting on his days off. He always had been a nature buff—constantly bugging Ryan to go hiking with him. But he had never gotten around to accepting. He preferred running along the lake where he could watch bikinis rather than birds.

By the time he arrived at Cedar Park, the snow had waned, already melting into slush on the streets. He pulled up to the gate and read the welcome sign, emblazoned with the hours of business. Summer hours on the left, winter on the right: Monday to Friday, 8:30 a.m. to 4:30 p.m. His cell phone displayed 6:57 p.m. He pounded the steering wheel, cursing the Kennedy's rush hour traffic, then flipped the Mustang into reverse and backed out. He'd come all this way, and he sure as hell wasn't about to turn around and get back on the highway.

Ryan turned right at the next corner, then again at the next, slowly circling the cemetery's outer gate until he found an under-lit section in the back. He parked at the curb and pulled a flashlight from the glove box. The green wrought-iron fence stood no higher than six feet, easily scalable with his training. He stuffed the bottle of scotch, the two shot glasses, and his cell phone into his backpack and got out, surveying the sidewalk and interior of the grounds for any potential witnesses. Satisfied that he was alone, Ryan took the fence in three moves, landing on a pile of wet leaves, slipping slightly until he found his footing. He made sure to illuminate the flashlight before he bumped into a tree or tripped over a low grave marker. In his head, he tried to imagine the layout of the place from above, re-calling how he got to Jon's funeral services from the en-trance, just twelve weeks and three days ago.

Slowly making his way through the park-like setting, he paused every so often and hid behind a larger tombstone to scope for guards. Either they had a small staff or they just didn't patrol frequently, because other than a couple of ducks, there was no life whatsoever. He followed the pe-riphery of the main drive to the left until he found the sec-tion of the cemetery that he recognized.

Small slush bundles fell from the branches overhead, causing Ryan to constantly check his six to make sure no one was following him. At one point he swore he heard footsteps coming out from behind a seven-foot concrete an-gel. He switched off the light and stood still, urging himself to breathe silently. Then something jumped out to his right. Ryan pulled his weapon and crouched, imagining some var-iant of walking dead. He flipped on the flashlight and shone it directly ahead of him. A large buck stood motionless, dazed, staring back for several seconds. Then it took off at full stride through the trees.

"Jesus, Mary and Joseph," he whispered to himself, holstering his gun. "Deer." He shook his head while scanning the light back down on the headstones. Row by row he followed the wet graves until he found the gravestone of his destination.

Jonathan Marcus Lange
Decorated Officer, Chicago Police Department
Beloved Son, Brother, and Friend

The Langes put that last word on just for him.

He pulled out the shot glasses and hunter green bottle of Glenfiddich and threw the backpack down next to the grave to protect his ass from the cold, wet ground. He sat down and poured a healthy shot of scotch into both glasses, placing one in front of the headstone.

"Happy Birthday, bud," he said, holding the glass up in a toast, and then downed it within seconds. The smooth whiskey warmed his throat and tingled through its journey from esophagus to belly. After two more shots, he took the glass he'd poured for Jon and trickled the whiskey onto his best friend's grave.

"That guy in the liquor store was right, this is good stuff," he proclaimed aloud. Ryan inched closer so that he could lean his back against the headstone. "I swear to God this is so fucked up. You should be there, at your desk, dude. Not that fuckin' Di-psycho kid. You should see this guy, Jon. What a piece of work. First of all, he won't wear anything but a fuckin' three-piece suit. Yep. Only Italian suits, and they're expensive, too. I'm like 'Dude, you know we police in tee shirts around here.' You know how it is, makes the perps more comfortable, more trusting. But no, every day this guy walks in looking like a fed...*Fuck!*" He poured himself two more shots and threw them back. "Not only that, but this kid looks like he's in high school. Smooth skin, beady little eyes, and scrawny as fuck. I have no idea how he got through the Academy." Ryan zipped his coat up a little higher to keep the Chicago wind from stinging his exposed skin. "And another thing—he's always up in my face, jabbering non-stop. Yak, yak, yak. About a case, about his patrol beat, about his family, about his love live. Yak, yak, yak. I can't get a minute's peace and quiet. You know me. I need my quiet. To think. To investigate. *Fuck,* I hate him."

Ryan stopped pouring shots and decided to swig straight from the bottle, awaiting Jon Lange's reply. A duck quacked in the distance.

"What, now you've got nothing to say? You interrupt my thoughts, blabbing in my head for the last three months, all outta nowhere, making me feel like I've lost my fucking mind. And now when I come visit you in your actual resting place, you won't talk to me?" He slammed a fist back into the stone. "Fuck you."

The outburst of anger released something in him, something liberating. He slammed his fist into the stone again. "Fuck you." And again, the pain in his bones resonating like a tuning fork. "Fuck you. *Fuck you! Fuck—*"

Without warning, a flood of tears emerged, his grief riding the wave, and he doubled forward, head in hands. The sobbing was a release, intoxicating, cathartic, lasting for about ten minutes until he curled into a fetal position, giving in to the exhaustion. Exhaustion from grieving. From fighting life. From analyzing what had gone wrong with Kelly to trying to act normal with the sarge. Debilitated, he let himself drift, eyes closed, to a place beyond. Anywhere but the present. His last thought as he drifted away was that he could die from exposure, but he just…didn't…care.

"Doherty!" a voice called out to him. "Get him up and into my car, and I can take it from there, Officers."

He attempted to open his eyes. "Jon? What's going—" Before he could finish the sentence he was lifted up off of the ground by the armpits.

"Can you walk? Ryan? *Hello?*" A cold slap stung his cheek as he tried to focus. Flashing blue lights spun in the background. A familiar face hovered before him. "Welcome to the land of the living," Di Santo said in his whiny boy voice.

Chuckles rang out in stereo, and Ryan turned his reeling head from side to side. Two uniformed officers stood flanking him, supporting his weight. Holding him up.

"There ya go! Now let's see if you can walk," Di Santo said.

The smells of the wet leaves and decaying flowers reminded him where he was, as darkness still enveloped the cemetery grounds. He suddenly got the joke: *Land of the living.*

"What...time is it?" Ryan's teeth chattered uncontrollably between syllables.

The officers wrapped an emergency blanket around his shoulders and began walking him toward the cemetery's paved drive.

"A little after nine, D. How long have you been here?" Without waiting for a response, Di Santo continued, "You know you're one lucky guy. One of the Cedar Park security guards found you, checked your ID, and called the Eighteenth. You could've died out here, it's gonna get below zero overnight!"

"You're not my mother," he attempted to say, but it came out more like "Yonomamurrrr."

Di Santo nodded. "Yeah, okay, Detective. Let's just get you into my warm car. Then we can have a conversation."

He let the officers support him as they walked him to a vehicle with its hazards blinking. They folded him into the passenger seat and shut the door. Ryan welcomed the car heater's warm air as it blew directly onto his face, thawing out his core.

He watched Di Santo with the officers, thanking them with a nod and a pat to the shoulders. When the guy got into the driver's seat, he tossed the backpack to Ryan.

"That was a very stupid thing to do, partner."

"You're not my partner."

Di Santo punched the dome light and Ryan winced, shutting one eye. "Listen, you miserable fuck. I *am* your partner whether you like it or not. You're lucky I was still at the station, working late. Working on that case that you refuse to touch because you'd have to...oh...*work with me*. You should see yourself now. How they found you. Killing yourself at his grave. Poisoning yourself with alcohol in your misery. Well, guess what? Jonathan Lange is not the first police officer in the world to bite it. You're not the first police officer to lose a partner, and you don't got the market cornered on grief, my friend. Get the fuck over it and start doing your job."

"Who the—"

"Shut. Up. I'm not hearing it from you, anymore. I've done my best coming into a hard situation, trying to follow Golden Boy back there." Di Santo started the car and put it into gear. Thank god, they were leaving. Ryan just wanted to get home. "You think I didn't know what I was getting into? I did. I knew Jon was well respected at the Eighteenth and I tiptoed around you when you came back on the job. And what did you do? Strangle me! Just because I existed. You know, I figured it would be hard coming back, so I did everything in my power to accommodate you. And you treat me like shit."

"I—"

"You *what?*" Di Santo shouted, coming to a stoplight. "*What?*"

Ryan forgot what he was about to retort. Di Santo hit the gas and the lights of the city flew by: liquor stores, Chinese food, gas stations, city buses.

"I'm telling you now. Tomorrow you're going to come in *on time* for once, and you're going to ask me 'Hey, Matt, how's it going?' like a decent human being and you're gonna work the cases with me like a decent fucking cop. You're going to acknowledge you have a partner. *A new partner.* And you're going to deal with it. Because if you don't, I have no problem going to Sarge and askin' to be reassigned. But once we cross that bridge, my friend, then it's on record. It's on record that you came back and couldn't deal with your shit. Let's see where that gets you in your career."

Ryan remained silent for the next portion of the drive, letting Di Santo's words sink in. He had to admit, he had a little more respect for the kid now that he had whipped out his balls along with his bravado. He realized that Di Santo had been tiptoeing around him, and maybe that's what had been pissing him off. Ryan didn't want to be treated any differently. He just wanted to do his job.

"That's it," Ryan said, pointing, as they turned onto his street. "That's my building right there." Di Santo slowed the car, pulling over across the street from his apartment. Ryan opened the backpack, taking inventory of its content. The two shot glasses were there, along with the flashlight and his cell. His keys jingled as he pulled them out from the side pocket.

"You finished the bottle. We threw it away," Di Santo said. "I'll take you back to get your car tomorrow after shift. Are you okay from here?"

Ryan nodded. He pushed the door open a couple of inches, stopped and looked back at his new partner.

"See you tomorrow," was all he could muster.

CHAPTER 12

Current Day:

Ryan arrived at Midway airport right on time and badged his way through the security line. He was directed to a private door that led to a secluded side of the tarmac, away from the commercial terminals. He spotted Di Santo loading a suitcase onto a luggage truck and jogged over to join him.

"Jensen went to find the plane," Di Santo said. "It should've been here by now. They said to put your stuff on here." He pointed to the luggage truck.

The rest of the task force agents arrived as a group, placed their luggage on the truck as well, and parted way for Jensen, who did the same.

"Detectives, agents, they're pulling the plane around now." As if on cue, a beautiful gleaming Gulfstream turned the corner and pulled up about two hundred feet from the group. "It's the 650 model, what do you think?" Jensen said, boasting, as feds are inclined to do. "Confiscated from a TV evangelist. Can you believe it?"

"Hallelujah!" Di Santo shouted.

Some agents chuckled, some just smiled. Ryan nodded his approval as the door cycled open and the plane's boarding stairs emerged. A flight attendant greeted them at the top of the staircase as the team filed into the plane. The interior was a mix of dark wood and creamy leather, with a bank of seating on the right side of the plane and club chairs on the left. Unlike a commercial aircraft, the chairs were arranged to face each other, specifically designed for executives—or in this case, agents—to work together during the flight. Video screens, strategically placed throughout the cabin, displayed the blue and gold FBI logo.

"Sit anywhere?" Ryan asked the flight attendant, who responded with a smile and scoop of her palm.

He and Di Santo took a seat in two of the leather swivel chairs while Jensen and Devin Doherty took the ones across from them. A highly lacquered mahogany table stood between them.

The agents plopped their laptop cases on it and proceeded to remove their computers in unison.

"Did you know that O'Hare Airport is named after the son of a mobster?" Devin asked the group. Jensen turned his head to listen, as did Ryan. "O'Hare Airport was named after Butch O'Hare, who was a decorated war hero in World War Two. One of the first flying aces for the US Navy. But his father, Eddie O'Hare, was just a typical Chicago gangster, a known associate of Al Capone's. Until he turned on Capone and provided evidence to the IRS during Al's trial. O'Hare actually helped put him away, believe it or not. So Family Secrets wasn't the first time the Outfit has turned on itself. Despite their supposed *omertá* code of silence, they've been ratting each other out since the beginning."

"That's actually very interesting," Ryan responded, giving the guy some kudos. "I had never heard that before, and I've lived here all my life." He pulled out his own computer. "What happened to the father O'Hare?"

"One of Capone's gang got to him. Gunned down in his own car."

"That's why I love this guy," Jensen declared, patting Devin on the back. "He's a never-ending font of information. I'm glad to have you on the team. Now we need to fast-forward to today's scumbags so we can plan our strategy for Vegas."

The video screens flickered and began a safety video, while the flight attendant gestured by rote to the emergency exits. At the end of the video, she announced that once they got into the air snacks were imminent. Apparently, there was no booze on government flights, at least not this one. Ryan texted Catharine that they were about to take off and said he'd text her again when they landed. Jensen took a moment to call in to DC and report the plan to his superior, whomever that might be. Ryan had worked with the FBI only one previous time, in the Jessica Way case, when Assistant Special Agent in Charge Hockett had been a complete dick to both him and Catharine. The guy's ego was about twice the size of Soldier Field. Devin, Jensen, and the task force team had been infinitely more respectful of the local cops and way easier to work with. Although Devin had made it clear he didn't believe in Catharine's abilities, he still made it clear that he respected her intelligence.

The pilot came over the loudspeaker, announcing that the plane was cruising at an altitude of 38,000 feet at a speed of approximately 500 miles per hour. His voice kept cutting in and out, punctuated with white noise, but Ryan understood most of it, doing the time calcs while spotting his watch. They took off at 3:23 p.m. and the total flight time was clocked at three hours and forty minutes, which would put them landing at just about 5:00 p.m. Vegas time.

Jensen got up and made his way to the back of the plane to make several more calls before the official meeting. Di Santo put in his ear buds and bobbed his head to a playlist, leaving only Devin to converse with. Ryan really wanted to ask the burning question and attempted an approach.

"You know, before Di Santo, I had another partner," he said to Devin, who was engrossed in something on his laptop screen. Probably email.

"Jonathan Lange," Devin responded, without a beat. He didn't even look up. "I read your file."

"Yes. Jon, actually. He went by Jon."

"He was a good cop." This time Devin looked him in the eyes, as if complimenting Ryan himself.

"Definitely one of the good ones." Ryan cleared his throat, closed his laptop, and leaned forward a bit, lowering his voice. "Catharine…she just gets things about a person. I was skeptical too, at first. I mean, hey, I'm a cop, right? When I first interrogated her, I thought she was a nutcase."

"You don't have to do that."

"Do what?"

"Try to get me to identify with you—or you with me. You did not think Catharine was a 'nutcase.' You wouldn't think that, because she's beautiful and you were attracted to her. You are a fairly attractive man by society's standards, and she probably had reciprocal feelings for you from the beginning."

"Okay, okay. I forgot you're an agent, and you know all the tricks with your data charts and everything. I'm trying to say that Cat's just *right on* sometimes, and there is absolutely no explanation how or why."

"Why are you trying to convince me of this again?" Devin said, going back to typing. "We already discussed the subject last night. You know I don't believe in psychic ability."

"Does Jon Lange speak to you?" Ryan asked, deciding to be blunt. Devin stopped typing. His gaze remained on the screen. "Catharine said when she was doing her reading, she got a feeling that Jon—my Jon—spoke to you." More silence. No eye contact.

Devin pushed his glasses up the bridge of his nose with one finger and was about to say something when Agent Jensen sat back down in his seat.

Shit.

Ryan's phone pinged and he checked the screen: a text from Catharine.

– Is everything ok?

The implication of the text drew concern, especially

since he'd just defended Catharine's sixth sense to the agent sitting across from him. Ryan glanced around the cabin at the working agents, Di Santo was still bobbing his head, and the flight attendant sat in a little flip-down seat, paging through a copy of *Fast Company*. The flight itself was smooth, no turbulence.

– Yes, everything is quiet here. All ok there?

– Yes. Have a safe flight and let me know when you land.

"Are you two Dohertys ready?" Jensen said with a perceptive gleam in his eye, betraying his knowledge of the brother theory. Ryan elbowed Di Santo to join the meeting. His partner pulled his ear buds out and turned off the music. Jensen slapped his hands on the table. "Great. So I just got off the phone with our guys in Vegas. We've got some physical eyes and ears inside The Chicago Resort, but since it's all Outfit-owned, we can't put in any wires or cameras in there, even with a warrant. The hotel management would alert the bosses and that would defeat the whole purpose. They said they have picked up rumblings of a Commission meeting tomorrow."

"Yeah, Danny Leone said something about that," Ryan said. "The Commission is a meeting with all of the bosses, right?"

"Yes. Ricci, Basso, Giordano, and Danny Leone…solo. They're going to decide what to do about The Ghost hits. Problem is, Joey Giordano's in the most imminent danger. His family is the last target, and if nothing happens by tomorrow then the other three families are going to be highly suspicious. We'll do everything in our power to protect him, but we need to hear what's being said in that room." He threw a deliberate glance at Di Santo.

"What?" Di Santo squawked. "You don't think *I* can go in there? You just said it was bosses only. And even if it were open to the families, that doesn't include me. I'm a cop, a clean cop, and I've made that extremely clear to them."

"No, of course you can't be in on the Commission *meet-

ing," Jensen responded. "But you can get into that conference room and plant a device for us. We want you to set up a meeting with Ricci prior to the Commission. You'll bring in our transmitting device and place it underneath the table." Jensen palmed the underside of the wood table between them to demonstrate.

"No, uh-uh," Ryan said. "I don't like this at all. You don't think they'll know that Matt is working for you? Ricci already admitted that he knew you guys were trying to recruit him. You're putting my partner in a clear line of fire, and that's fucked up."

"Detective Di Santo? Is Detective Doherty speaking for you?" Jensen said. Di Santo locked eyes with all three of them, in succession, ruminating on the plan.

Ryan glared at his partner. "D, you're not thinking of actually doing this?"

"What, you don't think I can pull it off? I think I can. Richie trusts me for some reason."

"What? You're nuts. What if Ricci sees you plant the bug?"

"I think Richie needs us and he's not going to jeopardize that," Di Santo responded. "Even if I'm caught, I can explain it away. I'll say I was coerced by the task force. Believe me, I can spin it. And like I said, he needs us. We'll keep dangling the Ghost's identity as a carrot, and he'll have to keep me alive."

"Yeah, but keeping you alive with all your fingers and toes…"

Di Santo winced and then quickly covered his apprehension with a dismissive wave. "Don't worry about me, I'll be fine. I'll do it. We have to find out what they're concocting in that meeting. And Jensen's right. We have to make sure they don't turn on Joey Bones."

"Shit," Ryan said, shaking his head. He had no way to respond to that. Jensen exhaled, clearly pleased at Di Santo's acceptance of the task while Devin had gone back to typing on his computer. Maybe he was taking notes on the decision. "So how's this going to work?" Ryan asked, finally giving in.

Jensen pulled out a floor plan of the mezzanine level of the Chicago Hotel. "The Gold Coast Ballroom is the one they use for all their Outfit meetings. It's huge, but that's why they like it—no one can eavesdrop from any adjacent room, since they meet toward the back, near the stage. The room should already be set up for the Commission meeting when you get there. All you have to do, Detective Di Santo, is get the transmitter placed in the room. That's it. We'll give you all the details after we check in."

"And what if they sweep the room before the meeting?" Di Santo asked. "Or worse, sweep me?"

Devin finally decided to participate in the conversation by responding. "We'll give you two transmitters. One you wear, one you place. If they sweep you, you show them the first one and plead the fifth. 'Hey, I'm a cop, they made me do it,' and all that. And while you're misdirecting their attention with the first bug, you'll be placing the second."

"Wow, you have this all figured out, don't you," Di Santo said, nodding at the plan. "Sounds like it should work."

"I want to go in with him," Ryan interjected. "For backup." Jensen sat back in his chair, contemplating the request. "If things get out of hand, at least Matt'll have a chance. I don't want him to go in there alone."

"We can't risk that," Jensen responded. "If two of you go in there, it looks more like an official police op. If Di Santo goes in alone, he'll look like he's decided to play ball with them. You have the choice of waiting somewhere on the mezzanine or in the surveillance room with us. We've requested a bank of rooms on the third floor, right above the ballroom. It's close enough to get the signal from the transmitter."

"And these guys are just going to let a bunch of federal agents rent rooms in their hotel?" Ryan asked, just a little too loud.

"We've reserved them under aliases, with General Electric as the corporate client. Their company's travel agent books the rooms for us."

Ryan sighed and rubbed his chin, accepting the plan for now. He'd do everything in his power to be as close as possible to that ballroom when Di Santo was in there. He opened up his laptop, connected to the in-flight Wi-Fi, and checked his email, zooming straight in on a message from Zach Sloane.

> Subject line: *Invisible Ink*
> *Hey, D –*
> *Nina Bhandari called with a positive on invisible ink on Desirée Leone's body. She took a black light to the room and found a BOO stamp all over the bed's headboard. Can you believe it? What does this even mean? Orlando body will be exhumed tomorrow— will let you know what we find. Hopefully the skin is still preserved. It should be.*
> *– Dr. Z.*

Ryan immediately shared the news with the table, bringing Jensen and Devin in on the invisible ink stamp that appeared on Robin Ricci's hand under black light. "We weren't sure it was even a viable clue until we connected it to one of the other crime scenes," Ryan explained. "Now that we found it all over Desirée Leone's headboard, they're going to check Sandy Orlando. Hard data, right?"

Devin nodded, his fingers flying a mile a minute over his laptop keyboard.

"And…" Di Santo said, burrowing around in his laptop case, "I even borrowed a black light from the tech team to bring along to Vegas!" He pulled out a battery operated black light bar, about the size of a cigar. "Just in case."

Di Santo switched it on to demonstrate and waved it over their table. His hand froze and Ryan's heart stopped.

Glowing green underneath the black light was the word *BOO*.

CHAPTER 13

H e was here," Ryan managed to say.

Jensen flew out of his chair. "There's been a securi-ty breach!" he announced to the team. "I want you all to spread out and conduct a search of the plane for explosives. *Now!*"

The team jumped into action while Ryan remained immobile. All he could think of was Cat's text. She knew. She knew something was wrong. Did she see a bomb? Were they going to die on this flight? If so, wouldn't she have seen it? Wouldn't she have told him? She would have instructed them to land as soon as possible. "What can we do?" he asked Jensen, snapping out of the haze.

"Nothing. Just stay seated and let us handle this."

Ryan felt both severely confined and endangered. Like Bae in the condo. He glanced over at Di Santo. "It'll be okay," he assured his partner, attempting to fight off his own terror. Di Santo's pallor betrayed his fear.

Visions of Catharine, his mom, his sisters, the mansion, all flew by in Ryan's head. This couldn't be the end. He wasn't ready for this to be the end.

"I want someone down in cargo now!" Jensen barked. He pointed to the blonde female agent. "Pendergrass, you have explosives training, so you're up. Take Martinez with you." Agent Martinez stopped thumbing his phone to catch the order. "And nothing—*nothing*—goes outside this plane," Jensen added. "I'll call HQ and inform them of the situation."

The detectives waited helplessly as the federal agents searched every corner and compartment of the aircraft. The flight attendant approached their table and asked calmly if they wanted anything to drink. They both declined. Ryan couldn't imagine how unaffected the woman was, but then realized she was most likely military herself, as were the pilots. They were trained for such emergencies.

"Let me see the light," he said to Di Santo. "Maybe he left more than this one clue. Maybe the stamps will lead us to the location of the..." He couldn't say the word *bomb*. He couldn't even bring himself to think it.

Di Santo handed over the light wand without a word and Ryan switched it on, getting up from his chair. He waved the stick over the table, now devoid of their laptops, as it was now evidence of a criminal act. The only BOO stamp visible was the one they had already discovered, glowing in the corner. He tried the walls of the plane. Nothing. He scanned the other tables, in succession. One *BOO* lit up on each, as almost a beacon, a taunt.

Jensen still stood at the rear of the cabin, alternating between talking quietly into his cell phone and shouting directions to his team.

Ryan discovered a line of BOO stamps on the carpet, spaced approximately twelve inches apart. "Agent Jensen! I think I've got something," he said.

The agent made his way through the team and watched as Ryan held the black light over the aisle. He followed the stamps to the front of the plane, causing the flight attendant to step aside into a cramped food prep section, angling her head to avoid a steaming pot of coffee. The line of *BOO* stamps ended in an arrow pointing directly at the cockpit door.

Jensen pounded on the door, but there was no response. He banged again with the heel of his fist. "Damn. This is a specially designed security door," he explained. "When it's locked, it's impenetrable. At least without a battering ram."

"What do you think it means? The arrow?" Di Santo asked. "You think the bomb's in the cockpit?" The flight attendant emitted an involuntary squeak in the corner.

"Don't jump to conclusions, Detective. We don't know for sure that there's an incendiary device on this plane. There's absolutely no reason to panic."

The craziest things ran through Ryan's brain, being trapped in this tin can of terror. Like if his partner was going to buy it this time, at least he'd go with him. He wouldn't have to suffer the loss again, because his body parts would be scattered across the Nevada desert with the rest of the team's. That particular image kept playing over and over in his head like a bad pop song.

"I would venture to say that there is *not* a bomb on the plane," Devin Doherty announced, approaching them. "Point one, the perpetrator left the stamps. If the plane had been wired to explode, there was really no way for his mark to be discovered, as the tables would be slivered and the carpet nonexistent in the crash debris." Creating that image didn't help alleviate his fright, but Ryan wasn't going to argue. He needed Devin to keep talking. "Point two, we're about fifteen minutes from beginning our descent. I checked, and we're still on course to Las Vegas. Why would he wait this long? If the perpetrator set an explosive on this plane, it would have gone off during takeoff, where he could watch, verify, and validate his work."

"So what is this?" Ryan said, grabbing Devin's elbow. "What are we up against?" He was losing his shit now. He couldn't help it.

The rest of the agents, with the exception of Pendergrass and Martinez, were idling behind Devin, awaiting the answer as well.

Devin took the black light from Di Santo, crouched down, and waved it over the carpet to study the pattern for himself. They stood back to let him study the glowing stamps. He took a moment, staring up at the cockpit door, then turned back to the team.

"I have quickly analyzed the hard data of the situation. *One:* The Ghost broke security protocol and was at some point on this aircraft. *Two:* he made his signature stamps point to the cockpit. And *three:* The pilots are not responding."

"And that equals…" Ryan asked.

Devin stood up, one knee cracking. "I believe our perpetrator is flying the plane," he stated, as casually as if he'd said, *I'll have some peanuts, please.*

"But we heard the pilot make an announcement," Di Santo said.

"Well, what you *thought* was the pilot," Devin answered. "It could have been anyone. We already deduced that The Ghost most probably has military training. He could have been Air Force."

Ryan tried to recall boarding the plane, and remembered that the cockpit door was closed the entire time. As opposed to a commercial flight, where the door to the cockpit was usually open upon boarding, he didn't remember seeing the pilot or co-pilot at all.

Jensen turned to the flight attendant. "Please show me how you communicate with the pilot through this thing." Jensen pointed to a navy blue phone set hanging on the wall. She pulled the handset off its cradle, punched in a code and handed it to him. No one dared breathe for seven seconds. "No answer. Shit, that doesn't bode well." Then after a beat, "Move back! Everyone back to their seats. We should be landing soon, and I have to call this in. Tell them it's a possibility the plane may be diverted." He grumbled the last phrase, already dialing.

Pendergrass and Martinez emerged from a small door in the back, a little more pale in complexion than when they had left. "Nothing out of order in cargo, sir," Pendergrass announced. "We even checked the suitcases."

Martinez confirmed her report with a nod. They took

their seats and buckled in like the rest of the team.

Three tones rang out and the flight attendant's eyes widened. She took the handset and made an announcement. "Please prepare for landing. Make sure your seatbelts are fastened and all electronic devices are on airplane-mode. Please secure your carry-ons under your seat or in an overhead bin." The woman was a rock, divulging no fear, not even a quiver in her voice.

Ryan thought about texting Cat. Maybe just an "I love you." But then she'd know. She'd know immediately that he was in trouble. He couldn't do that to her. He couldn't have her terrified with the burden of the unknown.

The plane began to descend and Ryan swallowed to alleviate the pressure in his ears. All of the passengers remained silent, and many eyes were on Jensen, as the agent in charge, as if he were God or Dad and could make everything better. He took his seat opposite the detectives and said quietly, "They'll have a tac team waiting for our plane at McCarran. We don't know if the perpetrator is going to let us off the plane. If he opens those doors, we let the tac team on first. If he doesn't, you let my team up front, and you three stay back."

"Me?" Devin asked. "Why do I have to hang back?"

"Because you're an analyst. You've been far removed from tactical for quite a while, Agent Doherty, whereas my team trains regularly."

Devin scowled, but didn't respond.

"I've trained in tac," Ryan said, a little eager to best his alleged brother. "I've got all my certifications."

The plane dipped suddenly and jerked to one side. Several of the agents emitted gasps of anxiety, but calmed when the aircraft righted itself. Di Santo had retreated into Neverland, his hands folded, eyes shut, mouthing a prayer.

For the next eleven minutes and twenty-two seconds, the cabin was quiet while the task force team peered out the windows, gauging whether they were landing or crashing or veering off, hijacked, in another direction. But the final descent was unexpectedly smooth and executed without incident.

As they flew over the Strip, Ryan tapped Di Santo's shoulder, pointing to the row of sparkling mega-resorts. From the last time he visited, he knew that the airport was located almost directly adjacent to the south end of Vegas Strip. The familiar sound of the wheels emerging from the plane was encouraging. The plane descended, foot by foot, until finally the wheels hit the tarmac and the reverse fans whirred, slowing the plane's velocity. The entire cabin resonated with sounds of relief, and soon after, the clatter of weapons prep.

Agent Jensen stood up from his seat and held up a silent palm. After several minutes, it was apparent that they were not pulling into any of the terminals. From the view out of the windows, both left and right side, it appeared as if the plane had taxied to a remote corner of the tarmac.

An announcement came from the cockpit. "Thank you for flying Spirit Airlines," a man's voice crackled over the PA system. "You will now wait five minutes before you open the door. Then you may leave. Have a sin-tastic time in Sin City!"

Jensen kept one hand on his gun and an eye on the cockpit. Ryan nodded to the front of the plane as a signal that they had to get into the cockpit ASAP. He wasn't about to wait their allotted five minutes, in which time the man could detonate a device and, as Devin described it, *watch, verify, and validate* his work. He surveyed the plane for anything he could use as a battering ram while Jensen flagged the flight attendant to open the plane's door. She pulled four levers and five locks and a rush of hot air swooshed in as the airlock released. The door mechanically released outward and turned into a stairway, down to the tarmac. No SWAT team boarded. They were probably rushing to make their way across the entire tarmac to plane's unintended remote location. Ryan quickly pulled together a plan. He could shoot his way through the cockpit door, but since it was reinforced, the bullets could easily ricochet back into the cabin. Too dangerous.

Jensen roared at Ryan to disembark the plane while he ushered the remaining agents out and down the stairs.

"The cart!" Ryan said, pushing the stewardess into Jensen. The agent was diverted enough to get her off the plane while Ryan grabbed the solid metal beverage cart, rolled it back into the main aisle and heaved it against the cockpit door. It made a slight dent, near the door handle. He pulled it back to strike again and Jensen decided to help, taking the opposite side of the cart into both hands.

Ryan shouted, "One, two, *three!*" and they slammed it into the door again. This time, the latch clicked. He tried the handle, still locked. "Again."

He counted to three and they crashed it again. The door buckled slightly, unlatching the lock. Ryan pulled with all of his strength and managed to heave the door outward, opening it. He rushed into the cockpit and the pilot's chair was empty. The second chair held a man in a pilot's uniform unconscious and slumped forward. Ryan felt a pulse still beating in the man's neck and noted shallow breathing. To the right of the man's feet a floor panel had been removed. The Ghost's escape hatch.

"He's gone!" Ryan shouted. "And we need a medic in here."

Jensen spun and scrambled off the plane, shouting commands, while five members of the Las Vegas SWAT team stormed onto the plane in full gear, weapons drawn. Ryan held up one hand and slowly put down his Glock.

"Chicago PD," he stated quickly. "ID and shield are in my front right pocket."

One of the men lowered his firearm, pulled Ryan's credentials, and then nodded to the team.

"This man needs medical attention, then we need an evidence team for the entire aircraft. The plane was hijacked by an armed and dangerous homicide suspect."

Once he was satisfied that they were handling the scene,

Ryan disembarked and made his way across the tarmac, where he spotted the task force members huddled near the terminal. The debilitating heat reflected off of the asphalt as Ryan realized how dehydrated he was. Vegas in September was like Chicago in June—probably a hundred and ten degrees in the shade. All Ryan wanted to do was call Cat and tell her he was safe, but he wanted to get far, far away from the plane first. He glanced back at the Gulfstream to make sure Jensen was okay. It appeared tiny in the distance.

As soon as he joined the group, out of the sun, he was offered a water bottle and downed a majority of it. He doubled over, hands on knees, taking a moment to exhale his relief. When he stood back up, Di Santo was coming in for a hug.

"I have never been so happy to have my feet on the ground," Di Santo said, during the embrace.

Ryan patted his partner's back and self-consciously pulled away. But none of the other team members could blame them for the outburst of affection. In fact, no one even noticed, as they were texting and phoning their own loved ones to assure them all was fine.

"We've landed and we're on our way to the hotel," Pendergrass said into her phone, her eyes shut in relief.

Another agent cooed, "I love you so much, honey. Give the kids hugs from me."

"We're in Vegas now!" Martinez exclaimed into his headset with false cheer.

The agents were trained well. Very well trained. As none gave even a hint of the danger they had just survived.

Devin stood to the side, calling no one, just swiping his cell phone.

They waited until Jensen eventually joined the group. "Perp got out through a maintenance panel," he announced, obviously frustrated. "LVPD is currently searching the airport, but since we have no idea what he looks like, he could easily be in the wind. I also have Midway pulling video of the private terminal. We've got to get an ID on this guy."

Di Santo paced in circles, having shed his suit coat from

the sweltering heat. "I don't get it. Why would he do that? Why would The Ghost risk being that close to us, flying a government jet to Vegas?"

"To show he's in charge," Devin responded. "It was a message. A power play."

"Well, at least we know he's here," Ryan said. "Left column. Hard data." Agent Doherty nodded with a flash of that creepy grin.

Ryan pulled out his cell phone out of his pocket and, taking a cue from the rest of the task force team, texted Cat.

– Landed in Vegas. All is well.

"Don't worry, we only kill each other."
~ Benjamin "Bugsy" Siegel

CHAPTER 14

The Las Vegas chapter of the Department of Homeland Security kept the entire Organized Crime Task Force and the two detectives at the airport for two hours and eleven minutes while they sorted out the story and filed a report. Even though the plane had kept to its original flight plan, it was still classified as a hijacking. After much inter-agency hoopla, Jensen won out and the case was handed back to the task force team.

They gathered their luggage and Jensen instructed everyone to check into their rooms at The Chicago, get a good night's sleep, and then meet at 08:30 at the Caesar's buffet. He made it clear that the Outfit families should not be aware of their presence in Vegas—with the exception of Di Santo and Ryan. That meant meetings took place at other hotels, and when any of the team members were at The Chicago, they were to be dressed like tourists or in their rooms. And no more than two team members were to be seen speaking to each other at any one time, so they coupled up and took separate taxis.

During their cab ride, Ryan ruminated aloud whether to call his mother and tell her about Devin. Di Santo riffed on the idea and called his mother, just to say hello and that he loved her very much.

"Wow, look at that," Di Santo said, pointing out the taxicab's window. The Chicago Hotel was a massive art deco structure, with vintage-looking awnings and several black 1920s Model-T automobiles in the turnaround. Each doorman dressed the part: head to toe in red, topped with a pillbox hat. One pulled open a door for the detectives, while another was waiting with a dolly for their luggage. Ryan had read about the resort when it first opened a mere five years ago, an attempt to create their windy city in the roaring twenties when—of course—the Outfit ruled the city. The place was designed down to the very last detail, even down to the brass door handles in the shape of tommy guns.

Flappers in fringe roamed the casino floor, taking and delivering drink orders. The male staff members, other than the doormen, sported period-perfect zoot suits and spats. Frank Sinatra crooned "My Kind of Town, Chicago Is..." over the sound system even though the song was incongruent with the decade. It almost made Ryan want to get a stack of twenties, fire up a stogie, and throw back a scotch. He'd settle for checking in.

The line was about fifteen long, and they checked their emails and messages during the wait. When they made it to the counter and checked in, a bespectacled reservation agent informed them that they were sharing a room. "Two king beds," she said. "General Electric."

"What? We have to share a room?" Ryan whined. "There's got to be some mistake. Could you check again? Maybe there are two rooms available?"

"Sorry," the woman responded. "We are completely booked because of ComTech. It's one of our largest conventions of the year. If you want, I could call some adjacent hotels—"

"Nah, that's okay," Di Santo said, making the decision for them.

The woman handed them each a key and a slip of paper with "gangster29" printed on it. "The key will get you into all guest amenities like the pool and the spa, and can be used at any of the restaurants. The password is for the hotel

Wi-Fi and the two hidden speakeasies around the resort. Knock three times and when asked, give them the password for entry."

A hokey gimmick, but as soon as she said it Ryan was intrigued. He loved authentic vintage jazz, and the whole secret password just made it even more exclusive and exciting. "So where are the speakeasies, exactly?" he asked her. The woman winked back, with no response. He nodded when he realized that finding them was the fun part.

They pulled their suitcases through the casino, for what seemed like miles, to the elevator bank. The interior of the resort was designed to look like the city a hundred or so years ago. Cobblestone "streets" with smoke coming up from fake manholes were lined with grocery carts, haberdashery shops, Irish pubs, and ethnic bakeries.

A roller coaster depicting the old El train, careened around the periphery, with the track both inside the building and out.

"This is the first time I've been to Vegas," Di Santo said, salivating at all the flashing, happily pinging slot machines. "It's crazy! I mean I knew it was big, but this is like a super playground for adults. I mean, despite who owns this place, you gotta admit this is very cool. You been here before, D?"

"To Vegas? Yeah, several times," Ryan griped. "The last time was about five years ago with Kelly. We got into a huge fight—I don't even remember what it was about. Money, probably. She always wanted to live large and play large, whether we had the money or not. But I've never been here, to The Chicago."

Di Santo pointed to a slot machine called "The Outfit" and they both shook their heads in disgust.

"I'd like to come back, though," Di Santo said. "You know, when I'm not working. I can see having a whole bunch of fun here."

"You would, D. You really would. This is your kind of town." His partner snickered at the song reference.

They finally made it to the eight-elevator bank rising into

the John Hancock Tower, which bore the diamond pattern of its namesake building.

"The feds fly in a sixty-five-million-dollar jet plane, and they can't pay for two rooms?" Ryan grumbled aloud in the elevator.

"How do you know that thing cost sixty-five million?"

"I looked it up on my phone before we took off."

Di Santo whistled through his teeth. "Well, like Jensen said, the agency confiscated it, so they got that thing free. Nice gig if you can get it! And what's wrong with rooming with me, anyway? I won't check out your tighty-whities, if that's what you're worried about."

Ryan was too tired to take the bait. It was nearing nine o'clock, and he was hoping to turn in by ten. "I'm a light sleeper, so you better not snore."

"Who the hell knows if they snore? They're asleep when they do it!"

The elevator doors opened and they found their way to room 1115, halfway down the hall. "Atlanta PD gave us our own rooms," Ryan said, as he inserted the cardkey into the slot. His mind traveled back to a couple of months ago when he'd entered the Atlanta hotel room, allowing Officer Heather Hill in behind him. He shook that mistake out of his head as they entered and perused the room. "Well, at least it's big." He shivered at the chilled air, and tapped a button on the thermostat to increase the target temp to seventy-two degrees.

Reproduction antique furniture and vintage photographs of Chicago represented the theme of the resort.

"These pictures are cool," Di Santo said, studying the framed images. "Look, here's Division Street, right down the street from the Eighteenth before our house was even there! Wow, even before Cabrini Green. I wonder where they got these?"

"Chicago Historical Society, probably." Ryan opened his suitcase, the contents in complete disarray from the bomb search. He fished out his black shaving bag, walked it to the bathroom, and closed the door. Not because he had to go, but because he couldn't take one more minute of Di Santo's jabbering, which had been ongoing since the airport. He needed five minutes of peace. "Showering!" he called out and started the water. The steam filled the bathroom as he shed his clothes and stepped in, relishing the hot water on his skin.

When he got out, dried off, and toweled his hair, Di Santo had chosen a bed and was watching the local news, scrubbing the remote with a small white cloth.

"What are you doing?" Ryan asked.

"Disinfecting! I brought along a bunch of these anti-bacterial wipes. I got all the light switches and handles while you were in your shower. But the remote—they say it has the most germs. And the phone, of course."

"Gee, thanks."

"Want me to bring out the black light? We can do like that guy on TV—"

"*No!*" Ryan's outburst caused his partner to giggle. He didn't care. Some things were better left unseen. He'd witnessed their evidence tech team as they scanned many a hotel room. It wasn't pretty.

He grabbed a clean pair of boxer-briefs from his suitcase and headed back to the bathroom to put them on. On the way, he picked up a cardboard advertising tent from the credenza.

"Did you see this? 'Get married by the mob. A real mobster—now ordained minister—will marry you in a mob-style wedding.'" He shook his head and threw the ad into the wastebasket. "I hate that they glorify these thugs. This isn't *The Godfather*. These guys are real criminals. The worst of the worst."

"Yeah, well, you think *you* hate it, think about how I feel," Di Santo replied at a higher decibel. "It sets us Italians back fifty years! You never see them idealizing Mickey Cohen, Mad Dog Sullivan, Meyer Lansky—it's always Capone, Luciano, Gotti! There were just as many Irish and

Jewish mobsters as there were Italians, but *we* get the bum's rush. All of it disgusts me."

In the bathroom, Ryan put on his boxers, brushed his teeth, and ran the blow drier through his hair so it was dry enough to get to bed. When he stepped out into the room again, Di Santo had already changed into the most ridiculous pair of purple silk pajamas, covered with the Ralph Lauren Polo logo.

"What?" his partner said, noticing his frozen frown. "You don't like them?"

"I have no opinion whatsoever on your sleepwear. Goodnight."

Three hours and twenty-two minutes later, Ryan rolled over in bed and checked the time on the clock: 1:03 a.m. Di Santo's chainsaw snoring had started almost from the moment they turned out the lights, and there was no way Ryan would be able to get to sleep without alcohol in his system. He pulled on jeans, a white tee shirt and a button-down, grabbed his phone, shield, and wallet, and ventured back down to the casino.

The long fake Chicago city street separated the lobby of the hotel and the casino. He studied the brick building façades that housed actual retail establishments, as several vintage automobiles cruised the cobblestone streets, carrying wide-eyed, wide-awake tourists, even at the early morning hour. Ragtime music now played over the sound system, a device to transport one back into the "good ol' days" of Chicago when Capone was king. Ryan shook his head and tried knocking on every unmarked doorway on the street, searching for one of the speakeasies. Nothing.

He mentally traveled back in time to 1929 and tried to figure out how a person might have found one of these joints back in the day without the benefit of an invite or word of mouth. *Money.*

He went to the ATM and took out $200 worth of twenties. He folded three of the bills and approached the largest spats-footed security guard he could find.

"This is to direct me to the speakeasy. The third speakeasy."

"What do you mean *third?*" the guy said, shuffling his feet.

"C'mon, there's got to be a third. One they don't promote, that's *not* open to the gen pop." The guy chuckled. Good, he was creating rapport, although the man didn't take the wad of bills…yet. So Ryan took out his gold shield and flashed it. "How about now?"

"Naw, man, that's surely going to keep you out."

Ryan decided to try a different tack. "I'm a friend of the family."

The man's eyebrows went up and he took out his phone. "Name?"

"Di Santo. Detective Matt Di Santo."

After a short, quiet conversation relaying the information, the goon held out two fingers and Ryan handed over the bills. He followed the guy into an artificial alley off of the main street, stopping at a phone booth—the kind that had been put out of business by cell phones. The security guard picked up the receiver of a vintage rotary phone and dialed several numbers, and a back panel opened. *So frickin' cool.* Ryan kind of wished Di Santo was seeing this too. He would've gotten a kick out of it.

The guy glanced back, beckoning Ryan to follow with a nod. Beyond the back panel of the phone booth was a set of stairs, descending down into a dimly lit hallway. Ryan wondered if he had just made a huge mistake until he heard a faint ragtime number emanating from behind a door at the end of the hall. The zoot-suited guy stood like Jacob Marley's ghost, pointing down the hall with a long finger.

"Valentine's Day," he mumbled before he turned and left, the weight of his footsteps echoing back down the staircase.

Ryan approached the door at the end of the hall and knocked. A small six-inch panel opened at eye level.

So frickin' cool.

"Yeah?" said an eyeball on the other side. It could have been male or female.

"Um—I was told I could—"

The person sighed through the peephole, already exasperated with the conversation. "*Password?*"

At 1:15 in the morning, Ryan's brain was fried from the day's events. He dug out the little slip of paper from his wallet.

"Gangster—"

"No."

"Oh. Then...*Valentine's Day?*"

The little panel closed, latches were thrown, and the door opened.

CHAPTER 15

The secret speakeasy was everything Ryan had envisioned, which he guessed was the point. Whether the design was truly authentic or not, this was how they were portrayed in the old gangster films: red velvet curtains lined the walls, with a stage in back and a bar along the right wall. A four-piece jazz ensemble wailed from the stage, while the patrons drank, danced, and laughed. The men in the crowd were primarily in suits and the women were gussied up. Ryan was way underdressed.

A zoot-suited bouncer carded him at the entrance and stamped the back of his hand, confirming that Ryan was way above drinking age.

"Table or booth, sweetie?" a flapper addressed him. She had a wide smile and was most definitely coached in the dialect of the era.

"Um, not sure. Which do you recommend?"

"Well, the tables are closer to the act, the booths are more private. You meetin' someone here? Ya' girl or an associate or sometin'?" She winked, smacking a gum wad of at least two sticks.

"No, no. Just me," he answered. "I'll take a table."

The woman led him through the club, the fringe of her dress flying to and fro across a tight ass. He couldn't *not* take in the view.

Ryan thanked her with a twenty. "You can start me on a scotch. Two fingers." The woman winked, stuffed the bill into her cleavage, and sashayed away. Subtle brass signs announced that no smoking was allowed in the club, although that would have been authentic for the era they were trying to recreate. He was grateful for it, though, and wished the entire casino had been smokeless.

The waitress delivered his tumbler of scotch along with change, and had disappeared before Ryan could even thank her. A muted trumpet wailed out the intro to the recognizable classic, "Ain't Misbehavin'," and after eight bars a heavyset black woman started crooning. Ryan sat back in his chair, letting the scotch warm his esophagus, and the music warm his soul.

"No one to talk with, all by myself,
No one to walk with, but I'm happy on the shelf.
Ain't misbehavin', I'm saving my love for yo-o-o-o-o-u."

The lyrics made him flash on Catharine and wished she were there enjoying the singer, the band, the drinks, and the whole experience with him. Maybe someday, when she was used to being out of the house, he'd bring her to Vegas. But not yet. She wasn't ready.

"Your kisses are worth waiting for…believe me!"

During a bass solo, Ryan's phone vibrated in his pocket. He checked the screen, and just seeing Catharine's name made him smile. She often felt him thinking about her and connected back in some way.

But it was three o'clock in the morning back in Evanston, and he grew concerned.

"Hey! Is everything okay?" he said, plugging an ear.

"Ryan? Are you there?"

He got up and moved farther away from the band. "Yes! Cat, what's wrong?"

"Well, I know this is crazy, and you are probably in bed—"

"No, not in bed. Couldn't get to sleep. What's up?"

"I couldn't sleep either," she said. "I had to let you know. I feel like he's there…with you. He's in the room with you. I know that sounds crazy because you're in your room."

"*Who's* here with me?"

"The killer! That 'ghost' person! I feel him in close proximity to you."

Ryan's attention went from the call to every male in the club. He scanned the bar, the tables, and the booths behind him.

"Cat, I'm not in my room. Matt was snoring like a warthog so I came down to a jazz club to grab a drink. You think The Ghost is here? In the club?"

"I know he is, Ryan. He's there. I've been feeling it for the last couple of minutes. He's with you. I'm sorry it's so late, but I had to call and make sure you were all right."

"Okay, okay. Let me work on this. You go to bed, okay?"

"Be careful!"

"I will. Love you." He disconnected and went back to his table. A second scotch sat next to the one he hadn't yet finished. "Excuse me," he said grabbing the elbow of his waitress as she went by. "I didn't order another drink."

"Compliments of that man—" she turned to the bar and pointed, then turned back confused. "Well, he was just there. He said to buy you whatever you're having. It's a gesture of respect, ya know."

"What did he look like?" Ryan said. The woman's eyes started to bug out when he realized he was shaking her by the shoulders. "I'm sorry, I'm police," he said, and pulled out his badge to prove it. "What did the man look like?"

"The man *looked* like Mr. Leone. Because it was," she said, jerking her arm away from him. "He said, 'Leave this for the policeman over there, he was good to my sister.' Then he choked up and left, the poor thing. Did you hear what happened to her? Eaten by a lion!" The woman *tsked* three times, exposing the pink gum in her mouth. "Are you okay now, mister? Officer?"

Desirée Leone's half-consumed body flashed into memory. "Yeah, yeah, thanks. You can go."

"Gee, thanks, boss," she said, throwing the phrase over her shoulder.

He stared at the two glasses of scotch, wanting more than anything to down one. But he couldn't take the chance. He now understood how women felt when they mistakenly left their drinks unattended. Vulnerable. He had just put out seventy dollars and change for two sips of scotch, including the bribe to find the place, so it was a shame to have both of the tumblers go to waste. But he wouldn't put it past The Ghost to slip him something. The guy had hijacked their plane. He was aware the team was in town and after him.

It might not have been a "hard data fact" that the guy was in the club with him, but Catharine's feelings were rarely off. He decided to treat it as such and work backward from the facts. If The Ghost was in the speakeasy, he must've had a way to gain access. For sure, he had connections to the Outfit, but he wouldn't use them, considering he was hunting them down one by one. So he had to have earned his way in through the big-money tables. He speculated that The Ghost played high-roller and, at some point, was given access to the exclusive speakeasy. Probably to continue the hunt. Ryan tried to recall the photos of Victor Basso and Joey Giordano that had been plastered on the task force's org chart back in River Forest. He scanned the crowd again, but none of the patrons appeared to be either of them.

He began a deliberate tour of the room, starting from the circular booths on the left side of the club, weaving through the tables in the middle, to the bar on the right. Not that he would be able to recognize the cold-blooded killer if the guy stepped on his foot, but he watched. Listened. And especially paid attention to anyone paying attention to him. Something would give the man away. Several people glanced at him as he passed, aware and uncomfortable at his creeping. He didn't care. Ryan took a seat at the end of the bar, where he had a view of the entire club, and ordered one more single malt, eyeing the bartender as he poured and delivered it personally. Clean chain of custody.

The bar ran the entire length of the wall, with classic chandeliers casting a glow every eight feet or so. To make sure its inhabitants were of drinking age, UV lights glowed purple on the bartender's side of the bar, performing the same duty as Di Santo's black light.

A group of three women laughed and screeched at the opposite end, a desperate cry for attention, all three of them scanning the men of the crowd to see if it was working. Next to that group sat two couples, one male/female, one male/male. In the middle of the bar sat one solo guy in a Hawaiian shirt sporting a thick gold chain around his neck and pinky rings. The man chatted up the bartender, who nodded and laughed back, while busting his ass filling orders from the waitresses. Hawaiian Shirt Guy was too heavy to have been Joey "Bones" Giordano, but he could very well have been Basso. Ryan couldn't be sure in the dim light of the club. Between the guy and Ryan sat one other couple, deep in conversation about diamonds, their various mines, and value. A flight of wine tumblers lined the bar between them. The man sat with his back to Ryan, wearing a trench coat that hung back over the stool like a cape. Both of them leaned in closely, completely engrossed in the conversation to the point where he couldn't see their faces or hear their words.

Until the woman raised a finger to catch the attention of the bartender. "I'll revisit the Cab," she said, flattening the A with a familiar Midwest twang. Ryan thought he recognized that voice. It sounded like the voice he'd lived with on and off for seventeen years. The voice that had told him "Jon's dead." But this woman's hair was three shades darker than Kelly's signature orange-red.

Without being too obvious, he leaned several inches to

the right, attempting to catch a glimpse of the woman's face behind the head of Mr. Trench Coat. But the man leaned with him to grab a napkin behind the bar, and when his hand passed under the UV light, it lit up in purple splotches. More than just the entry stamp.

Realizing this could be The Ghost, Ryan slowly placed his drink on the table and tapped the guy on the shoulder. "Excuse me, could you grab me a couple of those napkins too?"

Without turning, the man reached for the napkins and froze in the wake of the glowing evidence. In the fraction of a second that Ryan regretted not bringing his cuffs, the man flew off of his stool, toppling it to the floor, and ran to the door. Ryan followed, a few paces behind. The dude was fast and Ryan had been caught off-guard, not expecting a chase. When he exited the speakeasy, he stopped, scanning the dungeon of a hallway, his eyes adjusting. A shot rang out and he plastered himself against the wall. *Shit.* He hadn't even thought to bring his service weapon.

The man's hurried footsteps retreated up the stairs, and Ryan heard the door open into the phone booth. There was a chance it was a trick, but he had to pursue. He took off his shoes, padded silently to the bottom of the stairway, and rounded his head quickly to clear it. The one exposed light bulb cast a weak glow, but he could see he was alone. He slipped his shoes back on and ran up the staircase, bursting through the door, forgetting there was a second one, almost barreling through the glass of the phone booth. He folded the door aside and ran through the alley to the manufactured Chicago street. Checking left and right, he saw no man in a trench coat. *Fuck!* He'd lost him. All because he wasn't armed.

He made a mental note never to leave the room without his firearm. Ever. Not in this place.

He ran back to the phone booth, attempting to get back to the club—back to that Kelly voice—but the door had closed and locked behind him. Ryan slammed it with his fist. What the hell was she doing there with The Ghost? Had they just met? Was it deliberate?

He hadn't caught any of the man's features, but he could at least add some vitals to their chart: height, weight, hair color, race and tone of voice. He took out his cell and dialed Devin's number.

"Yeah?" Devin rasped. Ryan had clearly awakened him from a dead sleep. "Ryan? Why are you—"

"I just saw him, D—I mean, Devin. I believe I just saw The Ghost. I have more data for your chart. *Hard* data."

"Come up to my room," he instructed and gave him the number.

Up in the room, Ryan relayed everything that had transpired in the speakeasy. "He's Caucasian," he said, pacing between the two double beds as Devin typed. "Reddish-brown hair, didn't get a good look at his face, but I'd guess late twenties, early thirties. Five-nine, ten at the most. Fit build, but not muscle-bound. They were almost whispering, so I really couldn't catch the timber of his voice. You know, this was an exclusive speakeasy, only open to friends of the owners and high rollers."

"And how do you know this man was the one we're looking for?"

Ryan decided to be honest. "Cat texted me. She felt The Ghost was in the room with me, she could feel it. I scouted out the club, and this guy—he seemed suspicious. He had invisible ink all over his hand, I saw it glow in the black light. And when I tried to talk to him, he high-tailed it out of the place. I chased him, and he shot at me."

"Jesus! Are you okay?"

"I'm fine, I'm fine. But if it wasn't The Ghost, why would he run?"

Devin nodded, silently, while he took down some of the details. "Do you think he was scouting the place for mob members?" Devin asked. His hair was all over the place, not unlike Ryan's when he woke up in the morning.

"I don't know. He was with a...a woman. But she

could've been a cover. They seemed to be wine tasting, so put that in the chart. Soft data. Likes the better wines, or likes to look that way. They were talking about diamonds. Does that make any sense?" He racked his brain to pull the woman's face into view but he just hadn't gotten a good look.

"Why were you down there, anyway, at this time of night?"

Ryan explained the snoring situation as he sat down on the bed. "It's late, though, and after that chase I'm wiped out. I could probably sleep through the snoring now."

"Stay here. I guarantee I'm a quiet sleeper."

"No, I couldn't. I don't want to put you out."

"Jeez, Ryan, you're my brother. It's no problem at all."

Ryan still couldn't get used to the term, having only sisters his entire life, and he wasn't quite ready to accept a fourth sibling. For thirty-nine years, theirs was a family dominated by females, with his mother and three sisters at the helm.

Since his dad had died, he was used to being the only man. The Prince, as his mom had dubbed him.

Exhaustion and confusion, and maybe partly the scotch, all set in and helped make the decision. "Okay, I'll take you up on that," Ryan said, kicking off his shoes. He placed his shield, wallet, and phone on the bedside table, lay back on the pillow, and closed his eyes.

"Are things okay with you and your girlfriend?" Devin asked.

"Yeah, why?"

"You have the look of left."

"What's that?" Ryan was fading fast.

"The hard—and yet soft—look of a man who's been left by a woman."

'*I'm done,*' Kelly had said three and a half years ago. She'd packed and moved out in less than twenty-four hours.

"No, Cat and I are good."

Devin turned out the last light and got into the other bed.

"I must say, I didn't expect you to be with someone like Catharine. She's very kind. And beautiful."

"That's a strange thing to say," Ryan mumbled.

Devin said something else, ending with "Goodnight" as his voice faded into Humphrey Bogart's, narrating Ryan's dreams.

'*Of all the gin joints in all the towns in all the world...she walks into mine.*'

The cell phone rang out the bell of an old rotary phone. Ryan threw a hand out from under the sheets, blindly searching for it, feeling the bedside table until he found his phone and answered.

"You sonofabitch!" Di Santo screeched from the other side of the line. "You snuck out last night and then didn't come back. I kept waking up, every hour, so I know. And you know what? You've got the best woman in the world! *The best!* And you're already stepping out on her? What kind of—"

Ryan held the phone away from his ear, letting his partner rant, as he scanned the room, getting his bearings.

Devin was at the desk, already engrossed in his laptop.

"Devin, could you just...take this?" Ryan asked.

Agent Doherty turned and accepted the cell phone as Ryan fell back onto the bed and pulled a pillow over his face.

"Mmmm-hmmm. Mmmm-hmmm," he heard Devin say, although muffled through the pillow. "This is—uh, Detective? This is *Devin*. Ryan stayed here last night. In my room." Pause. "Yes, he's fine." Pause. "No, he didn't cheat on his girlfriend." Pause. "Okay, we'll see you at the breakfast meeting. Goodbye."

Ryan uncovered his face, scrubbing his eyes against the

sunlight. "See what I have to deal with? He's always up in my business. What time is it?"

"It's 7:47 a.m." Devin threw the cell back onto Ryan's bed and he checked the screen. "Detective Di Santo said to tell you he's going out for a walk before the meeting but he laid out an outfit for you."

Ryan's head shot up. "He—*what?!*"

"I'm just joshing," Devin said. His face was placid, but there was a definite sparkle in his eyes. He was turning out to have a sense of humor after all. "But you better go change. Our meeting starts in forty-two minutes and…fourteen seconds."

There was something about this guy that was beginning to grow on him.

CHAPTER 16

The agents—and detectives—ate like kings at the Caesar's buffet, while they discussed their strategy for the Outfit's Commission meeting.

Jensen announced that from what they'd gathered from their intel, it was scheduled to take place at 11:00 a.m. back at The Chicago. He handed Matt two small silvery disc-shaped objects. "Di Santo, here are the two transmitters. Put one in your pocket and one on your cell phone. If they do scan twice, you may be able to get away with just holding up your cell." Di Santo nodded. "There is no on and off switch, so be aware they are always broadcasting, and we are always listening." Di Santo accepted the bugs and showed off one to Ryan. They were about half the size of a dime. Jensen continued, "Agent Doherty and Detective Doherty can remain in the vicinity of the ballroom, just in case. It's perfectly believable that his partner would be close by. The rest of us will remain in the suite on the third floor. Upon completion of Di Santo's task, everyone will assume their positions for the Commission Meeting itself."

"So all's I gotta do is get one of the transmitters under the table?"

"Yes. The adhesive activates with plain saliva, and it's on both sides. So at some point, chew a fingernail or something, and then stick it."

For some reason Ryan found that really funny and chuckled aloud.

"Detective Doherty, do you have a question?" Every member of the task force turned toward him, awaiting an answer.

"No, sir," he said, feeling like a third grader.

"Okay. So now we need a code word, just in case you need assistance."

"How about 'Cow?' As in Mrs. O'Leary's cow!" Di Santo said, delighted by his idiotic suggestion.

"And how are you going to work that into a conversation?" Ryan asked.

"I don't have to work it into a conversation! If I'm in trouble, I'm just gonna shout it out! '*Cow! Cow!*'" he cried out, waving a fork of pancake wedges.

At that point, the rest of the table dissolved into hysterics. Maybe it was the residual tension from the hijacking, or the nervous energy before the Commission, but the comic relief felt good for a change and seemed to enhance the team's camaraderie.

"Okay, okay," Jensen said, waving a palm at the table. "Cow it is, but say something believable like, 'Don't have a cow,' so they're not tipped off." Di Santo agreed. "Okay, now Di Santo, you need to go call Ricci and tell him you have information about The Ghost and you want to meet with him at eleven."

"But you said the Commission meeting is at eleven..."

"Yes, this is intentional. He'll say he's busy at eleven, so you counter by asking if you can meet a couple minutes prior. You have to get him to invite you into the ballroom."

Di Santo nodded, stood up, and left the table.

Ryan followed him into the lobby, and they settled in the entryway of a high-end shoe store that had not yet opened for the day. In the window were brands labeled Louboutin and Jimmy Choo. "Twelve hundred dollars for a pair of shoes?" Ryan said, reading the price tag. "I'm glad that Cat has simple tastes. Why are all the soles red?"

"That's their trademark," his partner answered. "All Louboutin shoes have red soles."

"And how in God's name do you know that?" Ryan asked, squinting his eyes.

"Because I listen to my women, D. I *listen* and I *acknowledge* what they say. Because I respect them. And also, that's how I get laid."

Ryan slapped the back of his partner's head, smiling nonetheless. "Okay, are you ready to make the call?"

Di Santo took a deep breath, shaking off the joke. He pulled out a piece of paper with Ricci's number on it, lifted his cell, and dialed.

"Hey ya, Richie! This is Matt. Matt Di Santo. I'm here in Vegas because we have reason to believe that Robin's killer is here…yeah, we got special permission to follow him to Vegas." Di Santo glanced at Ryan for approval, he nodded for him to continue. "So, Rich: I need to meet with you. I can't say it all over the phone. You know, I'm not supposed to be tellin' you any of this." Pause. "How about eleven? I'm across town picking up some—shoes—for my girl-friend. But I can get there by eleven, maybe a little before." Pause. "Okay, where?" After one more pause, Di Santo put up a silent but aggressive thumbs up. "Okay, Richie. I'll see you there. Gold Coast Ballroom it is. See you soon."

He hung up and Ryan exhaled. "You did it?" Ryan asked.

"I did it! It was easier than I thought!"

They returned to the breakfast table to find the agents preparing to leave. Di Santo threw a thumbs-up to Jensen.

"Yes, I know. Good work."

"You know?" Di Santo said, confused for a moment. "Oh, right. Always transmitting."

As per instructed, the task force team broke off into twos and staggered their timing back to The Chicago Hotel, some taking the monorail, some walking along the strip, and some calling rides. Because Di Santo couldn't be seen at The Chicago until after 10:30, he and Ryan hung back, window shopping and discussing the plan.

"If all goes well, maybe we can catch a show tonight," Di Santo said, bouncing on his heels. He pointed to a poster for a new Cirque du Soleil production.

"We're not here to catch a show," Ryan answered. "If all goes well, we'll either have The Ghost in custody or have to get the Giordano family into *protective* custody."

"Too bad. I heard they do that show topless!"

Ryan turned to inspect the poster a tad more closely. "A topless circus?" All the women in the image looked fully clothed to him.

"I'm tellin' ya! We're in Sin City! Can't we have a little fun?"

Ryan slapped Di Santo's back. "Just concentrate on your mission. No boobies, no gambling, no distractions." The more he thought about the woman in the speakeasy last night, the more he convinced himself it couldn't have been Kelly. Maybe it was just a coincidence, some Midwest chick who sounded a lot like her.

"We could get married, even!" Di Santo said, interrupting his thoughts "By Elvis!"

"To who—each other?"

"Why not?"

"I'd never marry you. You snore."

"Small drawback. Speaking of which…when are you going to pop the question to Cat?"

"We haven't even been dating a year yet! Give me some time, geez."

"But you see it going there?"

"Possibly."

"You're an idiot if you don't."

"I know, I know, you're her biggest fan. I got that from the phone call this morning." Di Santo beamed, no shame at all. "Listen, I want to do this one right. Neither of us have any incentive to rush it. We don't want kids. Well, any more kids, that is. And she's got that multi-million dollar estate to protect. We'd have to get a prenup and all that mess."

"So you have been thinking about it. *Dude!*" Di Santo

held up his hand for a high-five, but Ryan didn't return it. "Wow, leave me hanging."

"There is no talk of marriage yet. We've just decided to take the next step—we're going to move in together."

"That's awesome! You're gonna be living in style, my man. Catharine is the perfect woman and you better marry her and I better be the best man. Fuck your new brother."

Ryan mouthed, "Always transmitting."

"Oh, shit," Di Santo said then held up the back of his cell phone. "Sorry, Devin!"

Ryan grinned and then beckoned Di Santo to walk with him out on the strip toward the Bellagio. He wanted to know more about the organization they were protecting and investigating at the same time. "So tell me about the Outfit's rackets. We just got an overview at the briefing, but tell me how they make their money."

"The task force is pretty clued in on them," Di Santo answered. "The Outfit make their dough through protection, unions, and bookmaking. The protection racket is as old as the families themselves. They have a territory, isolate the businesses making the most money in that territory, then squeeze them for a percentage of the profits. They'll go in and be like, 'You got a good thing here, we wanna partner with you.' If the proprietor knows what's best for them, they'll start kicking up a percentage to that family."

"And if they don't want to partner with the mob?"

"Yeah, then they get a warning," Di Santo responded. "And if they don't heed the warning, then…" He slit his throat with a finger.

"Just like that?" Ryan asked.

"Just like that."

"Okay, then what about the unions? I never quite understood that."

"Well, the unions have a lot of power. And money. Two things that the Outfit covets. So they get a guy in the management of the union. Let's say construction. This guy has control of the pension funds—bank accounts with cash,

cash, cash. They skim from these accounts. In addition, if they've got control of the unions, they've got control of big business. 'Cause without the workers, you've got no business."

"I don't get it."

"Okay, take Hollywood, for example. At one point, the Outfit controlled all the blue-collar union workers in moviemaking—set construction, decorators, gaffers, lighting, et cetera. So they go to Paramount Pictures, see. They say, 'You want this picture made? You give us twenty percent of the box office. If not, no one shows up Monday morning to make the picture.' So that's that. Management has to comply. When you have control of the labor, you have control of the corporation. Get it?"

"Yep. That's ingenious, actually."

"That was courtesy of Anthony Accardo, one of the most intelligent men of the Chicago Outfit. His legend lives on to this day. The current families, they're just copying his lead."

"So how does this relate to Vegas?" Ryan asked.

"Well, so after Capone got busted for tax evasion, the mob got smart. They needed legit businesses to cover their asses, to put on their tax returns. So then comes Vegas, Bugsy Siegel, and all that. It was a way to make a shitload of cash—legally. And when there's cash, there's a way to skim. All the families skimmed off the top. There was so much cash coming in, it was a cinch to alter the books and carry out hundreds of thousands of bills out of the casino in suitcases. I mean, I'm sure they're going straighter and straighter here, but I don't doubt there are bills leaving The Chicago in duffel bags and such. Bookmaking is bookmaking. Gambling, numbers running, horse racing, sports, you name it."

Ryan thought about the various rackets that these families perpetrated. "How come the CPD was never brought in on grabbing these guys and putting an end to all the rackets?"

Di Santo flashed him a smirk. "'Cause historically, D,

not all of the Chicago Police were as straight as you and me. Many of our ranks were on the take from the Outfit. It was an easy—and lucrative—business to be on both sides of the fence."

The thought of dirty cops pissed Ryan off. Every time a bad apple cop shot an unarmed suspect, bullied a kid, or got caught on a criminal's payroll, it affected the Department significantly. They relied heavily on a good relationship with the citizens, and if the citizens didn't trust them, the entire community policing system broke down. And the media didn't help, allowing the bad cops to go viral but failing to report on the good ones.

Ryan glanced at his watch. "Speaking of both sides of the fence, it's time."

Matt Di Santo never had butterflies conducting a police investigation, but this particular case was different. He was playing both sides, and when it came to the Outfit, that could be a lethal endeavor.

Luckily, traffic on the Strip was light. When they pulled up into the port cochère of The Chicago, Ryan informed him it was 10:41 a.m. Matt never understood his partner's obsession with time, but it came in handy at times like this when they had a sharp deadline. He had to get to that ballroom in four minutes so there was enough time to plant the bug. They met Devin on the landing of the Mezzanine, across from the Gold Coast Ballroom.

It was so obvious they were brothers, even if Ryan couldn't accept it yet. Despite the agent's geek-factor, the two of them could've almost been twins.

"Do I get an earpiece?" Ryan asked, pointing to the device in Agent D's ear.

"I'm sorry," Devin told him, "you cannot have a listening device. You're not officially on the task force, and therefore the warrant doesn't cover you."

"Are you frickin' kidding me? How am I supposed to go save him if I can't hear what's going on I there?"

"You're not going to have to *save* me, D. I can take care of myself," Di Santo interjected. It irked him that his partner always felt the need to protect him. He wasn't a newbie at police work, and he was proud of being one the youngest Chicago cops to make detective. He wished Ryan would just give him some props now and then.

"I don't like this." Ryan paced the hallway, a space made extra wide on the mezzanine to allow for conference crowds.

"So what exactly do I tell Richie about The Ghost?" Matt asked Devin.

"Well, the best lies are based in the truth," the agent responded. He held a finger to his earpiece and zoned for a couple of seconds. Jensen was instructing him through it. "Agent Jensen says you can tell Ricci about the BOO stamps and the black light, but not the plane. That's classified and we don't want that vulnerability getting out. Tell him that you think that the same perpetrator was behind Desirée Leone's death, but you're still awaiting autopsy results." He paused again. "And you can tell him about Sandy Orlando's exhumation order."

"What about last night? Ryan's bumping into the guy?"

"Well, that all comes from Catharine's phone call," Ryan said. "So I'm not sure we can say for sure it was the him."

"But he ran!"

"I know, D. But do you think The Ghost is the only criminal in Vegas?"

"True, true."

"Ricci doesn't have to know about that," Devin said. "Just say 'we have evidence that supports that The Ghost is in town, and we don't yet know why.'"

"And he'll say 'Yo, Di Santo, what kind of evidence?'" he said, mimicking the crime boss's dialect.

"Tell him you can't say, it's an ongoing investigation."

"Okay, okay. Sounds good. Think he'll buy it?"

Ryan put a hand on his shoulder. "Just tell him the truth...but not the whole truth."

Devin showed him the time on his phone. "Go, Di Santo!"

Finally he was up. Matt jogged across the mezzanine to the double doors of the ballroom and tried a handle. The door opened. Tootie was immediately all up in his face.

"Hey," the big guy said, holding out a hand.

Di Santo made a mental note to take his sister aside as soon as he got back home. "Hey to you too."

"Sorry, have to search you."

Matt raised his arms. "I've got my service weapon. It's in the holster," he said, raising a palm in greeting to Richie Rich, on the far side of the room. Tootie removed his gun and placed it on a nearby table.

"Di Santo!" Ricci shouted. "You shoulda told me you were going to be in Vegas, we woulda comped you a room!"

Tootie nodded that he was done with the security inspection, conveniently forgetting to take his phone. No bug scan either. Maybe they trusted him. Matt sauntered to the back of the ballroom and shook hands with Ricci.

"I appreciate the gesture, Richie, but you know I can't take no comps from you."

"Ha-ha! Always the cop. Love this guy, *love* this guy!" Ricci slapped him on the back just a little too hard to emphasize the fact that he did not, in fact, love him. Or trust him.

The round table that Ricci had been preparing held seats for four, with notebooks, pens and file folders at each place setting. Coffee and water were on a buffet against the wall. Two servers were bringing in warming dishes with brunch items.

"May I?" Matt said, pulling out a chair. "I think you should sit down when you hear this."

Ricci nodded.

"What's going on?" Ryan said to Devin, who sat on a bench about one hundred feet from the double doors of the ballroom.

"Hold on!" Devin answered. "Okay, Detective Di Santo and Mr. Ricci are sitting down at the table. He's relaying the information about the invisible ink and the black lights."

Ryan exhaled. His partner was good. Now all he had to do was lie a little, place the bug, and get the fuck out of there.

"He's now telling Ricci about Sandy Orlando's body...Ricci said Vic—meaning Victor Basso—won't be happy about that. Exhumation goes against the Catholic religion."

"That's why we have to get two orders—one legal, one religious," Ryan responded. "We have a priest who'll comply. What now?"

Devin held out a hand, so he could hear what was coming through the transmission. It drove Ryan crazy that he couldn't listen in.

"So you see, Rich, we think the guy's here in Vegas. We think he's going after the fourth family, now, the Giordanos. Do you think you could get Joey to accept our protection?"

"Fuck, no! He ain't gonna work with the cops. That goes against our code." Ricci sat thinking for a moment, giving him a chance to bite a thumbnail. "You really think he's in danger?"

"I think his family's in danger...wow, whatcha got going for lunch over there? Is that salmon?" Matt deliberately pointed to the spread of hot plates, causing Ricci to divert his attention and glance over at the food. As soon as the mobster's head turned, Matt pressed the transmitter up onto the underside of the table, and ran his fingertips over it to see if it stuck. It did. Fancy fed technology, with spit and all.

"Looks good, don't it?" Ricci replied "Sorry, Di Santo. Commission members only."

"Oh, that's okay, I already ate. So about Joey Giordano—"

"You are proving to be a good friend, Di Santo, a vital friend of the family. And I'm glad, because it took a lot to get you to where you are today. And once you understand that, then we'll be in a position to go a little further in this relationship. Know what I mean?"

Matt had no idea what he meant. "I like our relationship the way it is, Richie. I told you, I'm a cop first."

"But you're also one of us. A *paisan*!"

"I'm not one of you." Di Santo stood up, slightly agitated, needing to distance himself from the gangster, acutely aware that their conversation was going to end up on a federal transcript. "I'm here because I promised to keep you in the loop, you being a family member of one of our victims. That's all."

"Fuck, Di Santo, sit back down! We're not done here."

"I gotta go, Rich. I gotta meet my partner. We're here together."

"I said: *sedeti*." Ricci calmly aimed a palm at the chair. Tootie moved in closer to Di Santo, playing his role of Big Muscle.

"Really?" he said to his sister's boyfriend. But he agreed to take his seat again. "What, Richie? What do you want to tell me?"

Ricci leaned in closely, and beckoned Di Santo to do the same. "You are where you are because of us, see. Maybe we weren't so clear on this. We created that detective opening in the eighteenth district, encouraged you to go for it, and worked it out with the then-superintendent of the Chicago PD Shithead O'Malley for you to be placed there. So you see, you are where you are, Di Santo, because of us." He placed both palms on Di Santo's lapels and brushed away some imaginary fuzz.

"Yeah, right. And how would you have done that?" Matt was terrified at the potential answer, but also invigorated they were getting the first major offense on the wire.

Ricci sat back in his chair and grinned. "We had a Teamster member that owed us. Owed us big. Into the numbers for a hunner'd large. This guy, he had no record, clean as a whistle, so the judge gave him probation for vehicular manslaughter. Wiped his slate clean with us."

Matt froze. He couldn't absorb what Ricci was implying. "Are you saying that the truck driver who hit—"

"That *mulignan*, yeah. What was his name? Detective Lange."

"You're saying that Jon's death—"

"*Madòn*, look at the time! They're gonna be here any minute. This was a great talk, Di Santo, great talk. Thanks for the information." Ricci got up from the table and nodded to Tony to show him out.

Tootie stood next to Di Santo, waiting, until he shook off the fog that had enveloped his brain. His world had just imploded in the last thirty seconds. Tootie offered up Di Santo's weapon, and before he could exhale, Matt grabbed the gun and placed it directly on Ricci's temple.

"You fuckin' son-of-a-bitch," he seethed. "You killed a cop. You killed my—my best friend's best friend. And now, I'm gonna kill you."

Ryan sat next to Devin, studying his every breath, his every blink. "What, *what?*" Devin held up a finger as he cupped the ear with the receiver in it. "What is going on in there?"

Devin held his breath. "Wait…Oh, shit."

"*What?* Did he say cow?"

"*Go in, go in!*" Devin waved his hands toward the ball-room doors.

Ryan didn't need any more incentive. He flew off the bench, pulled his weapon and entered the ballroom, not knowing what kind of scene or how many people were going to be in there. He stopped in the middle of the floor, assessing the situation. Tootie had a gun to Di Santo's head, who in turn had a gun to Ricci's. *What the fuck had just happened?*

"Drop them!" he shouted, the cop kicking in. "Both of you! *Matt! Tony!* Drop your weapons. *Now!*"

He heard another person rush in behind him. With a quick glance over his shoulder he saw Devin backing him up, gun drawn. Tootie held up his hands and slowly put his .45 Valor on the table.

"Matt?" Ryan said, as if speaking to a child. "Could you please holster your weapon?"

Ricardo Ricci grinned at Di Santo. "Yeah, you better do what your best friend says."

After an excruciating three seconds, Di Santo dropped his arms and put his gun in the holster on his hip.

Ricci stood up slowly from his chair, unshaken, and took a hold of Di Santo's necktie. "I'm going to forgive you this time for that heinous mistake you just made," he said, leaning in close. "Because I understand you were caught off guard." He whispered something in Matt's ear that Ryan couldn't hear and then ended with a warning. "And if you ever do that again, Detective, you'll be sleeping in a hole in the desert."

"Get out of here, D," Ryan instructed, as he put his own gun away. Di Santo spit on the floor next to Ricci and strode out across the ballroom. Devin ushered him out with an arm. Ryan turned back to the mobster, "Keep it clean in here, guys. We don't want any trouble."

"Hey, I was just havin' a conversation and your guy—"

"Save it. We're watching you." He backed up with a hand on his weapon until he arrived at the double doors, then exited the room. The hallway was clear, and Ryan suspected Devin and Di Santo had headed up to the feds' suite, so he took an elevator to the third floor. Ryan knocked three times and was let in by Pendergrass, who gave him a weak smile.

"What in God's name happened in there?" Ryan asked the room, although aiming the question directly at his partner. Di Santo was leaning against the credenza, hand over his mouth. Nobody answered. "*D?*"

Di Santo shrugged. "I fucked up. Ricci just pissed me off. He...insulted my family." Even Matt wouldn't look at him. Ryan scanned the agents in the room—a feeling of pity and shame hung heavy in the air.

Jensen clapped his hands, shattering the silence. "The good news is: the wire is in place! Detective Di Santo completed the task, and now we'll have ears on the Commission. Stellar work, Detective. This is truly groundbreaking." He shook Di Santo's hand, but Matt didn't accept the commendation as he usually would, with a beaming smile, inflated chest, and nonstop chatter. Di Santo was as morose as if his mother had just died.

Something was seriously wrong.

CHAPTER 17

Catharine chose a light cotton sundress for her outing to the city and prepared herself for the trip. She descended the wooden staircase, trying to decide if she should attempt the outing alone, or have someone escort her downtown. As she made her way through the atrium, she encountered her sons, eating cereal at the table.

"Oh, hi, Ma. You look nice," Duke said, looking up at her. "Are you going out?"

"Yes, I'm going downtown to visit Jane."

"Ryan's Jane?" Hank asked.

She warded off the phrase with several blinks. "She's not *Ryan's* Jane, Hank. She's her own Jane."

"Yeah, well I just meant Ryan's *friend*, Jane. The lawyer?"

Catharine put a hand on his shoulder and sighed when he lifted the bowl to his mouth to finish off the milk. "Yes, Ryan asked me to check on her. I'm going to stop by the state's attorney's office, and then we may have lunch. Will one of you boys be available if I—need assistance?"

"Do you want me to take you?" Duke offered. "I have stuff to do downtown. I could go shopping while you meet with her. I could get some clothes for school."

Catharine did feel more comfortable knowing her son would be close by. Just in case. She hadn't been downtown without Ryan since her days at Town Red. And that had been almost ten years ago. She accepted the offer and Duke ran upstairs to get his keys.

"So Ryan's in Vegas, huh? With his brother?" Hank asked. "I bet they're having a blast."

Catharine didn't take the bait. "He's not having a blast, Hank, he's working. And what are you going to do today?"

Her son shrugged and carried the two cereal bowls out to the kitchen. When he emerged, he shouted across the atrium to his brother.

"Why don't you break it to her in the car?"

"Break *what* to me?" she said to Hank and then turned to his twin. "Duke? What are you supposed to break to me in the car?"

"C'mon, Mom," he said, waving her to the door. "I'll break it to you in the car."

As soon as he started up the engine to the hybrid SUV, she asked again. "So, what are you boys up to? Or is it Vanessa? She's not—you're not—"

"No, we're not pregnant."

Catharine exhaled.

"Hold on, let me get to Lake Shore Drive, first." He pretended to be an ultra-vigilant driver all the way to Sheridan Road, clearing his throat several times along the way.

"I don't like it already. If you're afraid to tell your mother, then it's not a good idea."

Her son lowered his voice until it settled into its usually soft timber. "Would you just hear me out, and don't react right away."

She sat up straighter, took a breath to prepare, and said, "Okay, go on."

"Hank and I need to choose our majors by the end of first quarter. They have to be filed at the registrar by December tenth. We talked about it, and it seems…well, I told you before, I want to go into Computer Science." She nodded, no surprise there. "Hank's going to go into Criminal Justice."

"That's great. Is he thinking pre-law? Oh, Hank would make a wonderful attorney."

"Well, no, Ma. That's the thing. After we graduate we both want to join the Academy."

"What academy?"

"The police academy."

Catharine's breath stopped in her chest.

"I want to do what Devin does. Stop criminals with computers. Data profiling and all that. It's exactly what I was interested in, and when I heard him describe his job...well, it all came together. And you know I've inherited some of your special talents too. My psychic abilities couldn't hurt with investigation." Catharine gazed out of the car window at the traffic light, her entire field of vision focusing on the red glowing glass. "As for Hank, he's more interested in the traditional law enforcement position. But he wants to—eventually—do tactical."

Catharine eventually found it within her soul to utter a response. "No."

"No?"

"No. Just no. I forbid it."

"Ma, you can't—"

She raised her voice to a decibel that she'd never heard from herself. "I will not have the *three men I love* be put in danger every day of their lives. I said no."

He dropped the subject and they rode in silence until Duke pulled up to the building that housed the offices of the Illinois State's Attorney. "Okay, Ma. Remember, you have to go through security. Don't freak out, okay? And if you need me, just call or text and I'll come pick you up."

Catharine nodded and exited the car with just an "I love you," back to her son. She had to block out the bombshell Duke had just dropped on her and check on Jane, as she'd promised.

The security line was light. She was able to send her purse through the conveyor line and step through the metal detector almost immediately. A woman waved a wand to her front and back and beckoned her through. But before she went up to Jane's office, Catharine needed a moment to gather her thoughts. She told herself to breathe.

As she continued through the clusters of people in the lobby, the thoughts of strangers flew by, second by second, like radio channels being flipped in rapid succession. A man worried about picking up his dry cleaning. A woman longed after a coworker. Credit card debt, what wine to have with dinner, who'll take care of the kids tonight. She blocked the thoughts, and their accompanying emotions, as she took the elevator up to the ninth floor.

Under the Illinois state seal, Catharine gave her name to the receptionist, who in turn summoned ASA Jane Steffen.

"Catharine!" Jane exclaimed, stepping out from a door. "What are you doing here? Is Ryan okay?" The spontaneous utterance reinforced what Cat's intuition had told her all along.

"Yes, he's fine. He actually sent me here to see if you were. Okay, that is."

Jane beckoned Catharine to follow her back to her office. They both took seats, Jane behind her desk and Catharine in front. The attorney wore a charcoal gray linen skirt paired with a pale pink button-down blouse. A matching suit jacket hung over the back of her chair.

As soon as they were seated Jane started her inquiry. "Are you okay? I thought you couldn't leave the house."

"I'm working on that, as you can see." Catharine smiled and spread her hands as if announcing her presence.

"But—agoraphobia. Isn't that a fear of going out in public? How can you do this? Are you on medication or something?"

"Having a phobia is more layered and complicated than just fearing something, Jane. For example, those who have a fear of flying are not actually afraid of flying. They are not even afraid of crashing, since that's proved to be instantaneous and painless. They fear—the *anticipation*—of impending death."

"I'm not following."

"My agoraphobia is not necessarily tied to the fear of leaving my house. Or people. It's about my empathic ability. When I'm out, I start hearing—feeling—the pain of everyone I come into contact with. It gets overwhelming and I shut down. So my fear of leaving the house is mostly a fear of being overwhelmed and not being able to get home. To my safe place."

"So, then, how did you work for Town Red Media? You worked for them for years, right? I always wondered about that."

"Almost five years, yes. During that time, my empathic abilities were not as strong. And when it did get bad, I medicated myself with anti-anxiety pharmaceuticals. But recently, I've made a concerted effort not to mask the problem, but to work on it. I've been working with my therapist on tuning out, so to speak, when I'm in public."

Jane nodded. "Well, welcome to the real world! What can I do for you?" She clasped her hands and gazed at Catharine, awaiting an explanation for the visit.

Catharine took a deep breath and exhaled before she spoke. "It's about Ryan, really. He said you haven't been returning his phone calls or text messages. He was worried."

Jane shuffled some papers on her desk, stacking a couple of them into a pile. "As you can see, I'm perfectly fine. I've just been extremely busy. A couple of large cases landed in my lap, and Stan's letting me take lead on them. It's a great opportunity, but I'm working non-stop."

Catharine studied her while she spoke, picking up the distinct impression that Jane wanted her to leave. "Do you know what I do, Jane?" she asked.

"Yes, of course. Ryan told me that you consult with the Department. You help them find people."

"I also do empathic healing. I can feel people's pain and take it away. Like I said, anytime I'm near someone, I can experience an empathic connection with them. It's a blessing but also a burden. I pick up on people's pain. When I'm in session with a client, I can absorb that person's fears, their stress, their losses…and their disappointments. It's not something I asked for, but it's something that's been with me for a long, long time. Since I was a little girl."

The attorney pressed her lips together. "I'm sorry."

"No, don't be sorry. I've learned to accept it, embrace it, and use it for good. And now I'm sensing there is some pain that you need to deal with, Jane. If you'd like, I can help you with that."

Jane took in a deep breath and responded. "You know, I think I'm good. I have a good life. A great job—where I get to put the bad guys in jail—and I've even started dating someone."

"No, you haven't."

"Wow, really?"

"I'm sorry, that was impolite. Sometimes, if I get an impression, it just tumbles out."

"Well, I'm dating several men, not anyone in particular. And that's why I've been so extremely busy—on top of these cases—and that's why I haven't had a chance to respond to the barrage of Ryan's calls and texts."

Like Hank, Jane had chosen her words deliberately. "He's a good man, Jane, and a good friend. He trusts you."

"It's funny you bring up that word: *trust*. Because every time you two have a fight, Ryan runs to me to tell me all about it. And each time it seems to center around trust." Catharine didn't respond. "And if he was so concerned about my welfare, then why didn't he come here himself?"

"Were you deliberately beckoning him with your silence?"

Jane leaned back, flustered with the accusation. "No. I meant why does he send you? You and I aren't particularly close. Maybe he likes having a woman on each arm. Maybe he's not as good a friend—or boyfriend—as you think."

"I know Ryan well, and am extremely comfortable with our relationship."

"You don't know Ryan outside of that house. That's the Ryan I know."

Catharine stood up. "I'm glad you're okay, Jane, and I will relay your message to him."

The attorney waved the back of her hand, dismissing Catharine like an assistant.

Before she left, though, she turned back one last time. "Oh, Jane? Don't give up on Paris."

CHAPTER 18

Di Santo was the first to leave the suite after the debriefing. Ryan ran after him but the little guy was too fast. He watched the numbers on Di Santo's elevator descend directly to the lobby, so Ryan took the stairs.

When he came out on the main floor, he spotted his partner heading for Alfonse's Bar and Grill.

The restaurant was designed to mimic an old-school Italian restaurant, with dark wood, red-checkered tablecloths, and the golden glow of period lighting. The walls displayed poster-sized photographs of Al Capone and his cohorts, along with newspaper headlines related to their exploits.

Ryan caught up with Di Santo as he was taking a stool at the bar and sat down next to him. "Again with the glorification of gangsters in this place," he said, breaking the silence. "They should post how Capone suffered from syphilis and had the mental capacity of a twelve year old." He glanced at his partner, but Di Santo didn't respond. "See, I can do my research. Like Devin."

His partner nodded in approval while signaling for the bartender. Across the restaurant an Asian tourist announced to his group, "*Bang, Bang! Al Capone!*" and pretended to mow them down, St. Valentine's Day style.

"Well, apparently the public loves it," Di Santo concluded. The bartender approached and he ordered. "Dutch Lemonade, please."

"You drinking already? It's not even noon yet."

"Hey, it's Vegas. There's no time here. No clocks in the casinos. I know that probably drives you crazy, but I'm going to order what I want."

"Seriously, D. Are you okay?"

Di Santo dropped his head into one palm. "I'm angry. Angry I let them pull me into this."

"Which side?"

"Both sides! Both fucking sides. I've got Richie thinking I'm working for him and Jensen pulling my strings because of my so-called 'connections.' They're stretching me in both directions and they're going to pull me apart like that Greek tragedy."

"Are you going to tell me what happened in that room?"

"No." The bartender delivered the piss-yellow drink and Di Santo thanked him with a nod. "I had a job to do and I lost my shit. I'm just a little down on myself now, and you don't have to be my nanny, Ry. You don't have to sit with me. I just want to—" He held up his drink and then downed half of it. "Cheers."

"You heard Jensen up there, you didn't fuck up. You did your job and placed the wire—"

"Can I just—" Di Santo held up a palm. "I just want to be alone for a while, okay? No offense. Go play with your brother or something. Get to know him. Do lunch. I'll circle back with you after the Commission meeting. Oh and here—" He handed Ryan the second bugging device. "Give this to Jensen."

Ryan nodded, retreating from the bar without a goodbye. He'd never seen his partner like this. Not even after the shootout where he'd almost lost his life. From the moment he left that ballroom, Matt appeared...deflated.

Ryan ascended the wide staircase up to the mezzanine and spotted several of the task force members attempting to blend in. Pendergrass and Martinez were pretending to be a couple at side-by-side slots. Agents White and Powell were chowing down subs at a nearby café table. Lefkowitz and Beerbelly—not his real name, but Ryan didn't quite catch it—stood a couple of feet from the ballroom doors, swiping their phones. Each agent had an almost indistinguishable earpiece connecting them to Jensen and the wire, and none of them acknowledged his presence. Two suited goombas flanked the double doors to the ballroom, making sure nobody disturbed the Commission meeting inside.

Devin wasn't anywhere to be seen, and Ryan figured he was probably up in the suite with Jensen, listening in on the wire. "I'm coming up," he said into the small silver disc. He had to find out what actually transpired between Di Santo and Ricci. This time Devin answered the door, let him in, and then returned to his laptop. Jensen sat across from him, taking physical notes in a spiral notebook.

"Anything interesting?" Ryan whispered, placing the bug on the table.

Devin teeter-tottered his hand. "So-so. They're going over what Di Santo told Ricci, and the three deaths. Dan Leone's a little manic. He says he wants to kill someone."

"Wow." Ryan tried to imagine the meeting taking place in the ballroom. "Do you want me down there? With your agents?"

"Where's Di Santo?" Jensen asked.

"Yeah, about my partner: he's a bit shaken. Taking some time for lunch at that Al Capone restaurant. What exactly happened with him?"

Jensen cleared his throat but didn't answer.

"We've been instructed not to inform you of what took place between Ricci and Di Santo," Devin responded. "It would hinder the investigation."

Ryan bristled. "Well, *my* investigation is to solve the homicides of the three women in Chicago. I really don't give a shit about your protocol. I'm here to catch a killer. And if you are withholding any information about my investigation, I'll report you for obstruction."

Jensen stood up from his chair. "We're here to bring down a criminal enterprise that's been responsible for *hundreds* of homicides in your fair city. And could be responsible for hundreds more in the future, if we don't stop them."

"So you're just *using* us to do your job?"

"It's best that you leave now, Detective. Let us handle the Outfit, and you keep searching for The Ghost. We'll be in touch." Jensen all but pushed him out of the door.

"Why can't I know what happened in there?" Ryan called back, as the door closed and locked behind him. "God *damn it!*" He pounded the door one last time, already regretting the trip to Vegas. He'd led his partner right into the feds' laps, unable to prevent them from making him an asset.

He took the elevator back down to the mezzanine and saw the six agents had all stopped play-acting and were facing the ballroom doors, on alert. The two mob guards had moved closer together, their massive shoulders almost touching.

Ryan unholstered his Glock and hovered behind the agents. A shot rang out and in less than two seconds one of the double doors flew open, thrusting the guards to the side. Joey Giordano ran out and barreled into Martinez, knocking him to the floor. Giordano took no notice as he ran to the staircase, with Danny Leone on his tail.

"You're dead, Giordano!" Danny shouted at the top of the landing. He sent two more shots down the stairs before resuming his chase. The agents played it safe and took cover, but Ryan went straight after Leone.

"Drop your weapon, Danny!" he shouted after the man. A crowd of tourists gathered in the lobby, watching the whole scene play out.

"This guy's done for! He killed my sister!"

Giordano fired several shots back up the staircase. Ryan ran after them, occasionally ducking for cover. The agents followed him down the staircase and commenced crowd control, directing the civilians to stay back. Giordano ran down the fake cobblestone street with Leone ten paces behind, firing off two more shots. Civilians screamed and retreated back into the stores.

"Leone! Listen to me!" Ryan shouted at Danny's back. "There is no evidence that Joe killed your sister. None! We have another suspect—"

"I don't believe you!" Leone let off another shot, shattering the glass of a luggage shop. Giordano slipped around a corner and escaped into Alfonse's Café. "Bones, come out and take it like a man!" he shouted.

He slowed his pace and began to whistle a tune as he approached the restaurant. Ryan came up behind him, his Glock less than a foot from Leone's head.

"Danny, just turn around and set down the gun. It doesn't have to end bad."

"Stay outta this, Detective," Leone called over his shoulder. "We take care of our own. Just walk away."

Ryan followed, ready to take the shot right into Leone's torso, but not really wanting to. Any time a PO discharged their weapon, there were forms to fill out, explanations to make, and a sitting with the review board. He was close enough to just sprint and cuff the guy. But just as he made the decision, something caught his eye: under the curtain of a nearby photo booth was the bottom of a trench coat. *Flash*—a light gleamed from the booth—a shot rang out from the restaurant in the same instant. When Ryan looked back, Leone had disappeared. He sprinted to the bar, where he found Leone on the floor staring up at Di Santo pointing a gun at his head. Leone groaned, clutching his shoulder. Not a fatal bullet wound, but enough to stop him.

"Wow, you must've been practicing at the range. You actually hit him," Ryan said, coming up to his partner.

"Yeah, and that was with a 'lemonade' already in me," Di Santo responded, as he rolled Leone and cuffed him. "By the way, don't tell that to the board." Ryan agreed. "So what just happened up there?"

"I don't know, but Giordano flew out of the meeting with

Leone at his heels. Danny, here, thinks Joey Bones had something to do with his sister's murder."

"He killed Desi. He killed *all of them!*" Leone spit out, his face parallel with the carpet. "His wife is still alive, so he's the one. He's got to be!"

"Get up, you piece of shit. You don't know nothing," Di Santo said.

He and Ryan each took one arm and lifted him to a standing position while a crowd of tourists began to applaud.

One older guy in a blue polo shirt came up to them and asked, "Excuse me, when's the next show? I seemed to have missed most of this one." Ryan and Di Santo glanced at each other and shook their heads simultaneously. *Vegas.*

"Bang, Bang! Al Capone!" the Asian man repeated from the corner of the bar. His group responded in a chorus of "Al Capone, Al Capone!"

Agent Jensen barked and badged his way through the crowd, with most of his team following, including Devin at the back. "Good work, gentlemen," he said to both detectives.

"It was Di Santo that got him," Ryan stated. "Small graze to the shoulder. He's going to need medical." They handed over custody of Danny Leone to the feds.

Jensen shook hands with Di Santo and instructed two of the agents to get Leone to Las Vegas PD. The rest of them were to search for Joey Giordano. "Find him and bring him to us on three. It's time."

"Time for what?" Ryan asked Devin.

"To turn him."

"*Ryan?*" a voice interrupted.

The voice from the speakeasy. He turned to see the woman he had feared and expected to see behind it. Kelly Riordan stood in a slim gray dress with black panels up the sides, but her hair was darker than her signature fire-orange mane. And shorter, just touching her shoulders.

"Ryan! I thought that was you, oh my God!"

He left the group to address her. "Kel? What are you doing here?"

"In Vegas? Yes, well, I'm here for ComTech," she said, pointing to a large poster for the conference on the wall. "What about you? Still catching bad guys, I see."

"Yeah, that was just one of them." He glanced back at Di Santo, who was watching them like a hawk. "Listen, was that you in the speakeasy last night? We're actually looking for the guy you were with. How do you know him? Where did you meet him?"

"I'm already getting the third degree, huh? I'm doing great, Ryan, thank you for asking."

He took her elbow and walked her out of the restaurant, farther from the crowd, as they dodged a strolling violinist. "This isn't a joke, Kel. The guy is dangerous, wanted by the FBI. Probably killed three women. And that's just in the past two weeks."

"*That guy?* No, that doesn't sound like him."

"So you were at the speakeasy?"

She nodded. "Yes. You were there?"

"Do you know his name?" Ryan pulled out his notebook. "Where did you meet him?"

Kelly glanced around at the crowd and lowered her voice. "We met in the casino, at the blackjack table. We struck up a conversation. He told me about the secret bars around this place and it sounded like fun. So we decided to look around and find one. That's all. Are you sure—"

"I'm sure. If we hooked you up with a sketch artist, could you give us a detailed description of the guy?"

"I—I suppose so. I'm not sure if I remember that much about him. I mean, he was kind of nondescript. Normal." She dug into a side pocket of her briefcase. "Here. Here's my card. That's a new cell number since, you know, since I left Chicago. A Boston number." Ryan took the card and handed her one of his. She perused it with a slight smile. "Still at the Eighteenth, I see?"

"Yeah, yeah. That's Matt over there," he said, pointing

him out. "He's my new—well not very new—partner. Matt Di Santo. He's good. We're good." Kelly nodded in approval.

Ryan checked out his ex-girlfriend from head to toe. "What's with the…" He motioned to her hair.

"Oh, yeah," she said, tucking a lock behind her ear. "I went brunette. I was ready for a change. It's funny, I feel like people take me more seriously like this. Especially at work. What do you think?"

"I don't like it," he answered honestly. "It's not you. I guess I'm just used to you being a redhead."

"There's the old Ryan," she snarked.

"I just don't understand. Why can't you be taken seriously with red hair?"

"Well, guess what, Ryan? You don't have to understand. It's my life, my hair, and I'm in charge of it."

"And *there's* the old Kelly," he fired back.

She threw him a sardonic smile, accepting the jibe. "How long are you going to be here? Maybe we can grab some coffee and catch up?"

He dug a toe into the multi-colored carpet. "Probably not a good idea. I'm seeing someone."

"Really? Is she here?" Kelly said and then scanned the crowd as if looking for her.

"No, she didn't come with me, since we're on a case. Her name's Catharine. Lives in Evanston. She's got two sons."

Her jaw dropped. "*Kids? You?*"

"I know, can you believe it? They're twins. Adults now, actually. Nineteen. Going into their sophomore year at Northwestern. It's good. We're cool. Two dogs…two cats." *In a mansion with thirty million dollars and she's psychic, too.* Sometimes Catharine was just a little too complicated to describe in casual conversation.

"Wow, Ryan with a family. And dogs and cats." She shook her head with an incredulous smile. "I never would've thought."

He smiled at her and nodded, comfortable with his new life and happy to relate that comfort to his ex.

"So, I guess it's serious, then?" she asked.

"We're moving in together."

Kelly jerked back, as if surprised, then settled into the idea with a sigh. "Wow! Well, good, Ryan. I'm really happy for you."

"And you? What about you?"

"Happily single."

It stung a bit that she was happier with no one than with him. Not that Ryan wanted her anymore, but it hurt his ego, nonetheless.

"Okay, then," she said, opening her arms for a hug. With their bodies pressed together he was struck at how much thinner she'd become. Lack of Chicago pizza, he guessed. Kelly used to order deep-dish twice a week. The embrace was short and awkward, ending with short pats on the back. Strange, considering how intimate they'd been for almost two decades. This girl whose frizzy orange braids he'd made a game of yanking in third grade. Part of him missed those braids.

"Take care, Kel. I'll have an agent follow up with you for the description of the guy."

"Bye, Ryan. Really great to run into you." She held up a palm as she turned and left them, red soles peeking out from the bottom of her high heels. *Louboutins,* according to Di Santo. Her new job must pay well.

"There it is again," Devin said, coming up to him. "The look of left."

Di Santo joined them. "Who was that hottie?" He turned a scowl on Ryan. "And why were you *hugging* her?"

Ryan handed him Kelly's card. "She's an eyewitness, who may have spent some time with The Ghost and could possibly identify him. We need to get her with a sketch artist over at LVPD."

"Kelly Riordan?" Di Santo said, staring down at the business card. "Not *the* Kelly Riordan? *Your* Kelly

Riordan?" Ryan threw his partner a death stare. "Oh, got it. And that's why *I'm* handling her!"

In the last three years, he'd often imagined running into Kelly, but assumed it would happen back in the old neighborhood visiting her folks, or maybe downtown, shopping at Field's. Yeah, he knew it was technically Macy's but every true Chicagoan still called it Marshall Field's. The actual encounter had gone almost as well as he'd imagined it. *Two dogs...two cats.* At least he'd had the chance to show her he was fine. Everything was fine post-Kelly.

And he was. Fine, happy. Life goes on.

"It all happens for a reason, bro," Jon would say. And now he understood that Kelly had to leave for him to have started a life with Catharine.

Ryan's thoughts were interrupted by the whir of the photo booth. It was currently developing the photo of the person who had caught his attention during the chase. That trench coat. He approached the booth cautiously, weapon drawn but at his side. He swiped the curtain back but it was empty. He encircled the machine, peering at the mechanics behind it. No Ghost. No trap door. When he came back around the front, a photo strip was being ejected into its receiving cage.

CHAPTER 19

Catharine could breathe easily now that they had made it home, and the fragrance of the flowers in the gardens calmed her. She bypassed her son Hank on the atrium path and went straight for the trowel that she had left in the asters, a blooming sea of purple and yellow.

Hank and Duke conversed within earshot. "She looks upset," Hank said. "So she didn't do well downtown?"

"She was actually doing okay until she met with Jane. I think they had some sort of a fight. I had the feeling something was going wrong, so I went back to the SA's offices and picked her up. But she didn't say one word on the drive home."

"Is that why she's in a mood? Because of Jane?"

"Well, that and the fact that I told her about our decision."

"Oh, you *told* her? And how did she take it?"

"Not too well. She forbids it."

Hank let out a short laugh. "She *forbids* it?" A silence.

"You know I can hear the two of you plain as day!" Catharine called out. "If you want to talk to me, then come talk to me."

She heard her boys' footsteps—once two pairs of small pattering feet, now size twelve clomps—down the path until they appeared in front of her. She stood up to face them.

"Ma, it's a career choice," Hank started in. "I thought you'd be proud. You're proud of Ryan's work."

She took their big hands and led them to the table in the center of the gardens. "Is this some sort of way to compete with Ryan...for my love or something? If so, then you should know that you boys will always come first in my life. I'm your mother. You will *always* come first."

"No, Ma. It isn't that," Duke replied. "We know you love us."

"Then what? What happened to football? Hank, didn't you want to play professionally?" She couldn't believe that professional football was now her preferred choice of career for her sons.

"We want to be cops," Hank stated. "We've put a lot of thought into this, it's not an impulsive decision, Ma. Duke and I have talked about it. Yeah, the NFL would be great, it's a nice dream. But we want to help people, not just entertain them."

"That is very noble of both of you," she responded. "I am proud of your intentions. But do you even understand how hard it is to have one loved one on the police force? And now Ryan is thousands of miles away, in the middle of a...a...*mafia war*! A real one, not like one of your video games. He could be shot—" A scene flashed before her. A city street, long ago. Almost a hundred years in the past. Guns, bullets, a chase. And yet the time frame was inconsistent, as she saw modern amenities as well: an ATM, a photo booth, high-heeled shoes with red soles. Green eyes. Red braids...

"Mom?" Duke shook her lightly and she came out of the vision.

"Please," she whispered. "The thought of all three of you putting your lives in danger, every day—"

"The majority of police officers never even fire their weapon in the line of duty, did you know that?" Hank said, squeezing her hand. "And if I applied for the Evanston force, it wouldn't be like I was working in the city. See, we can compromise. But we really want to do this."

Duke took her other hand. "Yeah, and I'll be on computers. Catching bad guys with code! No guns, Ma. I don't
even want to be on the street. Look at Devin. He's not in
danger at all."

Catharine took in her sons' pleading expressions. The
same expressions that asked if they could get a pair of Nerf
guns when they were eight. Or the newest video game system as teens. She'd had a policy of no toy weapons in the
house, but that soon gave way to virtual guns. *Call of Duty*,
God of War, *Halo Wars*, *Gears of War*...there was no shielding them, as much as she had tried. It was all too much for
her to handle in one day.

"Well, at least I have a three more years until you graduate. Maybe there will come a time when I'll get used to the
idea," she said, the acceptance weighing heavily on her
soul. She also secretly mused that the boys had that time to
change their minds. It was certainly possible that the cop
thing was a phase, and with Ryan living at the estate, maybe
they'd see that the job wasn't as glamorous as they'd imagined.

"I want to go to Las Vegas," she said, changing the subject.

Hank shook his head. "Are you kidding me? You can't
go to Vegas."

"Why not?"

"You just spent thirty minutes downtown and you were
shaking the whole ride back," Duke explained. "Even Ryan
said you're not ready for Vegas. Do you know how many
people are there? You wouldn't be able to handle it."

"I need to see him. Talk to him."

"I'm sure he'll be back soon," Duke said, patting her
hand.

An idea came to Catharine, a better idea of how she
could get there. She kissed both of her boys on the fore-
heads and turned toward the master staircase.

"The United States of America versus Anthony Spilotro...
now what kind of odds are those?"
~ *Anthony Spilotro*

CHAPTER 20

Ryan pulled the photo strip out of its delivery bay. The top image showed the back of the man—he recognized it as the same man from the speakeasy. In the second image, the man faced the camera with a fedora pulled down over his face, showing only his chin. The third had both hands in front of his face, like a game of peekaboo. But in the fourth, the booth was empty with just a blue background curtain taking up the frame. The photo strip was meant as a definite taunt for the detectives.

Di Santo came up to him. "Whatcha got?"

Ryan showed him the photo strip. "Where did Jensen go?"

"The whole team went to find Giordano and take him and his family over to a suite at Bally's. Get them outta this place filled with people who want to whack them."

They were interrupted by a text tone from Ryan's phone. It was from Zach.

– *Call Me!*

He dialed the ME's cell. "Hey, Z, what's up?"

"Well, three things. First, we got the body of Ms. Sandy Orlando sent to County hospital. Luckily there wasn't too much decomp, so I did a full review and a black light scan."

"And?"

"There were traces of ultra-violet ink on her hand."

"Boo?"

"Illegible. But it could have been. The smear was about two point five centimeters in length. Her skin had been covered with airbrush makeup, common for funeral parlors, so that most likely caused the smearing." Ryan wiped his own hand as an automatic reaction to the mental image. "Now, onto Desirée Leone. We processed the stomach contents and got her tox screen report. Ms. Leone had eaten a Caesar salad with anchovies and had imbibed a Cabernet blend. No beef stew in the stomach itself, although there were remnants of beef stew all over the remaining torso and limbs as well as the bed sheets. Her tox screen came back with an array of barbiturates, which would have rendered her completely comatose. The most significant was ketamine."

"The date-rape drug?"

"Yes."

"So what does that mean?"

"I'm thinking the killer somehow drugged her, laid her out on the bed, poured beef stew on her body and then let nature take its course with the...cat."

"Official COD?"

"Lion mauling, for sure. She was unconscious, but the drugs wouldn't have killed her."

Ryan inhaled deeply. "Can you match the barbiturates with what was found in Sandy Orlando? He must have drugged her somehow before she got in her car. Maybe that was ketamine too."

"Great minds think alike! I already went back and reviewed Ms. Orlando's tox screen and it was a positive for the same combination of pharmaceuticals. The exact same substances, slightly different quantities."

Ryan absorbed the implications of the match. "Got it. You said there were three things. That's two. What's three?"

"Oh, right. You had ordered a DNA test from the lab and they sent it to me. It had the Ricci case number on it, but no names." Ryan held his breath. "Anyway, subject one and subject two are not a match." He exhaled. "Well, not an *ex-*

act match. It's a filial match. They're siblings, same father. So who are they? Is one of them The Ghost?"

Ryan had to think fast. "No, well—maybe. I'll let you know. It's classified."

"Well, which is it? Yes, no, maybe, or it's classified?"

Devin was indeed his brother. "Classified. FBI stuff."

"Okay, well, good luck with the case."

Ryan disconnected the phone and stared at Di Santo. "What?" his partner asked. "You're as pale as a sheet. Zach give us bad news?"

Ryan shook his head like a dog shaking off water. "Not good or bad. More data for the chart. Sandy Orlando has been confirmed as victim number one. We've got invisible ink on all three women, tying them together, and Sandy Orlando was drugged with the same narcotics as Desi Leone. That makes three victims, same MO. So according to the feds, this is now officially a serial."

Ryan and Di Santo arrived at the newly-rented suite at Bally's just as Giordano was being led through the door in cuffs by Agent Beerbelly.

"What'd *I* do? Those guys just turned on me! You see them shootin'? I was the target, for fuck's sake," the mobster cried.

Beerbelly uncuffed the man once inside the room, and he ran right to his wife and daughter. Joey Giordano was about twenty years her senior, with a face too weathered for the shoe-polish-black hair on his head and the platinum blonde on hers. The man stood about five-foot-nine or -ten, with a lanky frame. "Hon', ya got any cigs?" he asked his wife. She shook her head, almost frowning, but the Botox wouldn't quite allow it.

"This is a non-smoking room," Jensen replied.

"Fuuuuu—" Joey whined, then glanced at his daughter. "—dge."

Jensen turned to the female agent. "Pendergrass, take Mrs. Giordano and her daughter to the next room. Order up some food."

She gathered up the family and ushered them through an adjoining door, closing it gently behind them. As soon as the door clicked, Jensen pushed Giordano down into a chair.

"Hey!" Giordano protested. "Like I said, I'm the victim here!" He rolled up the sleeves of his cotton shirt, revealing thin reedy arms under all of the wiry hair. *No wonder they call him Joey Bones*, Ryan thought. "Can you turn on the A/C? It's a little stuffy in here. Smells like pig." That earned him a short slap to the side of his head from Jensen.

The head of the task force then took a swig from a five-dollar water bottle and sat down on the bed, knee-to-knee with the mobster. "Mr. Giordano—Joey, if I may—this is how I see your situation. You, your lovely wife, and your daughter in there are the only one of the four families this Ghost guy hasn't hit. *Yet.* So either Danny Leone was right—and you were in on this whole thing—"

"No way! We had a good thing going on here. I wouldn't jeopardize this."

Jensen slapped him again, this time on the left side. "Shut up and listen." The guy sneered back, but silently. "Either you hired this Ghost, or your family is next. Do you understand me? Either way, you're fucked. And in a lot of people's crosshairs. You've got the other three families, with their capos, soldiers, associates—hundreds of guys, really—after you. Either that, or one of the best hit men in Chicago is now hunting down your wife. We know The Ghost is here, Joey. We've got witnesses."

The man squirmed and glanced out the eleventh story window. The "El Train" roller coaster whizzed around The Chicago hotel down the street.

"Whaddya offering?" he said, still staring out at the ride.

Jensen took another drink of water, letting the guy stew. "We're offering complete safety for your wife, your daughter. And you."

"What? Witness Protection Program?"

"Possibly. If it comes to that."

"And in return?"

"You testify in court."

"Fu-u-u-u-ck that. I'm no rat. I don't rat on my friends, I don't rat on my enemies. We don't rat."

Jensen smiled. "Yeah, that's what Sammy Gravano said at first. And Cantarella…"

"Massino, Lino, Tartaglione," Martinez chimed in.

"Scarpa Senior, Scarpa Junior, Vitale…" Beerbelly added. "Calabrese!"

Giordano spit on the carpet. "*Cacacazzi!* They're all scumbags. We have a code and they broke it."

"Yeah, yeah, we know. The old *omertá*. That doesn't seem to hold much water these days, Joey. If your associates aren't sticking to it, why should you? Is your precious *omertá* going to save your life? What about Lena's life? And your precious little girl? Not at this point. Think about this: do you want to send your beautiful family out there with only your guys to protect you? That didn't work too well for Robin Ricci or Sandy Orlando…or Desirée Leone. And she had a fucking lion."

Giordano jiggled his leg so furiously, his whole body quivered. Ryan could almost hear his bones knocking together like a skeleton at Halloween.

Jensen got up off of the bed. "I mean, if you don't want our help, Joe, we could just leave. Shut down the account for this room and happily shuttle the three of you back to The Chicago."

"No! No. Wait a minute," the mobster said, waving Jensen back to him. "There may be a way we can come to some kind of arrangement. Exactly…what is it you want to know?"

"Everything."

Giordano went into a coughing fit. Jensen motioned for Martinez to get him a water bottle. The man unscrewed the cap and downed half the bottle before exhaling another cough. "Don't nobody got a cigarette in here?"

"Maybe it's time to quit."

CHAPTER 21

Catharine had suspected there was a power emerging within her that she hadn't quite acknowledged. During what she called her "dream states," she felt as if she could journey out of her body to different physical locations. She could see people, and they appeared to see her. She participated in conversations, and even affected the situation at hand. When she awakened, she felt the experiences were so vivid they couldn't have been just dreams. These astral visits were something she hadn't disclosed to anyone. Not to her boys, not even to Ryan.

Sara had left for the day and there were no remaining appointments on Catharine's calendar. She climbed the dark wooden staircase, rounded the atrium to the rear wing, and entered her master bedroom. This was the bedroom she'd always wanted since childhood—a room she had created in her imagination—and when she was able to help design her estate, she had made it a reality. The entire bedroom was circular and completely white. White carpet, white vanity, white walls, white bedding. Catharine designed it after the bedrooms in the many classic 1940s movies she'd seen growing up. The types of rooms where Lana Turner or Jean Harlow would luxuriate in their negligées and retire on chaises. Where they'd received vases of red roses from tuxedoed gents. What glamor and luxury. She was able to realize this dream of a bedroom—of a house—when she sold her Town Red stock for thirty million dollars.

But the best part of her bedroom was the skylight. With a press of a button on a remote, the ceiling automatically opened to reveal the sky, where she watched the stars with Ryan the first night he stayed over. The night that she knew they were to be together.

She pressed another button and the automatic curtains closed on the west windows, blocking the afternoon sun. Catharine lay down in her bed, face up, and allowed herself to relax, concentrating on the bright tufts of clouds rolling by.

She'd never been to Las Vegas, physically, although she'd seen the neon signs and flashy casinos on television and in films. She let her imagination wander to the desert at first, with the city at its center, and then zoomed into the strip of resorts.

Cat and Ryan had always had a unique metaphysical connection, and many times she could get a feel for his location. She pictured his visage, listened for his voice, and followed his energy, his smell. The familiar sensation took hold as her body relaxed into the bedding and her inner spirit soared. She zoomed up, spiraling into space, and back down again, toward her destination. During these dream states, her senses were heightened: colors amplified, lights shone brighter, and noise louder.

Her conscious mind rematerialized in a shimmering corridor full of shops, bustling with people. Posters along the walls promoted a grand buffet, lively nightlife, and a local tech convention. Catharine was drawn to one of the shops where a woman had raised her voice to the salesman behind a glass counter.

"I have fifteen thousand dollars in that account, you asshole! How can it be declined?" The man had already pulled out a gift box for the diamond tennis bracelet the woman was attempting to purchase.

"I'm sorry, ma'am, but your bank is not approving the

sale. I've run it twice. This happens frequently to people on vacation. Did you tell your bank you were traveling?"

"You know what? Forget it, then!" she said, turning to leave. "You've just lost a sale." As if the store was responsible for her card being declined.

The man smirked as he lifted the diamond bracelet from the box and placed it back in the glass display. "Okay, then."

Catharine's spirit grounded as she approached the woman storming out into the corridor. She wore a fitted gray dress paired with expensive shoes. Catharine observed as the woman pulled her phone out of her Coach briefcase, sat down on a bench, and called her bank.

After she finished her call, the rage faded as she began to touch up her lipstick.

"Is this seat taken?" Catharine said, pointing to the spot beside her.

"No, go ahead," the woman said, pulling her briefcase over to make room for Cat.

There must be some reason Catharine needed to be here, with the angry woman who sat beside her. Her dream states always seemed to serve a purpose. Perhaps Ryan was close. Perhaps The Ghost was on his way. Catharine kept vigilant for anyone who felt familiar or ominous.

"I hope you didn't hear all that," the woman said to her. "I guess I just freaked out. I don't even want that bracelet anymore. Impulse buy." She chuckled, and Catharine smiled back. "Are you here shopping, too?"

"I guess so, yes. Just window shopping. My boyfriend is here for work, and I'm...killing time."

" I'm Kelly, by the way. You sound like you're from the Midwest."

"Yes, yes, I am." Catharine didn't want to give too much away. "Chicago area."

"Me too! Chicago born and raised."

Kelly from Chicago. Could this be *the* Kelly? It was a distinct possibility given their history, but Ryan had described her as a vibrant redhead with a sturdy frame. This woman was on the thin side, and a brunette. And then the suspicion hit her all at once—along with shock, uncertainty, vulnerability. *Was Ryan really in Vegas on a case?* She swatted the thought away to regain her composure. Kelly was a common name.

The woman jumped up. "Hey, let's window shop together. I can't buy anything anyway until my bank lifts this frickin' hold. They said it could be up to a half an hour." She got up from the bench and beckoned Catharine, who followed.

"Are you here for the conference?" Catharine asked her.

"Oh, no. But I am here on business. You?"

"I'm...I'm a consultant." She wasn't about to go into detail. Cat's attention was drawn to Kelly's hands. The woman was peering into a shoe store mindlessly picking at the cuticle of one of her thumbs. "You're bleeding," Catharine advised her.

"Oh my God." Kelly pulled a tissue from her briefcase and dabbed her thumb. "I guess I'm a little stressed. You see, I just ran into my ex. I can't believe it. Here in Vegas of all places. And you know, that's always awkward."

Catharine's exhaled her relief. If Kelly had just run into Ryan, then they weren't here together. "Your ex?" she inquired.

"My ex-boyfriend. He's a cop, a Chicago cop. We've known each other since we were kids." So this was *The Kelly*. There was the connection. Cat was definitely supposed to be in this woman's presence. "He said he's here on a case. It's been years since we've seen each other. Almost three years, actually."

"What was so stressful about it? Do you still have feelings—"

"Oh no, no, nothing like that. He did say he was seeing someone, though, and that it's pretty serious. I guess I'm happy for him. It's just so strange, thinking about him with someone else. We dated for a long, long time. Anyway, he told me I might have talked with some guy that they're hunting for a string of murders."

"That's frightening. How did that happen?"

Kelly went on to talk about meeting a man in the casino and then going to a secret jazz club. As she went on about the events of last evening, something struck Catharine as disingenuous—almost as if Kelly were rehearsing an alibi. "And now they want me to go to the police station and make a statement. I don't know. Maybe it's just his way of wanting to see me again. What do you think?"

A primal possessiveness swelled up and yet Catharine willed herself to remain neutral. "I think he probably just wants a statement from you," she answered. "So where did you leave it with him? With your ex?"

"Well, his partner called me. He wants to meet me at the police station at six."

"Well, there's your answer. If Ryan had wanted to see you again, he would be meeting you instead of Matthew."

"Wait," Kelly said, stopping their stroll. She turned to face Catharine. "How did you know their names?"

"I'm sorry, I have to go." Cat turned and ran toward the end of the corridor. Once she turned the corner, she could feel her astral body evaporate into the air. The shops below became smaller, fading into the distance, as she picked up on a sharp, brittle energy surrounding Kelly, swirling around her. Cat's spirit detached from the woman and rode the wind, floating, flying, and attempting to zero in on Ryan's location. Catharine had come here to find him, to make sure he was not injured...or worse. The duality of Ryan and his brother entered her consciousness as she perceived them becoming closer, bonding. But something was wrong with Matthew. His spirit was broken and far removed from Ryan and Devin, with a black aura enveloping him. Matthew was in pain. Or danger.

Catharine's out-of-body self floated up, up, and out of the humming city, into the clouds and with a deep, quick inhale, she opened her eyes and was back in her round, white room. She sat up and gasped for oxygen, her heart racing as if she'd just crossed a finish line. The clock displayed 4:32 p.m. She took a journal out from her bedside table and began scribbling her experience, attempting to make sense of the experience, writing the details so she could relay them to Ryan. Why hadn't she been able to reach him? Was the conversation with Kelly meant to be a warning about the case—or their relationship?

Catharine reached for her phone and almost called him until she heard Jane Steffen's words echo in her memory: '*It's funny you bring up that word: trust.*'

She replaced her phone on the bedside table.

She had to trust herself to trust Ryan.

CHAPTER 22

Ryan pulled Agent Jensen aside to a corner of the room. "Before you start in on this guy, we need him to draw The Ghost out of hiding."

Jensen furrowed his brows. "What are you thinking?"

"We need Giordano to give us the dark web info so we can message The Ghost on that secret Internet browser that Devin was talking about. Hopefully, we could set up a meeting with the guy, ask him what he wants. At the very least, we could get some more data on him, or a motive. Maybe we can even apprehend the sonofabitch. Once we put the three murders to bed, then you have free rein to use Giordano and put the rest of them away for life. But let's get this done first."

Devin and Di Santo joined the huddle. "I'm about eighty percent to an ID," Devin said. "Don't you want to wait?"

"We can't wait," Ryan responded. "The Ghost has proven he's extremely lethal and has the intelligence to get in and out of anywhere. I mean, look at what happened on the plane! And now Giordano and his family are targets—and who knows who else. He's been a step ahead of us the whole time and probably has a roster of the task force by now. Any one of our loved ones could be in danger."

Ryan could see the idea sinking in on Jensen's face, and finally the agent nodded approval. "Okay, you can get the login information from Giordano. The team will then be escorting him and his family back to Illinois tonight, as our plane's been inspected and cleared. You guys can book commercial flights back and bill us for reimbursement."

Devin cleared his throat. "If you don't mind, sir, I'd like to stay with Detectives Doherty and Di Santo," he said. "They'll need me to navigate the dark web and I can report back to you regarding The Ghost situation."

Jensen agreed to the plan and they approached Giordano, still jiggling in his chair. "Mr. Giordano, we're going to begin our relationship with some vital information. Tell Agent Doherty here the website on which you usually contact The Ghost for his services, and whatever login and password you use. Once we have that verified, we can get your family's belongings and prepare to return home under our protection."

The mobster shook his head. "You can try, but we've already attempted to draw the shithead out—see what he wants with all this—and so far we've received no response. If you're gonna try it, anyway, then you gotta get the login from Danny Leone. He knows all that Internet stuff. You can get it all from him."

Ryan, Di Santo, and Devin said their goodbyes to the team and proceeded back to The Chicago, with Devin calling Las Vegas Metro PD on the way. Danny Leone was being held at the county jail, awaiting arraignment, but they were able to get the officers to put him on the line. Devin promised him that the feds would recommend leniency if he'd help them catch The Ghost, emphasizing that they believed he was Desirée's murderer. Leone agreed and relayed the login information.

Devin, Di Santo, and Ryan settled in Devin's room as he unpacked his laptop and powered it up. "These sites are by invite only. As long as we have the password, they'll think I'm Danny Leone. I'm going to search his past messages to see how he worded them to contact The Ghost." His fingers flew like pistons on the keyboard, pausing occasionally for him to read the screen with a few "Mmm-hmmms" inter-spersed. "Okay, I see the account that Leone has been con-versing with. The username is Spectre519."

"A specter is a ghost. That must be him," Ryan said, looking over Devin's shoulder.

"I'll send this account a private message," Devin said, his fingers taking off again. "What do I say?"

"Tell him the families are all under federal protection," Ryan said. "Say we're ready to negotiate and ask what he wants. As simple as that."

"You think he'll tell us?" Di Santo asked.

"Can't hurt to try."

Devin typed the message almost verbatim, then hovered the mouse over the send button while Ryan and Di Santo reviewed it.

"Good," Ryan said, approving.

Devin clicked send and the detectives let out a sigh.

"Something's just not right with the data profile we put together and it's been bugging me," Devin said, rocking in his chair. "It's not adding up." He pulled out the chart from his briefcase. "We've got a guy who can fly a jet, is techie enough to navigate the dark web, has access to a variety of street and prescription narcotics, is a military-trained sharp-shooter, has the money to play the high-roller tables, and apparently can fight off a lion."

"Sounds superhuman," Di Santo said.

Devin pointed at him. "Exactly my point. No one guy in the world can do all this," he said. "As soon as I think I start narrowing down an ID, the perpetrator does something else fantastical and discredits the profile that we've carefully constructed."

"Wait…you said no *one* guy in the world can do all this," Ryan said, taking the printout of the chart from Devin. "What if it's *not* one guy? What if it's *more* than one guy?"

"A gang?" Devin asked.

"A family!" Di Santo shouted.

Ryan continued. "Of course! One guy can't do all this,

but a crew of guys could. Devin, what do you think about this theory?"

Devin started nodding and turned back to his laptop. "That makes total sense now," he said. "This isn't the profile of one perpetrator. It's the profile of a *group* of perpetrators. Why didn't I see that? I can use my algorithms that we've put together previously for terrorist cells and go from there. Good going, bro!" Devin held his hand up for a high-five and Ryan obliged.

After several minutes Devin closed the laptop. "Searches are running, now I'm hungry. Wow, it's already five fifteen," he said glancing at his phone. "You guys want to have dinner?"

"I could eat," Ryan responded.

"You two go ahead," Di Santo said. "I've got plans to meet Kelly Riordan over at Metro and get her statement. Pair her with a sketch artist. Meet you back here after, okay?"

Di Santo took off to meet Kelly while Ryan and Devin headed down to the buffet. It felt strange to have her name floating around in his orbit again. Strange to have *her* in his orbit again. Life was much easier when Kelly was out of sight, out of state, and out of mind.

They waited in the buffet line of name-tagged techies and Bermuda-shorted retirees, paid for their dinners, and then separated to choose their own mix and match cuisines. They met in back at a booth on the far side of the restaurant, away from children and the tour groups. They inspected each other's food choices and then ate in silence for a couple of minutes. The buffet had more of a Chicago city vibe rather than the mobster theme that permeated the rest of the resort. Framed posters of Chicago celebrities hung on the walls and the pillars throughout the buffet: Hugh Hefner and his bunnies, Oprah Winfrey, Richard Daley Senior, and sports celebs like Walter Payton, Ernie Banks, and of course, Ditka.

Ryan decided to rip off the proverbial bandage and get

the brother issue out in the open. "I got the DNA results today."

"Yeah?" Devin said, poking at his potato salad.

"It seems as if you were right. We're half-brothers."

Devin nodded as he finished off some macaroni and cheese. "I know. I had a DNA test done last year."

Ryan flinched. "How on earth did you manage that?" he said, dropping his fork on the table.

"Your DNA is on file with the Chicago Police Department to be ruled out at crime scenes, remember? You gave a sample when you became a detective."

Damn, he had forgotten about that. "And can you tell me how you got access to the Department's DNA files?" Devin shook his head while shoveling some sliced ham into his mouth. It wasn't like Ryan hadn't ever used police records for things that weren't quite work-related, but that was a hell of a breach. "So then why didn't you just show me the results of the test you performed?"

"Would you have believed it? You thought I had Photoshopped my birth certificate. So I let you run the DNA test for yourself, to be sure." Ryan stabbed a slab of roast beef on his plate without answering. Devin finally looked up at him. "So are you okay with this? Having a brother?"

"I suppose I don't have a choice, now, do I? I have a brother." It still felt strange to say it, that word he'd never used outside of the Department. His "brothers" had always been in blue, not anyone who shared his goddamned DNA. The closest thing he'd had to a brother up until this point had been Jon. '*My brotha from anotha motha*,' his partner would say when he introduced him to friends or family. Ryan wasn't ready for Devin to usurp that role. Not yet.

"You still say it like I'm a tumor growing from your neck," Devin said, wiping his mouth with a napkin. He placed it on top of a mound of food he wasn't going to finish.

"I'm sorry. I just need time to absorb it all. I've only known you a couple of days."

"Fair enough." Devin pushed his dinner plate out of the way to make room for a smaller plate holding a healthy slice of key-lime pie. He gestured to share it, but Ryan declined.

"So, as long as we're being real here," Ryan said, while Devin dug into the pie, "can you tell me what went on with Di Santo and Ricci?"

Devin held up his index finger. *Why does time always slow down when someone has food in their mouth?* After seven seconds, the man finally swallowed. "No, I cannot."

"Are you seriously pulling this with me? Matt Di Santo has been my partner for over two years. And you're my brother, apparently. You're not going to tell me?" He seemed to be breaking Devin down a bit and decided to continue to work that angle. "Look, Dev. I want to get to know you, and eventually we can get to the point when I introduce you to my mom and sisters. We have a really close family and I'm willing to bring you in, as much as I can. But we can't start off a relationship with secrecy. I need to be able to trust you."

"I'd really like that, and you can absolutely trust me. But this is a federal matter. What I can say is that Ricardo Ricci admitted to a major crime on that wire. The task force must now investigate thoroughly before it can be disclosed it to anyone outside of our unit. We've learned over the years that it's not prudent to release any information until we have all the evidence to convict. That's how we got all those convictions in *Operation Family Secrets*. They had no idea what we were doing or what evidence we had until *BAM!*" He smacked the table with the blunt side of his fork. "The shit storm came down upon the Chicago Outfit and we had them dead to rights. It was a beautiful thing. I wasn't a part of it the unit then, but I've heard many stories. Extremely efficient, perfectly executed. And that's why I cannot break protocol."

"Okay, I respect that," Ryan said. He figured he'd get it out of Di Santo eventually. He leaned back in his chair, patted his stomach, and let the mountain of food settle for a couple of moments. "So you never answered my question about Jon Lange."

"Which question was that?"

Ryan took a moment to figure out how to ask. "You know, after he died, I could have sworn I heard him talking to me. I mean I wasn't crazy or anything. Even went to the department shrink and got my head examined. I...well...Jon and I would have conversations."

Devin nodded as he scooped up a forkful of whipped cream. "Grief manifests itself in many different ways," he responded.

"Has that ever happened to you? Have you ever heard someone who wasn't exactly there? Catharine said that you might have experienced something similar. Maybe had even spoken to Jon. Like me."

Devin wiped his mouth with one of a stack of napkins that he had stashed next to his place setting. He contemplated the question for a moment and then answered. "As a federal agent if I ever admitted to hearing voices of people who were not present, I would lose my job."

"Is that a yes?"

Devin locked eyes with him. "As a federal agent if I *ever* admitted to hearing voices of people who were not present, I would lose my job." He paused. "But...if theoretically I had heard a voice...it might have said...to 'go find your brother. He needs you.'"

By the agent's severe expression, Ryan figured that was the end of the conversation. Those could've been Jon's words, or that could have been bullshit. He decided to shelve the subject for now.

"I might go back and get some of the cheesecake," Ryan said, putting an end to the inquiry. He was about to get up from his chair when the lights flickered and a wave of cheers rang out from the casino area. Screams, jubilation, and electronic bells in staccato succession. The pandemonium escalated as the buffet diners stopped eating, distracted by the uproar. Several people got up and headed toward the casino, Devin and Ryan included. When they got to the casino floor, they witnessed an unusual scene: every slot machine within sight was ringing a win. Lights flashing, credits compounding by pennies, nickels, dimes, and dollars. Many of the slot players were jumping up and down, while some stared incredulous at their machines. Twenty years ago, coins would have been spilling out onto the carpet in streams, but the machines were now digital and the little credit counters kept going up and up and up. When the other gamblers figured out what was happening, they fought for a spot at the machines, shoving bills and credit cards into them.

"This is not good," Ryan said, scoping out the wild-eyed grandmas and squealing tourists. He spotted Richie Rich and Victor Basso running down the staircase from the mezzanine with several security guards flanking them. He couldn't hear Ricci over the mayhem, but it was clear that he was shouting "Cut the power! Cut the power!" as he sliced a finger across his neck. The security guards tried unsuccessfully pulling the players away from the slots only to get kicked, punched, and have drinks thrown in their faces. When the guards heard Ricci's command over their walkie-talkies, they backed away, awaiting the power outage. It took another thirteen seconds for the entire casino to power down, and Ryan wondered how much money was lost in that time along with the preceding seven minutes of payout. Millions, considering the high-dollar slots.

As the lights dimmed and the slot machines groaned to a halt, the players frantically punched buttons attempting to cash out.

"Everybody out, folks!" the security guards commanded. Las Vegas Metro police filed into the building in crowd-control formation. Ryan and Devin hung out in the back of the casino watching it all play out—flashing their badges to the local PD so they could remain as bystanders while the rest were ordered off of the casino floor.

A backup generator had provided enough energy so that the security lights still illuminated the casino floor.

After all the players were cleared, the largest video screen in the racing pit powered back up on its own, grabbing the attention of the pit bosses, police, and security guards. On it was displayed one white word against a black background:

BOO!

CHAPTER 23

Ricci spotted Ryan and Devin on the casino floor and made a beeline straight to them, with Victor Basso trailing behind. "I want this sonofabitch Ghost, whatever it takes," he seethed, poking an index finger in Ryan's chest. "Where's Di Santo? And who's this jamoke?" Ricci nodded to Devin.

Ryan thought fast. "This is—my brother. Along for the trip. He likes blackjack." Devin held out a hand, but Ricci dismissed it with a wave. "Matt's at Metro PD, interviewing a witness," Ryan continued. "We're getting closer to this guy's identity, Mr. Ricci. Believe me, we want him just as much as you do."

"That's not possible. It's bad enough he's killing our families, but now he's killing our business? He's a dead man, I tell you. A *dead* man."

"Dead man," Victor Basso echoed. The two bosses stormed off, with two of their henchmen sending residual warning glares back at them.

"We are not going to identify the perpetrator to Ricardo Ricci until we have him safely in custody, right?" Devin asked.

"Of course not," Ryan replied. "We just have to tell him that so he keeps cooperating with us. And so he doesn't whack my partner."

As they made their way back to Devin's room, Ryan's cell pinged with a text from Di Santo.

– *Kelly's a no-show. No answer on her cell. Coming back to the hotel.*

Ryan texted his partner back to meet them in Devin's room while Devin checked the dark web for any messages. Ryan watched over his brother's shoulder as he logged back onto the message board. One unread message flashed in his inbox, elevating Ryan's heartbeat. "Is it from The Ghost?" he asked.

Devin clicked on it, revealing a message with only one link in it. He clicked on the link, which launched a live chat window.

– *Did you like my little prank?*

"It's him!" Ryan said.

Devin nodded, took a deep breath, and began typing in the chat box.

– Ingenious hack. We're impressed. What, exactly, do you want from us?

– *I'll only talk to Doherty and Di Santo. No mob. No feds. Stratosphere Outer Deck 8pm tonite.*

"Why us? How does he know our names?" Ryan asked aloud. Devin took it to the keyboard.

– Why Doherty & Di Santo?

– *Neutral parties.*

"Not really, we're hunting your ass," Ryan said, as if speaking directly to The Ghost.

"This is too dangerous. You can't go," Devin said, still staring at the screen. "If our theory is correct and it's a gang, we don't know how many will be up there. Just you and Detective Di Santo? You could be assassinated on the spot."

"What reason would they have to kill us? They obviously want something from the Outfit families, or they need to get a message to them. This way, we can find out their motives and see what he—or *they*—look like. More data,

Devin. More data." He shook his brother's shoulders from behind.

Devin wriggled out from under Ryan's grasp, pondered the rationale for several seconds, and then typed:

– Why the Stratosphere deck?

– *So neither party can set up snipers*

"That actually makes sense," Ryan said. "He's put some thought into this. I want to go. Tell him we'll be there, but we're going to be armed."

Devin hesitated. "It's too bad the task force team has already departed back to Chicago. I really would have liked you to have reinforcements."

"The Ghost said *no feds!* And we can't tell Richie, because he'll have his guys just mow them down and we'll have a massacre on our hands."

Bang-Bang, Al Capone.

Devin responded, "Fine. But I'm going to be close by. Just inside the Stratosphere's observation deck."

"Deal." They shook on it, and then Devin returned to the chat screen.

– We'll be armed, not negotiable.

– *Likewise. And I also have extra insurance.*

"What does that mean? What extra insurance?" Ryan asked.

Devin shook his head in response and was about to type when an image came through the chat window. It was Kelly Riordan, bound and gagged, with a gun to her head.

"Motherfuck—" Ryan whispered through his teeth. "I'll kill them myself."

– *If all goes well, I'll release Ms. Riordan at the end of the meeting.*

The chat window closed on its own and Ryan blew out a breath. "Jesus! Why Kelly?" He raked his fingers through his hair, wanting to tear at his scalp.

"He must have seen you two talking. Or she could have told The Ghost you were close when she had drinks with him. Maybe that's why he approached her in the first place.

He could've already known that you and she had a history."

Feeling completely thrown, Ryan began to pace the hotel room. "No wonder she didn't show up at the precinct. Matt's on his way back here. How long do we have?"

Devin glanced at the clock on his computer screen. "It's six-forty-three. We have one hour and seventeen minutes to plan this meeting. Do you guys have access to body armor?"

"Yeah, we brought our vests, but they say Chicago PD." He belatedly realized that it made no difference. His brain wasn't working. "She's tough. She can handle this," he added, trying to talk himself back into coherence, into *being a cop*. His thoughts went to Catharine, who wasn't as tough. She was a bit more frail and vulnerable than Kelly, as his ex had pretty much grown up on the streets of Chicago. "I have to call Cat. Make sure she's okay."

By the time Ryan was done ensuring that Catharine would lock all the windows and arm her security system, Di Santo had entered the room. Ryan ended the call and brought his partner up to date on Devin's chat conversation and Kelly's abduction. The three of them went back to Ryan and Di Santo's room to gather their vests, and then hailed a ride to the Stratosphere.

"Did you know that the Stratosphere is the only strip hotel that is technically in the city of Las Vegas?" Devin read from his phone. "And its tower is the tallest building west of the Mississippi. One thousand, one hundred and forty-nine feet tall."

"And we're going to be up on that? Outside?" Di Santo said, wiping a line of sweat from his brow. The body armor was not helping their body heat in Vegas's ninety-five degree weather, even with the cab's air conditioning blasting into the backseat.

"Is the Stratosphere tower higher than the Space Needle?" Ryan asked. The inane conversation calmed his nerves.

"Yes, almost twice the size."

"How big is the deck again?" Di Santo interjected. "And does it have safety bars like the Eiffel Tower?"

Devin continued to read from his phone, text scrolling at a rapid pace as he swiped up.

"Huh, it used to have a roller coaster at the top called the High Roller, but they removed that in 2005. And yes, there is a railing and—" He clicked the screen to display an image. "—it looks like the general public cannot get to the very edge. There is a maintenance walk around the outer periphery. But they do have the Sky Jump where people can pay to jump off of the tower."

"*What? Jump off of the tower?*" Di Santo screamed, at a decibel way too high for the taxicab.

"Controlled jump, of course, with a bungee."

"Since when are you scared of heights?" Ryan asked his partner. "You were all up in the Payton Arena catwalk a couple of months ago."

"Yeah, well, thirty feet is not a thousand, my friend. That's the difference between a broken leg and SPLAT!" Di Santo wiped his moist forehead with his sleeve again. He leaned forward to address the driver. "Could you turn up the air, please?"

After they exited the car, the three of them regrouped in the lobby of the Stratosphere. Just like every other casino on the strip, the colorful, ringing slots stood like soldiers on the front line, with one job only: to suck up the money.

"We're due up there in eleven minutes," Ryan said, checking his weapon. Di Santo did the same. "If they make any move to hurt Kelly, I'm drawing."

"Be careful," warned Devin. "He said he was going to be armed, and we don't know how many of them will show. If it's two against ten, then don't take the chance."

Di Santo spoke up. "Speaking of chances, what odds do you give us for coming down from that tower alive?"

Devin took the question very seriously, appearing to make the calculation in his head. "About eighty-five percent, I'd say. Look, I'll be just inside, pretending to be on my phone. They shouldn't be able to identify me, since I'm not a tactical member of the task force."

Ryan agreed with the plan and asked a security guard for directions to the tower. The three of them then proceeded up the main escalator, down the hallway of retail establishments, and then followed the signs to the main tourist attraction of the resort. They badged their way to the head of the line and had to walk in front of a green screen, where tourists would have an overpriced photo taken, superimposed onto the Stratosphere's view—strange, since the tourists were heading up to the *real* view. They were ushered through a line by one of the attraction's docents, who smiled and recited the tower's history. All of the statistics that Devin had just delivered in the car.

When the elevator doors opened, Ryan announced to the group of tourists, "Sorry, police business. You all will have to take the next one." The three stepped in and the elevator doors soon closed on the whines and complaints of the remaining tourists. "What are we going to do with the civilians on the observation deck?"

"Try to get them inside, I suppose," Devin responded. "I'll talk to security and get them to help us." He nodded to the Chicago badge on Ryan's body armor, implying that he had no jurisdiction here in Vegas. But Devin did, as a federal agent.

The doors opened on Level 108, and they stepped out to an indoor observation deck with floor-to-ceiling windows, framing an expansive view of the Las Vegas Strip. The sun had already begun to set, and streaks of orange and pink decorated the skyline. They followed the signs to a flight of stairs to Level 109. Two revolving doors flanked two frosted glass panel doors, with the words *871 Feet HIGH*. In the very center of those two doors was a yellow strip that instructed *NO SMOKING—NO GLASS* in big block letters.

Devin immediately separated himself from the detectives and headed off to the left. He approached the only visible security guard, a portly man who appeared to be on the greater side of seventy years. The detectives observed and scanned the surroundings while Devin convinced the guard to help him clear the deck and keep out the tourists for the next hour. Ryan was sure his brother had used the words "National Security" in there somewhere.

They watched as the tourists lined up to take the elevator, and when the deck was cleared, Ryan and Di Santo entered a revolving door and stepped outside. The view was impressive, especially with the neon signs starting to illuminate in the dusk. A low moon hung over the Eiffel Tower replica in the distance.

Ryan took out his cell and texted Devin.

– How will the ghost get up here if they're keeping all the tourists out?

– *Left word with the ticket taker to inform me of anyone insisting on coming up. I'll let you know when they're on their way.*

Ryan must have checked his watch seventeen times in the following seven minutes, with anxiety creeping in as the meeting drew closer. At exactly eight o'clock, he got a text from Devin.

– *They're here.*

Ryan took a deep breath, slightly amused at the *Poltergeist* reference. He'd known his brother for only two days, but he got the guy's intelligent yet dry sense of humor. He nodded to Di Santo, who stood about ten feet to his right, both facing the doors with their backs to the view, awaiting the appearance of The Ghost et al.

But it was Kelly who emerged first, with a gun to the back of her head. She stopped short just outside the doorframe, with her captor's arm behind her. The rest of the man was obscured by the frosted glass.

"Kel—"

"Ry—an…" She was weeping, with sobs in between the syllables of his name. But it wasn't the cry of grief or fear, as he'd seen every emotion Kelly had thrown at him in the seventeen years they had been together. These resembled her infamous "coercion tears," the kind she let loose when she wanted something. Easily discernible from the authentic type because these were accompanied with a jutted bottom lip and the trembling shoulders to evoke empathy. It made no sense, unless she was trying to convince her captor that she was more frightened than she really was.

Ryan unhooked the safety latch on his holster.

"He's not going to hurt you," Kelly called out. "He just wants to state his demands so you can take them to Ricci."

"Fine, if he lets you go."

Kelly shook her head. "No, he said he'll release me at the end. When he's done with the message." She had lost the shoulder-shaking and sobbing and was communicating particularly well for someone with a .45 at her head.

"Do you trust him, Kel? This is up to you."

She nodded. "Please, Ryan. Do what he says." She started to tear up again.

Ryan shouted to the man behind the door, "Okay, we're ready to listen. But you have to lower your weapon. No violence! We're here to talk."

Kelly was shoved out onto the deck, followed by a man in the same trench coat Ryan had seen in the speakeasy and the photo booth. His face was covered with a plain white plastic mask, the kind you could purchase in any costume or magic shop around town. He had one hand on the back of Kelly's neck while the other held the gun to her head. Ryan ran the man's personal stats through his head. He appeared to be about the same height as the guy in the bar, but the hair peeking out from the mask was lighter. Dirty blond.

"Who's the guy on the inside?" the man said. "I told you not to bring anyone." He shoved Kelly's head with the gun and Ryan wanted to jump and pound the guy to a pulp. But he took a breath, instead, and played contrite.

"I'm sorry, he's my brother. He's not—He's just protecting me. There's no one else. No one. I promise. Please, lower your weapon and I'll take that as a sign that you're serious about negotiating."

The man glanced at Di Santo, then back at Ryan for a long moment while Ryan continued to mentally record details about the masked man for Devin's chart. More data. He had slightly bowed legs, and wore a plain button-down shirt and jeans underneath the trench coat. But what was most recognizable was the Midwest Chicago twang in his voice. This guy was definitely from back home.

"Okay," the man said, coming back to life. He lowered his gun but kept a firm grip on Kelly's neck. "I want you to convey this to Richie Rich: I'm going to take over the North Side. Hear me? Lucky, there's now an opening. Leone's in jail, and the sister...well, she's been *digested*."

Ryan's stomach turned.

"What makes you think they're going to let you work a territory?" Di Santo said, inching closer to the conversation. "You are fuckin' enemy number one to the Outfit. You won't live twenty-four hours."

The man laughed a squealy, high-pitched laugh. "Oh, I think I'll survive. I've proven that I can get to anybody and anything. Their wives, their girlfriends, their sisters, their casino. Even your little ginger here," he said, shaking Kelly. She sobbed with the lurch. "Tell them that they will remain safe, their families will remain safe, and their business will remain safe—as long as they stay hands-off and allow The Ghost to run the North Side rackets. That's all. Easy-peasy."

"And why on earth do you think *we're* going to allow you set up shop in our district? On our watch?"

"Well, Detective Doherty, for one, you don't know who I am. And two, you need evidence in order to arrest anyone for any crime that I have—allegedly—perpetrated. And three, if I can hit the Outfit's families, just imagine how easily I could get to yours. Piece of cake."

Dusk was turning to dark on the deck, which had no lighting of its own intentionally so observers could appreciate the city's lights. Ryan had to forget the North Side for now. His number one priority was to protect his family and Catharine, and get Kelly released without injury.

"Okay. We'll relay the message. You're taking the North Side, and if they leave you alone, their loved ones are safe. *Our* loved ones are safe."

"Good job, Detective. That's all I want." The man backed up to the door, dragging Kelly back along with him. Ryan and Di Santo followed, keeping a safe distance. As they stepped into the lobby, the man replaced the gun barrel to Kelly's head until the elevator arrived. He stepped into the car and threw Kelly out at the very last second before the elevator doors closed behind her.

Kelly ran into Ryan's arms. "I'm so sorry, Ryan. I should have listened to you. I'm so sorry," she sobbed. He held her close, privately thanking their Irish-Catholic God that she was not harmed.

"It's okay. It's over now. He didn't hurt you, did he?"

"No," she said, pulling away. She wiped the remaining tears with the back of her hand. "No, I'm sure I'm just bruised." Ryan sat her down on a large stuffed banquette against the wall.

Devin appeared, speed walking around the periphery of the lobby. He began shouting at Kelly. "How did they abduct you? Did you see their faces? How many were there?"

She took a moment for a breath and then responded, "I was leaving my hotel and—and he just grabbed me. Shoved me into the back of a van and took off."

"Without any witnesses?" Ryan asked.

"I—I guess not. No one followed us. He had that mask on the whole time. I'm sorry, I was so scared…I'm not sure about all the details."

"How many were there?" Ryan asked her.

"How many? Just one, I think. That—that one guy. He gagged me, and then tied me up before we came over here. That's all I know."

Ryan was disappointed that his crew theory hadn't been validated. He inspected Kelly's wrists for ligature marks. There were none.

Devin squinted at her. "It's unusual that he didn't kill

you," he commented. "All the other women were murdered to make The Ghost's point. To send a message. I thought for sure they were going to execute you."

Kelly threw Devin a look like he was a species of alien life. Ryan moved in between them. "Don't mind him, he's—"

"Wait, you said this guy is your *brother?*" she asked, studying Devin. "But you don't have a brother."

"Long story," Ryan responded, grateful that the elevator finally made it back up.

When the four of them got down to the lobby, Devin left them to find the manager of security to view the Stratosphere's security video.

They decided that Di Santo had to be the one to relay The Ghost's message to Richie. "Tell him the instructions were delivered through the website," Ryan said. "Ricci would be super pissed if he found out we met with The Ghost and didn't give him a chance to put a bullet in his skull." Di Santo agreed, removed his body armor, and handed the vest to Ryan. He was soaked with sweat.

"Can I go now?" Kelly asked, when it was just the two of them left in front of a candy store. "I really want to take a shower and get that guy's smell off of me."

"No!" Ryan had barked so adamantly that she flinched. "You have to come to my room. Now."

CHAPTER 24

D on't touch anything," Ryan instructed, as he pulled Kelly into the original room that he shared with Di Santo. She sat down on the corner of a bed. "Stay still," he whispered and moved in to scrutinize her, tucking her hair behind her ear.

He went into Di Santo's black bag of wonders and pulled out a fingerprint card. Kneeling down in front of her, he pulled the sticky tape off of its backing and placed it on her neck, just under her ear lobe. He caught a whiff of Gucci Bamboo perfume, her signature scent, which prompted a flood of memories and emotions. They locked eyes for a moment before he went back to his task. He rubbed the tape with the edge of his palm and slowly lifted it from her skin. He held it up to the light and admired the print.

"We have at least three-quarters of a partial and another full one," Ryan told her, as he stood back up. "Let's just hope it's not yours." He replaced the tape onto the card and put the evidence into a manila envelope.

"Don't you need my prints, for elimination or something?" she asked him.

"I have them, remember? You let me roll them when I was training for detective. So they're in our system."

"Great. I'm in the system," she said with a smirk. Then, in an unexpected move, she reached out and took his hand.

"What happened to us, Ryan? How did it get so bad?"

"What happened to *us?*" he said, pulling away from her. "The way I remember it, *you* left *me*, Kel. At the time I needed you the most, you left me. My best friend had just died and I had to deal with it all by myself. By my fucking self."

Kelly paused and took a deep breath before responding. "You know our relationship had gone south way before then. We were fighting all the time. I wasn't happy, and neither were you. I guess I felt it was just time."

He started reliving it all over again. The worst week of his life. He recalled how she had told him that Jon died—she was pissed because she couldn't get a hold of him that night. He remembered how confused he had been was when she first broke the news—thinking that she was playing a cruel joke on him. Three days later, she'd said she was done. Done with the relationship, done with him, just *done*.

"We're done here," Ryan said. He walked to the door and held it open for her. "It's best not to rehash old stuff. If we couldn't work it out in two decades, then it can't be worked out."

Kelly took the cue and got up from the bed. "You know, I realized that I never said I was sorry," she said, pausing in front of him. "I'm sorry, Ryan, I really am. For losing Jon, for losing us. For leaving at such a bad time. But I want you to know that I'm thinking of moving back to Chicago, you know, my Dad's not doing too well. Alzheimer's."

"I'm sorry. I didn't know."

"So I'll be around and maybe we can hang out. Maybe we can be friends again. That's what was good about us, right? The friendship?"

Ryan had no feelings left for this person standing before him. "I don't think so, Kel. It's best we keep a clean break."

She nodded, placed a soft kiss on his cheek, and left. The phrase "Don't let the door hit you on the way out" ran through his head as he rushed to shut it, fighting the pneumatic hinge. He leaned against the door, shut his eyes, and rubbed them, scrubbing through the film of their tumultuous years together. Ever since elementary school, he'd been drawn to her wild red waves, perfectly befitting her wild, exuberant ways. She seemed to be a completely different person now, as subdued as her new brunette hair.

Ryan's detective gut suddenly stung with revelation. Up on the Stratosphere's deck, Kelly's abductor had called her a *ginger*.

Matt Di Santo knew he had to approach Ricci with caution. He was about to lie to one of the most powerful mob bosses in the history of Chicago. Not since Tony Accardo had anyone organized the Outfit so well. The crime families were not only making millions—possibly billions—a year, but Ricci had orchestrated it so the money all seemed to be earned by legitimate businesses. He wasn't just a goomba who grew up from the streets. Richie Rich was a well-educated financial wizard. And a ruthless killer.

Ricci informed him that a car would pick him up in The Chicago's valet stand at the front of the hotel. Before stepping out into the warm night air, Di Santo adjusted his tie and flapped his suit jacket, attempting to dry out the sweat-soaked shirt.

A black Town Car pulled up and Tootie got out, nodding at him through the glass doors of the hotel. Di Santo made his way through the turnstile and stopped short as Tootie opened the passenger door in front.

"Um, I think I'd feel more comfortable in back," he told the bodyguard. No way was he going to sit with his back to the number one gangster in Chicago. The big guy ducked his head in the car and got the permission he needed. He opened the door to the back seat and held out a palm. Di Santo climbed in next to Ricci while Tootie took shotgun, in front. Some guy he'd never met was driving. Oil-saturated hair, big honking scar down his right cheek, easily identified as an old knife wound.

Di Santo took a deep breath and said a silent prayer before the car started up. Ricci held his hand out to shake, dressed in full Italian pinstripe digs.

"Heya, Rich. We've got a message for you from The Ghost," Di Santo began, as the car pulled out of the turnaround.

"Yeah, yeah, so you said on the phone."

The driver pulled out of the drive and onto Las Vegas Boulevard. "So where are we going?" he asked.

"Just around," Ricci responded. "I don't want to take the chance of anyone listening, with all these fucking feds crawling around town like cockroaches. Which reminds me, you need to hand Toots your phone and take off your clothes."

"Take of my *clothes?* Why do I have to take off my clothes?"

"To make sure you're not wired. *Now!*" Di Santo did as Ricci instructed. Luckily the sedan's backseat was spacious enough for him to maneuver. When he got down to his blue boxers he asked, "Is this okay? Are we good?"

"Yeah, as long as you don't have anything up the wazoo," Ricci replied.

Tootie and the driver chuckled along with the boss's joke. Di Santo began to shiver from the car's air conditioning, or perhaps from the combination of that and his nerves. He could take Ricci's word on the stripping exercise being a wire check, or it could easily have been preparation for a burial. After the man inspected him up and down, he gave Di Santo the nod to redress.

"First off, Rich, I want to apologize for what happened earlier today," he said. "I was out of bounds. I made a huge mistake, and it was disrespectful. And I'd like you to know it will never happen again."

The man waved the air, dissipating the error. "Ahhh,

forget about it. What's done is done." He leaned forward on the edge of the car seat, waiting for the real news.

Di Santo hoped that the issue was really put to rest and that he wouldn't be. "So we spoke to The Ghost. *Online.*"

"And?"

"And, well, this isn't verified yet but we think it may be more than one guy we're dealing with. We have a theory that The Ghost might be a crew. A family." Ricci's eyes widened at the news, and he drew a deep breath. "We chatted with this guy on that underground web site—got him to talk a little—and he told us that the hits to your loved ones were made as an example of how they could get to you, Rich. Like you said, this guy can get in and out of everywhere. He's a sniper, he hacked into your slots, he can even friggin' fly a plane!"

"Fly a plane? Why the fuck do I care about someone who can fly a plane? Why would they tell you they could fly a plane?"

Shit. He wasn't supposed to have mentioned the plane.

"I—I don't know, Richie. Just to let us know that he can and will get to anyone. The murders were their way of saying that he could hit you where it hurts. Anytime. Anywhere."

"*Sonofabitch!*" Ricci gesticulated so madly that his seatbelt popped open. "I'll kill him! All of them! How dare they mess with the Outfit?"

"Richie, listen to me. There's more."

"There's more? How could there be more? What, does he want—to take me down or something? That will never happen! You hear me? Never! I'll beef up my guys, get more soldiers—"

"No, Rich. He doesn't want to take you down. He told us that he just wants control of the North Side. He wants to take over the Leone territory."

Ricci stopped ranting and took a moment to process the message. "The North Side, huh? And why would we give him the North Side?"

Di Santo kept an eye out the window, gauging their destination, as the driver hopped onto the highway. He knew the history of the mob in Vegas and that they did their hits in the desert.

He didn't want to end up a number in one of those statistics, so his best bet was to be truthful and to prove useful to the mobster.

"Well, my take is that he's pulling the protection racket on you. Seems kind of ironic, actually. But as long as you let him have the North Side, your loved ones—and your businesses—will remain safe. He'll stop the hits."

"That's what he said to you?" Ricci asked. Matt nodded. "So, do you believe this guy's on the up and up?"

"I don't know, Rich. We don't really know. We have no positive identity, and so there's no criminal history or rap sheet. But this is what we think you should do: accept his offer, officially, and then let the Chicago PD and the Federal Task Force do our jobs to take him down. Once we identify this guy, we're going to nail him for the homicides of your wife, Sandy Orlando, and Desirée Leone. I promise you."

Ricci finally leaned back on the leather seat and rebuckled his seatbelt. "Do your jobs, huh? You're asking us to leave this to the cops and the feds, then? Like, *cooperate* with yous?" He scrunched his face like someone had laid a stink.

"If you cooperate with us, we'll make The Ghost and his crew priority number one. You've got my word on this, Rich. And once we identify him, we'll let you know and, well, whatever you do with that information, I don't want to know. Catch my drift?" He slipped in a lie. They wouldn't let Ricci know the identities of the perp until after he was in custody.

The mob boss scratched his head, checked something on his cell phone, and then poked Tootie on the shoulder. "What do you think, Toots? You know this guy here. He good for his word or do I take him out?"

Di Santo's heart froze as the lights of the Las Vegas Strip faded into the distance.

"Just kidding! *'Uarda*, your face! Ha-ha-ha! I just pulled a Goodfellas on ya." Ricci continued the jibe as he slapped a knee. Di Santo chuckled, pretending to be amused while his heart tried to recover from the shock of impending death. "Tell you what we'll do. You can tell The Ghost that we fuckin' accept his offer. All's good. Then as soon as you've IDed him, you let us know. We'll take care of the rest."

Although Ricci had restated what Matt just said, he let the boss think it was his idea. "Okay, it's a deal, Rich. We'll get him. *Vi prometto.*"

The two shook hands, and Ricci pulled him in for a hug. "I knew you'd be good to us, Matteo. We did a good thing when we got you promoted. A good thing."

Di Santo's thoughts went back to Ricci's murder confession of Detective Jon Lange and he almost hurled right there in the car. The only thing that saved him was the driver finally taking an exit off of the freeway and into downtown Vegas.

"I'm taking you to the best Italian restaurant in town," Ricci said, picking up on his thoughts. "You did well, Matteo, and we need to celebrate with good food and wine! *Salud!*"

Di Santo had no choice. Other than being physically unable to escape, he had to break bread with this psychopath for the greater goal of their eventual collar. And that was when he realized he was already in too deep.

CHAPTER 25

The early evening sunset cast an amber glow throughout the atrium as Catharine finished clearing the dinner table. A buzz from the intercom sounded, someone calling from the front gate.

"Hank, can you see who that is?" she called to her son. Catharine took the dishes to the kitchen, rinsed them, and re-entered the atrium as Hank shouted back from the front of the house.

"Ma! It's Jane Steffen. She says she wants to talk to you."

After the confrontation earlier in the day, she was a bit shocked at the announcement. "Let her in," she said, as she smoothed her hair and removed her apron, placing it on a chair beside her. She made her way around the periphery of the atrium, turned the lights up, and arrived in the foyer as Hank was greeting the attorney at the front door.

"I'm Hank, Catharine's son," he cooed. "Wow, Ry told us how smart you were, but he never said you were gorgeous, too."

Jane beamed a wide smile, placed her briefcase on the floor, and shook his hand.

"Okay, Hank. That's enough," Catharine said, shooing him aside. She turned to Jane, "I'm sorry, he's an incorrigible flirt."

Hank retreated, backward, his attention still on Jane. "If you ever want to get lunch sometime—"

"Hank! Go!" Catharine commanded, shaking her head. The boy mouthed "call me" while signing it with his hand.

Jane laughed. "What a cutie," she said when Hank was out of earshot. "I bet he has no problems with the college girls."

"None," Catharine said, and then held out a welcoming palm toward her study. "Come, let's talk."

She led Jane to the east wing of the mansion. The last time they had both been in this room was when Catharine had given her deposition in the case against Todd Elliot. She shook off the sudden echo of the trauma and offered Jane a seat on the sofa, taking a chair to face her guest.

"I'm sorry it's so late," Jane began. "I just wanted to apologize for how I acted this morning. It wasn't a particularly good day, and I hadn't expected you." Even with the short pause, Catharine didn't reply, allowing Jane to state her business. "Well, anyway, I was extremely harsh this morning, and I regretted it after you left. You see, Ryan and I—we have a complicated friendship. And sometimes I just can't take his constant bullshit. Oh, sorry."

"Stop apologizing," Catharine responded. "I've heard worse. My rule about no profanity in the house was created mainly for my sons, to teach them respect and proper language skills. I can take a little bullshit here and there. After all, I'm dating a cop."

Jane displayed a wistful smile. "Yes. You are." She fumbled with a pearl ring on her right hand and then continued to speak. "So, this morning at my office when you were leaving and you said that thing about Paris? I thought that was your..." She waved her fingers at her temple. "...psychic thing. But then I went to check on my grant application and saw—"

"That I'm on the board of the Illinois Arts Council."

"Yes. And I'm here to ask you to recuse yourself from judging my application because you know me, and we have a personal history, and this is really important to me. I mean, between you and me, I'm just burnt out with making deals with these disgusting criminals who should be in prison the rest of their lives. I just need some time off. So that's why I applied for the Arts Council grant. I really need that half a year in Paris. And my plan was to set aside law for a while and just paint. Crazy, I know. But I thought I'd give it a shot."

Jane stopped to take a breath when Cat held up a palm.

"I would never let any personal relationship interfere with the Arts Council's decision."

"I know you say that but—"

"Jane. I cannot recuse myself."

"Why not?"

"Because the grants have already been made. They sent the response letters yesterday." The attorney's chest seemed to cave as she exhaled, staring at the floor. Catharine let her have a beat and then asked, "Would you still have apologized to me if the grant wasn't on the line?"

Jane nodded. "Yes. I felt like shit when you left my office. I mean, I wasn't really pissed at you, Catharine. My hostility was primarily aimed at Ryan. But since you came as his emissary, I took it out on you. And again, I apologize."

"Apology accepted. I realize you and I haven't exactly been close, but Ryan specifically asked me to do him this favor, and I saw it as an opportunity to practice getting out of the house."

Jane leaned back in her seat. "And you did well with that, as far as I could see. I'm happy for you."

Catharine smiled and took Jane's hand, searching for the truth. Jane flinched at first, but then relaxed, letting her have her moment. Catharine easily sensed Jane's pain when it came to Ryan: her deep affection for him as well as the unrequited desire.

"Ryan has never rejected you, Jane. He cares for you very much."

Jane blushed in response. "But sometimes he just dicks me around, you know? He plays me likes he plays all the other women on the job. In his life. He uses my feelings to get what he wants and that makes me...*irate*."

Catharine nodded in sympathy. "Yes, he can do that. Men want the best of both worlds, and Ryan, especially, thrives on female attention. It comes from being raised by a strong mother and three sisters. But he doesn't do it maliciously. In fact, he told me he never really had a female friend—*just* friend—until you, Jane. Not only does he care about you personally, but also he admires your intelligence and your work. He once said the two of you were like *Law & Order*. He's the law, you're the order."

Jane smirked, her antagonism slowly dissipating.

"Instead of concentrating on what you don't have with Ryan, you should concentrate on what you do have: a friend who will always give you the truth and support you when you need him. There are very few people he lets in, but once he does, he's as protective and loyal as anyone can be. I know because he's like that to me, my sons, to Jon, to Matt, and to you, Jane. And that's a pretty great friend to have."

"I know," she said, pulling her hand out from Cat's grasp. "I think I just need to get out of Chicago for a while—whether it's Paris or Mexico or the North Pole or wherever I end up." She lifted herself from the sofa and turned to leave, indicating that the visit was over.

As they arrived back in the front foyer, Catharine stopped Jane before she left and insisted on a hug. "*Ne vous inquiétez pas*," Catharine told her. "*Il sera Paris*."

Jane gasped, her eyes tearing with the news. "Oh, my god! Really? I got the grant?"

Cat nodded. "You don't know this until tomorrow, though."

"Thank you so much!" Jane gave her a hug back, more heartfelt this time, with gratitude.

"It was a wonderful proposal, Jane, and I wish you the best. Enjoy your six months in France. And please...keep in touch." She closed the door behind the attorney and heard her Lexus exit the gate.

While she wouldn't have acknowledged it aloud, there might have been a slight personal sway in her vote to send Jane away to Paris. After all, the woman got to share a world with Ryan that she couldn't. As evolved and compassionate as Cat tried to be, she was still human.

She couldn't help the words that emerged softly on her lips: "One down."

CHAPTER 26

When flying from west to east, you could count on almost a full day of travel with the time change. The detectives and Devin had headed out of Vegas on an 8:30 a.m. flight, and by the time Ryan pulled into the turnaround at the Catharine's estate, it was 3:10 in the afternoon. He was happy to be home. In the real Chicago, without Capone gazing down at him from every angle.

He parked Baby Blue, jogged up the marble steps, let himself in with his key, and called Cat's name. He was eager to see her, smell her, and hold her. With no response, he headed toward the atrium, but it too was empty. Classical music wafted faintly from the west wing, so utilizing his heightened sense of deduction, he headed toward Catharine's dance studio.

The door stood slightly ajar and he watched his woman move across the dance floor, making graceful art out of the movement of her petite body. Her long waves of brown hair billowed out behind her, as she preferred not to bind it while dancing. Even though he enjoyed watching the performance, he had to touch her, so he entered the studio without warning and swept her off her toe shoes. Catharine shrieked with a combination of surprise and glee, wrapping her arms around his neck. Ryan kissed her boldly before setting her feet back on the ground.

"How's life in Catville?" he asked. He'd recently coined the term for Catharine's world, so different than his own. Soon they were to merge.

She inhaled deeply and let out a heavy sigh.

"Uh, oh. That bad?"

"That *complicated*," she said, pulling aside the collar of his button down shirt and placing a small kiss on his chest.

That did it. He lifted her tiny ass up onto the barre and reached under her ballet skirt, while running his lips up the side of her neck to just under her earlobe. She mewed her pleasure.

"Right here," he said.

"But—" Cat moaned outright.

Someone cleared a throat at the studio door. "Hey, you two! Sorry to interrupt."

Ryan jumped back at the voice and turned to see Lisa, Catharine's naturalist, addressing them with a blush and a wide smile.

"Hey, Cat, just wanted to let you know I'm heading out. I had to pull some of the zinnias, as they were not surviving."

Catharine hopped off of the barre without shame and smoothed her skirt. "Thank you, Lis'. See you on Friday?"

"Yes indeedy! Did you tell him about 'you-know-who' yet?" Lisa loved gossip and often inserted her opinion in the middle of their affairs.

"Who?" Ryan asked, his gaze bouncing between the two women.

"No, I haven't. He just got home."

"Oh, right. Okay! Then have at it, you guys. See you in a couple of days." Lisa waved as she closed the door behind her, leaving the question lingering.

Cat sighed again. "Come on, let's have tea in the atrium, and I'll tell you what's been going on here while you were away."

"So are you telling me the mood has been killed?"

"Most definitely. Plus the boys are due home soon. We

don't want a repeat of the atrium incident!" Catharine went on tiptoes, kissed him lightly on the nose, and said, "Rain check."

Ryan huffed in mock frustration as she took his hand and led him out into the gardens where a tray of tea already sat on the long wooden table. He sat down, but before Catharine could take her own chair, he pulled her onto his lap. "I'm not letting you go."

She smiled and nestled up to him, accepting several more ardent kisses before their conversation began.

"I spoke to Jane. Twice, actually," Cat said, re-buttoning the button on his shirt. Ryan lifted his brows in inquiry. "The first time didn't go so well, but she came over last night and we had a longer conversation. She says she's tired of the criminal element. Of her job, you see."

"And?"

"She's going to Paris for six months to study her art."

"*What?*" Ryan let out a guffaw, thinking Cat was pranking him. "No, really, what's going on with her?"

"*Really.* She received a grant from the Illinois Arts Council, of which I'm on the board. I'd seen her application come through, but didn't want to reveal it to either of you before the decisions had been made. Jane needs this. She needs to regroup, go away for a while, and bask in her art. Did you know she was an art major before she studied law?"

Ryan was completely blown away by the news. Discombobulated. "Yeah, yeah. I saw some of it in her place. Not bad. But what do I know? So she's going away for a half a year? But what about her job at the SA's office?"

"I didn't ask."

"Wow. I didn't see that coming. So is that why she won't talk to me? She's worried that I'd discourage her or tease her or something?"

"Something," Catharine replied cryptically. "I think it's best to just let her do her thing and she'll reconnect with you when she's ready."

Ryan nodded as he gazed past his love and into her lovely gardens, not knowing what to feel. A bit abandoned, a bit offended that Jane hadn't confided any of this to him. That she was leaving without so much as a goodbye. He thought they were closer than that.

"And there's more."

"More about Jane?"

"No, about the boys. Me. You." Catharine got up from his lap. Her joy had dimmed. She took a deep breath as if she were about to break bad news. "The boys have to choose their major by December."

"Okay..."

"They told me that they want to be police officers," she said, her lower lip jutting out in disapproval.

Catharine's somber delivery of the news couldn't keep the grin off of Ryan's face. He couldn't have been more proud than if she had said the twins were biologically his.

"Really? Seriously? They want to be cops? *Both* of them?" A tear on Catharine's cheek stifled his immense pride. He stood up and went to her. "What? It's a compliment, Cat, a huge compliment! Why are you sad about this?"

"I won't be able to take it, Ryan. The three of you? The three people I love the most in my life—other than my dad, of course—out in the streets, risking their lives every day? How can you be happy about this? These are my babies, Ryan! And you, running after these horrible, horrible gangsters. I know you were in a shootout, I could see it in my mind's eye. I could see the guns and hear the pops! You risked your life in Las Vegas. And something happened in an airplane, I couldn't quite figure that out, but I know you were in danger. You never even told me about that. And then you drive that death trap of a car. It doesn't even have even air bags or proper seat belts or—"

"Wait, ho-ho-ho-hold on here." He took the babbling Cat into his arms and squeezed her shaking form for security. "How did this become about my car, now?"

"It's not about your car. I mean, not *just* about your car. It's everything, all together. Ryan, please don't let them be cops." She sobbed into the crook of his arm as he cooed and comforted her, sat her down in a chair, and pulled another close to her side.

"You should talk to my mom," he said quietly, wiping several wet strands of hair from her face. "We went through this exact same thing when I said I was considering enrollment in the police academy. She screamed, she cried. My dad, though, he was so proud—it was a couple months before he died. 'You see what you did to your father?' my mom told me when he had his heart attack." Ryan squeezed his eyes shut, recalling the pain. "Yeah, she actually said that. She outwardly blamed me for his death."

"Oh, Ryan. You never told me."

"Because I didn't really believe it. She didn't truly blame me. What she was trying to do was guilt me into changing my mind. It's a Catholic thing."

"Horrible."

"Maybe. But I understood she was just trying to protect me. She's my mom, and no mama wants to see their child in danger." That statement made Catharine shed another wave of tears. "Hey, hey. But look at me. I'm here, aren't I? Most of the time, I'm doing paperwork and looking things up on the computer. And when it's slow, I post selfies on Facebook. Tough job, but someone's gotta do it." He lifted her chin as Catharine attempted an obligatory smile. "And do you know why I'm still here? Because I'm a good cop. I'm trained, I take precautions, I wear my body armor, I practice at the range, and I know what I'm doing. Besko made sure of that, and he made a promise to *my* mom that he'd do his best to keep me safe by making me a good cop."

Catharine pulled a tissue out of somewhere and dabbed her nose. "Did that assuage her fears?"

"Of course not, but it did make her feel a little better. And I'll make that same promise to you. Those boys won't go anywhere or do anything in the Department without my knowledge and I'll make sure every FTO—field training officer—knows I'm watching."

"They still have three years to change their minds."

"Yes, they do. It's a huge decision to make. But you know what, Mama? It's their decision to make, and that's the hardest part about having grown kids."

Catharine smirked. "How do *you* know that?"

"Because I am one. A grown kid, that is. And I'm pretty smart, for a cop." He ran his fingers through her hair to calm her, relieved that she had stopped bawling.

"Will you take me to the ball? There's a ball," Catharine said, and pointed to a brightly-colored invitation in the middle of the table.

It was an odd non sequitur, but Ryan welcomed a way to distract Cat from her pain. He reached for the card and read it. "The Astor Ball. I've heard of that. Hoity-toity stuff at the Art Institute?"

"Yes, it's in two weeks. I think I might want to try going."

"I don't know, Cat. There will be hundreds of people there. I'm not sure you're ready for this big an event." He read the rest of the invite. "Black tie, huh? I'm not really a tux kinda person, you know that. I don't even own one."

Her pleading doe eyes could have rivaled Bambi's. *Dammit.*

Catharine's mood shifted as she became more animated. "Both the boys have tuxes, and I bet Duke's would fit you!"

"Okay, okay. Let me think about it."

"We could hire a car. And if, at any point, I felt I needed to leave, we could just go."

He squinted one detective eye at her. "You've already bought the tickets, haven't you?"

"I need to challenge myself. I need to get better," she answered, those blue eyes batting. "At least, that's what you told me..."

He realized he had no choice in the matter. He was going to the Astor Ball.

CHAPTER 27

Ryan and Di Santo met in the parking lot of the 18th District house the next morning. They greeted the desk sergeant and alighted the main steps together to the second floor.

"Your brother's here," Firenzo called out to the entire North Side.

"Great," Ryan mumbled under his breath. "I bet the entire force knows my private business."

Di Santo hit him on the arm. "He's not a totally bad guy. I mean, a little robotic at times, but you coulda done worse for a brother. I don't know what I'd do if I found out I had a brother. I guess you're the closest thing I have to one."

Ryan ignored the bonding attempt and burst through the double doors of the squad, ready to hunt down The Ghost. It sounded ridiculously cartoonish, like an episode of Scooby-Doo, but this story wouldn't end up with a quick arrest of the "mysterious innkeeper." If it was a crew, these were dangerous dudes with homicidal tendencies and military grade weapons.

Ryan noticed that Devin had completely taken over his desk, his laptop open on the right and papers and file folders on the left. "What's the haps?" he asked his new brother. "Are we having a task force meeting today?" Ryan put his own laptop case down by the side of his occupied desk.

"Good morning," Devin replied, taking a sip of coffee out of Ryan's homicide mug. "And no. I spoke with Jensen this morning. Now that they've got Joey Giordano turned, they're going to concentrate on working him back into the Outfit. They officially loaned me to you as a liaison to work The Ghost case."

Ryan didn't know if he was offended or relieved. He'd gotten used to being part of a team of ten—with eight feds at his disposal—and now it was down to just the three of them.

At least Devin still had the NSA resources for research purposes.

"*Triple-D! My office!*" Besko's voice rang out from the back of the squad. Ryan pulled out the case folder and a spiral notebook from his bag and headed back, with Di Santo and Devin following.

They swapped notes on the Vegas trip. Besko had already spoken with Agent Jensen, who'd brought him up to speed on the case, up and until the Stratosphere confrontation. Ryan filled him in on the rest.

"The guy held Kelly Riordan as a hostage," Ryan reported without revealing any residual emotion brought on by his ex. "Masked and armed, the perpetrator ordered us to present an ultimatum to the Outfit. To Ricci. His intention is to move in on the North Side. Our territory. He wants the rackets that were left open by the Leone family."

Besko rubbed his chin. "And?"

Ryan nodded to Di Santo to continue. "I relayed the message to Richie," Di Santo stated. "He wasn't happy with it, but they know The Ghost has them by the shorts. So they're complying. For now."

"I thought about it last night, Sarge," Ryan picked up. "And I think we need to wait for him to make the next move. We can't arrest this guy without evidence or it won't stick. We don't know his identity, although I am going to try to run prints from Kel—Ms. Riordan's neck, where he held her. I think we should put a BOLO on the street for any kind of new racketeering activities: street loans, protection extortion, anything."

"Maybe we should canvas the storefronts," Di Santo added.

The sarge appeared intrigued. "For what?"

"You know, the high-profit businesses: cars, bars, jewelry. Those are the kind of businesses the Outfit is likely to muscle in on. Hell, even the corner dry cleaner. If it's profitable, they'll want a cut. We can take a box of our cards and just pass them out."

"Why d'ya look so cynical, Doherty?"

"I'm not sure that's a good idea, Sarge. It may scare The Ghost off and then he's likely to lay low. And would the proprietors really tell us what's going on? From what Matt told me, these guys threaten their business, their families, and their lives. No one's going to take the chance that the next time they start their car, *kablam!*" Ryan mimed an explosion with his hands.

Besko leaned back in his seat. "I tend to agree with Doherty here. We need The Ghost to move in, so we can build a case against him. At least identify the motherfucker." Devin shifted at the squad room vocabulary. "Fed, what do you think?"

Devin put a hand to his chest. "*Me?*"

"I don't see any other fed in this room, Agent Doherty."

"I think we need to review all of the data that we collected from our Nevada investigation. There are quite a lot of data points that I can enter into the chart to help identify this man—or group of men. Ryan is correct that we should set a watch sheet for patrols to ascertain any new criminal activity in the area, especially that which looks like it could be part of an organized crime unit. As soon as we start seeing that activity, we move in."

Sarge slapped his desk and all three of them jumped. "Then that's the plan! No handing out cards, Di Santo, but talk to the uniformed officers and be on the lookout."

"Yes, sir," he agreed, and the three of them left the sarge's office to regroup at the desk pod.

In the next couple of days, several of the print results came through. The prints from Kelly's neck matched her own, on file. No prints on the tricycle at the Ricci scene. Nor were there any other prints in the condo other than Desirée and Danny Leone's. The Ghost took precautions.

Ryan made sure he spoke personally with every patrol at the 18th, on every shift. He explained the gravity of finding this perp and how he was wanted for a string of homicides—women and innocents—despite the victims' connection to organized crime. Although technically the Leones' area covered the entire North Side up to the Evanston border, the most lucrative high-end businesses were located right in their district, Lincoln Park.

Eight days after they'd returned from Vegas, Officer Ann Waleski came into the detective squad with a lead.

"*Doherty!*" she called out, less than two feet from his desk. "I think I got something that fits your extortion model." She sauntered up like a cowgirl who had just roped a calf and laid a pink phone slip down in front of him. "We got a call from Jeweler's Mutual Insurance Company about a theft over at Geitz Brothers Jewelry on Clybourne."

"A robbery?"

"Well, that's the thing. The insurance company called us for the police report, but there was none. Zippo. The Geitz Brothers apparently didn't file one. But they certainly made sure to file an insurance claim."

"That's strange," Ryan said. "Why do you think that's related to the mob?"

Di Santo jumped up from his chair. "It's the typical protection racket. Instead of the store owner giving the Outfit cash, they give merchandise, then file a claim of theft. The mob sells the loot, the store gets the insurance settlement, it's a win-win situation."

The six-foot patrol touched her nose. "Bingo! This is a fairly new retail shop. Moved in from Northbrook a coupla months ago. The way I see it, they made the deal with the mob, got nervous and forgot to file the police report."

"They were so focused on getting reimbursed by the insurance company?" Ryan asked.

"Bingo!" Waleski said again. "I've seen it happen before. Something in the back of their heads get them all nervous about contacting the police, 'cause they know deep down that they're participating in an illegal act."

Doherty thanked Waleski and gathered his gun and shield. "D, let's you and I go down to that jewelry store."

Throughout the week, certain details had bugged him about the meeting on the Stratosphere deck. For one, the guy was shorter than the man Ryan had chased at the speakeasy.

And then there was the ginger thing, nagging at the back of his mind for a week. And how did Kelly just happen to be in Vegas and manage to have drinks with the perp? Something was off.

On the way out of the station, he took out his cell and called Devin. "Could you do some background searches on Kelly Riordan?" he asked the agent. "Past six months. I don't know the extent of your capabilities, but phone records and credit card purchases would be great."

"With no warrant?" Di Santo asked, in that loud stage whisper of his.

Ryan nodded to his partner as Devin responded, "On it."

Di Santo at least waited until they were in the sedan and rolling until he started his interrogation. "D, what the hell are you doing with the Kelly background?"

"I'm going on a hunch. I think she may be involved."

"You think Kelly's in on this? *Your* Kelly?"

"She's not my Kelly."

"Seriously, D? I mean, because you're kinda too close to her to be making that assumption. I hope this isn't coming from a place of emotion—"

"When we were up on the Stratosphere, The Ghost called her a 'ginger.' He said 'We can get to anyone, even your little ginger, here.' Why would he call her that unless he knew she had red hair?"

Di Santo thought for a moment. "Maybe he did his research, found old pictures of you two online."

"This has been bothering me since we got back from Vegas. Things just aren't adding up. Like it seemed just too convenient that Kelly was there in Vegas when we were. She told me she was in town for ComTech, but I never saw a badge around her neck, did you?" Di Santo shook his head, frowning. "Every one of those conference people had badges. Then, I happen to catch her having drinks with The Ghost. What the fuck was that? And then later she tells me she's thinking of moving back to Chicago. I have no idea what's going on, but my cop radar's going off into the red, so I have to listen to it."

"So what are you thinking we'll get from her phone records?"

"I don't know, D. I'm just digging," Ryan said as he turned onto Clybourne. He slowed the car as they approached the jewelry store, scoping for a parking space. "I just want to see what she's up to."

"You promise it ain't personal?"

"I promise. I have no interest in that anymore."

He parked the Impala about a half a block down from Geitz Brothers Fine Jewelry. The shop had a double-security entrance, with an iron door on the outside and a small vestibule with a second door that led into the shop. Ryan knocked on the door with his badge to get the attention of an older man behind a glass case. The man jumped, reached under a desk, and buzzed them in.

As they entered the shop itself, Ryan took in the details of the establishment. A horseshoe of display cases held multi-colored sparkling pieces. The case on the left was filled entirely with diamond engagement sets. A significant notice on the wall stated that everything in the shop was under video surveillance.

"How can I help you gentlemen?" the man said.

Ryan introduced himself and Di Santo. "Do you own this store?"

The man appeared to be in his early-to-mid-seventies, in shirtsleeves and dress pants which were buckled to the north of his waistline. "I do, I do. I'm Shmuel Geitz and I own the store with my brother, he's in the back. *Harry!*"

Another man came out of a curtained doorway, appearing older than Shmuel. He took some time shuffling from the doorway to a spot beside his brother, a distance of only about two feet.

"We're investigating a robbery that you reported to your insurance company?" Ryan inquired. "They called our department and it appears that you failed to file a police report."

Shmuel Geitz opened the glass case from the rear and pulled out a gold watch, then proceeded to polish the dome. "I—I—was sure we had. Harry? Didn't you file that report?"

Harry Geitz looked like he had given up on life a couple of years ago. It would be a miracle if he could change his own adult diaper without assistance. "Huh? Why would we file a police report?"

"On that robbery last week, Har'. With that guy? Remember? I thought you were going to file the report." Poor Harry had no clue that Shmuel was attempting to place the negligence on him.

"Oh, oh, oh. That hoodlum in the mask. You shouldn't have buzzed him in, Shmuley, I told you not to let weirdoes into the store. Nope. Now we're out the cost of that necklace. That was a lot of diamonds, let me tell you. And emeralds, too!" The man hobbled over to a chair in the corner and took seventeen seconds to lower himself into it.

"He was in a mask? Can you tell me how many there were? Were they armed?" Ryan took out his notebook and poised a pen.

"There was just one guy…in a white mask. The kind adults wear for Halloween."

"Why *did* you let him in?"

"He had a big gun! Heavy duty artillery, like what I saw overseas during my service. He threatened to blow the doors in. I had to let him in."

Ryan glanced over at Harry for confirmation, but he had since drifted off into naptime. "Your brother said he took a necklace?"

Shmuel shook his head and clasped his hands in the prayer position. "One of our most expensive pieces. Forty-one carats of emeralds, ten-point-two of diamonds. Priced at eighty-four thousand dollars, retail." He hobbled to the desk and picked up a printed photograph, walked it back over to them, and placed it on the glass case. "Here. This is what I sent to the insurance company."

"They only took this one piece?"

"Yes, yes. Only this. I—I—well, that's all he wanted."

"Where was the necklace displayed in the store?" Di Santo asked.

"Oh, it wasn't on display. We keep it in our safe, usually, unless people ask to see something on the more expensive side."

Ryan ruminated on that detail. "Did he promise you protection or safety or anything in return?"

The man was visibly shaken by the question, puttering around to polish anything within arm's reach. "I don't remember, honestly. Everything is all jumbled up. Right, Harry?" He glanced at his brother, who had started to snore at this point. "We don't remember that well. We're old. It's fuzzy."

"How did the man know about the necklace if it wasn't on display?"

Geitz shrugged.

Di Santo stepped up to the case and addressed the man. "Mr. Geitz, if you were threatened or promised protection for yourself or your store in exchange for the necklace, that is extortion. This guy is extremely dangerous and we're working to get him behind bars. Any information you or your brother remember could really help us do that."

"I'm sorry, gentlemen, but we have family. Kids. Grand-kids! Therefore, we don't remember anything."

Ryan glanced up into the corner of the room. The video camera's lens stared back at him with a pinpoint red light underneath. "I'd like to see your video. Of the robbery, and of every customer interaction from the last two weeks. Someone must've come into the store previously to case it, and to know that you had the necklace in the safe."

"Oh, we don't keep video that far back. We review it every twenty-four hours and then record over it."

"And the insurance company allows that?"

"Yes, that meets their standard requirements. As long as the tape is reviewed by one of the owners. That would be us."

"Do you have the footage of the robbery at least?"

"Yes, on VHS tape. We sent that to the insurance com-pany."

Ryan sighed and massaged his temples with one hand. "Okay, then, had anyone asked to *see* the necklace in the last few weeks, prior to the robbery?"

"Oh, yes, yes. With the big ball coming up, I've shown it to several women looking to rent it for the event. Maybe two or three, even."

"The Astor Ball? At the Art Institute?" Ryan asked, as he started flipping through old photos on his phone.

"That's it! The Astor Ball. The biggest event in town. Tomorrow night! I went several times with my wife, in our younger days. It's a very good cause, The Children's Hospi-tal. And a very exciting event. I heard Oprah might be there this year!"

Ryan finally found a picture of Kelly from a hike up in Door County. "Is this one of the women who asked to see the necklace?"

Shmuel held up a finger and took his time grabbing a pair of reading glasses. He almost poked his eye out ma-neuvering them onto his nose. Angling his head back to glance through the lenses, he finally replied. "No, no. I don't recognize her."

"Could be the hair," Di Santo interjected.

Ryan kicked himself for not getting a picture of Kelly with her new brunette hair. Then he remembered she had dressed up as Xena, Warrior Princess one Halloween. McGinty's had a costume contest every year and they'd gone as Xena and Hercules. He swiped his phone with fervor until he went back to his archives and found photos of Kelly in the long black wig.

"Gotcha!" he exclaimed to no one, then turned the phone back around for the man. "What about this woman?"

"Hmmm…yes, yes, that could have been one of them. I don't know, really, my eyes sometimes fail me. But her eyes look familiar. Those pretty green eyes."

Ryan and Di Santo exchanged a look, with Di Santo's being more cautionary. "Okay, Mr. Geitz, I'll file the incident, but you'll have to come down to the station to make a formal report and to sign it. Until then, the insurance company will not be able to settle your claim."

Harry woke up with a snort and said, "Necklace! The man in a mask took a necklace. His name was Jake."

"Sir?" Di Santo said, writing down the name.

"When he was leaving the store, he got a call on his phone. He was out in the vestibule by that time, but I heard him. He answered it, 'This is Jake.' Or Jay. Something like that."

Shmuel waved a hand in the direction of his brother's ranting, obviously perturbed at the outburst. "He didn't hear anything. My brother is deaf as a doornail. There was no Jake. No Jake."

"My hearing is perfect, you schmuck. You don't know what you're talking about," Harry shot back. They were brothers, all right. Ryan tried to imagine himself and Devin at this age, bickering. He couldn't.

"Thank you, sir, that's really helpful," he said to the man in the corner. "If either of you remember anything else, please don't hesitate to call us." He left a card on the counter and the two detectives made their way back to the sedan. After both car doors shut, Ryan sat motionless, staring at the wheel.

"That's not really a positive ID, Ry." Di Santo said, noticing his discomfort. "You know that eyewitness testimony is greatly unreliable, and then add that to the fact that those guys were like a hundred years old. It could have been any woman with brown hair and green eyes." After a beat, Ryan started the car without a response. "Where are we going now? Back to the station?"

"No. We're going to the Riordans. Kelly's dad still lives in the same house where she grew up. I need to find out where her brother is."

"Kelly's brother? Why?"

"His name is Jake."

"There's no such thing as good money or bad money.
There's just money."
~ *Charles "Lucky" Luciano*

CHAPTER 28

Halloween, Five Years Ago:

I'm not going in that clunker of a car of yours," Kelly
said, as she adjusted her long black Xena wig. "It's em-
barrassing."

She just didn't know classic cars. "Baby Blue is a collec-
tor's item," Ryan responded as he adjusted his Hercules
cuffs. "You don't even have any idea what it's worth."

"Yes I do, about ten grand in that condition. I looked it
up." She had him on that one. As much as he tried to keep
the old girl running, the '66 Mustang he'd had since he was
a teenager wasn't in the best of shape. Especially the interi-
or, which was in desperate need of a full reupholster. "You
really need to dump it, Ryan. I think we need a Jaguar.
We'd look great in a Jaguar, don't you think?"

"I'm never going to dump it. I'll dump you before I
dump Baby Blue," he teased, coming up behind her.

He kissed her neck, extremely attracted to his woman in
the black breastplate. He was looking forward to a potential
role-play later on.

"Stop it!" Kelly squirmed out of his embrace. "I just got
the wig on straight. Now I have to do my makeup and I'll be
ready to go. Half-hour at the most, okay?"

He agreed to keep his hands off of her, for now.

The Hercules costume was pretty simple to put together, since he was already wearing his hair a little longer. He only had to procure a cut-off burlap top, some leather wrist plates, and a fake sword. Ryan was super-vigilant about hitting the gym lately, and the low-plunging V of the neckline showed off his proudly cut six-pack abs.

McGinty's was as rowdy as every other Halloween that had come before it, from the thumping bass of the DJ's sound system to the beer mugs flying across the bar. The law officer inside of him kept alerting that there were way too many people in the establishment—probably breaking fire code—but he stifled that voice to have a good time.

They found Jon and his date at a small round table to the right of the bar. Two chairs sat empty, reserved for them.

"My brotha!" his partner greeted him, playing the part of his costume. He was dressed as an authentic bell-bottomed Shaft, complete with an afro that took up a third of the bar. He slid the big seventies sunglasses halfway down his nose to take in their costumes.

"Super groovalicious, Dude," Ryan said, giving him a warm pat on the shoulder. He glanced at Jon's date, waiting for an introduction. A beautiful statuesque black woman stood to his partner's right, in orange bellbottoms and a halter top.

"Oh, sorry. Ryan, Kelly, this is Foxy Brown." Then to his date, "Iris, baby, this is the beautiful Kelly as Xena, and the illustrious Detective Ryan Doherty, my partner in crime-fighting."

Ryan took the woman's hand and kissed it, partly to match the chivalry of the sword he was carrying and partly to piss Jon off. The two detectives had had a long-standing bar rivalry on who could attract the most women.

"My lady," he said, keeping in character. "I am Hercules. Ready to fight crime with Shaft, here. Despite the difference in decade." Kelly rolled her eyes as Jon took her into his big arms for a hug. "Now where's the booze?"

Throughout the night, Ryan's abs drew the women in,

several offering to buy him drinks, several asking him to buy them drinks, completely disregarding the warrior princess beside him. As a city servant, he was trained to be accommodating to everyone, and the more he socialized, the darker Kelly had become. He attributed it to her not being able to imbibe, as she'd offered to be the designated driver.

At one point she stormed off to the bathroom and was gone for twenty-one minutes. Ryan made apologies to the table and eventually followed, knocking on the women's room door.

"Kel? You in there? You okay?" he said, inching the door open as not to embarrass any females inside.

"Oh, *now* you remember you came to the party with a date?"

"Kelly, please. Don't freak out. I'm just having a good time. It's a party!" She finally appeared, brushing past him and into the bar. When he caught up with her, she was standing at the coat check waving the ticket. "What, you're leaving? Already? They haven't even announced the winners."

"I have a headache. I might stop by Dave's party, this place is just a little too…crowded."

"Okay, we can go to Dave's. Hold up. Let me tell Jon we're leaving and I'll come with you."

"Whatever."

He never knew what to do when Kelly was in one of her moods. Any attempt to cheer her up would take the opposite effect. He made more apologies to Jon and his date, gave him a wink and thumbs-up for landing such a beauty, and met Kelly outside at the valet stand. They stood silently, waiting in the chilled October air until her Toyota rounded the corner and pulled up to the curb. Kelly tipped the valet, got behind the wheel, and waited all of three seconds before starting in on him.

"Whatever happened to the sergeant's exam? Wasn't that a couple of weeks ago?"

"What do you mean, 'what happened?'"

"Did you take it?"

"No, I told you, I have no interest in being a sergeant right now. I just made detective a year ago, and now I'm working on getting promoted to first grade."

"But wouldn't becoming a sergeant come with a big bump in salary?"

"And five times the paperwork. I don't want to be stuck behind a desk."

"Sergeant Besko gets out onto the street...when there's a big case."

"But most of the time he's writing reports and attending meetings with the lieus. That's not me. I'm not a politics-playing managerial type, you know that. It would drive me crazy." He let it hang for a while in the car while she drove. "And where's this all coming from, anyway? Why are you so interested in the sergeant's exam all of a sudden?"

"It's like you don't even care about advancing. About initiative. Are you going to stay a detective the rest of your life?"

"Maybe. What's wrong with that? I love investigation." Kelly *hmmmed* as she took a corner a little too fast. "Slow down, Kel, will you? There are drunk drivers out tonight."

"It's just that you've been in that miniscule apartment for how many years now, and if we're going to live together, we're going to need a nicer place. In a nicer neighborhood."

"If we're going to move in together, you're moving into my place. I like it. It's convenient. And I'm not paying thousands of dollars for a rental. You know I have to live in the city and I'm saving my money for a down payment on a house someday."

"A house in the *city*. Great."

"What's wrong with a house in the city?"

"It's just so...down-market. Ry, my family has struggled with money most of my life. At times we were months behind on the mortgage and one step away from being homeless. I swore to myself that I wasn't going to live like that. I want a condo on Lake Shore Drive. A boat in the marina. I want to have so much money at my disposal, I don't even have to think about the bills."

"I know, I know. I've heard that speech before. So if you don't want to be married to a cop, leave."

"*Married?* Who said anything about getting married? Are you asking me to marry you?"

"No. Most definitely not. I'm just looking down the line. If you want some multi-million-dollar future, you're dating the wrong guy."

She reached out and took his hand. "I want you, Ryan. We've been together since we were teenagers, friends since we were kids. We're meant for each other. I just want us to have the best life possible."

"Then you're going to have to be the breadwinner, Kel, because I'm a detective. And I have no plans on becoming anything else in the near future. Not a sergeant, not a boat captain, not Hugh Hefner."

"Maybe I will, then," Kelly said, braking hard at a stoplight. "After all, I paid enough for my MBA. It's time my degree starts paying me back."

CHAPTER 29

Current Day:

The Riordan family home was located in Ryan's old neighborhood on the northwest side of Chicago. Although the area was more progressive and liberal than Canaryville, it had remained just as Irish, even to this day. A semi-safe, family-oriented neighborhood, with children playing unsupervised in the front yards, staying out until the bells of St. James rang six times for dinner. His mind went back to high school when he strained to recall the street hoodlums Jake used to hang with: Iggy...something, Davey Tewes, and Patrick O'Hara. They were low-level thugs who did more than steal lunch money, but less than homicide. He made a mental note to have Devin check them out.

The old Riordan house itself had seen better days. He winced at the hanging shingles and aging aluminum siding that had slipped to reveal rotting wood underneath. Why hadn't Kelly or Jake helped their father with the upkeep? Surely Kelly was making enough money now.

Ryan pushed the yellowed doorbell and the familiar Westminster chime rang out. That memory of teenaged excitement resurfaced—the anticipation of picking up his girl for a date. And just as if it were twenty years ago, the curtains in the small window in the door parted and Mike

Riordan peered out. His face had aged, but he smiled, waved, and proceeded to unlock the front door just as he did so many times before.

"Ryan!" He took the detective into his arms for a hearty, unexpected hug. "How long has it been, eh? Two, three years?"

Four or five. "Something like that, sure. Nice to see you again, Mr. Riordan." Without prompting, Mike Riordan shook Di Santo's hand, too. "This is my partner, Matt Di Santo."

"Oh, oh, your partner, you say? What happened to that black fellow?"

Ryan and Di Santo exchanged looks. "That was my former partner, Jon Lange. He passed."

The man frowned as he shut the front door behind them, making sure to throw the deadbolt as if to keep out the horror of the dead black fellow. "Come in, come in." He led them into the living room to the left of the staircase, and Ryan marveled at how the house seemed to be frozen in time, still decorated with the flowered motif that Kelly's mom had instilled upon the entire house. Same wallpaper, same furniture. Family pictures were scattered throughout, with enlarged photos mounted in acrylic frames on the walls. He spotted a formal family portrait on the mantel taken approximately twenty years ago, about the time he and Kelly were in high school.

"Sorry to hear about Helen," Ryan said. "My mom told me she went peacefully, though."

Riordan responded with a nod and a melancholy smile. To the right of the family photo was a portrait of Jake in uniform. Marines. He took out his cell and snapped a photo of the photo.

"Oh—my—frickin'—God," Di Santo shouted from the hallway. Ryan heard a shutter click and turned to see what his partner had snapped. The junior prom picture. Kelly all freckle-faced, her smile twinkling with metal, with Ryan's arms circled awkwardly around her waist.

"You were so skinny!" Di Santo announced, with evil glee. "And you have a mullet! Ryan Doherty with a mullet!"

"Delete that."

"Oh, I am *so* not deleting this, D. And…it's already posted. Hashtag T-B-T!" He chuckled like a schoolgirl.

Fucking social media.

Riordan came up behind them and studied the picture. "Kelly tells me that prom is tomorrow. What time are you picking her up?"

Ryan turned to him. "Sir?"

"Prom! It's going to be a big event this year, at the Art Institute, she says! Do you have your tux, young man?"

Di Santo elbowed him. "He must mean the Astor Ball."

"Yes, sir. The ball. But Kelly and I aren't going together."

"Of course you are! You're sweethearts, aren't you? You've been planning on going to the senior prom together for three years now. She's even got her dress ready!"

"Yes, sir," he agreed, placating the man. He knew from his aunt that Alzheimer's sufferers could jump around in time, and the photograph must have triggered the flashback. "Sir, can I ask you where your son is now? Where does Jake live?"

"What do you mean, where does he live? He's sixteen. He lives here with us!"

God, Ryan had wished he had asked the question as soon as they arrived, when Mike had been more lucid and in the present. "Does he still have a room here, in your house?"

"Oh, he moved to the basement. It's finished, you know. Perfect place for a teenage boy, with video games and such. We let him move down there when he turned thirteen. Want to see it?"

Ryan and Di Santo nodded in unison. "Please."

"All righty, it's just down here."

Riordan opened a door in the hallway just before the kitchen and led them down a narrow staircase to the lower level of the home. "Careful of the railing," he warned. "There could be some old nails in it."

The lower level of the Riordans' home contained a moderately finished basement, a space that Ryan knew very well and like the rest of the house, hadn't changed much in the last twenty years. He and Kelly had come down here for their high school make out sessions. Jake was still in elementary school at the time. Since then, apparently, her brother had made it into a teen den, and that was how it had remained. Anchoring the room was the ancient checkered sofa on which Ryan had let his teen hormones rage, now with flattened cushions from many a butt. Across from it was an old pine entertainment center with a fat tube television bearing tentacles of abandoned game controllers. A doorway to the left led to the water heater, while a door to the right was the laundry room, if he'd remembered correctly.

"Jake made the old laundry room his bedroom," Riordan explained. "We moved the washer and dryer upstairs."

"Can we take a peek in his bedroom?" Ryan asked the old man. Then to Di Santo, "Maybe there's a clue to where Jake might be now."

Kelly's father nodded. "Sure, sure, be my guest. As long as you're not looking for contraband!" The man chuckled. "After all, you're a cop, right?" Mike Riordan had just returned to the twenty-first century.

"Yes, sir."

Ryan and Di Santo quickly started to search the place, now that they had the homeowner's permission. On one of the nightstands stood a beer bottle, half-full, indicating that someone had recently occupied the space.

"What's in there?" Di Santo asked, pointing to another door in the back of the room.

"Oh, that's my old workroom," Mike responded. "Tools and stuff. Jake uses it for his business now."

Ryan didn't remember the back room and quickly made his way over to find the door padlocked.

"Key's in the nightstand, I think," Mike added.

Ryan pulled a drawer next to the bed and found the silver key, unlocking the door to darkness.

Mike Riordan poked him in the back. "There's a chain above your head for the light."

Ryan felt around for the chain and pulled. As soon as the light revealed the sight of the workbench, Di Santo turned and gently backed Riordan away from the door.

"Mr. Riordan, what, exactly, *is* Jake's business?" Ryan called out, taking a mental inventory of the weapons lined up in succession.

"Oh, he's in security. Protection, really. Just like the old man!" Mike called back.

Ryan paused taking inventory. "I thought you were in construction?" Then it sank in: that's exactly what Tootie had told Di Santo's sister.

"Yes, well, that was an simpler explanation for the kids, of course, until they were old enough to understand."

Ryan swallowed that thought as he resumed his scrutiny of the arsenal of weapons. He searched for the M24 sniper rifle, but it was absent among the line of handguns, shotguns, and illegal automatics. On a worn wooden shelf behind the workbench he spotted several boxes of ammunition and snapped photos of each with his cell phone. Next to the bullets were manuals on car repair and engineering. A small white bottle peeked out from behind the manuals. Ryan could partially read the label, "Just Rite Ultraviolet—" with the last word obscured. Since they didn't have a warrant, he wasn't allowed to move anything.

"D, do you have the black light?" he called back to his partner.

"The black light? No, it's back at my desk."

"Hey, Ryan!" Riordan called out. "Jake has one right there on the desk. He plays with that stuff all the time. It's that desk lamp on the right."

Ryan locked eyes with Di Santo. He switched on the desk lamp just as his partner pulled the chain to turn off the overhead light. The workroom lit up like a million fireflies with purple splotches, interspersed BOO stamps, and hostile profanity-laden graffiti on the walls. He solemnly snapped a panoramic before switching off the black light and exiting the space.

"And you have no idea where your son is now?" he asked Riordan, re-locking the door to the workroom. Di Santo's right leg bounced as if he was itching to run a twenty-meter dash. Ryan silently willed him to stay calm.

"Well, let me see…I think Jake said he was going to get his outfit for the prom. You are taking Kelly, aren't you? It's tomorrow night. At the Art Institute. Should I tell him you stopped by?"

"*No!* No. In fact, let's keep it a secret that we were here, okay?" Ryan said, as he and Di Santo ushered the man back up the staircase to the main floor. "We wouldn't want him to think we were snooping in his private space. You know how teens are."

"Oh, yeah! I've got two of 'em!" Mike said, settling down into a powder blue recliner. "So, we'll see you tomorrow night?"

Ryan decided to play along again, if it would get information out of the man. "Sir, are you sure Kelly and Jake are *both* going to the…prom?"

The man picked up a remote and clicked on the television. Home shopping channel. "Oh, yes, they've been talking about it all week."

"Thank you, sir. Nice to see you again, we'll see ourselves out."

Back in the sedan, Ryan and Di Santo regrouped. "Was the M24 in there?" Di Santo asked, practically bouncing in his bucket seat.

"No, but I think I saw the bullets. With the extent of that arsenal and the invisible ink, Jake Riordan is looking good for the Robin Ricci homicide. It blows my mind what Mike admitted back there. I never thought—"

"That he was a mobster?"

"I never did see him with a hammer in his hand," Ryan said. "But it would explain Jake, I suppose. That would give him the connections to the Outfit. I wonder if Kelly knew?"

"Should we call Jensen and tell him about the guns?"

Ryan shook his head. "Not yet. For one, we can't let Jake know that *we* know about his workspace. That may not be his only weapons stash. And The Ghost made it clear that he could get to anyone. You and I can't risk the safety of our families."

"You think he'd come after us? My sister? My ma?"

"He would if he felt threatened. And although we received the homeowner's permission to search the basement, it could be argued that Mr. Riordan doesn't have the mental capacity to grant it. That search was gray-zone."

Di Santo started the car and Ryan called Devin on speakerphone as they rode back to the 18th and brought him up to speed on Jake's workshop.

"I'm sending you a photos of the ammunition now," he said, thumbing his phone. "And the shitload of invisible ink. All over the workbench and walls. He used it as a testing area. This is it, Dev. Jake Riordan has to be The Ghost."

After a pause, Devin replied, "I received the photos. Yes, I can spot the exact brand and caliber that fit the M24 sniper rifle." And then a pause. "Oh, my. The photo of the UV ink is blurry, but I believe it's enough to get a warrant. I have to ask...was the search legal?"

"We were invited in by the homeowner, Michael Riordan." Ryan left out the man's mental capacity, as they had no hard evidence that it was compromised in any way. At this point he would have called or texted Jane to verify that, but would she answer?

"Okay, good work, Detective."

A bit of pride swelled up in Ryan. Pride from the approval of his big brother. "One more thing," Ryan said into the phone. "We found a photo of Jake in a US Marines uniform, so he's definitely military. But I still don't think one guy could have pulled off all of this crap. Jake Riordan used to hang with some low-level guys in high school. Can you run a background on them? See what they're up to?" Devin agreed. "David Tewes, Patrick O'Hara, and...Donovan. Iggy Donovan. Not sure of Iggy's full name. All from the same neighborhood as Jake Riordan, if I remember correctly." He relayed the address.

They kept the call connected, waiting for a response, as they drove back, enduring long stretches of silence with the occasional clicking of Devin's keyboard. Ryan only hung up when they got back to the station and approached his brother in person.

"Oh, you're back," Devin said, acknowledging them hovering over his shoulders. "I believe now that you were correct about The Ghost being a group of individuals, rather than just one," he announced. "I found out that Jake Riordan served as a sniper in the Marines. He even received a medal of honor for sharpshooting. Per your instruction, I researched his known associates from high school, and they all fit the profiles as well: David Tewes is a licensed pilot, currently employed by Helo Air, a private jet company out of—get this—Midway Airport. *Ian* Donovan, a.k.a. Iggy, is employed by a computer security firm. He performs white hat hacking, which means he would easily know about and be able to navigate the dark web. Now, I couldn't find any occupation for Patrick O'Hara, but his parents own an established veterinary practice in Naperville, Illinois."

"The ketamine found in Desirée Leone's system," Ryan concluded.

"Exactly. He may be an assistant or something. But we know for sure that he can gain access to the drug."

Ryan let the new hard data sink in for a minute. "Can you run a quick background on Michael Riordan? Employment history? Any connections to the Outfit?"

"The father?" Devin responded.

Ryan nodded and the keys started clicking.

His brother clucked his tongue.

"What?"

"Damen Construction. It's a known front for the mob, owned by the Gillis gang. A lot of city contracts. Looks like he retired a good fifteen years ago, though."

Everything started to add up with Mike Riordan, Jake, and his crew. "So where does Kelly fit into all this?" Ryan said, thinking aloud.

Di Santo spoke up. "*Consigliere*, possibly. Every mob family has a consigliere. That means counselor. They're removed from the actual criminal activity, but advise the leader on how to manage the business—and avoid law enforcement. Consiglieri are difficult to nail, since they don't ever get their hands dirty."

It made sense. As far as Ryan could remember, Jake and his group of friends were low-level criminals and couldn't have formed such an elaborate organization with the intelligence and power to take on the Chicago Outfit. But Kelly had an MBA. And ambition. And a fundamental, compelling desire for money. And her father's connections.

Devin's voice pulled him out of his thoughts "Ryan? You knew her. Is that possible?"

He didn't want to believe it. "Consigliere," he murmured, mulling over the word and the implications that came along with it.

"I also pulled her credit card records," Devin added. "Kelly Anne Riordan bought a ticket from Vegas to Chicago on United. The flight was the day after we came back. Looking through her cell records, there are numerous calls to her father and brother, pinging off Chicago cell towers, so I would conclude there's a ninety to ninety-five percent chance that she's currently in town."

"Thanks for the info," Ryan responded, his cop sense firing up in his gut again. "Oh, and Dev: before we prep the warrant for a full search of the Riordan residence, see if we can get a receipt for the purchase of those bullets. It will help if we can tie them directly to Jake." He was about to turn to his desk before he added, "And can you just not tell Jensen about all of this right now? I don't want the task force mucking up the investigation until we're sure."

Devin nodded and the detectives regressed to their desk pod. Ryan fell down into his chair and pondered on the future vision of having to arrest Kelly. The woman who used to be his other half. Until she wasn't. He threw a tennis ball to Di Santo, who caught it with one hand. "Can you get a tux in twenty-four hours?" Ryan asked him.

"Yeah, I have a tux, why?"

"Mike Riordan said that Kelly and Jake were going to the prom at the Art Institute tomorrow. I think he was really referring to the Astor Ball. Cat and I are going." He caught the tennis ball and held it to his temple, trying to stave off a distant headache.

"Cat's going *out?* Downtown? To a *ball?*"

"She says she's ready." Ryan tossed the ball back, unwilling to go into Catharine's pathology. "Anyway, I have a feeling Kelly and Jake are going, too—along with some of the most influential and wealthy people in the city. That doesn't sit right with me."

"So you really think Kelly's involved in all of this?"

"You said it yourself: *Consigliere.*"

"Well, now we have proof that she's in Chicago, and I'd bet she was one of the women who asked about renting the necklace. She could have been the crew member who was casing the jewelry store."

They tossed the ball back and forth in silence, a habit that formed when deliberating the details of a case. Ryan had to look at Kelly as a perp rather than his ex-girlfriend. He shoved his disbelief aside and had to accept that she had it within her to run a criminal organization. To steal. To commit murder. With all the killers he'd arrested in his career, there was always someone close to them who said, "Never in a million years did I think she was capable of such an act," or "He seemed like a such a nice guy. He played ball with his kids, he coached the soccer team." *Until he took an Uzi and mowed down the parents in the stands.*

Ryan rotated the tennis ball in his hand. "I'll have Cat finagle another ticket to the ball. I want you there with us."

"Two more tickets, if you please. Amy-Jo would kill me if I didn't bring her to the event of the year."

Ryan groaned. Amy-Jo Slater served as the Department's Public Relations Liaison. The woman had always repelled him, mainly because she was responsible for reducing his cases into newsworthy sound bites. But since she and Di Santo had become a couple, Ryan bit the bullet and pretended to be decent to her.

"Okay, two tickets. But keep her away from me."

"You know, she adores you now. She's calling you Elliot Ness."

Ryan chucked the ball at his partner—hard. So hard, it flew past Di Santo and directly at Devin, who caught it without looking up from his screen.

"Elliot Ness just busted beer barrels," his brother announced. "It was Frank J. Wilson who actually brought down Al Capone. A forensic accountant."

"Well, hooray for the geeks!" Di Santo announced, and the squad broke out in laughter.

CHAPTER 30

Duke's tuxedo fit Ryan fairly well, with the exception of an extra inch of pant leg and two in the shoulders. To fix this, Cat had summoned a tailor who brought a team of five to the estate, complete with three industrial sewing machines. It only took two hours, thirty-seven minutes for them to measure, fit, tuck, sew, and perfect the penguin suit for Ryan's physique.

He finished dressing by inserting the cufflinks and running a comb through his hair. His jacket buttoned precisely over the gun holster—a detail the tailor was enthusiastic to perfect. Ryan admired his own visage. Not bad for a man of thirty-nine years and two months. He took a selfie in the mirror. For his mom, he justified.

Catharine was still in her dressing room when Ryan finished, so he went down to the library to call Devin.

"You shouldn't be going there without backup," his brother said.

"Di Santo will be there, and the two of us can arrest one man. You should see me, anyway, I'm the spitting image of James Bond." Ryan pulled his gun on the fireplace, accompanying the move with the theme song.

Devin wasn't impressed. "Nevertheless, Jake Riordan is a violent criminal. He's not just your girlfriend's brother."

"Ex-girlfriend."

"You know what I meant. You need perspective. We went back through Jake's credit card charges and found the M24 bullets, purchased from a local gun shop six weeks ago. We have enough for a warrant of the Riordans' house. Agent Jensen says he'll try to expedite it with the judge so we can go over there tonight."

"Okay, if Jake's at the ball, we'll make sure he stays there and occupied." He heard Catharine's heels on the staircase. "Look, gotta go, but keep me posted." Ryan disconnected and went out into the foyer in time to catch the vision of Catharine descending the staircase in a pale-blue full-length gown, her long hair clipped to one side with some kind of sparkly things interspersed into the curls. Her face was made up heavier than usual, enhancing her timeless beauty. She was perfect. Porcelain perfect.

"God, I've never seen you so beautiful. Except maybe after sex." He took her hand as a gentleman would, escorted her down the final two stairs and twirled her in a circle.

"Great dress. You are going to be the most beautiful woman at the ball."

"You don't look so bad yourself," she said, straightening his bow tie. "You clean up pretty good, Detective."

"I know, right?" He put a palm under the massive ruby and diamond necklace suspended from Catharine's neck. "This looks like the one that was stolen, although that one was green. Emeralds. Where did you get this?"

"Bought it for myself," she answered. *Eighty-four thousand retail*, the jeweler had said. Ryan whistled. "I figured it might be good bait tonight, to draw out Jake or Kelly."

"Smart *and* beautiful," he said, taking in the entirety of the woman. "Marry me?"

As soon as the phrase left his mouth, they both froze in place as if time stopped—Cat's eyes locked onto his, not a movement between them.

Ryan swallowed hard, breaking the silence. "I—"

"We—"

"It—"

"No."

It took him a moment to comprehend that Catharine had answered the proposal.

"No?"

"No." She stared up at him in apology with those damned blue eyes of hers.

"Um, is this a conversation for another day?"

"Yes," she replied on an exhale.

He took her into his arms. "Do you still love me?"

"Absolutely." She reinforced her affection with a kiss, and then wiped the residual lipstick off his mouth.

"That's good enough. For now." He was almost relieved she had declined. It was a spur-of-the-moment declaration. He wasn't even sure he was ready. Was he ready? At almost forty years old, it was definitely time for him to settle down. At least, according to his mother. He put the pink elephant away as he gathered their jackets. Catharine checked her purse to make sure she had all her necessities.

"There are two tickets waiting at the door for Matthew and his date," she said, although she had mentioned it several times earlier.

"Yes, I told him. He'll meet us there." Ryan opened the door for this enigma of a woman who was gloriously his—yet wasn't. Not really. They descended the mansion's front steps and entered the Town Car in the turnaround.

The drive from Evanston to the Art Institute took thirty-seven minutes via Lake Shore Drive. Enjoying the stunning fall evening, their conversation in the limo began with Ryan setting a plan for Catharine's exit, if necessary.

"I've instructed the chauffeur to keep the car close, and we can leave anytime," he said. "This is a big step for you, and I want you to feel safe and comfortable."

Catharine took his hand. "Thank you. This *is* a big step for me, and I feel I'm ready. I appreciate the escape plan and I promise to utilize it, if necessary."

On the second half of the drive, Cat gave Ryan the full details of her meeting with Jane, and he was still shocked at the career move. And the physical move as well. He thought of the future twelve months when he'd have no one in the SA's office to help him with cases, no one with whom he could run through the details of a grisly crime scene. The legal perspective was always valuable, but he was also going to miss her personally. She was smart and tough, and the only person who could put him in his place.

Catharine was definitely his equal in terms of character, intelligence, and willfulness, but she had never criticized him. If she disagreed with anything Ryan did or said, she'd throw out some New Age philosophical platitude like, "You'll find the right path when you're ready," or "Think on it a bit and I'm sure your heart will find the answer." Whereas Jane would say, "You're being a fucking idiot, Ryan, and here's why." Jane was also the only female friend who had remained just that: a friend. That was kind of huge for him, and he'd miss the benefit of having a relationship like that. Like her.

Catharine's excitement escalated as the driver pulled into the line of cars waiting to let their esteemed passengers out at the Art Institute of Chicago. She and Ryan peered out the passenger side window taking in the scene: search lights, a red carpet, and society photographers. She turned to him, smiling, and squeezed his hand with an intense feeling of both butterflies and joy.

In a museum filled with hundreds of people, it wouldn't be so easy to escape the assault of sensations that she was so used to perceiving. But she had worked on "turning down the radio" of emotions with her therapist and tonight was the big test.

When it was their turn, the driver pulled up to the Art In-stitute and a footman stepped up to open the car door. Catharine and Ryan got out, walked the red carpet to whispers of "*Who's that?*" posed briefly for the paparazzi and proceeded to ascend the white marble steps of the museum. As they reached the top of the steps, Catharine sent a silent request into the universe for the evening to go smoothly. If she could conquer an event like this, she'd be well on her way to recovery.

"You ready?" Ryan asked, as they paused outside of the museum's doors.

"Yes. And Ryan, during the evening, please don't ask me ten million times if I'm okay. That makes me feel like a mental patient. If I'm not okay, I'll let you know. Deal?"

"Deal." He kissed her and they opened the door to enter the world of the charity ball elite. Men in tuxes took the wraps of women in gowns as they chattered through the coat check and handed over their printed invitations. Catharine hadn't been to the museum for at least ten years, when it used to be one of her favorite places to escape the ad agency at lunchtime. She had remained a loyal member, even when she knew she couldn't make it physically to the exhibits. And now she was back, and it felt spectacular.

As they made their way through the museum's lobby, Matt Di Santo found them.

"Gorgeous, just gorgeous!" he shouted, and then planted a kiss on Catharine's cheek. "Both of you are gorgeous. Look at you, D! You two look like you belong on a wedding cake."

Catharine thanked him and blushed, recalling the awkward proposal earlier in the evening.

Ryan barreled past the moment by transforming into cop mode. "How long have you been here?" he asked his partner. "Have you seen Kelly yet? What about Jake?"

"No, no one who looked like the photograph," Matthew answered. "But we just got here."

Ryan appeared agitated. "And no Kelly? How many people are in there? Any celebrities?"

"Dude, like I said: we just got here only five minutes before you did." A petite blonde woman walked up and took Matt's arm.

"Cat, I'd like you to meet my girlfriend, Amy-Jo," he said.

Ryan seemed to flinch from her presence, muttering only a "Hey" to the woman. Catharine held out a hand, attempting more grace than her boorish date.

Amy-Jo was a small woman, but shook hands with a firm grip for her size. She stood several inches shorter than Matthew and had wavy golden hair and hazel eyes. She and Catharine complimented each other on their dresses, and then the four of them followed the other guests to the back of the museum's lobby, around the central staircase to the rear of the building where a grand ballroom was set up for the evening's event.

Chandeliers twinkled from the ceiling in a room large enough for three to five hundred of Chicago's elite to float about easily. A jazz ensemble played on the stage to the right, while the left wall was lined with a bar. A long row of draped tables stood holding silent auction items and small bar-height tables were peppered throughout the floor.

"Detective Doherty!" a voice boomed from behind them. Ryan and Catharine turned to see a tall statuesque man with a full head of white hair. He held out his hand and shook Ryan's with fervor.

Ryan introduced them. "Catharine, this is Superintendent Charles Grady. My boss's boss's boss." The man took her hand and kissed it.

"Catharine Lulling," she said, finishing the introduction, "So very nice to meet you, Superintendent Grady."

"Oh, please, call me Chuck." Ryan balked behind the Superintendent's back. "I must say, you are by far the most beautiful woman in this room."

She felt herself blush with the compliment. "Oh, my, I hope your wife doesn't hear you say that."

"Divorced, my dear. Happily divorced. So if you ever get tired of this guy, let me know." He slapped Ryan on the back. "Just...*beautiful!* Doherty, keep your eye on this one."

"Will do, sir. *Chuck,*" he added, knowing that the familiar was only meant for Cat. Grady let out a guffaw, slapped his back again, and proceeded to glad-hand a nearby state senator.

When the Superintendent was out of earshot, Matthew muttered, "Nice to meet you too, sir."

"Come on, let's get some drinks," Ryan said, looking around for one of the wandering waiters. The men each took two champagne flutes from a tray and then delivered them gently to their dates. "Are you in want of alcohol this evening, my lady?" Ryan asked, offering up the bubbly.

"I shall partake. After all, neither of us is driving, right?" She took her first sip as her gaze went up into the gallery. Ryan's followed. Like Catharine's atrium, the large room was several stories high with a gallery-like mezzanine around the periphery in a square, displaying some of the most prominent works in the Art Institute's collection.

"Oh, look, Ryan! There's that Degas that I love. With the ballerinas!" Catharine pointed up to the mezzanine. "Later let's go up there and check it out."

Ryan smiled to appease her. She was sure he was about to check in on her mental state, but when she raised an eyebrow, he wrapped an arm around her waist, and took a sip of champagne instead. His mind was elsewhere as he scanned the crowd.

"Are you looking for Kelly?" Catharine asked. She understood he was working a case, but hoped this evening could be just theirs.

"Yeah. I need to find out if her brother is here, and that's the easiest way. Sorry, I know that can't be easy for you."

"It's okay. You're mine now," she said with a smile. He kissed her on her head before continuing the investigation of the room. They moved through the crowd and toward the silent auction tables. Ryan stood with his back to the goodies, still surveying the guests, while Catharine wrote her name down for several items. An onyx and ruby bracelet—it would match her necklace beautifully, an architectural river cruise, and dinner for two at The Bohemian House. Tonight Catharine would be a normal woman, one who could go anywhere and do anything.

"Catharine Lulling?" A woman approached her. "Beatrice Allen, from the Arts Council! Great to see you...out! Here, I mean." Cat shook hands with Ms. Allen and several other members of the committee whom she had only conversed with over the phone and email. They chatted about the recent grants, the museum's exhibits, and the elegance of the evening.

"There she is," Ryan said, excusing Catharine from her group. He pointed out Kelly Riordan on the dance floor gliding to the jazz ensemble, led by an older man. Catharine recognized her as the woman she had conversed with during her dream-state in Las Vegas. But tonight she wore a black floor-length designer gown, with her brown hair swept up in a chignon.

Ryan flagged Di Santo over and nodded toward Kelly's location.

"Who's the guy she's with?" Matthew asked.

"I don't know. Never seen him. Definitely not her brother, he's too old." And as if Kelly had heard their conversation, her attention turned in their direction and she acknowledged Ryan with a grin. Catharine's empathic shield cracked as she felt waves of animosity from the woman aimed directly at her.

When the song ended, Kelly excused herself from her dancing partner and made her way over to them. Di Santo took Amy-Jo's hand and led her out to the dance floor, throwing back an expression of warning to Ryan. Whether they admitted it or believed in it, Ryan and Matt had gotten to the point in their relationship where they could communicate without words.

"Well, well," Kelly said. "This is the last place I'd expect to see you, Ryan. I didn't know you were into these kind of society events." She turned to Catharine. "Oh, hello again."

"Kelly, this is Catharine. Catharine, Kelly," Ryan introduced them without the expected awkwardness of introducing two women who had shared the same man.

"Hello," Cat said with a gracious nod.

"Didn't we—"

Ryan cleared his throat, thankfully ending the inquiry. "I didn't expect to see you either, at a Chicago event. Have you moved back for good now? Or just visiting?"

"Hoping for good," she answered. "Trying to line up a job and a place to live."

Catharine squeezed Ryan's arm, with the implicit message of *You didn't tell me your ex was moving back to town.*

"Kelly's dad is ill," he explained to Catharine, easing the sting a bit. "Alzheimer's."

"I'm so sorry," Catharine said to Kelly, a bit ashamed at her initial reaction.

"Thank you. He has good days and bad days. My brother and I are planning to take turns helping him out."

Catharine felt Ryan's pulse accelerate. "So...where is Jake nowadays?" he asked.

"Here," Kelly answered with a sly grin. "He's my date tonight as I try to network with the bigwigs for a job."

"Jake's here? I'd love to see him again. Catch up."

Catharine caught a microexpression of distrust on Kelly's face before she plastered on the false smile again. "Of course! He's around here somewhere. You can't miss him. He's got a red carnation in his lapel. Anyway, gotta run and schmooze."

But before Kelly could excuse herself, Catharine reached out and took the other woman's hand. "It was really lovely to meet you, Kelly," she made herself say, and hung on. She couldn't help it, she had to read her—for the good of Ryan's case, of course.

"A little violence never hurt anyone."
~ *Benjamin "Lefty Guns" Ruggiero*

CHAPTER 31

The ballroom faded away from Catharine's consciousness as she read Kelly's spirit from their touch. She perceived an image of a close, supportive family, and subsequently a great loss. The loss of the matriarch. The loss formed a catalyst for the darkness that enveloped this woman from the inside out, allowing the worst part of Kelly Riordan to flourish and prevail. She saw a boisterous, redheaded imp of a happy child superimposed upon this dark specter of a woman. *A ghost of her former self.* The driving force of The Ghost criminal organization. Flashes came, like photographs interspersed into Catharine's mind: the emerald necklace, a rifle, bullets, a lion roaring, and Desirée Leone's mauled body.

The jazz band's Lindy Hop seeped back into her senses, along with the heat of the hundreds of ball guests. Catharine swayed from the growing queasiness and removed her hand from Kelly's.

Ryan ducked down to be at eye level with her. "Cat, are you—"

"I—I just need to go to the ladies' room." She searched for the restrooms, feeling the panic rise within her.

"I know where it is," Kelly said. "I'll take her."

Catharine allowed Kelly to lead her back to the hallway and toward the restrooms to the right of the grand staircase.

The women's room was brightly lit, with elegant fixtures and full doors on the stalls, several of which were occupied. Cat just wanted water. She took several paper towels from the dispenser on the wall, ran them under cold water and held them against her forehead. After about half a minute she felt better and dabbed her forehead and cheeks several times before righting herself. Kelly stood about a foot away, inspecting her through the mirror.

"Thank you. I'm feeling better now," Catharine said, in hopes of discharging her. Their relationship would have been awkward anyway, given all the history, but the moment was compounded by the darkness Catharine had felt from the reading. The woman most certainly had a criminal side to her.

"You know, he's just going to lead you on," Kelly said, opening her clutch. "Ryan is famous for coercing women into believing they're 'the one' and leading them on ad infinitum. Don't think you're special in that respect."

Catharine didn't respond. She didn't have to.

Kelly pulled out a lipstick tube and proceeded to touch up. "You don't look like you're getting any younger, so if you're waiting for a marriage proposal, it may be a long, long, wait." She smacked her lips together for symmetry. "I concluded long ago that Ryan Andrew Doherty is a permanent bachelor."

Catharine could have responded that as a matter of fact, Ryan had just asked her to marry him this evening. However, in this particular case, that would have just sounded like a false retort. And anyway, she wasn't sure it was a genuine proposal or if he'd been caught up in the moment. "Each relationship is different, Kelly. You were involved with Ryan when he was a young man. I'd like to think he's matured."

The woman laughed. "We broke up *three* years ago, honey. You really think he's changed in three years? That's a bit delusional."

Cat had nothing to prove, so she chose silence once

again. A white-haired zaftig woman exited one of the stalls, washed her hands and loitered a bit to catch the end of the soap opera, but when they didn't oblige, she left.

Kelly turned back to her. "And just what was that whole scene at the Bellagio? Were you stalking me or something? Because that's pretty fucked up."

"No, Kelly, I wasn't stalking you." It was true. She had no control over whom she visited or where she went in her astral travels. "I honestly didn't even know who you were."

"Bullshit. You expect me to believe that in a city of millions of tourists, you happened to sit down right beside me?"

Catharine turned to face her. "You don't have to do this, you know."

"Do what?"

"You are at the brink of choosing the wrong path. And you have time to right it. You can back away from the darkness." Catharine reached for her hand a second time, and Kelly pulled something from her clutch. Something silver, shiny, that with the press of a button turned into a blade.

"You need to back away, *bitch.* Don't ever touch me again." Someone shifted in the last stall, distracting Catharine from the sight of the knife. Another person was in the room. Kelly couldn't hurt her. There'd be a witness.

"Please, you don't want to do this," Catharine said. "You are intelligent, brave. You could have a great life."

Kelly held the switchblade an inch from Catharine's neck and lifted the ruby necklace with her other hand. "This is one hell of a bauble. How did you manage this? I know Ryan can't afford anything close to this price range. Did you get it from another guy, I suppose? What on earth would make you lose the rich guy for a cop? Looks like you're the one on the wrong path." Kelly was enjoying the bullying, but Catharine remained strong.

"As a matter of fact, I bought it myself," she responded, lifting her chin in defiance. "I don't look for others to fulfill me, whether it's spiritually or monetarily."

Kelly squinted her eyes. "I don't like you."

"You don't have to like me," Catharine said. She shut her eyes to regain her composure. She couldn't let Kelly see her fear, but she was greatly aware of the capacity of this woman's violence. She felt the blade against her collarbone and willed herself to remain calm.

A third voice said, "Now *you* need to back away, bitch!" Cat opened her eyes to see Jane Steffen holding a pistol to Kelly Riordan's temple. Kelly threw her hands up to shoulder height as she closed the blade with one of them.

"Who the fuck are you? The bathroom police?" Kelly hissed.

Jane lowered her gun and took possession of the switchblade. "Assistant state's attorney. And you've just committed assault with a deadly weapon."

"I didn't touch her," Kelly said, backing away from them. "We were just talking." Then in a swift move, Kelly lifted her dress several inches and performed some kind of kick to the back of Jane's shin, causing her legs to buckle. Jane hit the floor as Kelly fled the bathroom.

Catharine rushed to help Jane. "Are you okay?" She took Jane's arm and helped her sit up.

Jane rubbed the back of her head and glanced toward the door, which was still closing on its hinge. "Yeah, I'm fine. How are you? Did she hurt you?"

"No, not at all," Catharine touched her neck with her fingertips and inspected them. "No blood. She didn't hurt me, but I'm not so sure she wouldn't have if you hadn't stepped in. Thank you," she said, helping Jane to her feet.

The attorney put her gun away in her handbag and turned on one of the faucets. She washed her hands, using some of the water to dampen her hair back into place. When she had recovered, she turned to Catharine and said, "So...that was Kelly."

Catharine dissolved into laughter, from the confrontational energy or possibly the absurdity of it all, and the mirth infected Jane with the giggles as well. The two of them fed off of each other as the laughter bounced off the tile and back at them.

"I have a question," Catharine said, trying to catch a breath. "Would you have saved my life if I hadn't sent you to Paris?"

That sent them both into another bout of hilarity, and when that died down Jane took out her phone and fired off a text.

Ryan stood near the bar, searching for the man with the red carnation, and took inventory of the guests whom he recognized: Stan Porter, the current state's attorney, was working his way through the politicos; Mayor Hogan and wife circulated the floor, arm in arm; Grady, of course, was trolling the attractive women, as if he was in a singles bar; almost every member of Chicago's billionaire Pritzker family; and the top local newscasters. No Oprah, despite the rumors.

A flash of red caught his eye and he studied a man with a red carnation in his lapel. He didn't appear to be Jake Riordan. His hair was two shades too light—more blondish than auburn, and he stood an inch and a half too tall. As far as Ryan remembered Jake and Kelly were about the same height, five-foot nine.

Within minutes, he spotted two more male individuals with matching flowers in their lapels, neither of them fitting his memory of Kelly's brother. He didn't believe in coincidences.

The Ghost isn't an individual, it's a crew.

He pulled out his cell and called Devin. "I think they're all here, Dev," he said, making his way to the hall. "Jake and his buddies. The entire ghost crew. Something's going down."

"I'll call Jensen. Be careful, and don't attempt to apprehend them alone."

He chastised himself for bringing Catharine into a dangerous situation and took off in search of the ladies' room. He had to get her out of the museum. As he was circling the corridor trying to find it, a text came in. It was from Jane.

– *Get to the women's room. STAT!*

Ryan found a security guard who pointed him to the door to the right of the main staircase. When he got there, Jane was exiting with Catharine behind her. They were both doubling over in laughter.

"Is everything okay?" he asked them. "What's going on?"

"Well," Jane answered, "Your *ex*-girlfriend just held a knife to your *current* girlfriend."

"And your *not*-girlfriend saved the day," Catharine added. The two women repeated their hysterics.

Ryan didn't get it. "Wait, *what?* Kelly held a knife on you? Did she hurt you? Why on *earth* are you two laughing?" His confusion seemed to further amuse the women. "Okay, maybe you've had too much champagne," he said, pulling Catharine to him. "Stop laughing and tell me what happened."

Catharine caught her breath with a sigh. "It really is exactly what we just said. Kelly got extremely aggressive in the powder room. She tried to bait me by saying that you were not serious about a relationship, that you'd never ask me to marry you…"

Ryan let out a *phfffft* at the statement. Jane coughed.

"And I saw the darkness in her, Ryan." Catharine quickly sobered up. "I tried telling her that she didn't have to choose the wrong path."

"Yeah, you can't tell Kelly what to do. So then what, she pulled a *knife* on you?"

"A switchblade," Jane said, and handed it over to him.

He took it, studying the weapon in his hand. "Like a street thug? I just don't understand. That's not Kelly."

"Apparently it is. Nice taste in women, Ry," Jane said, adjusting an undergarment through her dress.

"And you—"

"I saved Catharine's neck with my .22." Jane patted her handbag. "And before you ask, yes. I have my carry/concealed permit with me."

He ignored her comment and turned back in the direction of the ballroom. "I don't know what's happening here, but she is not allowed to mess with you like that," he called back to Catharine. "Jane, can you stick with Cat for a while and make sure she's okay? I'm going to go find Kelly."

"Yes, sir. You know, Kelly assaulted me too, but I'm fine, thank you very much…"

Ryan let Jane trail off as he jogged back to the event. He almost pushed the suits out of his way, first crisscrossing the dance floor, then circling the outer periphery of the room. He spotted her at the front of the bar, combing back some loose hair with her fingers. She smiled the same disingenuous smile as he approached her.

"What the hell? I just heard about the scene in the bathroom." He quietly flashed the switchblade. She reached out to take the knife back, but Ryan pocketed it.

Kelly pouted. "She started it."

"We're not eight years old, Kel. This isn't St. Athanasius. Seriously, what is going on with you? Why would you pull a knife on Catharine?" Kelly calmly accepted her glass of red wine from the bartender and took a sip, her eyes smiling back at Ryan. "Kelly, talk to me. I want to understand."

"Catharine antagonized me. I felt threatened. I pulled my knife in self-defense."

"Bullshit! She weighs a hundred and eight, soaking wet. You were not threatened by her. And anyway, she's not like that. She wouldn't threaten you."

"Maybe you don't really know her."

"I know her. And I *thought* I knew you. But now I'm not so sure. I have half a mind to arrest you right here on the spot."

"Yeah, I wouldn't do that if I were you. I'll just say you're my jealous ex-boyfriend, and it's all personal."

Shit, she had him. And by the way it sounded rehearsed, she'd planned this confrontation for a while.

"So she's pretty wealthy, eh?" Kelly asked. "That ruby necklace, the designer dress. I know you couldn't afford all that, not even with the bump to detective first grade. She's so far above your class. How'd you pull that off?"

"Next?" the bartender called out, interrupting Ryan's base instinct to slap the evil out of this woman. "Can I get you anything, sir?"

Ryan shook his head and pulled Kelly away from the bar, to a more secluded corner of the room. He was done with the small talk. "Where's Jake?"

Kelly smiled—a genuine grin this time. Smug. "Look up."

Ryan lifted his gaze to the ballroom's gallery and spotted the black M24 sniper rifle perched on one of the railings like a raven waiting to swoop. Before he could make an announcement to clear the ballroom, Kelly saluted the balcony and a shot rang out.

Ryan pulled his Glock and frantically searched the room for the victim. A group of people had pulled in to his left. Without letting go of Kelly's arm, he dragged her over to the formation. The mayor's wife had been hit. The band stopped playing. Screams of panic replaced the music. From the opposite side of the ballroom, he heard Di Santo calling for everyone to remain calm, initiating the first stages of crowd control.

Ryan angled himself behind Kelly, securing her as his shield as The Ghost had done on the Stratosphere. He'd never put anyone in danger, let alone a woman he once loved, but this was the only move he could make that would get Jake's attention. He wove through the panicked crowd to the stairs leading up to the gallery. He wanted desperately to call or text Jane to get Catharine out of the building, but with one hand around Kelly and one holding his weapon, there was no way to do so. He sent an urgent thought message to Catharine, hoping that, if they truly did share a psychic connection, she would receive it. *Get out! Get out!*

Halfway up the stairs, Di Santo came up behind them for backup.

"D, what's the plan?" Di Santo asked. Ryan could hear his partner's signature adrenaline rush in the cadence his voice.

"We've got a shooter on the balcony. Most likely Jake Riordan with the M24."

"Um, what are you doing with—" Di Santo pointed to Kelly.

"She's *our* insurance now."

Di Santo nodded acceptance and Kelly struggled as they continued up to the mezzanine level. Just as they made it to the top and turned the corner, Jake lined up another shot, his eye in the rifle sighting.

"Jake! Back away from the weapon. Now!" Ryan shouted. He stepped up to the sniper's right side with Kelly in tow, while Di Santo circled in on his left. This was definitely the man that he had chased out of the speakeasy. Same height, same hair. Sans trench coat.

Di Santo threw a cursory glance down to the floor, and Ryan followed, glancing over the railing to assess the scene below. Grady and the museum security staff had taken over, evacuating the guests, but most were panicking, running, searching for an exit.

Jake swept the rifle from person to person, attempting to lock in on a new target.

"What do you have against the ladies, Jake?" Di Santo said. "Someone break your heart? Or are you just one of those fucknuts who likes to hurt girls?"

When that got his attention, Ryan shoved Kelly off to Di Santo, who restrained her, and then pointed his Glock directly at the sharpshooter with both hands. "I said, *back away* from the weapon."

Jake took two paces back and pivoted to face the detectives. "Hey, Kelly. Nice company you keep," he said and then spit on Ryan's shoe.

"You are under arrest for the murder of Robin Ricci," Ryan said. He was about to recite Miranda when Jake busted out in laughter.

"Dude, we're *The Ghost*. You don't got us on anything." He then put two fingers in his mouth and let out a piercing whistle. One of his guys came up the stairs, and two came out from either side of the wings of the hallway. All armed, all with red carnations in their lapels.

One with Catharine.

CHAPTER 32

I—I—wanted to see the Degas," Catharine said, in apology. "Ballerinas. I wanted to see the ballerinas."

She was dissolving into agoraphobic shock. Ryan knew the signs. Her hands trembled and her beautiful blue eyes were fixed in a stare, disconnected from reality. He was pretty sure her captor was Iggy Donovan, the computer guy. He hadn't seen these guys for at least twenty years, but close up he could readily ID them.

"Let her go, and we'll release Kelly," he negotiated. He couldn't lose focus, not even with Catharine in danger.

"Well, Detective, I think we have the advantage here. You're going to let Kelly go, irregardless."

"Irregardless. Irregardless. That's not a word," Catharine responded to her captor. The repeated utterances confirmed that she was half way to gone.

"Shut up!" Donovan shouted, shaking her so violently that her limbs flopped like a rag doll. Ryan wished he had two weapons, one on Jake and one on Donovan. If they even scratched Catharine, he'd mow them down. Ryan attempted a step toward her when Donovan reached for her throat and ripped off the ruby necklace. She didn't flinch.

Catharine's voice rang out in Ryan's head. *'I can take him.'* But her mouth remained closed. *'You taught me self-defense. Just say when.'* His eyes flickered around the group, but no one else seemed to have caught her statement, and Donovan didn't seem particularly reactive. There had been other times when Ryan had sensed Catharine's "connection" with him, but he'd never heard her voice outright. Jon, yes, but not Cat. He studied her semi-catatonic form: no acknowledgement of the situation, no eye contact. Ryan decided to send a silent message back. Whether it was real or imaginary, he had to at least try. *'You are NOT to fight back. Stay still. Do you hear me?'* Catharine responded with an almost imperceptible nod.

Trained in hostage negotiation, Ryan decided on a different approach. "I have to admit, Jake, how you guys executed all of those stunts...we've been pretty impressed."

Jake accepted the compliment with a smirk as he exchanged glances with his crew. The guy whom Ryan knew as Davey Tewes beamed, his chest puffed up.

"And that whole lion thing? Genius. I've never seen anything like it."

"That was a big-ass sonofabitch cat," the fourth guy said. Patrick O'Hara. "Those paws!"

Ryan turned to the man. "So that was you who went on the date with Desirée Leone?" The man chuckled. "You guys drugged her, stamped the headboard, poured beef stew all over her body and then...what? Released the lion? That was pretty brave." Ryan gestured to the other three. "I bet it took all of you to pull that off."

"Naw, man. I'm an expert with animals. I did all of that myself—"

"*Shut up!*" Jake and Kelly shouted in unison.

They were getting agitated. Ryan could use this. "Look, Jake, we saw your collection of firearms in your workroom," he said, keeping his emotions in check. "The feds are there now, serving a warrant. This is over."

Kelly's head turned. "When were you at my dad's house?" She tried to squirm out of Di Santo's grasp, but he held tight.

"I think the correct response should have been '*what col-*

lection of firearms?' If you're in on this, Kelly, I swear to God, we will get you with the RICO act."

"I have no idea what you're talking about," she said, averting her gaze.

Jake inched his way back to the M24 as sirens approached the building. He dissembled the rifle with military precision and packed it into a black soft case.

"Hey, we're not cop-killers, like Ricci and them. I have no beef with you, Ryan," Jake said. "Just let us go and we're all good. The Ghost is done for the night. We've made our presence known."

"What was the purpose of all this, Jake?"

"We need access to government. To the powers that be in Chicago. You think I'd be happy with just the North Side? Nah, that was just leverage to get Ricci to let us in. We're shooting for the whole city. The whole shebang!"

Ryan grabbed Kelly back from Di Santo and marched her up to Iggy Donovan.

"Let Catharine go."

"Do what he says," Jake said to his guy. "We know where the lady lives. And the frat house where Hank and Duke Lulling live, too." Catharine let out a whimper, betraying her pretense of immobility. "And in case that all don't scare ya, we have a guy on retainer in Phoenix with the address of Mrs. Shirley Doherty." Ryan swallowed. Hard. "So you wouldn't dare fuck with us, would you, Ry?"

The threat to his own loved ones set him off. Ryan released Kelly and went for Jake, tackling him like a linebacker. "Now!" he shouted aloud to Catharine, and she elbowed Iggy Donovan while driving her three-inch heel into his instep.

O'Hara fired off a shot, but Di Santo plugged him in the shoulder and he went down fast. Davey Tewes tried to get away by running down the stairs, but yelped as he barreled into Jensen and the rest of the Federal Task Force, rushing up in full tactical. The headgear made them indistinguishable from each other but for the name strips on their vests:

MARTINEZ, POWELL, PENDERGRASS, WHITE, LEFKOWITZ, BIORDELLI.

By the time they hit the gallery with Tewes fully secured, Ryan had zip-cuffed Jake, Cat had done some damage to Donovan, and Patrick O'Hara lay writhing on the floor from Di Santo's bullet.

Ryan took Catharine into his arms. "Are you okay? I'm allowed to ask that now."

"Kelly," Catharine responded.

Ryan frowned, confused. "What about her?"

"She got away."

Ryan held Cat close to his body as he took inventory of the people in the gallery. He must have let Kelly go when he went to tackle Jake—it all went so fast, he couldn't even remember just minutes ago. "Don't worry about her, worry about yourself. You're shaking." Catharine didn't respond. He ran his fingers through her hair to calm her, then whispered into her ear. "Quite an inaugural evening out, my dear. I hope this doesn't mean you're never coming out of the house again." Catharine emitted a soft giggle in his arms. A good sign. "And about that proposal—"

Cat lifted her head, her trembling already beginning to subside. "It's just not time."

"I know. I was just overcome with—pride, your beauty, your strength. I love you."

She gave him that soft smile. "I love you, too. And, well, maybe this was a good inaugural night out. At least now I know I can handle anything!"

He moved Cat away from the scene, while Jensen recited Miranda to the perpetrators and marched them down to the main floor. Ryan waited a beat before following, holding Catharine close as they descended the steps back down to the ballroom. On the way, they passed the EMTs who had been dispatched for the wounded O'Hara. The ballroom had been evacuated of all guests, with only a few cops remaining. An evidence technician team had already roped off the periphery of where the mayor's wife was hit.

Ryan guided Cat toward the door, shielding her from the bloody scene. In the museum's entry, they ran into Superintendent Grady who was monitoring personnel in and out of the building.

"Good work, Doherty. You always get your man." Grady acknowledged him with a handshake.

"Not just me, *Chuck*," Ryan said, noticing Di Santo hovering to the left of them. "I couldn't do this without my partner, Matt Di Santo. He's a great detective and a loyal partner." Grady offered a palm to Di Santo, who shook it and nodded in appreciation—to both Grady and Ryan. "The Mayor's wife—is she okay?"

"Yes, it was an in-and-out, thank God the bullet missed all her vital organs."

"Jake Riordan is an expert sniper. He must have kept her alive on purpose."

The supe nodded solemnly. "I guess we all lucked out tonight. Oh, and, Doherty, the press is outside. I'd like you to make a statement. We can get the official paperwork done in the morning. No need for you and your lovely wife to stick around."

Ryan nodded, annoyed. Annoyed at having to face the press and annoyed at the Supe's arrogant inability to remember his relationship status that they had just discussed one hour and seventeen minutes ago.

"I'm going to go find Amy-Jo," Di Santo said, buttoning his overcoat.

"Tell her I may need backup with the press," Ryan said.

"Well, well, well! *Now* you need her services?" Di Santo jibed. Ryan shrugged. "I'll see if she'll oblige. Catch you outside." Matt kissed Cat on the cheek and saluted his POMP mentor.

As Di Santo exited the museum, Jane came running up the marble steps, flashing her badge to Grady for re-entrance. He allowed her in with a wave.

"Oh, thank God you guys are okay," she said on a heavy breath.

Ryan was surprised she was still here, suddenly register- ing the glamorous Jane, the model-like image that the wom- an rarely revealed during work hours. In fact, the last time he had even seen Jane all dressed up was when she had been called to a crime scene directly from a date.

"You look really nice, by the way," he told her. "I forgot to tell you that earlier."

"I'll go get our coats," Catharine stated. He knew Cat well enough to know she was allowing them a moment.

"I tried to keep Catharine out of the fray," Jane said. "But she kept insisting she had to be upstairs. In the gallery. Something about ballerinas—"

"That's okay, it's not your fault. And you should see what she did to one of the perps," he said, just a little bit proud. "Catharine can kick ass." They chuckled a bit and when it dissolved into silence he said, "Hey, Cat told me about the grant and your stint in Paris. I have to say, I was pretty surprised at the news. A whole *six months?*"

She shrugged, her bare shoulders sparkling with some kind of glitter. Possibly from the navy blue strapless dress. "It's what I want to do…until I figure out what I really want to do."

Ryan held out his arms and Jane came in for a hug. "I'm gonna miss you, kid."

She pulled back. "I'm a text away, Ryan, and yes I promise I'll respond. Whatever you need, you know, on the job. I still have a little pull in the ASA's office." Catharine came up and handed Ryan and Jane their coats. "And don't you dare get married until I come back, okay?" she said, addressing both of them. "I don't want to miss a wedding in those gardens."

"Who said anything about a wedding?" Ryan said, throwing a look to Catharine.

"Not I," Cat responded, with a hand over her heart.

Jane raised one eyebrow. "Yeah, yeah. I may be an at- torney, but I've learned a few investigative tricks from Ryan. I know it when I see it. Not till I get back!" She gracefully allowed Ryan to kiss her on the cheek, accepted a short hug from Catharine, and left the museum.

As Ryan and Cat helped each other with their coats, he picked up on a wave of concern. "I'll get Kelly," he told her. "*We'll* get Kelly. We've got the whole task force behind us, and I'm sure we'll get one of those idiot Ghost members to crack. If not her brother, then the one of the other guys."

Catharine nodded and took his arm. "I'm not worried about her. But I am worried about Matthew. Something is off with him."

"Don't worry about Matt. He bounces back quickly from things like this."

Cat went up on tiptoe and they shared a deep, comforting kiss. "Ready for the paparazzi?" she asked, looping her arm in his.

"Never."

They exited the Art Institute of Chicago into a swarm of lights and reporters.

CHAPTER 33

After a week of filing the reports from the Astor Ball and getting the four Ghost members arraigned, Ryan took a week of well-deserved vacation. He used the time off to move the majority of his belongings into the mansion, shore up its security, and shop for a new car. He adored his vintage Baby Blue, but it was time to grow up. He'd never had a new car in his life, and he had a blast going from dealership to dealership, negotiating with the salesmen, and eventually finding exactly what he wanted.

When he pulled up in his new baby, Catharine laughed and shook her head in incredulity. Sure, he'd spent over a year's salary on it, but it was perfect. And anyway, he was able to put down a decent down payment on the new car with the quick sale of the '66.

Ryan was eager to get back to work after his week of leisure. He was never one for just sitting around and doing nothing. That Monday finally arrived and he enjoyed a full breakfast before hitting the road. The meal was a far cry from grabbing a breakfast muffin and seven-hundred-degree coffee on the way in. He could easily get used to his big new life in the big new house.

At the station, Ryan was headed up the stairs when he got a call on his cell.

"Hey, Doherty, it's Pops from Central Files," the guy greeted him. Frank Popodopoulos was a veteran cop, happy to serve his pre-retirement days as a desk jockey amongst the boxes of police files. "Yeah, so you asked me to notify you if there was any activity on your old partner's file...Detective Jonathan Lange?"

It had been over two years since he'd made that particular request, and he'd long forgotten about it. "Yeah?"

"Well, I came in this morning and noticed that in the log that someone checked out his file late last night. The one with the truck crash, right?"

"Yes, that's right. Who checked it out?" He stopped his ascent up the stairs and plugged an ear.

"A...Detective Di Santo," he said, proceeding to read off the badge number. Ryan tried to compute why his current partner would need his former partner's files. Especially without notifying him. "Detective? You still there?"

"Yeah, still here. Thanks, Pops."

"Do you know the guy?"

"Yeah, he works with me here in the Eighteenth. I'll touch base with him."

"Glad I can help, Detective. And good luck with whatever you guys are looking for!"

What the hell was Di Santo looking for? Why would he request Jon's file without telling him? He ran up the steps two by two and made his way down the hall to the detective's squad, pausing slightly to say a silent 'Good morning' to Jon's picture. No response.

The first thing Ryan noticed when he entered the squad was that Devin had taken over Di Santo's desk. He had his laptop connected to Di Santo's monitor, staring at the screen while sharpening Di Santo's pencils one by one in Di Santo's electric pencil sharpener.

"What are you doing here?" Ryan asked, interrupting him from his task. "Now that we've wrapped up The Ghost case, aren't you going back to the task force?"

"Good morning to you too, Bro. May I call you that: Bro?"

"No. You can call me Ryan," he responded, scanning the squad room. "Where's other D?"

"Sergeant Besko will explain. Did you have a nice vacation?"

"Just dandy. I bought a new car..." He pulled his cell out of his pocket and swiped the screen until he got to the first photo of his new Mustang: Baby Blue II.

Devin frowned. "Looks exactly like your old one."

"Yeah, I know! It's a complete replica of the classic Mustang body, but a brand new vehicle on the inside. It has a modern electronic engine system, keyless entry, power everything and a digital message center. Car of the future." He swept the screen, showing off all angles of his new baby, including the sleek new shiny engine and lush interior. Devin was not as impressed as Ryan had anticipated. "And, well, Catharine's happy it has airbags and regulation seatbelts. Win-win."

"Ah! That's very good. It'll make a most suitable police car, once you get the light bar installed."

"I know, right?" Ryan said, beaming at his brother's approval. "So, where's Di Santo?"

"You will need to speak to your sergeant about that," Devin answered.

Ryan scrunched up his face. "O-kayyyyy," he replied, and made his way to Besko's office. The door was open, but he knocked on the jamb to get his boss's attention.

"D! Glad you're back," Sarge said, looking up from a stack of papers. "Sit down, sit down."

He didn't. "Where's my partner? Devin said you would explain in his weirdly ambiguous way."

"Here's the thing..." Every time Besko said *Here's the thing*, Ryan knew he was in for some bad news. "Di Santo has gone to the other side." Ryan froze. The sarge must have noticed Ryan's terror because he added, "No, no, no, he's not deceased."

Ryan blew out an exhale. "God, Sarge! Don't do that to me." He leaned over, recovering from the shock, his palms on the desk.

"I'm sorry, D. I didn't mean to scare you. What I meant to say was that he's gone over to the feds. As a loaner. And in return, we get your genius brother out there as a consultant."

Ryan shook his head as if that would jumble Besko's words into some kind of intelligible sequence. "Di Santo's going to work for—the *feds*? That makes no sense. He didn't say anything to me about it."

"Well, he made the decision last week, while you were on vacation. He said he didn't want no parties or nothing, he just wanted to leave quietly. But I assumed he was going to let you know. Sorry you had to find out like this."

Ryan couldn't wrap his head around the concept. He flashed back to when he returned to the squad after Jon's death and Di Santo was the newcomer. How he'd fought the partnership, kicking and screaming. It took them almost two years to get into a groove, and now Ryan had gotten used to it. Irritating as he was, Di Santo was sharp. Ryan meant what he'd said to the Supe—Matt was a good cop and a good detective. And despite their rocky start, they had become good friends.

He pulled out his cell to text Di Santo.

– Where are you?

His partner texted back almost immediately.

– *My house.*

– Stay there!

Ryan headed straight out of the sarge's office, nodded to a startled Devin, and headed back out of the station house. He jumped in Baby Blue II, hit the gas and made it to Di Santo's house on the west side in seventeen minutes flat. He might have broken a couple of speed limits, but he didn't particularly care.

As he pulled into Di Santo's driveway, his partner was waiting for him on the steps of his little yellow-brick bungalow, the kind that looked plucked out of a storybook. In the driveway next to the house stood an open moving pod. "No," Ryan mumbled to himself. "This can't be happening now."

As soon as he got out of his car, he started in on his partner. "So when were you going to tell me you were bailing on us and going to work for the feds, D? *What the fuck?* I have to find out from Besko? When did this happen? And why? Why would you go want to work for those guys? We're a team. You're my partner. You're my...*partner.*" His tirade deflated a bit with no response from its target. When Di Santo broke eye contact, Ryan let out a sigh and sat down next to him.

After a pause, Di Santo spoke up. "This is something I have to do, D. I have to get those guys. It's been over a hundred years that these shitheads have been lording over our city. There was only that short time in the nineties that they were crippled, but it's like whack-a-mole. You take one guy down, and another pops up in his place. We need to stop it for good."

"But why *you*?" Ryan asked. "Why do *you* have to do it? Is it the family thing? Your connections? Is it Tootie?"

Di Santo scrubbed the bottom of his face with one hand. "Yeah, yeah. It's the family thing."

"You are such a lousy liar, you know that?"

Di Santo chuckled. "Okay, maybe so. But there are some things you just don't wanna know."

Ryan couldn't imagine partnering with anyone else. Not after all they'd gone through in the past three years: Town Red, Jessica Way, Terrico James, The Ghost. And now Kelly. It had taken him a while to accept Matthew X. Di Santo on the squad, and now he wasn't about to lose another partner.

"Look, I'll help you. I'll go too. We'll do it together. Bring down the mob, you and me, as a team."

Di Santo shook his head. "Nah, D. You can't help with this one. I have to do it alone."

Ryan ran his fingers through his hair. "Does this have something to do with Jon Lange? They told me you requested his file. What's that about?"

Di Santo shifted a bit and fixed his gaze at a tree line in the distance. "I'm sorry, Ry. I can't say right now. Just something came up in the feds' investigation. But I promise you, if anything comes of it, you'll be the first to know."

"Is there new evidence that it wasn't an accident?"

"I really don't have any information for you right now, I'm just riffing on something and need to check it out."

Ryan turned Di Santo's shoulder to force eye contact. "Let *me* check it out! He was my partner. *My* best friend."

"That's exactly why you can't. You're too close."

Ryan took a moment to let that sink in. "So you absolutely promise to tell me if anything comes up? Bro-to-bro?"

"Promise. You're my bestie, you know? It's been great working with you. I've learned a lot. You were a good POMP mentor, and I'm gonna m—"

"Don't say that. Don't talk like we're never going to see each other again. Sarge said this was a temporary assignment, so you'll be back at the Eighteenth when you take these guys down, right? You'll be back."

"I really don't know. I can't make any promises."

They sat in silence for several minutes, and for once Ryan wasn't keeping track of the time. "So you're moving to Washington?"

"Washington? No, I'll be working here, in the Chicago branch of the FBI. I'm moving downtown to a security building. These Outfit dudes don't mess around, D, and I can't be staying in this shitty little bungalow I inherited from Aunt Domenica. I wouldn't be safe."

"What're you going to do with the house?"

"Rent it out, I guess. I've already got a family that's interested. My sister Gina said she'd help manage it."

"How's she doing, by the way? Did you tell her about Tootie?"

"Yep. She's okay. Better off without that mook, know

what I mean? Broke up with him as soon as I told her the whole story. She cried, my ma cried, even the dog cried. But it's for the best, you know? They don't need that kind of affiliation in their lives."

"Yep. Jane's gone, too, did you know that? She's gone to study art in Paris. What am I going to do without two of my best friends? This is really going to suck."

Di Santo rubbed his hands together. "Yeah, I know, Jane told me about the grant. Par-ee, France! Maybe we can go visit her sometime."

Ryan's world had just flipped a hundred and eighty degrees. His ex-girlfriend was now a mobster, his two best friends were leaving him, and then there was Devin. "And now I have to work with my long-lost brother. Thanks a lot for that."

"Aw, that dude's not so bad," Di Santo responded. "I kind of took a shining to him. Smart as a whip. He must've gotten all the brains in the family."

Ryan shot him a fist in the shoulder for the jibe. They both laughed.

"I have one request," Ryan said, sobering. Di Santo turned to look at him. "If and when it comes to putting the cuffs on Kelly, you'll let me do it?"

"I'm sure Jensen wouldn't object to that. That woman sure is a piece of work. I can't even picture the two of you together."

"Maybe, deep down, I always knew she was a little off. Maybe that's why I never took the plunge and asked her to marry me." Di Santo nodded, and with nothing left to say Ryan held out a hand. "So don't be a stranger, okay?"

Di Santo shook his hand. Ryan reached over to pat him on the back, but Di Santo moved in for a tight hug. "I'll still be around. We'll meet every so often, compare notes, and do drinks at McGinty's."

"And you're always welcome for Sunday dinner." He stood up and Di Santo did as well, with a sigh that signaled the end of an era.

"Oh, I'll be by," Di Santo said. "Making sure you don't fuck up that relationship! You so don't deserve Catharine Lulling."

Ryan flipped Di Santo the bird as he made his way back to Baby Blue II. He turned around to show it off. "Hey, didja see my new car?"

But Di Santo had already closed the door to the little yellow brick house.

EPILOGUE

Ryan tapped his foot as he sat in the waiting room. It hadn't really changed in three years. Same fountain, same magazines, same meditative music with the airy chimes. At exactly 5:00 on the nose the inner door opened and Dr. Jamie Sullivan greeted him.

"Detective! Nice to see you again. Come on in." Like his office, the doc hadn't aged much. Maybe a few extra gray hairs on his temples, a wedding ring on his finger, and eight to ten pounds of marriage weight around his middle.

Ryan automatically took a seat on the couch while Doc Sullivan grabbed a notebook and file from his desk and sat himself down in the leather club chair across from his patient. "Thanks for seeing me on such short notice," he said.

"No problem. What brings you here today?"

Ryan's gaze dropped to his shoes. "Well it was either here or the liquor store."

"Good news, then, Detective. You've made the right choice."

ACKNOWLEDGEMENTS

This book is about friendship, and I'd like to thank my friends old and new: Carolyn Mather, who gave me the idea of The Ghost's calling card. Nancy Pendergrass , Doug Susu-Mago, Tracey Meyers, and Lynette Stuhlmacher, who never let distance or time get in the way of a great friendship. Thanks to the entire community of Oakhurst for championing me and my work. Thank you to my writing student, Blake Action, for the idea of using a fedora on the cover and Chuck Reaume for the amazing cover design— again. I, of course, have to thank my amazing editor, Idria Barone Knecht, for keeping me and my characters in check. Thanks, again, to Kathleen Puckett, Special Agent, FBI (ret)—so great to be able to talk shop and get our hair done at the same time. Continuous gratitude to Officers Casey O'Neill and Karen Wojcikowsi of the real Chicago 18th for putting up with me and becoming super-supportive fans. And to my dearest departed friends, Joanne and Suzhanna Elam, my heart constantly aches with the loss of both of you. ~ JAM

About the Author

Jennifer Moss was born and raised in Evanston, Illinois and is a graduate of Northwestern University. Moss began her writing career as a freelance author for articles about the Internet industry. In 2008, she published her first book, *The One-in-a-Million Baby Name Book* (Perigee Press) as a companion to her website. She has published three novels in her *Ryan Doherty Mystery* series, *Town Red* (Black Opal Books, 2012), *Way to Go* (Black Opal Books, 2013), and *Taking the Rap* (Black Opal Books, 2014).

Moss has served on the board of directors for the Northwestern University Club of Los Angeles, Los Angeles Female Business Owners (LAFBO), The Crescendo Young Musicians' Guild, Planet MedAlert, and The Bully Police Squad, an organization founded by police officers to help schools define and enforce their bully prevention strategies.

Moss resides in the mountains near Yosemite National Park and divides her time between writing and web development.

For more information about Jennifer Moss, visit her website: www.JenniferMoss.com and follow her on Facebook, Twitter, LinkedIn, and GoodReads.

Made in the USA
San Bernardino, CA
17 April 2016